"We need to get some sleep," said Laura, getting to her feet.

Craig rose at that same moment, and their bodies touched. She turned to move away, but before she could, Craig had her in his arms.

She gazed up at his face; his eyes, filled with desire, met hers. She tried to still the erratic pounding of her heart, but her pulse was racing too wildly. When he bent his head, she met his lips halfway.

His demanding kiss triggered her passion, and entwining her arms about his neck, she pressed her body against his. She was conscious only of his nearness, his lips, and a tingling effect that was running through her like wildfire.

Craig's hand swept to the back of her neck, pressing her lips ever closer. He drew her against him so tightly that she was aware of his entire length.

He kissed the soft hollow of her throat, then his lips were suddenly back on hers, sending stronger and more vivid desire coursing through them.

Craig lifted her into his arms, knelt, and placed her gently on the blanket. "Laura," he whispered thickly, "I want you. God, how much I want you!"

ROCHELLE WAYNE

NEVADA FLAME

PINNACLE BOOKS
WINDSOR PUBLISHING CORP.

*This book is dedicated to my
good friend — Carol Glatz*

PINNACLE BOOKS

are published by

Windsor Publishing Corp.
475 Park Avenue South
New York, NY 10016

First printing: July, 1992

Printed in the United States of America

One

Laura Mills watched the Nevada sun dip into the west. She stood on the veranda, then moved to the porch steps, and sat down. She propped her elbows on her knees, cupped her chin in her hands, and thought about the way things used to be, when her ranch had been prosperous. As her mind skimmed back into the past, she gazed fleetingly at the empty corral; it had once been filled with horses. Slowly, she turned her eyes to the quiet bunkhouse, she remembered better days, when the boisterous voices of wranglers could be heard. Now, only silence prevailed. Last week, she had insisted that the last four ranch hands leave and look for work elsewhere. They had worked at the Diamond Cross for years, they were very fond of Laura, and their concern had compelled them to hang on. But there was no work, and Laura certainly couldn't afford to pay them wages, so the wranglers had finally packed up and moved on.

Laura sighed deeply, peered into the distance, and tried to imagine that her ranch was again prosperous and overflowing with cattle. But the vision was too depressing, so she quickly cast it aside. She wasn't one to feel sorry for herself, and if she continued to long for the past, she'd certainly sink into a state of self-destruction.

The past was gone, she couldn't bring it back. She must concentrate on the present. She gave it serious thought — it didn't look very promising.

She tried to control the direction of her thoughts, they nonetheless wandered to her father. A bitter frown sharpened her otherwise soft features. Although she had loved her father, she hadn't respected him. He had been weak, self-indulgent, and unbelievably selfish. She often wondered why her mother had married him. The two had been so different. Her mother had been emotionally strong, dependable, and responsible; her father had been the complete opposite. Laura never doubted that it had been her mother who had kept the ranch operating prosperously. Late in life, she had become pregnant, and died giving birth to a stillborn son. The woman had now been gone for two years, but Laura still missed her acutely.

Following his wife's death, Laura's father gave in to his weakness and began to drink heavily and gamble compulsively. He was more successful at drinking than at gambling, and his debts soon drained his finances, until finally, depleted, he began to sell his cattle. In time, the cattle were gone, and the Diamond Cross was destitute. Laura knew that if her father hadn't died, he would certainly have mortgaged the house and the land, but two months ago, he had suffered a fatal heart attack.

Now Laura was living alone. She had an older brother, but he was off with their uncle prospecting in the region known as Death Valley. Almost a year had passed since Laura's uncle had visited the Diamond Cross. A prospector, he was always searching for that big strike. His visit was short, and when he left, Laura's brother went with him. She had asked him not to leave, but certain of staking a rich claim, he assured her that he'd return a wealthy man. Laura, more levelheaded than her brother, feared he was chasing a foolish dream that might inevitably cost him his life.

She gazed off into the distant hills; dusk had filled them with a purple mist. Remaining on the porch, she watched as full darkness descended, and a myriad of stars dotted the cloudless sky in all their majestic splendor. A gentle breeze stirred, ruffling Laura's long, golden tresses. She brushed the wayward locks back away from her face, and got to her feet. The warmth of day had ebbed into a faint but balmy chill, and she rubbed her bare arms to warm them. Her eyes scanned her surroundings, as she searched for her only companion. Seeing no movement, she whistled loudly, and within moments a large gray shadow streaked across the landscape. Running at full speed, it swiftly covered the distance, leapt the porch steps, sat at Laura's feet, and wagged its tail.

Smiling, she reached down and patted the creature's head. "You're a good boy, Lobo." Lobo was a fitting name for her companion, for he was a full-blooded wolf. Four years ago, during an extra-frigid winter, packs of wolves had ventured in from the hills, searching for food. The starving packs had stalked the cattle, which made it necessary for the wranglers to shoot them. One wrangler, who was a soft touch, had found a litter of pups in a small cave at the foot of the hills. Their mother had most likely been one of the unfortunate wolves killed by the wranglers. The puppies—except for one who was stronger and bigger than the others—had died from hunger. The wrangler brought the surviving pup back to the ranch, and knowing that Laura shared his love for animals, he gave her the half-starved wolf. It had seemed doubtful that it would live, but the young wolf was a survivor and pulled through. Laura named it Lobo, and despite its wild heritage, it grew to be as trustworthy and tame as a domesticated dog. Laura was very fond of her pet, and now that she was living alone, his presence was not only comforting, but necessary as well. She slept better at night knowing that Lobo was there to keep a vigil.

Laura, followed by Lobo, went into the house. Despite her father's poor management, Laura's home was still in good condition. The one-story, clapboard house had large rooms, a huge kitchen, and an office with a side entrance.

Now, as Laura's steps wandered to the office, she had no conscious thought of why she was going there. She opened the solid oak door, moved inside, lit a lamp, and sat at the desk. Laura wondered what her mother would do in her place. She most likely would have borrowed money, putting the land and house up as collateral. But when Laura had tried that at the bank, she had been turned down. Mr. Lancaster, the bank's president, considered her a bad investment, in fact, he had treated her as though she were incompetent. Simply because she was a woman—and a young one at that—he was certain she had no head for business. He had advised her to sell out, find a man who could provide for her, marry, and have children.

The man's biased opinion had infuriated Laura, but there had been nothing she could do about it. If only her brother hadn't left! He was a man, and Mr. Lancaster might have agreed to give him the loan.

Laura knew there was only one option left. However, it was one that she dreaded. Somehow, she had to find a way to put her pride behind her and ask Harry Talbert for a loan. He could afford it, for he was the wealthiest man in the territory. She didn't want to ask her neighbor for money, but what other choice had the bank left her? She didn't know Harry Talbert all that well, and she suspected that years ago a rift had taken place between her parents and Talbert. Several times she had questioned her mother and father about their cold relationship with Harry Talbert, but she never received a satisfactory answer. Their association with Talbert was a topic they avoided.

Personally, Laura had no grievance against Harry Talbert, but his two youngest sons were a different matter. She knew Doyce and Lee Talbert well, for she and her brother had gone to school with them. She hadn't liked the boys then, and nothing had happened in the years since to change her mind. In her opinion, they were arrogant, overbearing, and totally insensitive. The oldest son was somewhat of a mystery to Laura. Unlike his brothers, Ed Talbert was well mannered, but he was also reticent, and Laura barely knew him.

Now, set on visiting Harry Talbert, Laura left the office and went to her bedroom to change into a riding skirt and a long-sleeved blouse. She pitched the garments on the bed, slipped off her dress and petticoat, filled the wash basin, and took a sponge bath.

As she put on the clean clothes, her thoughts were running fluidly. She experienced a pang of guilt, for she knew asking Harry Talbert for a loan was something her mother would never have considered. A bemused frown creased Laura's brow, if she only knew *why* her mother had felt that way. What had Harry Talbert done to warrant her mother's disfavor? She didn't have the vaguest idea, but she did know that it had happened many years ago.

Laura moved to her vanity and began to brush her hair. She remained deep in thought, causing her to pay little attention to her reflection. But even if she hadn't been sidetracked, she would have failed to fully appreciate her own beauty. Although she was modest, she wasn't blind, and she knew fate had been kind to her. Laura was well aware that she was attractive, however, she was too guileless to realize that her beauty was very sensual.

Standing, she gave her reflection a quick appraisal. The mauve-colored skirt, complimented by a pink blouse, fit her tall, slender frame flawlessly, enhancing her seductive curves. She had left her golden tresses unbound, and the silky waves cascaded radiantly past her shoulders.

She slipped on her riding boots, then returned to the wardrobe, where she found a wide-brimmed hat and a jacket that matched her skirt. Dressed in western fashion, Laura Mills was indeed a fetching sight. She opened a vanity drawer, delved inside, and brought out a pair of riding gloves.

She was bolstered by her resolution to make a business

transaction with Harry Talbert, and she lifted her chin proudly. After all, she wasn't asking for charity, she would pay him back with interest. In addition, she intended to put her land up as collateral. Harry Talbert wouldn't be taking a risk. A hopeful glint lit up her blue eyes; Talbert would surely cooperate. He had nothing to lose, and much to gain.

She left the bedroom, stopped at the office, picked up her Winchester, then with Lobo trotting at her heels, she hurried to the stables. The place was empty except for Laura's roan mare. The horse whinnied a friendly welcome at its owner's approach.

The faint rumble of thunder sounded in the distance. Certain a storm was advancing, Laura saddled the mare as quickly as possible. She hoped to make the trip to Talbert's ranch, discuss business, and return before it started raining.

She slipped her rifle into a tooled-leather scabbard attached to the saddle, then swung agilely onto the horse's back. She held the reins in one gloved hand, and as she kneed the mare gently, it obediently galloped from the stable.

Laura glanced up at the night sky; it was still clear, but on the horizon clouds were forming. A streak of lightning zigzagged across the heavens, followed by roaring thunder. The storm would probably hit before she could complete her errand. For a moment, she considered unsaddling the horse, and going back into the house; she could always visit Harry Talbert tomorrow. She decided against waiting, now that she had made up her mind to ask him for a loan, she was anxious to do so.

Still hoping the rain would hold off until she returned, Laura coaxed the mare into a steady canter and headed toward Talbert's ranch. Lobo, his strong legs moving swiftly, had no trouble keeping up with the horse's fast gait.

Talbert's ranch, called the Circle T, bordered Laura's

land, and it didn't take her long to arrive at the winding lane that led to the main house. Harry Talbert was a thriving rancher, and a highly successful businessman. His elaborate home attested to his prosperity. The mammoth, two-story house sat atop a hill overlooking the bunkhouse, corrals, and several small outbuildings.

Laura had visited the Circle T before. Twice every year, Talbert invited his friends to a large barbecue, and despite the mysterious rift between him and Laura's parents, he always extended them an invitation, which included Laura and her brother. The Mills family, however, was always the last to arrive, and the first to leave. It was as though Talbert and Laura's parents could barely stand such proximity. As Laura grew older, she came to realize that Talbert's invitations, and her parents' acceptances, were carried out to curb gossip. Apparently, they didn't want the townspeople or their fellow ranchers to know that hard feelings existed.

A few wranglers were lingering about as Laura rode up to their boss's house. Oblivious to the admiring eyes of the men, she halted her horse at the hitching rail, ordered Lobo to stay, then with long, determined strides, she walked to the front door.

She knocked firmly, and a minute or so later, the door was opened by the butler. An elderly Negro, with curly white hair, smiled pleasantly. He liked Laura, for she was always friendly. Occasionally, their paths crossed in town, and she never failed to stop and chat.

"Evenin', Miss Laura. What can I do for you?" he asked.

"Good evening, Joshua. I'd like to see Mr. Harry Talbert."

He motioned her inside. "The masta's not home, but Mista Lee's here. Would you care to see him instead?"

She certainly had no desire to see the youngest Talbert. Since her father's death, she had encountered Lee on more than one occasion, and each time he had tried to make advances. Fortunately, she had always succeeded in warding off his less than subtle moves. But one of these days she might have to deal with him more forcefully.

She was about to tell the butler that she'd come back to-morrow, but before she could, Lee suddenly appeared at the top of the stairs.

The sight of Laura placed a big smile on his face. Lee Talbert was tall, slim, and handsome. "Well, well," he said to Laura, hurrying down the steps. "Whatever prompted you to grace our threshold?"

She ignored his tone. He was perfectly aware that she could barely tolerate him. "I wanted to see your father."

Lee spoke sternly to the butler. "Why are you standing around? Haven't you got work to do?"

"Yes, suh, Mista Lee," he mumbled, hurrying on his way.

Smiling again, Talbert looked at Laura and said amicably, "My father's not home, but maybe I can help you."

"I don't think so."

"Nonsense," he replied. He gestured down the hall. "Let me show you to the study. You can tell me why you need to see my father, and I'll pass the information on to him."

Laura consented somewhat hesitantly. She didn't relish discussing business with Lee, but he would at least let his father know what she wanted.

She allowed Lee to escort her to the study. She had never been in this room before, and she looked about with interest. The study was huge, its decor exclusively masculine, the furniture consisting of large, bulky pieces. A painting of Harry Talbert hung over the fireplace. Laura scrutinized it closely, it was obviously done some years ago, for the figure in the painting was still a young man. An inexplicable sensation passed over her as she continued to view the picture. She couldn't understand why she felt so odd, but there was something about the painting that had a strange effect on her. Harry Talbert had been a handsome man in his youth, but it was more than his looks that held her attention. It was as though she were seeing someone she had once known or dreamt about. A face she couldn't quite place. She shook the feeling aside. That was crazy, she had known Harry Talbert all her life. Not well perhaps, but he was certainly no enigma!

"Would you care for a glass of sherry?" Lee asked, breaking into her thoughts.

"No, thank you." She didn't want to dally, and came straight to the point. "I need to speak to your father about obtaining a loan. I plan to put up my land as collateral, and I also intend to pay him back with interest."

Lee responded with a hearty laugh, which provoked Laura's anger. With a toss of her head, she brushed past him on her way to the door. But Lee moved alertly and caught her arm.

"Take your hands off me!" she ordered.

He simply tightened his grip. He was no longer laughing, but merriment shone in his eyes. "Pa's not going to loan you any money. Your land borders on ours, and we're just waiting for you to sell out. You can't make it on your own. Soon now you'll have no choice but to ask us to *buy* your ranch, and we'll be only too glad to accommodate you."

"Is that why Mr. Lancaster wouldn't give me a loan? Did you Talberts tell him to turn me down? Your wealth runs the town, and it probably runs Mr. Lancaster as well! You've got more land now than you need! Why do you want mine?"

"Why not?" He was grinning smugly.

She jerked free of his grip, and fire suddenly flashed in her blue eyes. "You'll never get my ranch!" she swore firmly. "My brother will be back soon, and he'll find a way to save our home!"

"Johnny's never coming back. He's been gone almost a year. By now, his bones are probably rotting in the middle of the desert! He was stupid to go with that crazy uncle of yours to Death Valley."

"Johnny isn't dead!" she retorted. But the statement lacked conviction. She hadn't heard from him in such a long time; she knew that he and her uncle could very well have died.

"Laura," Lee began, his lips smiling with confidence. "I have a proposition for you."

She eyed him guardedly. "Oh?"

"Since you're alone without a provider, I'll take care of you. When Pa buys your ranch, I'll see to it that he allows you to remain in your house. I'll give you money for food, clothes, and whatever trinkets that might please you. In return, all you have to do is be my mistress."

"I'd rather be dead!" she spat. Outside, the storm was drawing closer, and a large clap of thunder nearly drowned out her words.

Lee's temper was short-fused. "You uppity bitch! Just wait and see! You'll come crawling, begging for my help!"

"Never!" she replied tersely, once again heading for the door.

This time, his arm snaked out and grasped her about the waist. Turning her about, he drew her against him. "Since you won't cooperate, I guess I'll just have to take what I want. After all, there's no one to protect you."

"I can take care of myself!" she spat. Then, taking him unawares, she brought up her knee, and slammed it into his groin. Groaning, he released her and doubled over in pain.

She opened the door, went into the hall, and hurried outside. A jagged streak of lightning severed the sky, succeeded immediately by deafening thunder.

She untied the reins, swung up onto the mare, and with Lobo following, she galloped away from the house. A pleased smile was on her face. In her opinion, Lee Talbert got what he deserved.

Two

Sheets of rain were falling as Harry Talbert and his oldest son returned home, stabled their horses, and headed for the house. They had been at the saloon in town, and still feeling their drinks, they stumbled up the porch steps.

As they put away their rain-soaked slickers, Harry suggested, "Ed, let's have a nightcap before turning in."

Agreeing, Ed followed his father to the study. The sight that confronted them there had a sobering effect. Lee was sprawled on the floor beside the desk, dead, a bullet hole in his chest. His pistol was lying at his side.

As Harry knelt beside his son's body, Ed went into the hall, yelling loudly, "Joshua! Joshua, where the hell are you?"

The servant responded at once, and entering the hall, he said eagerly, "Yes, suh, Mista Ed! I's here! Whatcha need?"

He practically pushed Joshua into the study. "Lee's dead! Who the hell killed him?"

Shocked, the butler stuttered, "I . . . I don't know!"

"Didn't you hear a gunshot?"

"No, suh! Not with all this thunder."

They were suddenly interrupted by the third brother. "What's all the commotion?" Doyce asked, stifling a yawn. He wore a robe, was barefoot, and his hair was tousled.

"Lee's been murdered!" Ed replied.

"What?" Doyce exclaimed.

Ed returned to questioning Joshua. "Did anyone come to the house tonight?"

"Yes, suh. Miss Laura was here."

"When did she leave?"

"I don't know. I didn't hear her leave."

Harry moved away from Lee's body. A note was partially concealed in his hand. He looked at Doyce and asked, "How long have you been home?"

"About thirty minutes, I guess. I'm not sure, I was asleep." He gestured toward his father's hand. "What do you have?"

He seemed hesitant to answer. "It's a piece of paper. I found it beside Lee."

Doyce jerked it from his hand. He looked at it, then showed it to Ed. "Lee lived long enough to tell us who killed him. There's one word on this paper—*Laura!*" A terrible rage burned in his eyes. "We oughta wrap a rope around her murdering little neck!"

"That's enough!" Harry suddenly bellowed. "There will be no lynching! I want you and Ed to ride to town and get the sheriff."

"But that'll take over an hour," Doyce complained. "In the meantime, Laura's liable to get away."

"Just do as I told you!" Harry demanded.

Doyce gave in reluctantly. "All right. I'll hurry and get dressed."

"While you're doing that," Ed said, "I'll saddle two fresh horses."

The moment they were gone, Harry turned to Joshua. "As soon as Ed and Doyce leave for town, I want you to ride to the Diamond Cross, and if Miss Laura is there, tell her to leave at once."

Joshua could barely believe what he was hearing. "You

mean, you wants me to warn her?"

"Yes, that's exactly what I mean."

"But, Mista Harry, you helpin' her don't make no sense. Not that I ain't willin' to do likes you say. Regardless of that note, I don't think Miss Laura killed Mista Lee. She's too nice a lady to kill anyone. Is that why you wants me to warn her? Do you think she's innocent, too?"

"If she were innocent, Lee wouldn't have written her name on that note."

Joshua was more confused. "If you think she done it, then why is you helpin' her?"

"Never mind why. Just carry out my instructions. And, Joshua . . ."

"Yes, suh?"

"Never tell anyone about this. Never!"

"I won't, Mista Harry. You can count on me."

Satisfied that the butler would keep their secret, Harry moved back to his son's body. Grief etched his face, and tears filled his eyes. He knew Lee's several faults, but had loved him in spite of them.

Laura was preparing for bed when she was suddenly alerted by Lobo's deep growl. She hastily slipped a robe over her nightgown, grabbed her rifle, and with Lobo at her side, hurried into the parlor. Drawing aside the curtain, she peeked outside. The storm had passed, but the sky was still cloudy, and she could barely make out a lone rider approaching the house. She watched as he halted his horse, dismounted, and flung the reins over the hitching rail. She squinted against the darkness and tried to recognize him. As he moved up the porch steps, she got a better look, and seeing that it was Joshua, she put aside her rifle. She wondered why he was calling at such a late hour. Had Harry Talbert agreed to the loan? But why would he send his butler to her house *now?* Why not wait until morning?

Joshua was raising a hand to knock when Laura swung open the door. "Come in," she said, motioning for him to do so.

He stepped inside, removed his hat, and began fidgeting nervously with the brim. "Miss Laura, you gots to get away from here."

She was puzzled. "Get away? What are you talking about?"

"Mista Lee's been murdered. Someone shot him dead. They killed him in the study. Mista Harry found a piece of paper beside Mista Lee's body. 'Fore he died, he wrote your name on that paper."

It took a moment for his words to sink in. "My name? I don't understand! I didn't kill him!"

"I don't think you did either, but that piece of paper's mighty incriminatin'. It don't look good for you, Miss Laura. I's afraid a jury would find you guilty. I reckon Mista Harry feels the same way, that's why he sent me here. He said that you better leave right away." Joshua reached into his pocket and brought out a sealed envelope. He handed it to Laura. "Mista Harry told me to give you this. It's some money to help tide you over."

Laura accepted the envelope numbly. "Mr. Talbert . . . sent you here? He . . . he wants to help me? But why? Why?"

Joshua shrugged. "I don't know. He didn't tell me why. I's just as confused as you."

"He must think I'm innocent!"

"No, ma'am. He don't think that at all."

"But I didn't kill Lee, and there's no reason for me to run. If I leave, it'll only make me look guilty."

"Miss Laura, you ain't thinkin' very smart. Mista Doyce, he's already wantin' to *lynch* you. You bein' a woman ain't gonna save you from him. Mista Doyce has got too much evil inside him. Please, Miss Laura, get away from here, 'fore that man can do you any harm."

Joshua's warning made headway. Laura knew he was right. What chance would she have against Doyce Talbert? Even if he didn't lynch her, he'd buy the jury's vote. She'd be found guilty, and most likely sentenced to hang.

"All right, Joshua, I'll leave. But this is my home, and I don't intend to stay gone forever. Somehow, I'll find the person who really killed Lee and clear myself."

"You hurry and pack what you needs to take with you, and I'll saddle your horse."

Laura hurried to her bedroom, took a carpetbag, and began to fill it. Her thoughts were swirling. Lee dead? A piece of paper with her name on it? But why had Lee named her as his killer? Or had the real murderer written her name? That, she decided, was a distinct possibility. Her thoughts swung to Harry Talbert. Why in the world was *he* helping her? If he truly believed she killed Lee, then he should want to see her brought to justice! Harry Talbert's aid made no sense whatsoever, and for the moment she stopped thinking about it—she couldn't even begin to solve the puzzle!

Laura decided it would be safer if she traveled in men's clothing. Seen from a distance, she might not be recognized as a woman. She had already made up her mind to try and find her brother and uncle. It would be a long and dangerous journey, but if she could pass as a teenage boy, it might save her from any lecherous characters along the way. She knew the disguise wouldn't be flawless, but it was all she could come up with.

She went to her brother's room, searched through his wardrobe, and found a pair of trousers and a shirt that he had worn years ago. Removing her nightwear, she quickly slipped into the clothes. Her brother had been quite slim when he had worn the pants and shirt, thus, the garments were a good fit on Laura. She found a pair of his boots, which were, of course, too large, so she looked through the dresser drawers until she located two pairs of socks. She stuffed one pair into the toes of the boots, put the other pair on her feet, and finished getting dressed. She slipped on one of her brother's jackets, and on her way out, grabbed a hat hanging on a peg by the door.

Back in her own room, she completed her packing, went to her vanity, pinned up her hair, and put on the wide-brimmed hat. She stepped back so that she could view her full reflection. She was disappointed; she didn't look very much like a boy. She shrugged; there wasn't anything she could do about it. Still, at a distance, her disguise might work.

Taking her carpetbag, she went to the kitchen to pack provisions. She was in the act of doing so when Joshua found her.

"Miss Laura, you gots to hurry up. Mista Doyce and Mista Ed done gone to get the sheriff. They'll be here 'fore much longer." His eyes traveled over her manly attire.

Aware of his scrutiny, she asked, "I don't look much like a boy, do I?"

He smiled haltingly. "If you travel by night, you might fool people."

"Joshua, that's a great idea! I'll ride at night! That way, I'll be less apt to run into anyone."

"Miss Laura, where you aimin' to go?"

"I intend to find my brother and uncle."

Joshua was anxious for her to leave. "Is you done packin', Miss Laura?"

"Yes, I guess I am. Traveling horseback, I can only take so much."

"Then you best get goin'."

"Wait. There's something I forgot."

Joshua, following her to the study, watched as she went to the desk, opened a drawer, and brought out a sheathed bowie knife. She hid it in her boot.

"You know how to use that, Miss Laura?" he asked, evidently surprised.

"Yes, I do," she replied, leaving it at that. She didn't have time to explain. She remembered to get extra ammunition for her rifle, then she and Joshua hurried outside.

Joshua helped her put her belongings on the horse, gave her a hand up, and said, "Goodbye, Miss Laura. I'll be prayin' for you."

"Thank you, Joshua." Her gaze swept ruefully over her house. "I wonder what will happen to my home? There won't be anyone here to protect it."

"Don't you worry 'bout that. You just worry 'bout yourself. Now, get on out of here!"

As she turned the mare away from the hitching rail, Joshua slapped the horse's flank, sending it on its way. Laura, with Lobo following close behind, fled into the darkness.

About an hour later, the sheriff, accompanied by the Talberts, rode up to Laura's home. Harry, for appearance's sake, had decided to ride along, even though he knew Laura wouldn't be there. But staying at his ranch might arouse suspicion. After all, he should be as anxious as his sons to apprehend Lee's murderer.

Harry had thought Doyce would be enraged to find Laura gone, but, to his surprise, her absence didn't seem to bother him all that much. His oldest son, on the other hand, was livid. He insisted that the sheriff round up a posse. The man assured him that he would, but not until morning. It would be foolish to try and pursue Laura in the dark. Furthermore, it was starting to rain again, which meant her tracks would wash away.

As Ed made plans to meet with the sheriff at sunrise, his father took a lit lantern and wandered through the house. Harry moved aimlessly from room to room, not really searching for anything in particular, merely looking the place over. More than twenty years had passed since he had stepped foot inside this home, and he was a little surprised to see that it hadn't changed all that much.

His wandering eventually took him to the largest of the three bedrooms, the one that had belonged to Laura's parents. His gaze swept over the huge bed where the couple had slept, and a look of pain came to his eyes; for a moment, it seemed as though he were about to weep. He quickly took hold of himself, and was about to leave, when he caught sight of a framed picture. It was on the nightstand, and he picked it up. The picture was small, and he held it close to the lantern so that he could see it better. It was a photograph of Laura's mother. It had been taken shortly after she married.

The woman in the photograph was lovely, and, for a long moment, Harry studied her delicate features. He softly rubbed his thumb across her face, as though he could actually feel her. He soon became lost in the past.

Suddenly, Ed's voice called to him, bringing him back to reality. Slipping the picture inside his jacket pocket, Harry left the room, closing the door behind him.

The others were ready to leave; they extinguished the lamps that they had lit, but as Harry started to put out the lantern he carried, Doyce reached out a hand to stop him.

"Give me that," he said, a cruel grin curling his lips. "I'm gonna torch this house!"

"You'll do no such thing!" Harry remarked angrily.

"Why not?"

"This house will not be burned, vandalized, or damaged

in any way! In fact, to make sure of that, I'm going to hire a couple to stay here as caretakers."

Doyce was confused. "Pa, why do you care if this place is destroyed or not?"

"Never mind why I care!" He brushed past his son, saying firmly, "To destroy this home would be a terrible waste, and I'll not stand for it!"

Harry didn't ride with the posse the next morning; he stayed home hoping that Laura wouldn't be found. Ed and Doyce showed up at sunset, discouraged and tired, for they had failed to apprehend Laura. The sheriff had refused to ride out of his jurisdiction, and when he had reached that point, he demanded that they turn around and return to town. The Talberts, especially Ed, had tried to convince him to continue, but he had flatly refused, insisting that Laura's arrest was now up to the federal marshals. He did suggest, however, that they might consider hiring a bounty hunter. Also, he assured them that wanted posters would be distributed throughout the west. He told them not to worry, Laura Mills would be brought to justice—it was only a matter of time.

Lee's funeral took place the following morning, attended by the townspeople and ranchers from miles around. Harry buried his youngest son in the town's cemetery; following the burial, everyone was invited to the Circle T. Food and drinks were plentiful, and Harry's multitude of guests began to enjoy themselves. Harry took no offense, it was customary for funerals, as well as weddings and christenings, to be a reason for people to gather. The gatherings, even when brought about by a funeral, always took on a festive flair.

* * *

As the Circle T was overflowing with guests, Laura Mills, miles away, was sitting alone in a narrow cave. She had gotten as far as the foothills, when her mare pulled up lame. She had no choice but to stop and let the horse rest. The mare had picked up a stone, and it had become embedded in her hoof. By the time Laura became aware of it, she had ridden the horse several miles. Now the mare's hoof was badly bruised, and Laura knew she would have to hole up for at least two days.

She was very worried that the delay would lead to her eventual arrest. She was familiar with the sheriff's border lines, and knew she was out of his jurisdiction, however, she feared that he and his posse might venture beyond that point. Especially if the Talbert brothers were riding along. She didn't think border lines would keep them from insisting that the sheriff continue his pursuit.

Thinking about the Talberts made Laura suddenly remember the envelope from Harry. She had almost forgotten about it. It was in her saddlebags; she took it out and opened it. She counted the bills and was amazed to find that she had five hundred dollars. Good Lord, why would Harry Talbert give her so much money? After all, Joshua had said that the man didn't even think she was innocent! It made absolutely no sense!

She put the envelope inside her coat pocket. Such ample funds certainly made her feel better. At least she didn't have to worry about money.

Sitting at the mouth of the cave, she watched as the sun sank into the west. She dreaded the advancing night. A frightful chill coursed through her, and as she thought about the dark, she was tempted to build a fire. But, no, she mustn't! If a posse was out there, a fire might give her away! Yesterday, she had traveled by night, but riding through the dark seemed less scary than sitting inside a damp, pitch-black cave.

She wished she was braver, after all, it was childish to fear the dark! But Laura couldn't help but be afraid.

Gradually, the sun disappeared and soon thereafter, full darkness set in. The sky was cloudy, causing the night to be extremely black and threatening. Laura drew Lobo close to her side; his presence had never been so comforting.

She couldn't see in the dark, but she knew the wolf could. Moreover, he could hear and smell danger long before it arrived.

She hugged her pet gratefully, murmuring, "Lobo, thank God I have you."

Three

As Craig Branston rode past the sign Welcome to Silver Star, he merely gave it a cursory glance. He had ridden through town a couple of years back, and was again planning to simply pass through. He was stopping for one reason—a hot meal.

Reining in at a clapboard building that advertised nourishing, home-cooked meals, he dismounted, and moved lithely inside the restaurant. It was dinner time, and the establishment was crowded. Craig found an empty table, sat down, removed his hat, and placed it on an extra chair.

Craig Branston had caught the attention of several diners, but if he was aware of their scrutiny, one couldn't tell by his relaxed manner.

The patrons were indeed curious about the stranger. He was exceptionally good-looking, yet, at the same time, there was an intimidating aura about him. He was tall, and his tightly muscled frame exuded strength. A close-clipped moustache, its color as coal black as his hair, shadowed mobile lips that blended into a strong chin. His dark eyes, their lashes noticeably long, were framed by thick, arched brows. His suede shirt was partially unlaced, revealing an apex of curly hair that grew abundantly across his wide chest. He wore black trousers, which adhered tightly to his slim hips and long, muscular legs. A short-barrel Peacemaker .45 was strapped on securely, but worn low, in the traditional gunslinger's fashion.

Sheriff Longley, sitting at a table with Ed and Doyce Talbert, recognized Branston, for he had once done business with him. He quickly filled his companions in on Branston, and the three discussed him for a few minutes. As Craig was ordering dinner, the sheriff left the restaurant to hurry to his office. He returned shortly with a wanted poster on Laura. Accompanied by the Talberts, he approached Craig's table.

Branston remembered the lawman. "Good evenin', Sheriff," he said cordially.

"May we join you?" Longley asked.

He nodded his consent.

The three men pulled out chairs, and sat down.

"What can I do for you, Sheriff?" Branston asked.

Longley introduced Ed and Doyce before explaining, "Three days ago, the Talberts' youngest brother was murdered." He reached into his jacket pocket, brought out the wanted poster, and laid it on the table. The sheriff pointed at Laura's picture, and said, "That's the murderer."

"Ed here drew the picture of her," Doyce put in. "He's good at drawing faces."

"That poster's fresh off the press," the sheriff continued. "Getting it now will give you a jump on other bounty hunters."

Branston didn't say anything; he was looking at the face on the poster. She certainly didn't look like a killer.

"Mr. Branston," Ed began, "as you can see, I've posted a reward of five hundred dollars on Laura Mills—alive. However, Sheriff Longley has informed me that you are

27

very good at your job. When you decide to pursue a murderer, you usually succeed. Therefore, I'm willing to pay you eight hundred dollars for your time and effort. Find Laura Mills, bring her to me, and the money's yours."

Craig tore his eyes away from the drawing. "How do you know she killed your brother?"

Ed told him about Lee writing her name before he died. "She undoubtedly murdered him."

"It could've been self-defense," Craig replied.

"If she wasn't guilty, then why did she run?"

"Maybe she was afraid."

Ed was losing his patience. "Mr. Branston, do you intend to find Miss Mills or not? Capturing her shouldn't pose a problem. She'll be easy to recognize. Furthermore, she's traveling with a wolf. Anyone who sees her will no doubt remember her."

Craig cocked a brow, his expression questioning. "A wolf?"

"Yes, she raised it from a pup."

The sheriff decided to intervene. "Branston, this should be a piece of cake for you. You're a damned good bounty hunter."

"I *was* a damned good bounty hunter," Craig said, setting the record straight. "I'm not in that line of work anymore. I quit over a year ago."

"I didn't know," the sheriff replied.

Ed pushed back his chair, and got abruptly to his feet. "Excuse us for bothering you, Mr. Branston. However, my offer of eight hundred dollars still stands."

He left the restaurant, followed closely by Doyce. The sheriff remained for a few minutes, chatting easily with Branston. Then he, too, departed.

The wanted poster on Laura was still on the table. As

the waiter was bringing Craig's dinner, he shoved the poster aside. Despite his hunger, the steak and fried potatoes failed to keep his full attention, for his eyes were continually drawn back to the face on the wanted poster. Ed, sketching a good likeness, had captured Laura's vulnerable beauty. Craig couldn't help but find her enchanting.

Branston soon finished his dinner, paid for it, picked up the poster, and left the restaurant. He slipped the poster into his saddlebags. He wasn't sure why he couldn't leave it behind, but for some reason, he wanted to hold onto it. He certainly had no intentions of pursuing Laura Mills, but, nevertheless, he couldn't part with the lovely face that Ed Talbert's talent had duplicated.

It took three days for the mare's hoof to heal, during which time, Laura had stayed holed up in the cave. Still determined to travel at night, she left on the third evening. The long delay had unsettled her nerves, and she was terribly tense as she journeyed across the dark landscape. She had lost three days! She should be miles and miles farther away from Silver Star, the sheriff, and the Talberts! She was jumpy and expected a posse to appear at any moment. However, as the night wore on and she came upon only nocturnal creatures, her apprehensions began to wane.

She stopped at sunrise in an area well-concealed by foliage and trees. For the first time, she dared to build a small campfire, brew coffee, and cook a meal. Her hunger satiated, she spread out her bedroll, placed her Winchester within easy reach, lay down, and hoped she would soon fall asleep. Since the night she had been forced to run away, sleep hadn't come easily. She was scared, lonely, and filled with anxiety. Now, as she tossed and turned on her blanket, she waited impatiently for fatigue to conquer her worries and allow her to fall into a deep slumber.

Lobo came to her side and snuggled against her. She welcomed his closeness, and put an arm about him. A long time thereafter, she finally fell asleep.

The sun was beginning to set when Laura was suddenly awakened by Lobo's deep growl. Alerted, she sat up with a start, grabbed her rifle, and cocked it. Her long hair was still pinned up, and she threw on her hat. As she got quickly to her feet, her eyes scanned her surroundings. Meanwhile, a vicious snarl curled Lobo's mouth, baring his long, deadly fangs. Laura stood tense, her heart beating rapidly. Someone was certainly approaching, she listened closely, but couldn't hear a thing. The wolf, however, had picked up a strange scent, and, now, as his acute hearing warned him of possible danger, his growl deepened ferociously.

Laura, her body rigid, stood as though fastened to the ground. She wondered if a posse was close by. She had a fearful feeling that she was about to come face to face with the Talberts and Sheriff Longley. She felt sick inside; her desperate flight had been for nothing! Her arrest was inevitable, and running away was only going to make her look guilty!

She heard the sound of a horse approaching, and it sent her heart pounding even harder. Despite her fear, though, she realized only one rider was coming her way. It gave her hope. Maybe there was no posse nearby, only a traveler who meant her no harm.

She stared into the surrounding thicket, but she

couldn't make out a form of any kind. Thus, when a man's voice suddenly called out, she jumped as though she had been physically struck.

"Hello, in the camp! Mind if I ride in?"

Laura's thoughts were swirling. If she refused him entry, he might try to force his way into camp. Furthermore, inhospitality would make it seem as though she had something to hide. That would surely raise the man's curiosity. No, it would be best to invite him to join her, and hope he wouldn't see through her boy's disguise. She wouldn't linger, however. She'd let him know that she was leaving, but that he was welcome to use her campsite.

Lowering her voice an octave, she called back to him, "Come on in, but keep both hands where I can see them."

She watched as man and horse came into view. He was riding a black Arabian stallion, and, for a moment, Laura's gaze swept over the horse. She then turned her eyes to the rider, and his astounding good looks jolted her. She couldn't recall ever seeing a man so handsome.

"Howdy," he said warmly. "My name's Craig Branston." He recognized Laura from the wanted poster. He hid a smile, for he found her disguise humorous. Her lovely face and softly contoured frame could never be mistaken as a boy's. He decided, though, to go along with her masquerade. He was sure it would put her more at ease. "What's your name, son?" he asked, watching her closely.

Laura sighed inwardly. Thank goodness, her disguise had fooled him! Her brother's name was the first to pop into her mind. "My name's Johnny," she said, remembering to lower her voice.

Craig grinned wryly. "If I get down, that wolf won't attack me, will he?"

"Not unless I tell him to."

31

The implication didn't seem to faze him, for he dismounted carelessly without keeping a watchful eye on Lobo. He gestured toward the burned-out fire. "Mind if I build that back up and make some coffee?"

"Go right ahead. You can camp here for the night, if you want. I'm leavin'."

"Leaving?" Craig questioned. "But it'll be dark soon."

"That's all right. I prefer to travel at night."

"You shouldn't ride at night. It can be dangerous. A robber could waylay you before you had a chance to see him."

"I'm not afraid." She pointed at the wolf. "Lobo's my eyes at night."

Craig knew why she didn't want to travel during daylight hours; she hoped to avoid coming into contact with other people. Obviously, she wasn't too sure of her boy's disguise. He understood her reasoning, but didn't agree with it. Traveling at night could prove to be more dangerous than riding during the day. He wondered if he could convince her to change her tactics.

"It isn't dark yet," he said. "So why don't you share some grub with me? After all, you need to eat before you leave, don't you?"

Laura was hungry, and she did need nourishment before embarking on her night's journey. "Sure, I'll stay and eat. But then I gotta get goin'."

"I'll gather up some more firewood," he said, moving toward the thicket. The kindling about the camp was still damp from the past rain, and he ventured into a more dense area where he knew he'd find drier branches and twigs. He was soon deep in thought, as he tried to figure out a way to talk Laura into traveling by day. He supposed the only logical way to convince her was to be perfectly honest. He'd let her know that he knew her true

32

identity, but meant her no harm. Also, he couldn't let her travel alone; he'd offer to ride with her. That, of course, would mean a change in his own plans, unless for some uncanny reason they were going in the same direction. Regardless, Craig was now determined to escort her. He couldn't leave this woman to fend for herself.

Meanwhile, as Craig was gathering kindling, Laura was going through his saddlebags. She was too cautious not to be suspicious, and wasn't about to blindly trust Craig Branston or anyone else. The wanted poster was quickly found, read, and returned to the saddlebags. Had Branston seen through her disguise? Did he know who she was? Of course, he knew! She wondered why he was carrying the wanted poster. He was probably a lawman, or, even worse, a bounty hunter! But why hadn't he taken her prisoner? What kind of game was he playing?

Her first impulse was to run, but fleeing was impossible. Her mare wasn't even saddled, and Branston would be back any moment. Moving quickly, she went to Craig's horse, took his rifle, and hid it under her bedroll. She grabbed her Winchester, re-cocked it, and waited expectantly.

Craig emerged from the thicket, his arms laden with small branches. He was startled to find himself at gunpoint.

Laura smiled inwardly. She definitely had the drop on him; carrying kindling, he couldn't draw his gun.

"Real easy-like, I want you to put the wood on the ground, then unbuckle your gun belt, drop it, and kick it over here by me."

He put down the kindling, then slowly undid his holster, lowered it to the ground, and kicked it toward Laura. It came to a stop at her feet.

33

Carefully, she picked it up. "Now unsaddle your horse."

"Do you mind telling me why you're doing this?"

"Don't act as though you don't know! Are you a lawman or a bounty hunter?"

He looked at her questioningly, but a somewhat devilish grin was on his face.

"I went through your saddlebags," she explained.

"I take it you found the wanted poster."

She had nothing more to say. Furthermore, she was impatient to be on her way. "Do like I said, and unsaddle your horse." When he didn't move to do so, she threatened, "Don't think I won't shoot you!"

He put up his hands in a don't-shoot pose, but she knew he wasn't afraid, for his dark eyes were mocking her. He went to his stallion and removed its saddle.

She walked cautiously to her belongings; a lariat was beside her own saddle. She picked it up and pitched it to Craig. "Remove your horse's bridle, then slip that rope about its neck."

He did as he was told and, for a moment, considered making a lurch for Laura's rifle. But he quickly decided such a move wouldn't be wise. He had a feeling that she not only knew how to use her weapon, but wouldn't hesitate to do so. However, she had his admiration.

"Now saddle my horse," she told him.

Again, he complied. When he was finished, she ordered him to stand back. Telling Lobo to watch him, she hastily put her belongings, plus Craig's rifle and holster, on the mare. She mounted, grabbed the stallion's rope, then spoke to Craig, "There's a small town about three miles straight south. Since it'll soon be dark, I suggest you start walking there in the morning. I'll turn your horse loose a few miles from here. When you reach the town, you can rent a horse, and if you're lucky, you might find your stallion. Regardless, you won't be able to follow me for at least a day or longer. By then, I'll be a long way in front of you."

"What about my guns?" he asked. "You wouldn't leave a man alone and unarmed, would you?"

She studied him thoughtfully. She couldn't help but find him disturbingly handsome, and the woman in her was powerless against his masculinity. She wished they had met under different circumstances.

Craig's thoughts were coinciding with Laura's, for he, too, was feeling an intense attraction. Despite her boyish clothes, he was physically aware of her.

Laura tore her gaze away from his, for there was something about him that stirred a weakness in her. She couldn't succumb to this man simply because he was so good-looking. After all, she was nothing to him but a five-hundred-dollar bounty. She had decided that he wasn't a lawman. If he were, he'd certainly have told her so. By now, he'd undoubtedly have flashed his badge.

"I'll leave your guns close by, where you can find them. Without them, you might come to harm, and I wouldn't want to be responsible."

"That's very kind of you, ma'am." His eyes seemed to be laughing at her. "By the way, Miss Mills, horse stealing is a hanging offense."

She lifted her chin defiantly. "What difference does that make? The Talberts can only hang me once!" With that, she slapped the reins against the mare's neck, and taking the stallion with her, she left in a quick gallop. She could have sworn Branston was laughing as she rode away, but she couldn't be sure.

Craig had eaten a hot meal and was sitting at the fire

drinking a second cup of coffee, when his stallion returned. He wasn't at all surprised to see the horse, for he had known it would come back. The stallion was well trained, and had been taught to always return to its master.

He finished his coffee, then thoroughly smothered the fire. As he saddled his horse, his gun was again strapped to his hip. Earlier, seeing his way with a lit torch, he had located his rifle and holster. Laura, true to her word, had left them close by.

Branston was very impressed with Laura Mills, and he didn't blame her for taking his horse and weapons. The stallion's return had foiled her maneuver, but it was nonetheless a good strategic move. In Craig's opinion, Laura was quite a woman! He not only admired her, but was also attracted to her physically.

As he stuffed his belongings inside his bedroll, he wondered if Laura had really shot Lee Talbert. If so, he was certain it had been self-defense. Craig considered himself a good judge of character, and believed Laura wasn't capable of cold-blooded murder.

Mounting his horse, he headed in the direction Laura had taken. She had only a couple of hours head start, and he was set on finding her. Somehow, he'd convince her that he wasn't interested in collecting the bounty, then he'd offer to ride with her. She was independent, cautious, and most likely a skilled shot, but, nevertheless, Craig kept telling himself that she was a woman and needed protection.

Laura, stopping at sunrise, was relieved that she had safely made another's night journey. She unsaddled her mare, turned her loose to graze, then built a small fire.

She hadn't eaten supper last night and was very hungry.

Her provisions were running low, though, and she knew she'd have to stop at a town along the way. She hoped the town's sheriff wouldn't have a wanted poster on her. Just in case, she would wear her disguise, and hope no one would see through it.

She ate breakfast, fed Lobo, then spread her blanket beneath a tree. She removed her cumbersome hat, settled herself down, and waited to be overtaken by sleep. However, she was soon tossing and turning, for slumber eluded her. If she could only put her mind at rest, but thoughts kept flowing ceaselessly. Her present situation was dangerous, and her immediate future was uncertain. If she couldn't find her brother and uncle, what would she do? Returning home would only lead to her arrest. She remembered telling Joshua that she would find Lee's murderer. A testy frown creased her brow. How in the world could she accomplish such a feat? She certainly couldn't do it alone! She would need help. Her spirits lifted somewhat—maybe her brother could find a way to clear her name! But, first, she had to locate him!

Laura's spirits suddenly took a downward plunge. She was grasping at straws. She loved Johnny, but she couldn't really depend on him, for he was too much like their father. He wasn't emotionally strong, intimidating, or even very brave. No, Johnny could never find the real killer—it would be up to her!

Her troublesome thoughts suddenly switched to Craig Branston. She was pleased that she had delayed his pursuit, but she didn't doubt that he'd continue to look for her. Thank goodness, he'd be at least two days behind!

A vision of Branston flashed across her mind. The man was undeniably handsome. His image was captivating, and it sent unwanted sparks of excitement through her. But her vulnerability made her furious, the man was undoubtedly a bounty hunter bent on turning her over to the Talberts! She was angry at herself for finding him attractive! Forcefully, she thrust him from her thoughts.

Laura, remaining tense, tossed restively for at least two hours, before she finally gave up on sleep. Surely, later, fatigue would set in. She went back to the campfire; it was now only burning embers. A slight chill was in the air, and wanting to warm herself, she went in search of kindling. Lobo trotted at her heels.

As a stiff breeze ruffled her hair, she realized that she had forgotten to put on her hat. Unconcerned, she reached up, removed the pins, and let the long, golden mane fall free. Once she had a fire going, she'd give her hair a good brushing. Locating dry branches, she knelt to pick them up when, all at once, her heart lurched! She had left her rifle behind! She could hardly believe that she had made such a foolish mistake.

She turned to rush back for her weapon, but Lobo's sudden growl gave her reason to pause. She stood perfectly still and listened. The unmistakable sounds of horses caused a pang of fear to writhe in her stomach.

Deciding her only chance was to reach her rifle, she made a dash back to camp. As she emerged into the small clearing, however, two horsemen appeared at the same time. One drew his pistol and held it on her. There could be no mistaking her for a boy; her long blond hair falling past her shoulders was a dead giveaway!

"Don't make a move for that rifle, little gal!" The warning came from the man holding the gun.

Laura stared at the strangers. They were a loathsome pair, both unkempt and threatening-looking. Their eyes traveled over her licentiously, and their sexual intentions were obvious. She watched intensely as they dismounted.

38

The man still had her at gunpoint, and she was powerless to try and defend herself. The other man, keeping his pistol holstered, said gruffly to his companion, "Shoot that damned wolf!"

Laura had been expecting such an order, for Lobo was growling fiercely. She stepped in front of her pet, sheltering him with her own body.

"Run, Lobo! Run!" she shouted suddenly.

Obeying, the wolf scurried into the bordering thicket. The man got off a shot, but missed. "To hell with the wolf!" he muttered. His close-set eyes raked over Laura's delicate curves. "Get them clothes off, sweetie! Me and my friend are gonna give you some real good lovin'."

"You heard him, gal!" his companion chipped in harshly. "Start strippin'!"

Four

The dense foliage concealed Lobo as he crept back toward Laura and the two men. He crouched close to the ground, and a low growl sounded deep in his throat as he readied himself to strike. The wolf instinctively knew that his mistress was in danger, and he was willing to risk his life to save hers.

Laura and the men had Lobo's full attention, causing his acute senses to miss another's presence. Craig, following Laura's trail, had heard the gunshot. He dismounted and advanced stealthily on foot.

Meanwhile, Laura was defying her adversaries. "I'll not take off my clothes!" she uttered. She wasn't intimidated.

"Then I reckon we'll have to do it for you," one of them replied.

She watched intently as they moved closer. One man still had his pistol drawn; the other's gun had remained holstered. Laura's body was tense, and she took a long, calming breath. She knew her wolf was close by and would attack at any moment. She had trained Lobo for incidents such as this one, and was aware that he would lurch for the man holding the gun. She was prepared to stop the other one.

Suddenly, taking the men totally by surprise, Lobo sprang from the thicket. The wolf's strong jaws encircled his opponent's arm before he knew what had happened. Falling to the ground, the man fought furiously against his attacker, but as Lobo's sharp teeth cut through his shirt and into his flesh, he dropped his pistol and screamed in agony.

The man's friend reached quickly for his gun, but Laura moved faster. With lightning speed, she slid her hand down to her boot, removed the hidden knife, and sent it soaring through the air. Her aim was accurate, and the razor-sharp blade pierced the man's shoulder. He didn't see the knife coming, and, for a moment, he looked at it as though it were something alien.

Meanwhile, Laura dashed for her rifle, picked it up, cocked it, and yelled loudly, "Lobo! Turn him loose, Lobo!"

Obeying, the wolf let go and backed away.

The man, holding onto his bleeding arm, got awkwardly to his feet. The expression in his eyes was murderous, as they flitted back and forth from Laura to the wolf.

Laura spoke to the other man. "Pull the knife out! Then drop it to the ground. If you make one fast move, I'll blow you straight to hell!"

Grimacing, for the pain was severe, he drew the blade from his flesh, then let the knife fall at his feet.

Laura felt she was in control of the situation, but Lobo's sudden growl put her on edge. She caught a movement out of the corner of her eye, and dared to look away. She was indeed surprised to see Craig Branston. He was leaning leisurely against a tree, his arms folded across his chest, and a rakish smile on his face.

Laura, turning her eyes back to her captives, said to Craig, "I didn't expect to see you so soon."

"But you were expecting me?" His dark eyes glinted with humor.

"Yes, but I was hoping it would be later and not sooner."

"Sorry to disappoint you," he murmured, coming toward her. He gestured toward the two men. "What do you plan to do with them?"

"Take their guns and horses."

Craig said with a chuckle, "I should have known."

She turned her rifle on him. "Don't come any closer."

His steps slowed, but he kept coming. "There's no reason to shoot me, Laura. I don't mean you any harm. In fact, I followed you to offer you my protection." He smiled broadly. "But, considering what has just happened, such chivalry seems unwarranted. You're perfectly capable of taking care of yourself. Nonetheless, there is safety in numbers, even if the number is only two." He pointed at Lobo. "Make that two and a half."

Laura wanted to trust him, but she wasn't about to throw caution to the wind. She didn't, however, threaten to shoot him instead, she watched, amazed, as he reached down and petted Lobo. She had never known the wolf to take to someone so quickly.

"Since Lobo seems to trust you," she said, "I'll give you the benefit of the doubt. But I'm going to be watching you closely, Mr. Branston. This doesn't mean, however, that I want you traveling with me. We'll talk about it later."

"Yes, ma'am," he agreed, smiling. "Whatever you say."

Laura was somewhat perturbed, for it seemed as though he were secretly laughing at her.

Craig wasn't laughing, but he was amused. He found Laura delightfully charming, and because he had never met a woman like her, he didn't quite know how to take her. Nonetheless, she had his complete admiration.

Laura and Craig took the men's horses and weapons. They dropped the guns close by, but didn't turn the horses loose until they had traveled a good distance from the campsite.

They rode in silence. Laura, remaining cautious, didn't sheathe her rifle, but kept it cradled across her arms. She was worried and very tense. Allowing Branston to ride along might be a serious mistake. After all, she didn't know the man! He could very well plan to turn her over to the Talberts. What if he were merely laying some kind of trap—one that she was foolishly falling into? The more she thought about it, the more her anxieties increased.

She suddenly reined in, and Craig brought his horse to a stop alongside hers. Laura, moving quickly, pointed her Winchester at him. "I'm not sure I can trust you, Mr. Branston. And until I make up my mind, I'll take your pistol and rifle."

He quirked a brow, and his dark eyes twinkled. Apparently, he wasn't bothered that Laura had him at gunpoint. "Miss Mills," he began calmly, "I let you take my guns once; there won't be a second time."

"You let me!" she exclaimed. Oh, the man had his nerve!

"Yes, I let you," he replied softly. Then, with the

43

quickness of a snake, his hand shot forward, grasped Laura's rifle, and jerked it out of her grip. "Let this be a valuable lesson, Miss Mills. When holding your opponent at bay with a rifle, keep out of his reach. A rifle's too easy to grab."

Laura was not only fuming, but was also embarrassed. He had taken her gun so easily.

"If I give this rifle back, do I have your word that you won't aim it at me?"

She wasn't sure she could make such a promise. "Mr. Branston, if you aren't interested in collecting the bounty, then why are you carrying that wanted poster?"

"I stopped in Silver Star for a hot meal. The sheriff, along with Ed and Doyce Talbert, were in the restaurant. The sheriff knew that I used to be a bounty hunter. He and the Talberts gave me the wanted poster. They figured I might be interested."

"Do you really expect me to believe that you aren't interested? Five hundred dollars is a lot of money."

"Eight hundred," he told her. "Ed Talbert thought raising the ante might change my mind."

"I don't understand why you didn't accept his offer."

"Hasn't it occurred to you that I might think you're innocent?"

"Why would you think such a thing?"

He smiled charmingly. "You're a suspicious little vixen, aren't you?"

"You'd be suspicious, too, if you were on the run."

"Laura," he said gently. His tone, caressing her name, made Laura feel strange inside. "I can't prove that I'm not your enemy; you'll simply have to trust me." He gave her back her rifle.

She slipped it into its leather sheath. "This doesn't

44

mean I completely trust you, Mr. Branston."

"The name's Craig."

"If you weren't pursuing me when you left Silver Star, then exactly where were you headed?"

"California."

She looked at him with surprise. "That's where I'm going!"

"What part?"

"Death Valley."

"You can't be serious!" he exclaimed. "That's no place for a woman!"

She frowned testily. "You know, I was just beginning to like you, but after a remark like that one, I'm not so sure. Just because I'm a woman, doesn't mean I'm incompetent."

"Laura, Death Valley is a hot, deadly region. It's the closest thing to hell on this earth."

"Not this time of year. It's still spring."

"Why do you want to go to such a place?"

"I hope to find my brother and uncle." She was eager to change the subject, for she could tell by his expression that he wanted to talk her out of it. "Where in California are you going?"

"San Francisco."

"Is that your home?"

"No. Actually, I'm from Abilene."

"Then why are you going to San Francisco?"

"My fiancée is there, and I plan to get married."

His answer made her heart sink, almost literally. She didn't know why. After all, Craig Branston was nothing to her. Why should she care if he was getting married?

She kneed her horse gently. "We'd better keep moving."

45

Riding at a steady pace, they put several miles behind them. Conversation, however, was short and sporadic; neither seemed to have much to say.

Ed Talbert was in the study relaxing with a glass of brandy, when his father, returning from town, suddenly barged inside. Furious, Harry slapped Laura's wanted poster on the desk in front of his son's eyes, and demanded, "Was this your idea?"

Ed was puzzled by his father's anger. "I sketched the picture, but the poster was Sheriff Longley's idea. Wanted posters are common procedures, and they usually do the job. I'm sure Laura will be apprehended."

"Well, at least you specified that she be brought in alive."

"I thought it more proper, considering she's a woman."

"And hasn't been found guilty," Harry added.

Ed studied him quizzically. "You don't think she's guilty, do you?"

"I believe she shot Lee, yes. If she hadn't, Lee wouldn't have written her name. However, I'm not so sure that he didn't somehow cause his own demise."

"What do you mean?"

Harry eased into a chair. "I loved Lee, but I wasn't blind to his faults, and, God knows, he had several. Maybe he tried to force his intentions on Laura, and she shot him in self-defense."

Ed was also aware of his youngest brother's unscrupulous character, and he couldn't completely disregard what his father said. "But if she shot him to protect herself, why did she run away? Apparently, Lee was still alive. Why didn't she have Joshua send for the doctor?"

"I don't know," Harry sighed. "Maybe she ran out of fear."

"That's absurd! Laura Mills isn't like other women. She never ran from anything in her life. She'd tangle head on with a grizzly bear, if she had a mind to."

Harry eyed his son dubiously. "That's quite an observation. I didn't realize you knew Laura that well."

"I don't." He shrugged. "But I know a lot about her."

"Did you ever consider courting her?" Harry awaited his answer intently.

"It crossed my mind a couple of times, but I didn't do anything about it."

"Why not?"

"I knew you wouldn't approve. You didn't like Laura's parents, and I don't think you care all that much for Laura and her brother."

"I have nothing against Laura and Johnny."

Ed's brow wrinkled as he regarded his father with curiosity. It didn't mar his good looks; it merely lent his angular face a thoughtful expression. He was an attractive man with pleasant features and a tall, slender frame. "Do you ever intend to tell me what happened between you and Laura's parents? Which one did you hate? Her father? Her mother? Or did you hate them both?"

"I didn't hate either one of them," he replied, getting to his feet. He turned to leave, but Ed detained him.

"Pa, satisfy my curiosity, will you? What caused the feud between you and the Millses?"

He didn't answer.

"Damn it, Pa! Are you going to take the secret to

47

the grave with you?" Ed wasn't angry, he was merely impatient.

Harry, on his way to the door, said over his shoulder, "That's right, son. I just might take it to my grave."

Ed returned to sipping his brandy. He thought about his father and Laura's parents, but he couldn't imagine what had caused their rift. He routed it from his mind; what difference did it make? Furthermore, his father was determined to keep it to himself. If he had intended to confide in him, he would have done so years ago. Ed turned his thoughts exclusively to Laura. He wondered if he should pursue her himself. He was sure she was heading for California to find her brother. Ed was disappointed in his father's apparent disinterest; he should be hell-bent on apprehending Lee's murderer, even if she was a woman! Murder was murder, damn it, and Laura shouldn't get off scot-free! Well, if need be, he'd hunt her down himself! He didn't want her to hang, but he did want her to pay!

Laura and Craig made camp at sunset. They found a good area surrounded by thick foliage, built a fire, and cooked a warm meal. They discussed Lee's death, the Talberts, and Harry's part in aiding Laura's escape. By the time they were on their second cups of coffee, full darkness had set in, and silence had come between them. Both were immersed in their own thoughts.

Laura, sitting beside Craig, suddenly sensed his perusal. She cast him a sidelong glance; he was indeed watching her. "Why are you staring at me?"

"Several reasons," he replied, grinning.

His smile was contagious, causing her to respond in kind. "For instance?"

"Well, for starters, you're a very beautiful woman."

She blushed; she couldn't help it. "Thank you," she murmured softly. Somewhat embarrassed, she looked away.

"You're not only beautiful," he continued, "but you're also a very remarkable young lady. For instance, how did you learn to throw a knife so handily? Jim Bowie, himself, couldn't have done better."

"A wrangler who used to work for my father taught me how to use a knife."

"What drove you to learn such a thing? I mean, handling a knife isn't normally something a woman wants to learn."

"The wrangler's name was Pete. He worked at the Diamond Cross a long time. He was always showing off good-naturedly with his knife. I was fascinated, and I asked him to teach me."

"I bet you're good with a rifle, too, aren't you?"

"I could be a lot better."

"Do you know how to use a handgun?"

"A little."

She was gazing into the fire. Placing a hand under her chin, Craig turned her face to his. He looked deeply into her azure eyes and found them enchanting. "You're a very unique lady, Laura Mills." A sensuous smile touched his lips. "I wish I had met you sooner."

"Sooner? What do you mean?"

His mood took a sudden switch. He no longer seemed interested in tender amenities. He drained his cup in one swallow, got to his feet, and said tersely, "I'll tend to the horses."

"Craig!" she called. "Why do you wish you had met me sooner?" Coyness wasn't a part of Laura's nature, her question was straightforward.

"You really don't know, do you?"

"Should I?"

"Laura, I never dreamed a woman with your charm and character existed. And now that I found you, it's too late."

This time, she understood. She tried not to show her feelings, but still her cheeks reddened. Also, she wasn't sure if she liked the course of their conversation. She hadn't decided yet how she felt about Craig Branston. He had dropped into her life too unexpectedly.

As he walked away to take care of the horses, she found a spot close to the fire, spread her blanket, and lay down. Lobo quickly took his place beside her.

A few minutes later, she heard Craig return to the fire. She was lying on her side, with her back facing him. She decided to keep it that way.

"Laura?" he said softly. "Forgive me, if I spoke out of turn. I shouldn't have said anything. I plan to get married as soon as I reach San Francisco, and nothing's going to change my mind." It sounded as though he were trying to convince himself, as well as Laura. She didn't say anything, and he wondered if she was sleeping. "Laura, did you hear me?" he whispered.

She feigned sleep, and told herself she didn't care if he got married or not. It didn't work, however, for deep inside she did care.

Sheriff Longley was seated at his desk drinking his third cup of morning coffee, when the door opened, and Harry Talbert came inside. Longley was surprised to see him; he wondered if there was trouble.

"What brings you here so early?" he asked Talbert.

"This!" Harry replied, showing Longley the wanted poster. "I want you to call all these back."

"I can't do that. There's too many of 'em. Another shipment went out yesterday. Also, a description of Laura has been widely telegraphed."

Harry pulled out a chair and sat down. He was obviously troubled.

"There's something you should know," Longley began. "That last shipment of posters reads alive or dead." He had one on his desk, and he handed it to Harry. "I don't know how the mistake was made, but by the time I realized it, the shipment was gone. These posters are going by stage and railroad, and they'll be widely distributed."

Talbert, his face livid, bounded from his chair. "Ed specified he wanted Laura returned *alive!* How could you have let something like this happen?"

Longley sighed deeply. "I'm sorry, but mistakes happen."

Harry sank back into his chair, clearly worried.

The sheriff studied him thoughtfully. The two men had been close friends for years, and Longley was concerned. "Harry, there's something going on here that you haven't told me. Do you want to talk about it?"

"I'm not sure," he murmured.

"Harry, you can trust me. We've been pals for a helluva long time. What's bothering you? Why are you so concerned about Laura Mills? She killed your son; you should want to see her apprehended. Why are you acting as though you hope she won't get caught?"

Talbert got slowly to his feet and moved hesitantly toward the door. He started to leave, but, pausing, he turned back to the sheriff. "I know I can trust you, George. What I'm about to say must be kept confidential. No one must know, not even my sons."

"You have my word." He meant it.

"I have reason to believe that Laura Mills is my daughter."

Five

Laura awoke shortly before dawn. The campfire had burned down, so she placed a couple of branches on the hot embers. Craig was in his bedroll; he appeared to be asleep. Telling Lobo to stay, Laura went into the thick foliage for privacy. When she returned, she filled the coffeepot and put it on the fire. She glanced over at Craig; he was watching her.

"Good morning," she said.

He smiled warmly. "How did you sleep?"

"For the first time since all this happened, I slept soundly."

"My presence must make you feel safe." There was a twinkle in his dark eyes.

"I think I was just completely worn-out."

Craig left his bedroll, went to the fire, and sat beside Laura. "You make it very difficult for me to feel chivalrous."

"I'm not a damsel in distress."

"So I've noticed."

"Do you disapprove?"

"Not in the least. I admire a woman who can take care of herself. However, I don't think she should be *too* independent. A man likes to feel that he's taking care of a woman."

"Well, my father never took care of my mother, nor did he take care of me. My brother is just like him. In order to survive, I had to be independent, and so did my mother."

"Tell me about your family."

"There's not much to tell. My parents are dead, and my brother's somewhere in Death Valley." She sounded a little bitter.

"What about you, Laura? I'd like to know you better. Tell me about yourself."

"What do you want to know?"

"Have you ever been in love?"

She smiled disarmingly. "Isn't that question a little personal?"

"No, I don't think so."

She decided to answer it. "I thought I was in love with a man named Chad, he was a wrangler and worked for my family."

"You only *thought* you were in love? Are you saying that you weren't?"

"I was seventeen; Chad was twenty. I was completely infatuated with him. He was very handsome and had a winning personality. I thought he felt the same way about me, until one day he quit his job, left town, and ran away with a saloon girl. When I realized that my pride was hurting more than my heart, I knew I wasn't really in love."

"Were there any other beaux?"

"A couple here and there, but nothing ever came of the relationships. You see, by the time I was eighteen, I didn't have time for romance. My mother had become pregnant, the doctor told her that she'd have a hard time carrying the child. She had to stay in bed. Her chores became mine, and there was a lot of work to do. You see, it was my mother, not my father, who successfully operated the Diamond Cross. My brother Johnny had no interest in the ranch at all. Mama died giving birth, and the baby never lived. After that, Papa started spending his time in town gambling, drinking, and womanizing. He lost all our money, then sold the cattle. It was about this time that Uncle Zeb stopped by for a visit, and Johnny left with him. Zeb is really our grand-uncle on my mother's side. He claims to be a man of many trades, mostly he's a prospector."

"When did your father die?"

"Two months ago. He died of a heart attack."

The coffee was ready; Craig poured two cups, and handed one to Laura. He couldn't help but feel sorry for her, but he knew if he offered her sympathy, she'd be offended. Laura Mills was too proud!

"You have my admiration, and I hope someday you'll meet a man who's worthy of you. Someone who will make life's burdens a little easier to bear."

"I know there are men like that, but there's been only three men in my life, and none of them was strong enough to carry many burdens. Quite the contrary, they were the burdens."

Craig chuckled good-naturedly. "Don't judge all men by your father, Chad, and Johnny."

"Don't you think we should make breakfast, and be on our way? We're wasting time."

"I don't think the time was wasted at all. I got to know you better."

"Well, the next time we decide to sit around talking, we'll talk about you."

"When it comes to myself, I'm a man of few words."

He got up, went over to the horses, and began to saddle them.

Harry, looking for Ed, found him in the study. He was sitting at the desk, taking care of paperwork. "I'm leaving in the morning," Harry told him.

"Leaving?" Ed queried, confused. "Where are you going?"

"To find Laura."

"What!" he exclaimed, bounding from his chair. "I can't believe you're serious!"

"I'm serious, all right!" He went to the liquor cabinet and poured a glass of brandy, saying calmly, "I know you'll take care of things while I'm away."

"You don't plan to go alone?"

"No, I'll take Joshua with me. That is, if he agrees."

"Pa, I wish you wouldn't go."

"It's something I have to do."

"Why?"

"That wanted poster reads dead or alive. I intend to find Laura before someone kills her for the reward."

"But why do you feel that it's something you have to do?"

"Never mind why."

Ed lost his patience. "Why can't you give me a simple answer?"

Harry finished his brandy, and as he headed for the door, he said firmly, "There are some things I'd rather not talk about, and my concern for Laura Mills is one of them."

Ed sat back down, his paperwork now forgotten. He was deeply worried. Harry Talbert was no longer a young man, and neither was Joshua. The two had no business pursuing Laura Mills. However, Ed knew his father was stubborn, and once his mind was made up, nothing or no one could change it.

Smoky Gulch was a small, rowdy town close to the California-Nevada border. It had a sheriff and a deputy, but most of their time was spent on gambling and drinking. Enforcing law and order was not a top priority. The undisciplined town was frequented by rovers, drifters, outlaws, and all kinds of other unsavory characters.

Craig was hesitant to stop at Smoky Gulch, but he and Laura were running low on supplies. He advised Laura to continue her boy's disguise; the town might have a wanted poster on her.

They rode into Smoky Gulch at dusk, but a brewing storm darkening the landscape made it seem much later. Streaks of lightning, severing the swirling clouds, were accompanied by roaring thunder. Due to the threatening weather, Craig and Laura decided to spend the night in town. They stabled their horses, and took their carpetbags to the hotel.

Laura was glad to find that the establishment was clean and in good condition. She stood back as Craig went to the front desk.

"I need two rooms," he told the clerk.

The man shook his head. "Sorry, but I have only one room left." He glanced at Laura. "It's got a bed big enough for you and the boy to share." Then, as his gaze fell across Lobo, a deep frown creased his brow. "If you expect to keep that wolf with you, it'll cost you double."

57

"Double!" Craig remarked. "Isn't that a little stiff?"

"Take it or leave it."

Craig didn't see where he had any other choice. "I'll take it."

He signed the register, paid for the room, and gestured for Laura to follow him to the stairs.

With a boy's ungainly gait, she crossed the lobby and climbed the steps behind Craig. They moved down the hall to the third room on the right.

Craig unlocked the door and stepped aside for Laura to enter ahead of him. She went inside, put her bag on the bed, and looked about the room. It was small, but neat and clean.

"Where's your room?" she asked Craig.

"Here," he said, closing the door.

"You can't stay here!" she said sharply.

"Why not?" Amusement shone in his eyes.

"There's only one bed, that's why not!"

"This was the last room for rent," he replied. He placed his carpetbag beside hers. "If you don't want to share the bed, I guess I'll have to sleep on the floor. However, it's a mighty big bed. There's more than enough room."

Laura couldn't help but smile. "Craig Branston, I do believe you're a rogue."

"Me?" he questioned innocently. "Ma'am, I'm a perfect gentleman."

"In that case, you won't object to sleeping on the floor."

"Right," he replied, opening his bag and removing a change of clothes. "I can get a shave and a bath at the barbershop. However, I'll have the clerk send a tub up here for you." He went to the door, opened it, looked

58

back at Laura, and said, "When I come back, I'll take you to dinner."

The moment he left, she moved to a mirror that hung over the dresser. As she studied her reflection, a frown of distaste wrinkled her brow, for her clothes were coated with trail dust.

"A lot of good a bath will do," she mumbled aloud. "I'll just have to put these dirty clothes back on. I wish I had brought more than one set of Johnny's things." She shrugged; there was nothing she could do about it. She could at least wash her hair, and soak in a hot tub—it sounded heavenly!

An hour later, Craig knocked on the door, and received permission to enter. Laura had taken her bath; now she had a towel wrapped about her, and was kneeling beside the tub, washing Lobo. The wolf's head was bowed, and his tail was stuck between his legs.

Craig chuckled. "I don't think Lobo's too happy."

"He hates baths."

Craig was carrying a wrapped bundle, he pitched it on the bed, went to the tub, and told Laura that he'd finish washing the wolf. She was glad to hand over the chore. As she stood up, Craig tried not to look at her too closely. But his willpower wasn't quite that strong. The huge towel wrapped about her was adequate cover, but it revealed her soft shoulders, and came down just past her knees, baring her slender legs. Her hair was still damp, and the long, golden strands fell about her face in seductive disarray.

"What's in the package?" she asked, noticing the bundle.

"I bought you a change of clothes." Craig forced himself to concentrate fully on bathing Lobo. If he continued to admire Laura, he might throw reason to the wind and try to seduce her.

Laura, opening the package, found a pair of trousers and a shirt. The clothes looked as though they would fit perfectly. She cast Craig a sidelong glance; he was totally involved in his chore. A warm blush colored her cheeks, she knew that for Branston to buy her the correct size, he had to be familiar with her body. Apparently, his eyes had measured her very thoroughly.

Realizing this was somewhat embarrassing, yet, at the same time, it made her feel warm and tingly inside. Moreover, she couldn't help but wonder if Craig Branston liked what he saw.

She watched as Craig lifted the wolf from the tub, took a towel, and dried him as much as possible. "I'll take Lobo for a walk, while you get dressed."

"Has it stopped raining?"

"Yeah, but it looks like it'll start up again."

Taking Lobo with him, Craig left the room, went down the rear stairs, and out the back door. He allowed the wolf to roam freely, but kept a watchful eye on him. The alleyway behind the hotel was dark, and Craig doubted if anyone would pass by.

As he walked a distance behind Lobo, Craig's thoughts turned to Laura. He couldn't deny that she had come to mean a great deal to him. How could he help but be drawn to her? After all, she was not only beautiful, but the most unique woman he had ever met.

Craig took one look at Laura, and said, "It won't

work." He and Lobo had just returned to the room.

Laura was confused. "What won't work?"

"No one's going to mistake you for a boy." His eyes swept over her attire, the long-sleeved shirt fit snugly across her full bosom, and the trousers hugged her feminine hips. "You were able to fool the desk clerk because he barely looked at you, he was more interested in Lobo. But in a well-lit restaurant the disguise won't work. There's a place to eat across the street, I'll get a couple of dinners and bring them to the room."

Laura was disappointed, for she was looking forward to eating in a restaurant. "Craig, what difference does it make if people know I'm a woman?"

"It'll make a big difference if the sheriff has that wanted poster on you."

She sighed heavily. "You're right, of course."

He tried to cheer her up. "Spread a blanket on the floor, we're gonna have a picnic by candlelight." He went to the door, saying over his shoulder, "I'll be right back with chicken, bread, and wine."

"I'm famished, so hurry up." Laura removed a blanket from the bed, spread it on the floor, and lit two candles. With the lamps extinguished, the room took on a cozy, romantic hue.

Craig soon returned; he had a basket filled with chicken, all the trimmings, and a bottle of wine. They were hungry, and giving Lobo his fair share, they did justice to the meal. Conversation ran smoothly, but Laura and Craig avoided discussing anything serious.

Laura had finished eating, and was on her second glass of wine, when she asked, "Craig, will you tell me about your fiancée?"

The query seemed to take him by surprise. "Wh . . .

61

what do you want to know?"

"What's her name?"

"Deborah."

"How long have you been engaged?"

"Almost a year."

"Why aren't you in San Francisco with her?"

"She's attending a school."

"School?" Laura repeated, puzzled. "What kind of school?"

"A school for the blind."

Laura didn't say anything for a moment. "I'm sorry. Has she been blind all her life?"

"No, she hasn't. Her blindness was caused by an accident."

"What happened?"

"She fell from her horse and hit her head."

"Were you with her?"

"Yes, I was."

"Would you care to talk about it?"

He shook his head. "I'd rather not."

"Craig, I have one last question. Do you mind?"

"What is it?"

"Do you love her?" Laura awaited his answer intently.

He started gathering up their plates and utensils, putting them back into the basket. "I'm going to marry her, so what difference does it make whether I love her or not?"

"It makes all the difference in the world. Craig, if you don't love her, you shouldn't marry her. You aren't being fair to her or to yourself."

"You don't know what you're talking about!" he said testily. Laura had finished her wine, he took the glass from her hand and packed it away. "I'll return these things to the restaurant, then I think I'll stop at the saloon and have a couple of drinks."

She didn't say anything as he left the room.

Craig hurried across the street, returned the basket, and was on his way to the saloon when three men suddenly blocked his path. They had their pistols drawn.

"Hello, Branston," the largest of the three said gruffly.

Craig recognized them; they were brothers. Four years ago, he had collected a bounty on their father. The man was a cold-blooded murderer, and his sons were just like him.

"We're gonna kill you, Branston!" the large one said. "We saw you before, when you was goin' into the hotel. We figured you'd be comin' back out." A murderous snarl curled his thick lips. "Usin' your left hand, Branston, slowly unbuckle your gun belt, and let it fall to the ground."

Laura was thinking about Craig when Lobo's sudden whine got her attention. She could tell something was bothering the wolf. She watched as he went to the window, placed his front paws on the sill, and whimpered.

She went over, drew aside the curtain, and glanced outside. She looked on anxiously as three men held Craig at gunpoint. Moving decisively, she got her rifle, raised the window as quietly as possible, and took aim.

The man's voice carried upstairs. "Usin' your left hand, Branston, slowly unbuckle your gun belt and let it fall to the ground."

"Hold it right there!" Laura yelled down to the street.

The one holding Craig at gunpoint looked up at the window, then raised his pistol to shoot.

At that moment, Laura opened fire. She aimed for the man's arm, and the force of the bullet sent him whirling before he fell to the ground.

Simultaneously, Craig drew his pistol, shot one brother, and was about to shoot the other one, but he quickly dropped his weapon, held up his hands, and gave up.

Laura, with Lobo at her side, rushed out of the hotel and into the street. She had forgotten to put on her hat, and her long hair was falling about her shoulders.

The sheriff arrived at that moment. He had met Craig before, and he believed him when he said that the Mitchell brothers had tried to kill him. The sheriff knew the Mitchells were always causing trouble. The two brothers who had been shot weren't badly wounded, and the sheriff told them to go see the doc, then get the hell out of town.

It was then that the sheriff took notice of Laura and Lobo. She was carrying her rifle; the lawman quickly drew his pistol, aimed it at her, and ordered, "Put down that gun, ma'am!"

Laura, confused, did as she was told.

"You're under arrest, Miss Mills." The sheriff grinned. "That is your name, ain't it? I got a wire on you this afternoon. There ain't no mistaking who you are, a blond-headed woman travelin' with a wolf. That description fits you perfectly, don't it? Come with me, lady! I'm puttin' you in jail!" He stepped to her rifle and picked it up.

Laura turned to Craig, her expression anxious.

"You'd better go with him," he said gently, giving her a small, encouraging smile.

Craig, keeping Lobo, watched as Laura left with the

sheriff. He was impressed, for she moved proudly, her head high and her shoulders straight. A great warmth filled his heart, and suddenly he knew that he was in love with Laura Mills. It was, however, a disturbing revelation!

Six

Craig waited as the sheriff took Laura into his office. He followed; the window was open, and he could hear what was being said. He hoped to break Laura out, but he wasn't sure how to go about it. He suddenly remembered the knife she kept hidden in her boot. A smile crossed his face; he didn't doubt that Laura would instigate her own escape!

Inside, Laura had her eyes glued to the sheriff as he went to his desk, opened a drawer, and pulled out a set of keys. There were two empty cells; he gestured toward one, saying gruffly, "Get inside, young lady."

Laura didn't move. She knew the man had been drinking heavily, for the smell of whiskey was overwhelming.

Impatient with his prisoner, the sheriff holstered his pistol, placed the Winchester on his desk, frowned angrily, and asked, "Do I have to force you inside that cell?" He moved toward her to do just that; she was unarmed and he didn't consider her a threat.

She backed away.

"Miss Mills," he began testily, "I'm gonna hold you for this bounty hunter I know. He'll be passin' through here day after tomorrow."

"The two of you will split the bounty, no doubt. You're not much of a sheriff, are you?"

He was feeling his liquor, which caused him to reach clumsily for her. She stepped quickly to the side, and, losing his balance, he stumbled.

Laura darted behind him, withdrew the knife from her boot, and held the pointed blade to his back. "Don't move," she ordered.

At this moment, Craig, followed by Lobo, came inside. He was smiling; Laura never failed to impress him.

"It's about time you showed up," she remarked. A teasing note was in her voice.

"I figured you could handle the situation," he replied calmly. He took the sheriff's pistol, then gagged the man with his own neckerchief, and tied his hands behind him. Taking him to the nearest cell, he locked the sheriff inside. To Laura, he said briskly, "We'd better get the hell out of here!"

Remembering to get her Winchester, Laura followed Craig outside. She went to the hotel and got their belongings, while Craig hurried to the stables. By the time she reappeared, he had the horses saddled.

They rode out of town, and keeping to a steady gallop, they traveled a long distance before slowing down.

"Do you think the sheriff will come after us?" Laura asked.

"I doubt it, not in this weather." Storm clouds had formed, causing the night to be pitch-dark. Craig could barely see Laura, but he nonetheless turned his eyes in her direction, and said, "You handled yourself real well back there."

"Thanks," she murmured. "But we stopped in Smoky Gulch to buy supplies, and we didn't get any."

"We'll manage. We can always tighten our belts."

"How far to the next town?"

"About two day's ride from here. It's more a settlement

than a town. It's called Peaceful, and it's the last stop before entering no-man's-land."

"Death Valley?" Laura exclaimed.

"Death Valley covers a big area, but, yes, Peaceful is a stopping place for prospectors."

"Then I expect Johnny and Uncle Zeb stopped there."

"More than likely." A flash of lightning suddenly lit up the sky, followed almost immediately by thunder. "It's getting ready to storm, we'd better find a place to hole up."

As lightning again brightened the sky, Laura spotted a distant cabin. "That looks abandoned," she yelled over a clap of thunder. "Let's check it out."

They veered their course and rode to the shelter. The cabin was in poor condition, and looked as though it had been deserted for years. After Craig helped Laura carry in their supplies, he took the horses to the lean-to built close by.

He returned momentarily, and—to Laura's surprise—had an armful of firewood. He dropped the kindling in front of the fireplace. "The last person to use this cabin left this wood stacked in the lean-to. I'll have a fire going soon."

Outside, the storm had arrived; the wind was now blowing fiercely, sending sheets of rain pounding against the cabin. Laura checked the windows; they were only covered by broken shutters, but they still kept out most of the rain. She looked about the cabin; it consisted of only one room and was completely devoid of furniture.

Craig had a blazing fire going. Laura placed a blanket on the floor, close to the warm flames. She shivered; the storm had brought a chill to the air.

"You'll be warm in a moment," Craig told her. He sat beside her, took her hand, and squeezed it gently.

She glanced down at their hands; the contact intensified her physical awareness of him. She was terribly attracted to

68

Craig Branston, but she felt she had to fight these feelings. After all, he was planning to marry another woman! She drew her hand away.

Craig understood her reserve. "I'm sorry," he murmured. "I wasn't trying to be fresh."

She smiled hesitantly. "If only things were different . . ."

"For instance?"

"If I wasn't running from the law, and if you weren't engaged to be married, we might stay together . . . always."

"Laura Mills, you don't hedge, do you? You're a lady who says it like it really is."

"Mama used to tell me that I should always think before I talk. As you can see, it's a habit she never managed to change."

"I'm glad. A person should be honest and straightforward."

"In that case, why don't you try being honest? Why are you marrying a woman you don't love?"

"I never said that I didn't love her."

"You didn't say that you did."

Craig grew quiet, in fact, he remained that way for so long that Laura was beginning to find the silence uncomfortable. Finally, he said, "I've known Deborah all her life. She was an only child, and she lived in Abilene with her parents. Her father was a reverend; her mother passed away when she was still a young child. I was eight years older, so I always thought of her as a youngster. My parents died two years apart; I was in my late teens at the time. I have an older brother, and after my father's death, he started running our ranch. I didn't really have much interest in it; I was more interested in sowing my wild oats. To make a long story short, I wandered back to the ranch off and on, during which time, Deborah grew up.

"She'd had a crush on me since she was a child. I was

aware of it, but I never took it too seriously. The last time I went home, I stayed a long time. I was through being a bounty hunter. I had a lot of money saved, and was considering buying a ranch of my own. I started seeing Deborah. I was very fond of her, but I wasn't in love. When I realized that she was thinking our relationship was leading to marriage, I knew I had to stop seeing her. I was about to tell her this when her father died quite suddenly. Two weeks after the funeral, Deborah and I went horseback riding. That was when I told her that I didn't love her. She was hurt and angry, and took off racing her horse. It stumbled; Deborah fell and hit her head. I took her to the doctor, and when she regained consciousness, she was blind."

The fire was burning down, and Craig put on another log. "Deborah was all alone; she didn't have any kin. I told her I'd take care of her. She said she didn't want my charity. So I offered her marriage, and she accepted. The doctor told us about a school for the blind in San Francisco. I convinced Deborah to let me take her there. I promised her that I'd come back in six months and we'd be married, and in the meantime, I'd look for some land to buy, or maybe a ranch that was for sale. Well, I didn't find either one, but I plan to keep on looking. Until I can make a home for us, I figure we can stay with my brother."

"Craig, offering to marry Deborah was noble, but very foolish. Didn't you realize you were taking on an obligation that you'd regret for a lifetime?"

"Not really. I thought I could live with it. Maybe I could have, if I hadn't met you."

"Me?" she questioned. "Craig, are you saying—?"

"That I love you? I think I loved you from the first moment I set eyes on you."

"But you intend to honor your commitment to Deborah, don't you?"

"What kind of man would I be if I didn't? She's alone, has no money, and is blind!"

Laura didn't argue; he had made a valid point. She had a feeling that she, too, was in love, but their love wasn't meant to be.

She didn't want to discuss his upcoming marriage—it depressed her. "We need to get some sleep," she said, getting to her feet.

Craig rose at that same moment, and their bodies touched. She turned to move away, but before she could, Craig had her in his arms. She gazed up into his face; his eyes, filled with desire, met hers. She tried to still the erratic pounding of her heart, but her pulse was racing too wildly. When he bent his head, she met his lips halfway.

His demanding kiss triggered her passion, and entwining her arms about his neck, she pressed her body against his. She was conscious only of his nearness, his lips, and a tingling effect that was running through her like wildfire.

Craig's hand swept to the back of her neck, pressing her lips ever closer. He drew her against him so tightly that she was aware of his entire length.

He kissed the soft hollow of her throat, then his lips were suddenly back on hers, sending stronger and more vivid desire coursing through them.

Craig lifted her into his arms, knelt, and placed her gently on the blanket. "Laura," he whispered thickly, "I want you. God, how much I want you!"

She wanted him, too! But not like this! After all, he was determined to marry another woman. The thought sobered her passion, she pushed him away and sat up. "Craig, please! I can't! I just can't!"

His own desire began to ebb. "I understand. I'm sorry; I had no right to take advantage of you."

"You didn't," she replied. "However, when we reach

71

Peaceful, I think we should part company. You have a fiancée waiting, and I don't think you should keep her waiting any longer."

"If I leave, you'll be alone."

"So what?" she spat, a little sharper than she had intended. "By now, it should be obvious that I'm capable of taking care of myself." She bounded to her feet, glared down at him, and added, "I don't need a nursemaid!"

With that, she moved away, got a blanket, and spread it in a corner. Hereafter, she would avoid close proximity to Branston! She was angry, but her anger was directed at herself more than at Craig. She had been a fool to succumb to his kisses!

At that moment, a loud banging sounded at the door. Laura bounded to her feet, and looked anxiously at Craig. She was sure the sheriff had followed them.

"Hello inside the cabin!" a man called strongly. "Branston, I know you're in there, and I'm coming in!"

Craig smiled, for he recognized the voice.

As the man came inside, sheets of rain blew in behind him. The wind was powerful; he had to drop his bedroll and use both hands to close the door. He was wearing a slicker, he removed it along with his hat, pitched them in the corner, then went to Craig and shook hands.

"Slade, what the hell are you doing here?" Branston asked, his tone friendly.

"I was in Smoky Gulch having a drink at the saloon, when the sheriff came inside and said Craig Branston broke his prisoner out of jail. I was hoping I'd catch up to you." Slade turned to Laura, and smiled tenderly. "You must be the prisoner. The sheriff said you were a murderer." His smile broadened. "You don't look like a killer to me."

"I'm not," Laura replied firmly. She studied the stranger closely. He was very handsome; his tall frame heavily mus-

72

cled, his hair—the color of ripe wheat—was thick and curly.

He came toward her, carrying himself with vigor and grace. She looked up into his clean-shaven face, and met a pair of eyes as blue as her own.

"How do you do, ma'am? My name's Jim Slade."

"I'm Laura Mills."

"Yes, I know. I've seen the wanted poster on you."

"That wanted poster certainly gets around," she mumbled.

Jim laughed. "But the drawing doesn't really do you justice. You're much prettier in person."

The compliment made her cheeks redden. "Thank you, Mr. Slade. Tell me, does the sheriff intend to pursue me?"

"I don't think so. When I left the saloon, he was keeping company with a bottle of whiskey."

"Laura," Craig said. "It'll interest you to know that Slade's a federal marshal."

Laura's eyes widened in surprise. "No wonder the sheriff isn't chasing me, he sent you instead!" She brushed past Slade, and moved over to stand beside Craig.

Following her, the marshal replied, "I'm on the trail of a bank robber, Miss Mills. Although I should arrest you, I'm not going to."

"Why not?"

"Apparently, you're innocent. Otherwise, Branston wouldn't be helping you."

"Laura," Craig explained, "Slade and I are good friends. If he says he's not going to arrest you, he won't." He looked at Jim. "Tell me about this bank robber you're after."

"His name is Jerry Donaldson. He was a bank teller in Carson City. He embezzled quite a sum of money, then left town with his wife. I've been trailing them for some time. They're heading for California. I have a feeling that in order to avoid pursuit, they're going to travel through part of

Death Valley."

"It seems we're headed in the same direction," Craig said.

"In that case," Jim replied, "there's no reason why we can't ride together." His eyes went to Laura. "I'm looking forward to such charming and beautiful company."

Jealousy was a new emotion to Craig, and it hit him with a sudden and jolting force.

They left at dawn. The storm had passed, and the day promised to be sunny and warm. Laura took an instant liking to Jim Slade; he was friendly and had a winning personality. Also, with Jim along, she didn't have to worry about being alone with Craig. She didn't trust her emotions. If she were to find herself in Craig's embrace again, she might give in completely. But, now, with Slade traveling with them, such an encounter was unlikely.

The journey to Peaceful went pleasantly, for the weather remained warm and dry. They arrived at the settlement in the late afternoon. Laura could see why it was called Peaceful. The settlement, which consisted of log homes and buildings, was nestled among tall, billowing trees. A stunning backdrop of rugged cliffs overlooked the settlement, and a babbling brook, bordered by spring flowers, enhanced the area. It was indeed peaceful!

They rode to the trader's store, which was in the heart of the village. The building served many purposes; it was not only a store, but also a saloon, barbershop, and a post office. Laura wondered if she'd find her picture posted inside.

The sunlight was bright, and as Laura walked into the establishment, it took a moment for her eyes to adjust. She looked about with interest, and was relieved not to find a wanted poster. Thank goodness, they hadn't gotten this far!

The place was fairly crowded; a group of prospectors

were sitting about a table, chewing tobacco, and comparing stories. A few men were standing at the bar, drinking whiskey.

"Howdy, folks," the proprietor said heartily. Then, recognizing Craig, he continued, "How you doin', Mr. Branston? I ain't seen you in a long time."

"I'm fine, Elmer. How are the kids and the wife?"

"They're doin' just great."

Jim reached into his shirt pocket, withdrew his badge, and showed it to Elmer. "I'm looking for a man and his wife. They're in their twenties, the wife's very pretty, and the man's quite polished. Has anyone like that passed through here?"

"A couple of days ago, a couple fittin' that description stopped here and stayed for a day. The man bought up some supplies, then they left. They was travelin' in a covered wagon. He asked a lot of questions about gettin' to California. Said he wanted to cut through the desert. This time of year, he'll probably make it."

"Thanks," Jim replied. "You've been very helpful."

"Elmer," Craig began, "the young lady here is looking for her brother and uncle. Johnny Mills and Zeb—?"

"Zeb Douglas," Laura said.

Elmer responded with a toothless grin. "Is Zeb your uncle?"

"Yes, he is."

"I've known Zeb for years. He was here with his nephew 'bout a year ago. They was goin' to do some prospectin'. I ain't seen 'em since the day they left."

Laura couldn't hide her concern.

"Don't you fret, ma'am," Elmer told her. "Just 'cause they didn't come back here, don't mean they ain't all right. If they staked themselves a claim, they probably got rich and took off for San Francisco."

Craig put an arm about Laura's shoulders, and drew her to his side. "You look tired. There's a boardinghouse across the street. Let's go get you a room. I bet you'd like a hot bath and a good meal, wouldn't you?"

She smiled warmly. "Sounds wonderful."

Craig, telling Slade he'd be back, escorted Laura outside. "I might as well see if I can get a room for myself and Jim."

"When are you leaving?" she asked.

They were crossing the street, but Craig stopped to ask, "What do you mean?"

"Don't you think you have delayed long enough? I'm sure your fiancée is eagerly awaiting your arrival."

He took her arm and led her across the street to the boardinghouse. He didn't take her to the door; instead, he paused, looked deeply into her eyes, and asked, "Why are you so anxious for me to leave? Are you afraid I might take you into my arms and kiss you into submission?"

"Maybe," she murmured. She lowered her eyes.

"Look at me, Laura."

She did as he asked.

"I promise, if I ever kiss you again, it'll be because you want me to." He smiled disarmingly. "You have my word. Now, let's see about getting you a room."

His promise did little to ease Laura's anxieties. She wasn't worried that Craig would betray her; she was worried that she'd betray herself!

Seven

Laura had dinner in the dining room along with Craig, Jim, three other boarders, and Mrs. Nelson, who owned the rooming house. One of the boarders was a young woman, Karen Darnell; she and Laura shared a bedroom. Laura had barely had time to introduce herself to Karen, before it was time for them to leave their room and go down for dinner. Although their meeting had been short, Laura had taken an instant liking to the young woman. Karen was from Boston, and she had come westward with her father. On their journey, he met some prospectors who told him there were riches to be found in Death Valley. He pooled his money with these prospectors, left his daughter in Peaceful, and headed into the arid region with hopes of staking a rich claim. He had now been gone nine months, and Karen hadn't heard anything from him.

Laura also took an immediate liking to Mrs. Nelson. The matronly woman was warm-hearted and friendly. During dinner, she advised Laura to look for Johnny and Zeb in the mining settlement called Seclusion; so named because it was hard to find. She knew Zeb fairly well, and told Laura that he often stayed in this settlement. Knowing that Jim was searching for the Donaldsons, she said that the couple would certainly stop at Seclusion to buy provisions. Laura, with Craig and Jim in complete accord, decided that they would leave in the morning and travel to the settlement. Laura hoped, prayed, that she would find her brother and uncle there.

Following dinner, Laura and Karen bid everyone good night and retired. The room they shared was small, and the large featherbed seemed to dominate the entire space. However, the room was clean, and the bed looked wonderfully comfortable.

The moment they entered their quarters, Karen asked anxiously, "Laura, may I ride to Seclusion with you?"

The question took her by surprise. "Why do you want to go there?"

"For the same reason you do! You hope to find your brother and uncle, and I want to find my father."

Laura, uncertain, sat on the edge of the bed. Her eyes closely examined her new friend. Karen was small, fragile-looking, and terribly thin. Laura doubted if she was strong enough to make an arduous journey. The young woman wasn't especially pretty; Laura supposed most people would say that she was plain. Her brown hair was pinned into a bun so tight that no wayward tendril could possibly escape. She had a heart-shaped face, high cheekbones, and a delicate nose. She was wearing a gingham dress that was too large, and it fit her slender frame unbecomingly. Karen's eyes, however, were enchanting. They were huge, round, and dark in color.

Now, with anxiety shining in her large eyes, she sat beside Laura, grasped her hand, and pleaded, "Please let me go with you! I'm so worried about my father! Even if he isn't there, maybe someone will know where he is!" A sob caught in her throat. "Or if he's . . . if he's . . ." She paused and wiped at her eyes, for they were filling up with tears. "If something terrible has happened to him, maybe someone in Seclusion will know."

Laura hadn't the heart to refuse. "All right, you can come with us. But, Karen, surely you realize that the journey won't be easy. You'll have to ride horseback all day, and sleep on the ground at night."

"I know that," she replied. "Believe me, I'm not as fragile as I appear."

"Do you have any riding clothes?"

"Yes, I do have one outfit."

"With boots and a hat?"

"I'll show it to you," she said, hurrying to her cedar chest. She opened it and removed the attire.

The riding dress was dark blue, with a mauve-colored, long-sleeved jacket. A black felt hat with plumes completed the outfit. There was also a pair of black boots.

Laura, suppressing a giggle, said, "Karen, you can't wear that! In Boston, I'm sure it's very fashionable, but it's totally unsuited for this part of the country. Furthermore, if you were to wear it, you'd have to ride sidesaddle. The boots, however, will do."

Laura went to her carpetbag. Although she had packed lightly, she had managed to squeeze in two sets of riding clothes. She took out a set for Karen, and put the garments on the bed.

"Here. Wear these."

Karen looked the garments over carefully. "Laura, this outfit is very stunning."

"Perhaps, but it's also very practical. You'd better try it on; you're so small that it might have to be altered."

Karen, her gaze sweeping over Laura, asked curiously, "With clothes like these, why are you dressed the way you are?"

"Like a boy?"

"Yes. I don't want to sound rude, but what you're wearing isn't very flattering."

Laura laughed warmly. "I'm dressed like a boy, because I was pretending to be one."

"But why?" Karen was astonished.

"I'll explain later. First, we need to get you packed. By the way, do you have a horse?"

"Yes, I have a horse at the stables. My father took the rest of the horses and our wagon with him."

"Do you have a saddle?"

"My father's."

"Then I guess all we have to do is pack you a bag. You'll have to leave most of your things here."

"That's all right. I can get them later."

"I'm going to the stables, but I'll be back soon."

"At this hour?"

"Mrs. Nelson doesn't allow pets, so Craig took Lobo to the stables. I want to check on him."

"Lobo?" Karen questioned. "That's Spanish for wolf."

"Lobo *is* a wolf."

"Good Lord! Are you saying, you have a wolf as a pet?"

"Don't worry, he's as tame as a dog, and just as lovable." Laura left the bedroom, and moved quietly through the house, but as she stepped outside, she came face to face with Jim. He had been about to open the front door.

"Where are you going?" he asked.

"To check on Lobo."

"I'll go with you," he offered. He slipped Laura's arm into his, and they started down the street to the stables.

Jim was a big admirer of Laura's; he found her not

only beautiful, but refreshingly charming. He knew it wouldn't take much effort on his part to fall in love with her, but he wasn't blind—he had seen the way she and Craig looked at each other. It was obvious that they were in love. He also knew why they were fighting their feelings, for Craig had told him that he was planning to marry Deborah. Jim, liking and respecting both Laura and Craig, hoped things would somehow work out in their favor.

They entered the stables, and Laura found Lobo tied in a stall. The wolf wagged his tail, and whined a friendly welcome. She hated to see him tied, but, in this case, it was necessary. If he was loose, he'd leave the stables and try to find her.

She sat beside her pet and rubbed him behind his ears. Enjoying her affection, Lobo placed his head in her lap and wagged his tail even more vigorously.

Jim, watching, pointed toward Lobo's bucket of water. "Craig fed him, and left the water in case he got thirsty."

"I think Craig's as fond of Lobo as I am." A sadness shadowed her face. "He'll miss Lobo."

"Not nearly as much as he'll miss you."

Laura looked up with surprise.

"Branston's in love with you, but I guess you already know that."

"He doesn't love me enough to break off his engagement."

"I don't think it's a question of breaking his engagement, so much as destroying a young lady's life."

"Deborah's life," Laura whispered.

Jim smiled sadly. "It's a no-win situation, isn't it?"

Laura agreed. She hugged Lobo, patted his head fondly, then moved out of the stall.

She headed outside, and Jim fell into step beside her. "I'm sorry," he murmured.

"Sorry?" she asked.

"About you and Craig. I wish things were different, for you're both fine people."

"Do you know Deborah?"

"No, I've never met her."

It was a short distance to the boardinghouse, and they walked the rest of the way in silence. As they stepped up onto the porch, Jim took Laura's hand, and she paused to look up into his face.

"Keep your chin up, hon. I have a feeling that you and Craig are gonna end up together."

She smiled wistfully. "I sure hope your feelings generally come true."

"They do," he replied with a smile. He brought her into his arms, hugged her tightly, then gave her a chaste kiss on the lips. Arm in arm, they went into the house; both unaware that Craig was standing across the street watching.

He had just left the trader's store, and was about to cross the street when he spotted Laura and Jim. Their tender intimacy hit him with a force so hard it jolted him to the core. He wondered if Laura was falling in love with Slade. The man was handsome, charming, and he supposed most women found the marshal irresistible. Anger stirred within him, but it wasn't aimed at Jim or Laura, he was angry at fate. He was also painfully jealous.

Slowly, he moved across the street, went into the house, and to the room he shared with Jim. He didn't say anything about seeing him with Laura.

They were about to get undressed for bed when a soft

knock sounded on the door.

"May I come in?" Laura called in a low voice.

Jim was closest to the door, and he let her in.

"Karen will be leaving with us in the morning." She spoke directly to Jim. "I should have told you this evening, but I forgot."

Slade frowned dubiously. "Are you sure Miss—Miss Darnell—is that her name?"

"Yes, Karen Darnell."

"Are you sure she's up to making such a trip? She doesn't look very strong."

"I'm sure she'll do fine." Laura was well aware that Craig hadn't said a word. She turned to him. He was watching her with an expression she couldn't define, but it nonetheless made her uneasy. "Do you care if Karen rides along?"

"Does my opinion matter?" He sounded bitter.

"Of course, it matters." She didn't like his attitude, and meeting his hard gaze without flinching, she replied, "Then it's settled. Karen will join us." With that, she left.

She wondered why Craig had seemed so unfriendly. Had she done something to displease him? If so, she couldn't imagine what it might be. She shrugged it aside, if he was still behaving strangely tomorrow, she'd insist that he tell her what was bothering him.

The travelers left Peaceful early the next morning, and by late afternoon, the landscape began to change. Trees, shrubbery, and grassy plains became scarce, and were eventually replaced with coarse sand, a cactus here and there, and an open, barren desert. Laura could well imagine why the region was considered hell on earth.

During the summer months, it was most assuredly a place of death.

They made camp at sunset. The area was wide open, and Laura missed the protection afforded by surrounding foliage. They cooked a scant meal, for no one was very hungry. Following dinner, Laura and Karen had to walk a long way from camp to achieve privacy. Laura was grateful for Karen's company, another woman's presence made her feel less apprehensive.

When they returned, Craig and Jim had laid out the ladies' bedrolls, as well as their own. Tired, Karen crawled in between her blankets. Despite her fatigue, she had a feeling it would take her a long time to fall asleep. She was worried about her father, but she was also very aware of Jim Slade. Thoughts of her father and Jim swirled through her mind. She considered what she would do if her father was dead. She had very little money, but she did have enough to get back to Boston. She didn't want to go back there, but she was beginning to feel that she would have no other choice. She had an aunt living in Boston, and the woman would undoubtedly take her into her home. Karen's musings gradually drifted to Jim Slade. She had never met a man so charming; also, he was very exciting! A federal marshal! His job alone made him more fiery than the men she had known in Boston. Not that she had known that many; men didn't seem to find her all that attractive. Her father, sensing his daughter might be doomed to spinsterhood, had advised her to be more vivacious, to wear brighter clothes, and with an impatient wave of his hand, he'd tell her to do something with her hair! Karen wished she could improve herself, but she was too self-conscious to do so.

While Karen lay in her bedroll, deep in thought, Laura sat by the fire, studying Craig. He had been withdrawn all day. She was ready to get to the heart of the matter. "Craig," she said, getting to her feet. "Let's take a walk. I'd like to talk to you."

"All right," he said. They moved into the distance with Lobo following, but the wolf was soon loping ahead.

Karen was unnerved to find herself alone with Jim. She was painfully shy around men, and if he attempted to make conversation, she was afraid she'd fail to keep his interest.

"Miss Darnell?" he called softly.

"Yes?" she responded, her heart suddenly pounding.

"Whatever prompted your father to leave Boston?"

"He was an accountant for a shipping company. He had worked there for years, but was fired so that the owner could give the position to his nephew. Father always dreamed of going to California, and when he lost his job, he decided to move to San Francisco." She sighed regretfully. "If only he hadn't met up with those prospectors."

"He's chasing rainbows."

"What?" Karen asked, sitting up.

"Your father's chasing rainbows, and he's not going to find that pot of gold. Exactly how long has he been gone?"

"A little over nine months."

"Then it was still summer when he left?"

"Well, it was September."

"Which means this desert was still ungodly hot."

"Mr. Slade, you think my father's dead, don't you?"

"For your sake, I hope he isn't. But I advise you to prepare yourself for the worst."

"I am prepared," she replied, her tone sad, yet, somehow unemotional, as though she were talking about something that wasn't real.

"What will you do if you learn he's dead?"

"I'll have to return to Boston and live with my aunt. I'm a teacher, and I'll find employment."

He smiled easily. "I'd have bet money that you were a schoolteacher."

"Why? Do I look the part? Most people see teachers as old maids."

Her acrimonious reply startled him. "Miss Darnell, I wasn't trying to be rude."

"I'm sorry," she was quick to apologize. "I shouldn't be so sensitive."

A warm twinkle shone in his blue eyes. "Besides, you aren't old enough to be an old maid."

She responded with a bright smile. "I'm twenty years old."

"You're still a young woman, Miss Darnell."

She swallowed, took a deep breath, and dared to say, "Please call me Karen."

"I'd be honored, ma'am. And I'm Jim."

"Jim Slade," she murmured, savoring the sound of it. "It's a nice name, so masculine and strong."

He chuckled warmly. "No one's ever complimented me on my name before."

She blushed, for she was certain she had made a foolish remark. Embarrassed, she stammered, "Good . . . Good night, Ji—Jim." She lay down, and turned her back.

"Good night," he murmured.

Karen, fighting back tears, wished she were witty and charming.

* * *

The full moon, resplendent in the cloudless sky, cast a golden hue upon the land. Craig, walking beside Laura, could see her clearly. She had discarded her boyish attire for her own clothes, and was wearing a stylish, divided skirt and blouse. She saw no reason to continue her disguise; there would be no wanted posters in this desolate region.

Laura was a natural beauty, and Craig knew she would look lovely in anything she wore. After all, she had been beautiful in boys' clothes. But, now, dressed in feminine attire, she was more desirable than ever. Craig could barely control the urge to take her into his arms and kiss her.

They had strolled quite a distance before Laura stopped, turned to Craig, and asked point-blank, "What's bothering you?"

He was confused. "What do you mean?"

"You aren't acting like yourself. Something's on your mind. What is it?"

"You know me very well, don't you?"

"I'm not sure if I do or not."

It was a moment before he replied, "Laura, I saw you with Jim."

"And?" She was at a complete loss.

"He held you in his arms and kissed you."

She forced herself not to smile—Craig was jealous! She couldn't help but be delighted. "That's right. We embraced and we kissed. Was that wrong?"

"No, it wasn't wrong." He looked miserable. "Laura, are you falling in love with him?"

"I like Jim as a friend, but that's all. He feels the same

way about me. We merely hugged and kissed as friends."

"God, I feel like a fool," he groaned.

She touched his arm. "Craig, you apparently care about me, and I know I care about you. What are we going to do?"

"I wish I knew."

"You'll have to make a choice, you know. Deborah or me."

"If it were only that simple."

Laura wasn't angry, how could she fault his compassion? Deborah was wholly dependent on him. Could he possibly shatter the woman's dreams, her very future? Was it possible for him to do that to a blind woman? If he did, would Laura think less of him? Wasn't his compassion one of the reasons she loved him so much?

"Jim said it was a no-win situation," Laura murmured. "He was so right."

"We either hurt Deborah, or we hurt ourselves."

"Oh Craig!" she cried, flinging herself into his arms. "Hold me! Please hold me close!"

He was more than willing to oblige.

"I've dreamed of falling in love," Laura murmured. "But I always thought it would be such an happy occasion. But, now, in reality, it's so heartbreaking!"

He brushed his lips across her brow. "I know what you mean. My heart virtually aches."

She slid her arms about his neck, encouraging his kiss, which was immediately forthcoming. His mouth caressed hers in a hungry, aggressive exchange that left them breathless.

Reluctantly, they broke apart. Their passion was burning fiercely, but this was not the time nor the place to fulfill their desire. Their gazes locked hopelessly; there might never be a right time or place for their love.

Craig took her hand, and they began walking back. "I'll always love you, Laura," he said softly.

"I love you, Craig Branston. And I will love you until the day I die."

Depression accompanied them back to camp.

Eight

The next day, Jim rode ahead, hoping to find tracks left by the Donaldsons' wagon. Luck was with him, and the day was only hours old when he rode back to the others and reported that he had found a trail.

"The tracks are fresh," he said to Craig. He was puzzled, for the Donaldsons should be much farther ahead. "Maybe they had to hole up for some reason."

"Or else they got lost," Craig replied.

A warm breeze had been blowing all morning, but it was now growing stronger. In quick bursts, it swept across the desert, stirring up sand and sending the particles swirling. A look of concern came to Jim's face. "It looks like a real storm is brewing."

Craig, agreeing, pointed toward a steep dune in the distance. "We'd better ride over and take shelter, these sandstorms can blow up mighty fast."

The group galloped toward the sandy hill. Farther westward, Jerry Donaldson was bringing his covered wagon to a stop. The wind was picking up speed; securing the wagon's brake, he turned to his wife, and said, "Let's get under the canvas."

She didn't say anything; she merely cast him a disdainful glare, as though the storm was somehow his fault.

With a petulant toss of her head, she climbed over the seat and into the back of the wagon.

Jerry, sighing miserably, followed. He drew the canvas opening together, then laced it closed tightly. He sat huddled, his shoulders slumped and his eyes downcast. He was a small man, but he now appeared even smaller. Withholding his gaze from his wife's, he said, "Marsha, my mind is made up. I'm turning the wagon around, and we're going back to Carson City."

"How do you intend to find your way to Carson City?" she asked querulously. "You can't even find Seclusion! We've been lost for days. We're probably traveling in circles!"

He lifted his gaze and met her eyes, which were flashing with rage. Despite her anger, she was lovely. As always, her beauty overwhelmed him. Until last night, he marveled that a woman so beautiful had married a homely man like himself. He had literally worshipped his wife, and had tried very hard to please her—he had even gone against his own principles and embezzled funds. The crime had been her idea, she had formulated the plan and had pressured him into carrying it out. Money meant everything to Marsha Donaldson!

"Darling," she murmured, her tone suddenly as sweet as honey. "You can't be serious about turning around. If you go back to Carson City, you'll go to prison."

"I don't care," he replied. He sounded resolute. "All my life I prided myself on being an honest man." Jerry's conscience was plaguing him terribly. "Now, because of you, I'm running from the law. I don't know why I let you talk me into this." A hardness came to his eyes, and he glowered at her through his rimless spectacles. "Why do I lie to myself? I did this because I believed you actually loved me. But last night, when I told you I wanted to go

91

back, you revealed your true feelings. You not only threatened to leave me, but you said things that hurt me very deeply."

"Jerry, I didn't mean all those cruel things I said. I was overwrought."

"Overwrought!" he exclaimed. "Marsha, you swore you only married me so you could inveigle me into embezzling from my employer."

"But that isn't true!" she said, feigning a wounded expression. "I was saying things I didn't really mean."

"Then prove it," he told her.

"But how?"

"Tell me you want me to return to Carson City, give back the money, and pay for my crime. Then tell me you'll wait for me."

"You fool!" she hissed, her real feelings surfacing. "You can go back, but the money stays with *me!*"

"I'm sorry, Marsha, but I'm returning every cent I stole. That way, my punishment will be lighter—and so will my conscience."

"To hell with your conscience!" she retorted furiously. "And to hell with you!"

Outside, the wind was swirling, causing the canvas top to billow and sway. Jerry could hear the horses neighing frightfully, and he hoped they would make it through the storm. This was his first trip into the desert, and he was unfamiliar with windstorms, thus, he had no way of knowing that the gale was comparatively mild.

Marsha's anger was much stronger than her fear of the storm, and it barely fazed her. She could think of nothing except the money.

They had purchased their wagon in Carson City, and knowing they would need a safe place to hide their money, Jerry had torn up the floorboard, installed a small compartment, then nailed the boards back together. Now, the stolen funds were ensconced beneath the wagon.

Marsha stared at the floorboard as though she could see through to the compartment below. Greed glinted in her emerald green eyes, and she ran her tongue across her lips as if she could actually taste her hidden wealth.

The storm continued its gusty assault; still, Marsha couldn't have cared less. She turned her gaze to her husband; he was staring down at his lap, and his lips were moving. She wondered if he was praying. An inward laugh caused her to smile cruelly. If the bastard was praying, it would be his last conference with God, unless he saw Him in the hereafter! Marsha's mind was made up—she would kill Jerry Donaldson! Murder, like the storm, didn't faze her in the least. She shrugged calmly; she had known all along that Jerry's demise was inevitable. She certainly never planned to spend her life with him. The man was intolerable.

Last night, the things she had said to her husband had been true. She had indeed married him for only one reason—to inveigle him into committing the embezzlement. She had known the crime would be easy, for the bank's president had trusted Jerry completely.

As a long sigh escaped her lips, she leaned back, relaxed, and reflected on her life. She had been born in Chicago, and her parents were domestic servants; thus, she had grown up in an expensive home surrounded by wealth. From the time she was twelve, she had decided that someday she, too, would be rich. She had left home at seventeen to seek her fortune. She went to New Orleans, where she planned to marry a rich man, preferably an old one who would soon die and leave her a wealthy widow. But Marsha soon realized, bitterly, that marrying for money was easier said than done. There were no proposals forthcoming, in fact, she failed to even meet any rich bachelors. Finally, penniless, she had no choice but to look for work. In Chicago, she had worked for her parents' employers and was experienced as a maid. Deciding it would be best to search for that kind of work, she answered an advertisement in a New Orleans paper. She had no money to waste on a public conveyance, so she walked to the address she had written down. The house was located at the edge of town; it was mammoth and ostentatious. Marsha was still somewhat naive, otherwise, she would have known that it was a house of ill repute. The madam, impressed with Marsha's beauty, successfully influenced her into becoming a prostitute. It hadn't been too difficult for the woman to convince her—prostitutes made a lot more money than maids! Greed, the great motivator in Marsha's life, made the decision for her. She took the job and soon became one of the madam's most popular girls.

Marsha had been a prostitute for about two years, when her employer learned that she was secretly taking extra money from her customers and keeping it for herself. She was fired on the spot. Marsha didn't care, for she had been planning to leave anyhow. A couple of months back, one of her customers, Jack Merrill, a middle-aged widower from Carson City, had made a lasting impression on her. He visited New Orleans for two weeks, during which he spent a lot of time with Marsha. Bragging about his riches, he told Marsha that in his youth he had made his fortune panning for gold near San Francisco. Now he owned a prosperous ranch outside Carson City. The night before he left for home, he promised to write, and said he hoped their correspondence would lead to matrimony. She hadn't heard from him, but that was understandable. After all, he had to make the long trip home, and, of course, it would take quite awhile for a letter to reach her.

Certain she was about to marry a wealthy man, Marsha packed her bags and undertook the lengthy, arduous journey to Carson City. Once there, she asked about Jack Merill, and learned that he had died two weeks earlier, leaving his estate to his married daughter. Marsha was devastated; she was also practically broke. The madam had kept Marsha's back salary as payment for the money she had secretly withheld.

Now Marsha had no choice but to look for work. There were saloons in Carson City that employed prostitutes, but Marsha considered herself too good to work in such places. Western saloons, in her opinion, were too crude and wild. After all, she had worked in New Orleans' finest establishment!

She found a job at a ladies' dress shop, and moved from the hotel and into a boardinghouse, where she met Jerry Donaldson, who was also living there. At first, Marsha's only plan was to save enough money to travel to St. Louis, where she hoped to resume her former profession in a classy establishment worthy of her talents. Her plans, however, were soon forgotten. Jerry Donaldson was completely smitten with her, and, she, in turn, was fascinated with his job. She told him that she was a widow, and had come to Carson City to start a new life. She could have told Jerry that the sky was green, and he would have believed her, for he was totally under her spell.

They were soon married. Marsha weaved her web, and

Jerry became helplessly entangled. He embezzled a small fortune, they hid it in the wagon, and took off for San Francisco. Marsha had no intention of staying with Jerry. Once they were in San Francisco, she planned to get rid of him—one way or another!

Now, as Marsha brought her musings back from the past, she looked at her husband with hate in her eyes. She despised the little man, and pretending to love him had been the hardest thing she had ever done in her life.

The windstorm had died down. Jerry opened the canvas, and climbing over the backboard, he went to check on the horses. Marsha, moving decisively, got her husband's loaded shotgun and followed him outside.

He was heading toward the front of the wagon, when she called to him, "Jerry, wait!"

He stopped, turned around, and was shocked to find himself at gunpoint. Fear knotted and writhed in his stomach, his mouth felt as dry as cotton, and his whole body tightened. He had never been so afraid, for cold-blooded murder was in his wife's eyes.

"Marsha!" he gasped hoarsely. "For God's sake, put the gun down! Don't shoot me—*please!* I'll do anything you say! If you want the money, you can have it!"

"You sniveling little coward!" she uttered coldly. Those were the last words Jerry Donaldson was to hear. His wife pulled the trigger. She wasn't a good shot, but at such close range, she couldn't miss, not with a shotgun!

She watched, unmoved, as her husband toppled to the ground and drew a final, agonizing gasp for breath. Slowly, she stepped to his body and looked down at him. She felt almost giddy. At last, she was rid of the little bastard!

She went back inside the wagon, put away the shotgun, and sat down. The storm had passed, and now an eerie stillness had come over the land. For a long time, she sat perfectly still, her face expressionless; then fear slowly set in. She was alone in the middle of the desert, lost, and totally inexperienced. Good Lord, she thought, I don't even know how to unharness the team, let alone tend to them! She wasn't sure if she could drive the team either; Jerry had taken care of that. The more she considered her situation, the more she realized that Jerry had done just about everything. By killing her husband, she had put herself in a desperate situation! Marsha was suddenly afraid.

Craig and the others had waited out the storm behind the steep sand dune. Afterwards, their clothes were covered with grit and their faces were noticeably dirty, but, otherwise, they were no worse for wear. They brushed at their clothes, washed the sand from their faces, and continued onward.

The storm had blown away the tracks Jim had found earlier, but he wasn't too disappointed. He was hopeful that he'd catch up to the Donaldsons in Seclusion.

The sun had passed its meridian when they spotted a covered wagon in the distant plain. As they drew closer, they could see that the team was hitched and that a body was lying on the ground. Craig and Jim drew their pistols, told the women to stay behind, and rode up to the wagon.

As Craig checked the body, Jim crept to the back of the wagon, jerked open the canvas, and ready to fire at a moment's notice, he peeked inside.

Marsha, her feelings numb, looked at Jim as though

his unexpected presence was no reason for alarm. She had worried herself into a state of shock, but now it suddenly began to wane. "Who are you, and what do you want?" she asked weakly, her heart starting to pound.

"Mrs. Donaldson, I presume?" Jim had never seen the fugitives he pursued, but the sheriff in Carson City had given him a good description. He had also told him that Marsha Donaldson was attractive, but he had failed to emphasize that she was strikingly beautiful. Jim couldn't help but be physically drawn to such a lovely woman.

He offered her his hand, she took it, and he helped her down from the wagon. He spoke gently, "Ma'am, my name is Jim Slade, and I'm a federal marshal. I've been trailing you and your husband for several days."

Marsha's heart sank. A federal marshal! He would no doubt take her back to Carson City, where she'd face a trial and a possible jail sentence. Well, she'd find a way out of this — somehow! Her calculating mind went instantly to work.

"Mr. Slade, thank God you found me!" she exclaimed, her enchanting eyes filling with tears. Then, becoming aware of another's presence, she whirled about and saw Craig. The woman in Marsha responded to both men, she could hardly believe that two such handsome gentlemen had appeared out of nowhere. She immediately decided that she'd have an affair with one of them, she just didn't know which one — choosing between them would be a hard, but delightful, task!

Craig waved his hand in the air, a signal for Laura and Karen to join them. The sight of the women dampened Marsha's spirits. Damn the luck! She was probably about to meet their wives!

The ladies rode in and dismounted. Marsha watched

as Laura went to Craig and stood beside him. Their eye contact was brief, but Marsha nonetheless recognized love in their gazes. She then took a close look at Karen. She was pleased to note that the woman didn't move to Jim, but stood back. Apparently the federal marshal was available! Which, she supposed was better for her, he was the one she really needed to seduce. After all, he had the power to arrest her or set her free! Lobo had been a distance behind Laura and Karen, and he now loped into sight. Marsha eyed the wolf cautiously—animals frightened her.

"Who shot your husband?" Jim asked, taking her mind off the wolf.

She forced tears back to her eyes, and sobbed, "Three men overtook us! They killed Jerry!"

"Would you mind explaining exactly what happened?" Jim requested kindly. "Also, where's the money?"

She pretended to compose herself. "Mr. Slade, believe me, I didn't know that my husband stole that money from the bank. He didn't even tell me about it until yesterday. I was shocked. I never dreamed that Jerry would do something like that! He said we were going to San Francisco, because he had an offer for a better job." She paused, feigned a whimper, and continued, "This morning, three men rode up to our wagon. They went through our belongings and found the money from the bank. Jerry tried to take it back, and they shot him. I thought they would kill me, too, but they just rode away. After that, a windstorm blew up and I took shelter in the wagon. When it passed, I went outside and cleaned the sand off poor Jerry." She put her hands over her face, and with deep, shoulder-wracking sobs, she cried, "I was so terrified! Thank God you found me!"

Jim wanted to console her—she seemed so helpless and frightened—but with effort he restrained the urge. "Mrs. Donaldson, why don't you go back into the wagon? Craig and I will bury your husband." He signaled for Laura and Karen to accompany her.

Marsha, still sobbing, allowed Jim to help her inside; he then gave Laura and Karen a hand.

A shovel and a pickax were hanging on the side of the wagon. Craig and Jim removed the tools, then walked a short way into the distance.

Inside the wagon, the ladies found a place to sit, but for a long moment, they didn't say anything. Karen wanted to express her condolences, but Marsha was still crying heavily, and she wasn't sure if the woman would even hear her. Meanwhile, Laura, more perceptive than Karen, was doubting Marsha's sincerity. But she didn't want to pass judgment too hastily, and decided to withhold her opinion. She would give the woman the benefit of the doubt, but she intended to watch her closely.

Marsha quieted her sobs slowly, for she needed time to prepare herself to make conversation with these two women. She was apprehensive and unsure of herself. Pulling the wool over a man's eyes was easy as pie, but she had no such power over her own sex. Managing a shaky smile, she looked at Karen, and then to Laura. "My name is Marsha."

"I'm Laura, and this is Karen."

"I'm sorry about your husband," Karen murmured.

"Thank you. Are you two married to the gentlemen outside?"

"No," Laura answered. "We're traveling with them to Seclusion."

"What I said to Mr. Slade was true," Marsha said, her

tone pleading. "I didn't know my husband stole that money. Please . . . please don't think I'm a criminal!"

"We don't think any such thing!" Karen was quick to reply. "Do we, Laura?"

She wished Karen hadn't put her on the spot. "It's not our place to judge you, Marsha. If you two will excuse me, I'll see if Craig and Jim need any help."

Marsha watched as she left the wagon, her senses on full alert. Laura was no fool and could very well become an adversary. She would keep a close eye on her, and foil any attempt she might make to influence Jim Slade. At this point, the federal marshal was her key to freedom, and she would not let Laura turn him against her!

Outside, Craig and Jim were digging Jerry's grave. Laura walked over to them.

"How's Mrs. Donaldson?" Slade asked her.

"She's all right." Laura paused, then regarding Jim closely, she asked, "Do you believe she didn't know her husband stole from the bank?"

Jim shrugged. "I don't know. I suppose she could be innocent." He stopped digging, leaned on the shovel, turned to Laura, and said, "You don't believe her, do you?"

"Well, I don't disbelieve her. But there's something about her that doesn't ring true. It's probably just my imagination."

"There's no way I can dispute her claim that three men waylaid her and Donaldson. That windstorm wouldn't leave any tracks."

"If she's lying," Craig put in, "then the money has to be inside the wagon."

"After we bury her husband, I'll search the wagon," Jim decided. "If I don't find it, then I'll have to assume that Mrs. Donaldson is telling the truth."

Jim failed to find the money, the hidden compartment was too well camouflaged. Inwardly, he was glad that his search had come up empty, for he was falling prey to Marsha's beguiling charms.

They moved onward; there were still several miles to cover before sunset. Jim tied his horse to the back of the wagon, and drove the team. This, of course, elated Marsha. Having Jim to herself gave her free rein to work her magic spell. He would soon be putty in her hands.

Dusk was cloaking the landscape when they stopped to make camp beside a small watering hole. In the far distance, barren mountains loomed over the plains, which were desolate except for the wretched little watering hole where they were camped.

After dinner, Jim left to check on the horses. Marsha soon followed him. "I hope you don't think I'm terribly forward, but I need to talk to you."

"Of course," he replied gently.

She batted her long lashes. "May I call you Jim?"

"I wish you would."

"And you must call me Marsha."

"Marsha's a beautiful name."

She pretended to blush. "Jim, for some reason I have this compulsion to tell you about my marriage. I'm not sure why, but I do so terribly need to confide in you."

He smiled tenderly. "I'm a good listener."

"I knew I didn't love Jerry when I married him, but I was awfully fond of him. He was a very kind, gentle man, and I thought he was honest as well. I intended to be a good and loyal wife. You see, I was married before

102

and I loved my husband with all my heart. When he died, I felt as though I died with him. I didn't think I could ever love another man. I married Jerry for companionship. I never deceived him; he knew my feelings."

"Why do you want me to know this?"

"I can't truly grieve for Jerry as a wife should, and I don't want you to think badly of me. I'm very sad, and I wish he hadn't died, but my heart isn't broken. Do you understand what I'm trying to say?"

"Yes, I do."

"If those men hadn't robbed us and killed Jerry, I would have insisted that he return the money; or else, I would have left him. I mean that sincerely."

"I believe you, Marsha. I really do." He meant it wholeheartedly.

Victorious, she smiled inwardly. "Thank you, Jim. Your faith means a lot to me."

The moon's luminous rays slanted across her face, and Jim could easily see her. Her green eyes, cat-shaped, were mirror brilliant, and they sparkled like a pair of matching emeralds. Strawberry blond curls framed her oval face, and the shiny tresses danced with reddish highlights. Her lips were full, sensual, and seemed to beckon a man's kiss.

Jim, mesmerized, raked her with an admiring, yet hungry gaze. She was tall, and her slender frame was perfectly contoured. Her cotton traveling dress was plain in design, but it nonetheless emphasized the fullness of her breasts, her tiny waist, and the feminine curve of her hips.

Marsha was fully aware of his intense scrutiny, and she responded in kind. She was, however, more discreet, and her gaze was slanted. She liked what she saw, for Jim

Slade was indeed attractive. His heavily muscled frame exuded powerful strength, but for such a big man, he moved with uncanny grace. He was hatless, and Marsha sensed an almost uncontrollable urge to run her fingers through his curly blond hair, stand on tiptoe, and encourage his lips to take hers in a heated exchange. She was passionate, and her passion had gone unassuaged for a long time. Jerry Donaldson had been a poor, limpid lover. Marsha liked her men virile and aggressive.

Jim took her arm and began leading her back to camp. "You need to get some sleep. We'll be leaving early in the morning."

When they returned, Craig suggested that the women sleep inside the wagon; it would be more comfortable and safer. Karen was in complete accord, Marsha had never intended to sleep anywhere else, Laura, on the other hand, was somewhat hesitant. For some reason that she couldn't quite put her finger on, she didn't like Marsha Donaldson, nor did she trust her. She preferred to avoid the woman as much as possible. But she understood Craig's reasoning, and didn't argue with his decision.

As she followed Karen and Marsha to the wagon, Lobo trotted at her heels.

"I cannot sleep with that wolf in my wagon," Marsha remarked sternly.

Craig called Lobo to his side, telling Laura that he would take care of him.

The women, with Jim's assistance, climbed into the wagon.

"That wolf of yours gives me the creeps," Marsha told Laura.

"He's very tame. He won't hurt you."

"Well, I don't like animals, and I want you to keep that creature away from me."

"That creature, as you call him, is traveling with us whether you like it or not. If you don't bother him, he won't bother you."

Marsha's eyes met Laura's, and, for a moment, their gazes locked—not a measure of friendliness was visible.

Nine

Laura awoke early the next morning, slipped hastily into her clothes, put on her boots, ran a brush through her hair, and left the wagon. Jim was still in his bedroll, but Craig was sitting beside the fire. A pot of coffee was brewing.

He smiled at Laura. "You're an early riser."

"So are you," she replied, sitting beside him.

"Didn't you sleep well?"

"No, not really." She looked about the campsite. "Where's Lobo?"

"He was here a minute ago. I guess he's wandering."

"Are there wolves in this region?"

"Not as far as I know. There are some half-starved coyotes." He reached over and took her hand. "Why did you have trouble sleeping?"

"Several reasons," she replied, sighing. "There are so many problems, and they kept swirling through my mind."

"I understand," he said considerately.

Lowering her voice in case Jim might wake up and hear, she asked, "Craig, what do you think of Marsha Donaldson?"

"What do you mean?"

"I don't trust her, and I'm worried that she'll manipulate Jim."

Craig grinned. "Honey, Jim's a grown man, he can take care of himself. Besides, you have too many problems without taking on any more."

"You're right, of course." Catching a movement in the distance, she said, "There's Lobo!"

The wolf was scurrying across the desert, his nose to the ground, and his tail wagging vigorously.

"He's chasing something," Laura said, standing. It was obvious that the wolf was toying with a victim.

Craig rose also, and they watched as Lobo chased his prey into camp. It was a rodent, and its small legs were moving as fast as possible.

"That's a scorpion mouse," Craig told Laura. "The creatures live on scorpions, and get fat doing it." He yelled to the wolf. "Lobo, come here!"

The wolf forgot his quarry and loped over to Craig. Petting the top of Lobo's head, he said laughingly, "Boy, you don't want to kill anything that eats scorpions."

"Are there many scorpions in the desert?" Laura asked, her tone a little frightened.

"Too many," Craig answered. "Not only scorpions, but lizards, rattlesnakes, tarantulas, and the deadly Gila monster."

A chill ran up Laura's spine. "No wonder you wanted me and the others to sleep inside the wagon."

He took her arm, and they sat back down. The coffee was ready, and Craig poured two cups. "This place is often referred to as the Kingdom of Death, and rightfully so. It's not too bad this time of year, but in a few more weeks, it'll be like a red-hot oven."

"In that case, I must find Johnny and Uncle Zeb very soon."

"If they aren't in Seclusion, you'll have to make different plans. You can't wander around this desert looking for them. That would be certain suicide."

"But if I don't find them, what will I do?"

"Well, we know you can't go back home. I think you should come with me to San Francisco."

"And do what?" she exclaimed. "Watch you marry another woman?" Her words had a bite to them.

Jim, now awake, threw off his top blanket and got up. He had overheard the last of their conversation. "Laura," he began, "the only way you're going to clear your name is to find the person who really killed Lee Talbert." He walked over, bowed gallantly from the waist, and with a smile, remarked, "Madam, I'm offering you my professional services."

Craig scowled. He had wanted to offer his services, but, first, damn it, he had to settle his personal life! If only he hadn't promised to marry Deborah!

"Thank you, Jim," Laura was saying. "I appreciate your offer, and I gratefully accept."

The marshal poured a cup of coffee, sat beside Laura, and said, "Tell me about Lee Talbert. In fact, tell me about all the Talberts."

Harry Talbert and Joshua, arriving in Smoky Gulch late at night, had gone straight to the hotel. Now, following an early breakfast, they walked down the street to the sheriff's office.

The lawman was sitting at his desk, staring at a cup of coffee. He was suffering a harrowing headache; last night he had gone on a drinking spree. His stomach was churning, and just the thought of taking a sip of coffee made him nauseous. He picked up the cup, for he was

108

determined to force himself to drink it. He believed it would somehow make him feel better.

He heard the front door open, but he was in no hurry to glance up. He got down a swallow of coffee, then raised his gaze. He looked the two strangers over curiously. "What can I do for you gents?"

"My name is Harry Talbert, and this is Joshua."

The sheriff stood, shook hands with Harry, but ignored Joshua. He wasn't about to recognize a Negro as an equal.

"I'm looking for a young lady named Laura Mills," Harry continued. "She allegedly killed my son, Lee Talbert."

"So you're one of them Talberts, huh? I received a wire about her, then yesterday I got some wanted posters."

"I was hoping that she might have passed through here."

"She was here, all right. I even had her in my jail, but the sneaky little tart drew a knife on me. Then her boyfriend, Craig Branston, helped break her out."

"Branston?" Harry questioned. He turned to Joshua. "Didn't Ed say that he tried to hire Branston to find Laura?"

"Yes, suh. He said that Mr. Branston's a bounty hunter."

"Well, he ain't huntin' no bounty on her," the sheriff remarked. "She done persuaded him to take her side. I reckon she spread her legs for him." He chuckled heartily. "Can't say I really blame Branston, that Laura Mills is a fine-lookin' woman."

Harry controlled the urge to slam his fist into the sheriff's dirty mouth. "How long ago were they here?"

"A couple days or so."

"Thank you for your time," Talbert replied. He and Joshua left the office and returned to their hotel room.

"You still reckon Miss Laura's a-headed for Death Valley?" Joshua asked.

"I'm certain that she is. Well, I'm glad she has Branston riding with her, she'll be a lot safer."

"Are we still goin' to try and find her?"

"Yes, of course." He handed Joshua some money. "Buy more supplies, we'll leave in an hour." A small frown crossed Harry's face, and thinking of his ranch, he murmured vaguely, "I hope everything's all right at home."

Ed was sitting in the dining room alone. He had finished breakfast and was having a second cup of coffee. His expression was testy, for he was growing angrier by the moment. Damn Doyce! He hadn't come home all night! Ed's patience with his brother was just about gone. All the man thought about was drinking, gambling, and womanizing! The Circle T was nothing more to him than a place to sleep, free meals, and limitless funds! Owning a ranch of this size was demanding, and it took not only Ed's time, but also his father's to keep it operating successfully. Doyce reaped all the rewards, but never gave anything back. Ed was at the end of his rope. Doyce would start doing his share, or he'd find himself without a home!

Ed wondered what his father would say if he returned to find that he had forced Doyce to leave. He'd no doubt be very upset. He loved Doyce, the same as he had loved Lee, and neither one of them was worth a grain of salt.

A knock sounded on the front door, Ed waited for the butler, who was taking Joshua's place, to answer it. A moment later, the servant came into the dining room and announced Sheriff Longley.

Ed asked the lawman to be seated, and gave him a cup of coffee. "What brings you here so early?" Talbert asked. "Is Doyce in trouble again?"

Longley smiled hesitantly. "You guessed it."

"Damn! What did he do this time? Was it another barroom brawl?"

"No, I'm afraid it's a lot worse than that."

A concerned frown wrinkled Ed's brow. "Go on."

"My deputy was in the saloon last night, and he learned that Doyce is in debt to Bret Ganey."

Ed, enraged, slammed his fist against the table. Bret Ganey was a professional gambler, but an honest one. The man didn't need to cheat, he was too damned good at his trade. Although Ganey was aboveboard when playing cards, he was nonetheless very dangerous.

"Ganey will kill Doyce if he doesn't settle his debt," Longley said. "And, as you know, Ganey's smart. Doyce will show up dead, but I won't find a piece of evidence against Ganey. I have a feeling he's killed more than once, I just can't prove it."

"How much does Doyce owe him?"

"I'm not sure, but I think it's a helluva lot."

"Thanks, Sheriff, for coming by and letting me know."

"Have you heard from Harry?"

"No, I haven't."

"I'm worried about him. He's too damned old to be runnin' around the countryside."

"I agree completely. I'm seriously considering going after him."

At that moment the dining room door opened and Doyce, followed by two strangers, came inside. He was with the two men who had attacked Laura.

Sheriff Longley quickly excused himself and left.

"Ed," Doyce began, gesturing toward his companions, "I met these two guys last night. They're lookin' for work, and I thought we might give them a job."

Ed regarded the two men carefully. They looked more like gunmen than wranglers.

Doyce continued, "Ed, you ain't gonna believe this, but they came across Laura. And guess who she's travelin' with?"

"Just tell me, damn it!" He was in no mood to play guessing games.

"Craig Branston! Some bounty hunter *he* is!"

Ed bounded to his feet. "Branston! Good God, that man's dangerous! If Pa meets up with him and Laura, he's liable to get killed!" He spoke to the strangers, "Where did you see Laura?"

"She was campin' out," one of them replied. He distractedly rubbed his sore shoulder where Laura's knife had penetrated. "We didn't know she was a fugitive, so we just passed the time of day with her and Branston, then left." He wasn't about to confess that he and his friend had tried to rape her.

"Are you certain she was with Craig Branston?"

"Yes, sir. I heard her call 'im by name."

Ed, worried about his father, sank back into his chair. He became immersed in thought for a long moment, then looked at Doyce and said, "We're going after Pa. The foreman is perfectly capable of taking care of things here."

"What!" Doyce exclaimed. "Ed, I don't want to go chasin' after the old man!"

"You're going whether you like it or not! And don't call our father an old man! I hate that expression!" Staring coldly at his brother, he debated if he should tell him that he knew about his gambling debt. He decided not to say anything for the time being. He turned to the strangers. "If you two want a job, I'll hire you to ride with us. You look as though you can handle those guns you're wearing."

"We'll take the job, and you're right, we do know how to use our guns." The man, massaging his wounded shoulder, grinned inwardly. He hoped they would find Laura Mills, for he had a score to settle with her!

Laura was relieved to get another day's journey behind her, for it meant she was that much closer to Seclusion. A warm meal was prepared over the campfire, but not much of it was eaten. The desert had a way of stealing one's appetite.

The night was still young when Craig asked Laura to take a walk. Hand in hand they strolled away from camp; Lobo, of course, followed. Marsha was inside the wagon, which left Karen sitting at the fire with Jim. Finding herself alone with the marshal unnerved her, yet, at the same time, she was thrilled.

"Karen," Jim said quite casually. "You've held up remarkably well during this trip. To be honest, I had my reservations." His eyes traveled briefly over her small frame. "You look as though you'd be very fragile."

She smiled cleverly. "A stick of dynamite isn't all that big either, but it's mighty powerful."

His sudden laugh was deep and good-natured. "I'll remember what you said."

Responding to his chipper mood, her smile brightened. She was finding it easy to talk to him, men usually made her nervous and tongue-tied. "Jim," she began curiously, "tell me about your job."

He was evidently taken off guard. "No woman has ever

asked me that before. Are you sure you're interested, and you aren't just making polite conversation?"

She was indeed interested, everything about Jim Slade fascinated her. "Yes, I want to know. Please tell me."

"I work on a territorywide basis, and I enforce federal laws. I pursue mail thieves, Army deserters, and bank robbers. Also, if a town or county lawman needs help—or an extra gun—I'm there for him."

"You must spend a lot of time away from home."

"I do, but I don't mind. I have a small homestead outside a little town called Winding Creek, it's not far from Carson City. When I'm not on a case, that's where I hang my hat."

"When you marry, your wife will spend a lot of time alone."

"Yes, she will. But I know several marshals who are married, and their wives manage fine."

"Have you ever considered getting married?"

"Not yet, but when I meet the right woman, I won't hesitate to ask her to marry me." His thoughts went to Marsha.

"Whoever she is, she'll be very lucky."

Jim looked closely at Karen, he saw only sincerity on her face. "Thank you, Karen. That was a very nice thing to say. And I return the compliment. Your husband will also be very lucky, for you're a fine woman."

Karen's cheeks turned scarlet-red, and she averted her gaze from his. Inside, though, she was beaming. Jim Slade's flattery had delighted her. She was about to ask him more about his life, but, at that moment, Marsha left her wagon. At her approach, Jim got quickly to his feet. Karen arched her neck, and as she looked up at him, her spirits sank. His gaze, locked on Marsha, was filled with desire.

Marsha cast Jim her most sensuous smile. "Mind if I join you?"

"Of course not," he answered at once. Taking her hand, he helped her sit beside him.

"Where are the others?" she asked.

"They took a walk," Jim replied.

"Oh? Well, I feel much safer beside the fire." Her green eyes sparkled flirtatiously. "But I wouldn't be afraid if I was walking with you."

Karen murmured an excuse, hurried to the wagon, and climbed inside. Tears smarted her eyes, but she held them back. Crying wouldn't change anything! She had no chance with Jim Slade, for she couldn't possibly compete with a woman as charming and beautiful as Marsha Donaldson.

Craig and Laura walked a good distance from camp before stopping. They hadn't said much, they had been comfortable simply holding hands and enjoying the other's company. Now, gazing down into her dark blue eyes, Craig murmured sincerely, "Laura, I'm sorry about this morning."

"I don't understand."

"When I suggested that you come with me to San Francisco, I didn't mean it the way it sounded. I don't know what I was thinking."

"That's all right, Craig. I shouldn't have snapped at you. I'm sorry, too."

He sighed deeply. "God, Laura, what's going to become of us?"

"I don't know."

Taking her by surprise, he suddenly drew her into his arms. "I don't want to lose you!"

She held him tightly. "Craig, we can't be together unless you break your engagement to Deborah. Can you bring yourself to do that?"

"Would you think less of me if I did?"

She pushed out of his arms, looked up into his face, and replied softly, "What I think doesn't matter. It's what you think of yourself."

He smiled admiringly. "You have a lot of wisdom for one so young."

Her composure snapped, and with tears brimming, she cried, "Craig, I want so badly to tell you to forget Deborah! I wish I could say that her feelings don't count, and we must think only of ourselves! But can we destroy Deborah's life? Is it possible for us to do that to a blind woman, who is completely dependent on you? If we did, could we build happiness on someone else's misfortune?"

"I'm not sure I can answer those questions," he replied heavily.

"In the final analysis, we're damned if we do, and we're damned if we don't."

He brought her back into his embrace. "Maybe losing me wouldn't break Deborah's heart."

"Yes, and maybe the sun will rise in the west tomorrow."

His lips brushed across her brow. "I can't bear the thought of losing you."

"I know," she whispered. She slid her arms about his neck, and lifted her mouth to his.

Initially, their kiss was whisper-light, but the contact soon intensified. Her lips were now smothered by his, and when his tongue sought entrance, she welcomed such intimacy.

He held her closer, and as she pressed her thighs to his, she could feel his superb hardness. Instinctively, she

116

rubbed against him, and the erotic motion stimulated her passion beyond her wildest dreams.

Craig stopped their kiss long enough to draw a breath, and then his mouth was again fervently assaulting hers. His hand cupped one of her breasts, and then the other; his touch sent fire blazing through every nerve in her body.

Suddenly, without warning, he released her. He was breathing heavily, and she was startled to see that he was actually trembling.

"Laura!" he groaned.

"Craig? What's wrong?"

"Honey, I think we'd better go back to camp. If we stay here any longer, I might forget myself."

"We might both forget ourselves."

A flicker of a smile touched his lips.

"What are you thinking about?"

"I was thinking about you. I hope you never change. Your honesty is so refreshing. Most well-bred young ladies would never admit that their passion was about to get the best of them."

"Maybe I'm not a well-bred young lady," she said pertly. "I probably know more about cattle and guns than parlor etiquette."

Chuckling, he slipped an arm about her shoulders, and they started back to camp. Craig was in awe of his own feelings. With each passing minute, he loved Laura all the more.

Ten

The remainder of the journey to Seclusion passed uneventfully, and the travelers came upon the thriving settlement in the late afternoon. The barren desert had been left behind, and the tableau was now pastoral and verdant. They had infiltrated only a narrow portion of Death Valley, but even that small part had made a powerful impression on Laura: she never wanted to see the desert again!

Seclusion, surrounded by mountains, was located in a fertile, unblemished valley. Wooded bluffs overlooked the village, and a waterfall, rippling gently over deep ravines, emptied into the meandering river below.

Seclusion was popular with prospectors. They often stayed there during the summer months, then in early autumn they would pack provisions, and traveling by muleback, return to Death Valley and continue their endless search for a "rich lead." Mining expeditions was Seclusion's biggest source of income, for these large parties always spent huge amounts buying supplies. Seclusion's permanent residents were mostly merchants and farmers, the stores did a thriving business, and the fertile area was ideal for growing crops. The secluded settlement was indeed prosperous!

As Laura and the others entered Seclusion, they received curious glances from the people mingling about town. It was obvious that they weren't prospectors or a mining party, and their presence was a curiosity.

They stopped in front of a two-story, clapboard building sporting a hotel sign. Craig tied Lobo to the wagon, then the group went inside where they were welcomed by the desk clerk. He was a middle-aged, bearded man with twinkling eyes and a friendly smile.

"Howdy, folks," he said cheerfully.

"Do you have five available rooms?" Craig asked.

"As a matter of fact, I do! Normally, I wouldn't have so many vacancies, but no mining expedition is in town, and most of the prospectors are still in the desert."

"Excuse me," Laura said. "Do you know a prospector named Zeb Douglas?"

"Sure, I know Zeb."

"Have you seen him lately?"

"I saw him a few minutes ago. He's staying here."

Laura could hardly believe her good luck. "Is he here now?"

"He just went up to his room."

"Which room is his?"

"Number three, it's marked on the door."

"Laura," Craig began, "I'll take care of things here. Go on up and see your uncle."

Laura, her heart pounding excitedly, fled up the stairs, found room three, and knocked.

"Come on in," she heard Zeb say. "The door's open."

She stepped inside, and her uncle, sitting in a chair beside the window, stared at her as though he couldn't believe his own eyes.

"Laura!" he burst out suddenly, his expression incredulous.

She rushed across the room and into his awaiting arms. "Uncle Zeb!" she cried. "I'm so glad to see you!"

He held her tightly. "Laura, what are you doin' here?"

She pushed gently out of his arms, her eyes were misty, and she gazed at him through a teary blur. Zeb, at the age of fifty, was still a fine figure of a man. His tall, lanky frame, as firm as a man in his thirties, belied his years. A full, well-groomed beard, dappled with gray, matched the color of his hair.

"Uncle Zeb," Laura began, "I'll explain later why I'm here. But I want to see Johnny. Where is he?"

"Johnny's in San Francisco."

"He isn't with you?" she exclaimed.

"No, I'm afraid not."

"But why is he in San Francisco?"

He took her hand, and they sat on the bed. "Last fall, Johnny and I found a silver ledge, and we took some specimens to San Francisco to have them assayed. The yield even surpassed my anticipation—it was a rich find! Well, these gentlemen who work for a mining company offered to buy us out. I didn't want to sell, but Johnny did. He didn't want anything more to do with prospectin'. To please Johnny, I gave in. By sellin', though, we took a big loss. Johnny said he wanted to stay in San Francisco, but that city's too big for me, so Johnny and I parted company. Before I left, I gave him my part of the money and told him to send it to you. When I visited you last year, I could see that the Diamond Cross was in financial trouble. That's why I told Johnny to send you the money, I figured you'd need it." He frowned testily. "I hope that father of yours didn't get his hands on it. If he did, I'm sure he gambled it away."

"I never received any money from Johnny, and Papa's dead. He died of a heart attack."

"A heart attack!" he remarked, surprised. "He didn't seem in bad health."

"I know, that's why it was such a shock."

He patted her hand. "I'm not gonna pretend grief I don't feel. As you know, I never liked your pa. But, hon, I'm sorry for you. Losin' him must've been awfully hard." He rose, went to the dresser, got a cigar, and lit it. He puffed on it for a minute or so, then turning back to Laura, he said gruffly, "It seems Johnny kept your part of the money. I hate to say this, but that boy's too much like his father."

Laura didn't say anything, but she agreed with her uncle. Anger grew within her—damn Johnny! If he had sent the money, she could have used it to salvage the Diamond Cross!

Zeb dragged a small, hard-back chair to the bed, sat down, and said, "Tell me what's goin' on. Why are you here, and how the hell did you manage such a trip? You couldn't get here by yourself, who's travelin' with you?"

Laura drew a long breath, then, in detail, explained everything.

A restaurant was adjacent to the hotel, Laura had dinner there with Craig, Karen, and Zeb. Marsha and Jim planned to dine later.

Earlier, with Craig accompanying her, Karen had inquired about town, hoping to learn something about her father. No one had even heard of him.

She discussed her father with Zeb; he wished he could ease her mind, but he didn't want to give her false hope. He did suggest that her father might be in San Francisco. Intuitively, however, he suspected that the man had perished in the desert. Karen talked a great deal about the prospectors he had left with, and, to Zeb, they sounded inexperienced. More than likely, they were *all* dead.

Following dinner, Karen went upstairs to her room. Zeb excused himself and retired soon thereafter. Before leaving, however, he paused at Laura's chair and whispered into her ear that he liked Branston. Laura had told him that she and Craig were in love, but that he was obligated to marry Deborah.

"What did Zeb say?" Craig asked.

"He said that he likes you."

"That goes both ways. I like him, too."

Laura's expression turned thoughtful.

"Are you thinking about Johnny?" Craig guessed.

She nodded. "I'm so disappointed in him." She had told Craig that her brother **had** stayed in San Francisco. "If he had sent the money, I could've used it to restore the Diamond Cross." She scowled. "Johnny's so much like Papa!"

"Laura, I have money—a great deal of it. My former profession provided me with lots of money. Just tell me how much you need and—"

"Thanks, Craig," she interrupted. "But I don't want handouts."

"Then consider it a loan."

She smiled warmly. "I appreciate your offer, Craig. But, at present, clearing my name is more important than the Diamond Cross. First, I must find Lee's murderer, then I can concentrate on my ranch."

Craig pushed back his chair, stood, and suggested, "Let's take a walk and check on Lobo." Again the wolf had been confined to the stables.

They encountered Marsha and Jim on the way out.

The couples exchanged amenities, then went their separate ways.

Jim and Marsha chose a corner table that was romantically secluded. Marsha had gone to great lengths to look her best. Her reddish blond hair was unbound, and the shiny tresses softly framed her face. She had chosen an evening gown, it was too formal for Seclusion's only restaurant—the establishment wasn't very refined. Marsha knew she was overdressed, but she didn't care. She had a purpose for enhancing her beauty: she wanted Jim to become infatuated with her.

She got what she wanted, for he was hopelessly enamored. Now, as his eyes met hers, desire radiated in their blue depths. "Marsha," he murmured, "you're very beautiful."

"Thank you, Jim," she said, smiling sweetly.

The waiter approached, they ordered dinner, then Jim remembered to tell Marsha, "I talked to the desk clerk earlier, and he said that yesterday three men checked in. They left early this morning. The clerk had never seen them before, he also said they looked rough and unkempt. They're probably the men who killed your husband and stole the money."

Marsha blessed her good fortune. She had made up three men, and, now, as though fate was in her corner, three strangers had materialized. Such a coincidence certainly added substance to her story.

With excitement in her eyes, she said breathlessly, "Yes, they must be the same men!"

"They told the clerk they were going to San Francisco. I intend to pursue them." He reached across the table and placed his hand atop hers. "That is, if you'll come with me. I need you to identify them." A halfway smile touched his lips. "It'll also give us a chance to know each other better. Marsha, I'm very attracted to you, but, then, I suppose you already know that. I don't mean to be pushy, I realize it's still too soon for you to think of me in that way. After all, you just lost your husband."

"Jim," she said, clasping his hand. "It isn't too soon. As you know, I wasn't in love with Jerry. I cared about him, but that was as far as my feelings went." She smiled demurely. "I find you attractive, too. And, of course, I'll go to San Francisco." Her smile was suddenly bright and teasing. "Does this mean you don't plan to arrest me?"

"You never can tell," he replied, playing the game. "I might put a ring on your finger, and place you in my custody for a lifetime."

She laughed coquettishly, inwardly, however, she was gloating. Jim Slade was such a fool, and manipulating him had been so easy! She certainly didn't plan to marry him, she still intended to find a rich husband—her stolen funds wouldn't last forever! In the meantime, she was looking forward to seducing Jim; after all, he was indeed handsome, and most likely a superb lover!

"I intend to go to San Francisco," Laura remarked. She and Craig had left the stables and were on their way back to the hotel.

"Do you think Johnny still has your share of the money?"

"Ha!" she laughed bitterly. "Johnny's too much like Papa. By now he's gambled it away! I want to see Johnny, but the money has nothing to do with it."

"I'll take you to San Francisco," he said, his hand slipping into hers.

"I don't think that's a good idea," she replied. Craig was startled when she drew away her hand.

"Laura, what's wrong?"

They had reached the hotel, and standing in front of the door, Laura gazed up into Craig's dark eyes, and replied with a calm she didn't really feel, "There's no reason for us to continue seeing each other. Why must we subject ourselves to that? It only makes everything worse. I fall more in love with each passing day, so I want us to part company now, while I'm still strong enough to take losing you. I can make it to San Francisco without you, Uncle Zeb has offered to go with me."

"Laura, you don't mean that."

"Yes, I do!" she replied firmly.

Craig understood, but he didn't necessarily agree, for more reasons than one: He felt she needed his protection as well as her uncle's, also, going their separate ways wouldn't settle their problems. They were too much in love.

"I plan to go to San Francisco, so I might as well travel with you and Zeb. As I've said before, there's safety in numbers." He placed his hands gently on her shoulders. "And, as for our love, I will find some way for us to be together. I don't want to spend my life without you."

"What about Deborah?"

"I don't know!" he groaned. "But there must be a way to work this out!"

It was at that moment that a man's voice suddenly rang out, "Mr. Branston!"

Craig whirled about cautiously. He never knew when he might encounter someone harboring revenge; as a bounty hunter he had sent many men to prison. It wasn't an enemy, however, but a pleasant-looking gentleman and his wife. Craig recognized the man, and said politely, "How do you do, Mr. Worthy?"

"I'm fine, thank you." He introduced his wife, and Craig responded in kind by introducing Laura.

"Mr. Worthy works at the blind school in San Francisco," Craig told Laura. He turned to Worthy. "I'm surprised to see you in Seclusion."

"My wife has relatives here, and we came for a visit. We plan to leave next week."

"How's Deborah?" Craig asked.

"She's fine, and is adjusting remarkably well to her blindness. At first, it was very difficult for her, but that's to be expected. Now she's very anxious to get married and embark on a new life."

"Anxious?" his wife said, smiling. "Why, I've never seen a young woman so enthused, or so much in love. If something happened to stop her marriage, I do believe she would shrivel up and die."

Laura could bear no more. "Excuse me," she murmured, and, turning, went into the hotel.

Craig, going after her, quickly mumbled his own excuses.

The Worthys thought such abrupt conduct was quite rude.

"Their manners leave much to be desired," Mrs. Worthy complained.

"Yes," her husband agreed. "But, you know, I got the feeling that Mr. Branston doesn't know about Deborah."

"Of course, he knows. She sent him a letter weeks ago. I wrote it for her myself."

He took her arm and began escorting her away from the hotel. "I'll probably come across Mr. Branston tomorrow, and then I'll ask him if he received the letter."

Inside the hotel lobby, Craig had caught up to Laura. He clutched her arm, and turned her around so that she was facing him. "Laura, we must talk!"

She drew away. "There's nothing more to discuss. You heard what Mrs. Worthy said—if Deborah loses you, she'll shrivel up and die. Oh Craig, you're probably all she lives for! I won't take you away from her! I can't be responsible for ruining her life! My God, I can't be that cruel, or that selfish!"

"Our love isn't selfish, and you don't have a cruel bone in your body!"

"Neither do you." Her voice had dropped to a whisper. As she headed for the stairs, he didn't try to stop her. Instead, he left the hotel and went across the street to the saloon.

Laura had bought a nightgown and a robe at the mercantile. She had bathed earlier, so when she returned to her room, she got undressed for bed. She slipped into the new nightwear, then went to the dresser and brushed her long, golden tresses.

She was miserable, but her expression was strangely vacant, as though all emotion had been swept away. A heavy dullness filled her being, causing her to move languorously to the bed. She sat on the edge, shoulders drooped, and head bowed in defeat. Such depression, however, went against Laura's grain, and she fought back. After all, losing Craig wasn't the end of the world, and she would find a way to go on without him! Maybe, in time, she'd fall in love again!

A small, bitter laugh escaped her lips. Fall in love again? Yes, it was possible, but she would never love any man as much as she loved Craig Branston!

Laura drew back the covers, took off her robe, then after extinguishing the lamp, got into bed. She lay there a long time, tossing and turning. She couldn't sleep, for her heart was aching too severely. She propped up the pillows, leaned against them, and stared into the darkness. She remembered the kisses she and Craig had shared, and just thinking about them stirred her passion. She had so desperately wanted to make love to him. Now she would never experience such ecstasy! She knew that only in Craig's arms would she achieve total rapture, for she loved him with all her heart and soul! She would never again love so completely!

Laura suddenly threw off the covers, leapt from the bed, and put on her robe and slippers. Craig's and Deborah's marriage might be inevitable, but they weren't married yet! He wasn't yet bound by marriage vows to remain faithful. In a way, he was still free!

Moving decisively, she left her room, hurried down the hall to Craig's door, and knocked lightly.

It was opened almost immediately. Craig was visibly surprised. "Laura!" he exclaimed, taking her arm and drawing her inside.

Her eyes swept over him with desire. Apparently, he was getting ready for bed, for he was in his stocking feet, and his shirt was unbuttoned. She caught a whiff of alcohol and knew that he had been drinking.

"Why are you here?" he asked.

"Craig, I want you to make love to me."

He didn't say anything, for her words had taken him totally by surprise. In fact, he was so startled that, at first, he wasn't sure if he had heard her correctly. There was nothing he wanted more in this world than to make love to Laura. Now, incredibly, she was here granting him what he wanted the most.

"Craig, say something." Her voice was timorous, and her courage was beginning to falter. She lowered her gaze from his. She wondered if she had gone too far?

Was Craig finding such brazen behavior distasteful?

He placed a hand under her chin, and tilted her face up to his. A wry smile was on his lips, curling the corners of his black moustache. "Laura, again you have amazed me. No wonder I love you so much. I've never known a woman like you. You're not only beautiful, but brave, honest, compassionate, and wonderfully unique."

"And I'm entirely too bold," she added, blushing somewhat. "Forgive me, Craig. I feel so foolish. I can imagine what you must think. A lady certainly wouldn't come to a man's room and make the request I just made."

Taking her unawares, he suddenly lifted her into his arms. Holding her tightly against his chest, he looked down into her azure eyes, and murmured, "Laura Mills, you are indeed a lady, and I love you more than words can express. You can't imagine how often I've dreamed of this moment."

"Yes, I can," she replied huskily. "It's been my dream, too."

He carried her to the bed. The covers were already drawn back, and as he laid her down gently, her long blond hair fanned out across the pillows. Taking his place beside her, he leaned over and kissed her demandingly.

Lacing her arms about his neck, she returned his ardor with a need equal to his. As his mouth ravaged hers, his kiss grew more intense, and she accepted his tongue with wild abandon.

A moan of wonder sounded deep in her throat, when Craig's hand moved to cup one of her breasts. His fingers tenderly massaged their fullness, and his caress sent sparks of desire coursing through her.

"Laura," he whispered thickly. "I love you so much!"

She loved him, too, and she declared her feelings by kissing him aggressively and intimately. Craig, inspired

129

by her passion, slipped his hand beneath her nightwear, and traced a gentle path up her legs, across her thighs, and to her womanly softness. His touch, though pleasant, made Laura tense; no man had ever touched her there.

Craig, understanding, murmured soothingly, "Don't be afraid, darling. I want to love you completely. I want to touch and kiss every inch of you. You're so beautiful, so perfect!"

Again, his mouth was on hers, his lips driving her crazy with desire. As his intimate caress continued, she surrendered to the ecstasy of his touch, and was soon engulfed in mindless rapture.

"My love," he moaned later, moving his hand to the tie securing her robe. He quickly removed the garment, then he freed her of her gown. A lone lamp was burning softly, and its saffron glow fell across her lovely body. Craig's dark eyes drank in her beauty, and then his lips followed the path his gaze had formed.

Laura, her passion unbridled, writhed and moaned as she responded to his ravishing ministrations. She had never experienced such heavenly wonder, and she wished it would never end.

Craig's desire was raging as he left the bed to shed his clothes. Laura watched, unashamed, as his masculine body was revealed, and she marveled at such male perfection. His wide shoulders were visibly strong, and dark, curly hair grew thickly across his muscular chest. Her passion-glazed perusal traveled downward to his erect manhood and back to his desire-filled eyes. She opened her arms to him; though a virgin, she wanted him deep inside her.

He went into her beckoning embrace, and their lips came together in a wild, hungry caress that stimulated their passion all the more.

Wanting to know his body as well as he knew hers, Laura's hand explored his flesh. Her searching fingers feathered over his lean, muscled flesh, and when she rested her palm against his throbbing hardness, he gasped with pleasure. His response thrilled her, for she longed desperately to please him. She caressed his maleness, and her touch almost drove him beyond control.

He could wait no longer, and moving over her slender frame, he positioned himself between her legs. His chest was melded to her naked breasts, and she could actually feel the rapid beat of his heart.

He entered her slowly, and when he encountered the barrier of her virginity, he paused, then penetrated fully . . . stealing her innocence in one swift thrust.

She gasped softly, and his lips touched her brow in a caring gesture. Tenderly, he pledged his undying love, then kissed her deeply, as though he could kiss away the pain his penetration had caused.

Laura's discomfort was soon supplanted by a feeling of glorious ecstasy, and she turned their kiss into one of fiery passion. He moved against her, and her hips instinctively matched his rhythm. Together they became lost in the fathomless rapture of their love, and reality melted away as their hearts and bodies merged into one. Nothing else mattered; this moment in time was forever!

Eleven

Laura lay snuggled in Craig's arms, her head on his shoulder, one leg thrown across his. She was finding their intimacy thrilling, and the feel of his naked flesh against hers had her pulse racing with excitement. "If I were to die this very minute," she murmured to Craig, "I would die happier than I've ever been in my life."

He chuckled softly. "I know what you mean. But let's not talk about dying, we have too much to live for."

"Umm," she hummed, sounding content. "For instance?"

He gently fondled her breasts. "Like this, for instance."

"And?" she teased.

His hand moved between her thighs. "And this."

Her fingertips feathered across his chest. "Craig Branston, if you don't stop, you're going to have a wanton woman on your hands."

"Promise?" he asked, his smile filled with anticipation.

"You have my word."

"Then prove it."

"Gladly," she responded, leaning over and kissing him with deep longing.

Their passion was quickly rekindled, and with each kiss and touch their desire burned more fiercely. Their bodies, now on fire, came together as one. Craig's deep thrusts fanned Laura's passion into leaping, consuming flames.

Holding her man tightly, she wrapped her legs about his waist, loving the feel of his hardness slipping ever deeper inside her. Her hips moved rapidly, arching to meet his steady thrusts until, uncontrollably, she was engulfed in ecstasy.

Craig drew her body flush as he, too, achieved total fulfillment. He kissed her lips softly, then moved to lie at her side.

They lay silent, catching their breaths, and basking in the afterglow of their union. Then Craig drew her close, and whispered, "I love you, Laura."

"I love you, too," she murmured. Her earlier happiness was beginning to fade, and she no longer felt so pert. She would treasure this night forever, for she knew that she and Craig might never be together like this again. She supposed she could talk him out of marrying Deborah, but did she really have that right? He had promised to marry Deborah months before she had met him. If she stole him away, could she live with her conscience? Certainly she could, if only—if only Deborah wasn't completely dependent on Craig! She wondered if Mrs. Worthy's words were true. If Deborah lost Craig, would she shrivel up and die? Not literally perhaps, but she could very well lose the will to live.

Laura sighed sadly. Craig wasn't hers . . . not really. He belonged to Deborah, and she had known that from the very start. She could compete for him, and undoubtedly win, for he was in love with her. But it wouldn't be a fair battle, for Deborah had no way to fight back.

Laura couldn't help but ponder if she were making a serious mistake. Giving Craig back to a woman she didn't even know was a sacrifice beyond measure. Was

133

she being too noble, too unselfish? Laura didn't know the answers to these questions, and she thrust them from her thoughts.

One of Zeb's favorite sayings came to mind: let the cards fall where they may. Yes, that's what she would do! For now, she wouldn't make any plans, nor would she make any sacrifices, she'd simply take each day as it came. Whatever happens, will happen, she thought.

Craig was now breathing deeply and evenly, and Laura knew that he was asleep. Softly, so she wouldn't awaken him, she leaned up and placed a light kiss on his lips. "Good night, my love," she whispered, then she snuggled closer and was soon lost in slumber.

Dawn was over an hour away when Craig and Laura awoke. They made love, then Laura went to her own room to pack. It had already been decided by everyone involved that they would leave this morning to start their journey to San Francisco. Karen, hoping to find her father there, had asked to come along.

The group wanted to leave early, and the morning was still young when the travelers started out of Seclusion. Jim, his horse tied to the rear of the wagon, drove the team. Marsha was on the seat beside him. The others rode horseback.

They were at the edge of town when Mr. Worthy, leaving his in-laws' house, spotted them. He called out to Craig, but he wasn't heard. The man didn't yell again but went on his way. He supposed his wife was right, Mr. Branston had certainly received Deborah's letter. If not, he'd learn the truth soon enough, for Worthy was sure Craig was on his way to San Francisco.

Later that day, four horsemen, their clothes covered with trail dust, rode into the town of Smoky Gulch. They went straight to the sheriff's office, where the man in charge introduced himself as Ed Talbert. Questioning the lawman about Laura and Harry Talbert, he learned they had both passed through the town.

They got rooms at the hotel, for Ed had decided to remain in Smoky Gulch for the remainder of the day. The men had dinner in the restaurant across the street, then Ed told his brother he wanted to talk to him alone.

As Doyce accompanied Ed to his hotel room, the two hired gunmen went to the saloon.

Doyce pulled up a hard-backed chair, sat down, and watched as his brother paced back and forth. He was impatient with Ed, and wished he'd hurry up and say what was on his mind. He was anxious to visit the saloon, he could use a few drinks; also, and more importantly, he hoped the establishment furnished prostitutes. Doyce had a strong sex drive, and needed a woman badly.

"What do you want, Ed?" he finally asked, his patience gone.

"I know you owe Ganey money."

"So what?" he spat defensively. "That's my problem, not yours!"

"How much do you owe him?" Ed's expression was stern.

Doyce bounded angrily to his feet. "Damn it, Ed! Don't start treatin' me like I don't have enough sense to take care of myself!"

"Apparently, you don't have enough sense. Otherwise, you wouldn't play cards with Ganey! You fool! Don't you realize he'll kill you, if you don't pay up?"

"I'll pay him."

"Where do you intend to get the money?"

"I don't know. Maybe I'll get it from Pa."

"How much?" Ed demanded. "Tell me exactly how far you're in debt."

"It's none of your business!" Doyce headed out of the room, mumbling over his shoulder, "Keep your god-damned nose out of my life!"

He left, slamming the door behind him. Doyce was steaming as he walked to the saloon. He had never liked Ed. Even when they were children, Ed had always acted superior. In Doyce's opinion, Ed was his father's favorite. He supposed Harry had chosen Ed because he was not only the oldest, but was a lot like him. Doyce and Lee had taken more after their mother, in their looks, as well as their personalities. Doyce barely tolerated his father, but he had worshipped his mother. His childhood flashed across his mind. His mother had been extraordinarily beautiful, and he had idolized her. As he grew older, he came to realize that she was unhappy. She loathed life in Nevada, and longed desperately to return to her home in New Orleans. He remembered overhearing an argument between his parents. Harry, losing his composure, had heatedly told his wife to pack her clothes and leave if she wished, but their sons were to remain with him. Soon after that, she had suffered a terrible accident and was left a cripple. Unable to cope with her paralysis, she sank into a state of depression. Two years later, she died.

Reaching the saloon, Doyce pushed aside the bat-wing doors, thoughts of his mother now forgotten. The place was crowded, and looking about, he spotted his companions sitting at a back table.

Joining them, he pulled out a chair and sat down. A bottle of whiskey was on the table, he picked it up and took a large gulp. His gaze passed fleetingly over the two

136

men watching him. He got along well with these two, for they were the kind of men he liked to associate with. They knew what was important in life—money, whiskey, and women. Furthermore, he was sure they would do anything if the price was right.

"I have a proposition for you two," he remarked, taking another drink of whiskey.

Their names were Morgan and Elias, they looked enough alike to be brothers. Both men were burly, sported unkempt beards, and had hair that grew down past their necks.

"What's your proposition?" Morgan asked.

"My pa is a very rich man. If he and Ed were to die, I'd get everything. I'd be wealthy beyond your imagination. How would you two like to share in my riches?"

"We'd be only too glad to help you spend all that money," Elias replied, grinning. "What do you want us to do?"

"Help me kill Ed and my old man."

Asking them to help murder his brother and father didn't faze them in the least. In fact, they didn't even blink an eye.

"When do you wanna do it?" Morgan asked calmly.

"Well, first we have to find Pa. Then I'll know when the time is right."

"You just let us know when you're ready, and we'll blow their brains out," Morgan remarked coolly.

Doyce smiled with satisfaction. "You two will be well rewarded." He glanced about the crowded room, and finding a flashily dressed woman standing close by, he waved her over. She moved toward him, her hips swaying provocatively. Murder was no longer on Doyce's mind, it was now occupied with lust.

He offered the woman a couple of drinks, then asked

her price. Agreeing to her terms, he followed her upstairs to her room. Once there, he ordered her to remove her clothes. Doyce slipped off his boots and trousers, then threw the prostitute down on the bed, fell on top of her, and took her roughly. His harsh treatment made her cry out, but her obvious pain merely whetted his appetite. He pounded into her unmercifully, then, gasping with animal-like lust, he achieved satisfaction.

"You brute!" she cried, pushing his body off hers.

"Shut up, you goddamned whore!" he uttered angrily. Drawing back an arm, he shoved her off the bed and onto the floor. Retrieving his boots and trousers, he put them on quickly and headed for the door.

"Where's my money?" she screeched.

"Are you kiddin'? As lousy as you were, you oughta pay me!" Laughing, he walked out.

He had barely rejoined his friends when the woman came downstairs, went to his table, and demanded her money. She was making quite a scene.

Ed, entering the saloon, heard the commotion. That his brother was involved certainly didn't surprise him. He quickly took care of the situation by paying the woman double her price.

Doyce had remained in his chair. Ed glared down at him, and said sternly, "It's time you went to the hotel."

"I'll leave here when I'm damned good and ready."

"You'll leave now or else!"

"Or else what?"

"Don't push me, Doyce! I've had it up to here with you!" He moved a gesturing hand up to his chin. "You either leave now, or you'll find yourself on the streets for good!"

Doyce knew Ed didn't have the power to carry out his threat, but he decided to pacify him. After all, Ed

138

Talbert would soon be dead, and he'd never again have to put up with his arrogance. He exchanged conspiring glances with Morgan and Elias, then got up, and followed his brother outside.

Harry and Joshua, stopping at Peaceful, learned that Laura and her party had left for Seclusion. The pair moved onward, for they had arrived early and still had hours of daylight ahead.

Now, camped for the night, they sat about the fire, drinking coffee. Fatigued, they didn't have much to say. The two men, however, didn't find the lack of conversation uncomfortable — they had been friends all their lives. The night air was warm, and now that the coffeepot had been drained, Joshua smothered the hot flames. With only the moon to furnish light, darkness drew down upon them like a heavy cloak.

Joshua, finding the blackness eerie, said to Harry, "Maybe I oughta build the fire back up."

"No," he replied. "At least this way it's cooler. In a few more weeks, this desert will be as hot as an oven. We need to find Laura soon, and return home before summer sets in."

"Mista Harry, I don't mean to pry, but why is you so determined to find Miss Laura? I know you's worried 'bout that wanted poster, but findin' her ain't gonna change nothin'."

Talbert didn't answer for quite some time, and Joshua figured he wasn't going to offer a reply. He was about to get up, when suddenly Harry said, "There's something I must tell Laura. I think she has a right to know the truth."

"Whatcha aimin' to tell her?"

"That she's my daughter."

Joshua's mouth dropped open, and his eyes widened with surprise. "Mista Harry, is you sure?"

"Well, I can't prove it, if that's what you mean. But in my heart, I know it's true."

Joshua brought an image of Laura to mind. "You know, Mista Harry, she does look a lot like you. I never thought about it before, but now that you claim she's your daughter, I reckon she does resemble the Talberts."

"She reminds me a little of my mother," Harry said softly.

"How come you's waited so long to tell Miss Laura that you're her pappy?"

"I'm not sure why. I'm not even sure why I want to tell her now."

"But, Mista Harry, if you've known all these years that Miss Laura belongs to you, how come you ain't paid more attention to her?"

"All things considered, I thought it best."

"Is you sure that's the reason, Mista Harry?"

Talbert smiled ruefully. "You know me very well, don't you, Joshua?"

"I reckon maybe I do."

"What you said before is true, Laura does resemble the Talberts. However, she looks very much like her mother. When I see Laura, I see Beth, and, God knows how much that hurts! Joshua, I loved Beth Mills from the depth of my heart! The kind of love I felt for Beth only happens once in a lifetime. Sadly, some people go their whole lives without experiencing it."

"Did Miss Beth feel the same way 'bout you?"

"Yes, she did. No two people could have loved more than we did."

"Then how come you two didn't end up together?"

"We found each other too late," he replied pensively. "Our love was never meant to be."

Talbert, moving slowly, got to his feet, found his bedroll, and spread it on the ground. Using his saddle as a pillow, he lay down and gazed dreamily at the myriad of stars dotting the heavens. His thoughts meandered back in time, and he was again a young man in his prime. The Circle T was prosperous, he was the father of three sons, and his future was indeed secure. Only one dark cloud hovered over his otherwise bright existence; his wife, Charlene, wanted a divorce. The love between them had died a slow, agonizing death, and Harry was willing to set her free, but she refused to leave without her children. Harry loved his sons and wasn't about to lose them. Thus, the three boys held the marriage together.

Now, as Harry looked up at the stars, he remembered the first time he set eyes on Beth Mills. The ranch bordering his had been sold, and he had ridden over to welcome the new owners to the community.

It was midsummer, the day was sunny and extremely warm. The two properties were separated by a river, and as Harry crested a hill that overlooked the body of water, he was astounded to see a beautiful, naked woman wading through the rippling waves. She stepped onto the bank and was reaching for a towel, when she sensed another's presence. Her eyes flew in Harry's direction, and, for a moment, she was too stunned to move. Harry, taking full advantage, thoroughly relished the woman's lovely flesh.

Coming to her senses, Beth quickly grabbed her towel and drew it about her. Harry rode down the hillside, dismounted, tipped his hat, and said, "How do you, ma'am? My name's Harry Talbert."

Beth's response was a hard slap across his face.

Now, recalling that moment in vivid detail caused Harry to laugh softly. "Joshua?"

"Yes, suh?" the servant replied. He was spreading a blanket on the ground.

"Laura doesn't only have her mother's beauty, she also has her spunk." Harry closed his eyes, but sleep was a long time coming. But not even in slumber was he free of Beth's memory, for she dominated his dreams.

Twelve

Laura and the others had been traveling for two days when they stopped to make camp beside a meandering river. The rapidly flowing water was bordered on both sides by thick shrubbery, and the fertile area was an ideal place to stop. Darkness was still a couple of hours away, so Craig and Jim, taking Lobo with them, decided to hunt wild game.

Zeb had noticed that the wagon's wheels were a little rusty, and he set about greasing them. Laura was watching him work when Marsha asked her if she'd like to bathe in the river. It wasn't a friendly gesture, she simply didn't want to go alone.

Marsha's offer was tempting, for the day was warm and a dip in the cool water sounded heavenly to Laura. Zeb advised them not to go too far. They asked Karen to come along, but she was busy writing in her journal, and said she'd join them later.

Laura had replenished her wardrobe in Seclusion, and taking a change of clothes and a bar of soap, she accompanied Marsha downstream. They didn't go far, but they were out of sight of the wagon when they decided to stop.

They undressed hastily, for the rippling water was inviting. Leaving the grassy bank, the ladies waded into the river. The waves lapping about their ankles felt wonderfully cool.

"Can you swim?" Laura asked Marsha.

"Not a lick," she replied.

"Then don't wade too far out. This river might be narrow, but I have a feeling it's deep in the middle."

Laura was an experienced swimmer, and she ventured farther out. When the water was up to her waist, she plunged headlong into the undulating waves.

In the meantime, Marsha had daringly made her way into deeper water. She stopped when it was up to her breasts, and keeping her feet planted firmly on the bottom, she began to rub the soap over her shoulders and arms. The bar was soon sudsy, causing it to slip from her hand. She tried to grab it, but it floated out of reach. As she moved forward to retrieve the soap, she stepped into a deep hole, and the water was now over her head. Her arms floundered wildly before she was pulled down into the river's deadly depths. Somehow, she fought her way back to the surface. Gagging, she managed a small cry for help, then she again sank to the bottom.

Laura, swimming leisurely, heard Marsha's feeble cry. Treading water, she looked about, but Marsha was nowhere in sight. Then, all at once, the woman's head popped up out of the river; she was gasping, and her arms were splashing to no avail.

The water drew Marsha back down, and her whole body was now immersed. Diving deeply, Laura swam underwater, reached the drowning woman, grabbed her, and took her to the surface.

Panicking, Marsha fought for air, her arms flailing furiously.

"Stop it!" Laura yelled. "Calm down before you drown us both!"

Marsha was too frightened to take heed, and she continued to fight wildly. Her desperate struggles sent them both sinking, and the water was suddenly over their heads. Laura, holding onto Marsha, fought their way back to the surface. She filled her lungs with needed air, then constraining Marsha with one armhold, she managed to draw back a hand and slap her face sharply.

The stinging whack jolted Marsha to her senses, and she calmed down enough for Laura to get them to shallow water. The moment Marsha's feet touched ground, she jerked away from Laura, and said hatefully, "How dare you slap me! Who do you think you are?"

"The woman who just saved your ungrateful life!" she retorted, angry enough to hit her again.

They waded through the water and were almost to the bank before they noticed a lone horseman watching them. His drawn pistol was aimed in their direction.

"Scream," he threatened, "and I will kill you!" He nodded toward their folded clothes, which were placed on the grass. "Get dressed!"

Laura's first reaction was embarrassment, for she was naked before this man's intense scrutiny. The feeling, however, was quickly replaced by fear. She had never encountered a man so forbidding. She could tell that he wasn't very tall, but his frame was huge. He was obviously an Indian, for his complexion was dark, and his features were broad. A long, jagged-shaped scar ran the entire length of one cheek. It wasn't his appearance, though, that was so frightening; it was the stoical expression in his dark eyes.

The women dressed as quickly as possible, it was a difficult task for Marsha, for she was trembling uncontrollably. Like Laura, she suspected the man was extremely dangerous.

Laura was also unnerved, nevertheless, she stealthily slipped her knife inside her boot.

The man had an extra horse, it was saddled, as though

he had been expecting to find a rider. "Mount up!" the Indian said gruffly.

Laura got on first, then Marsha managed to climb up awkwardly behind her. The man had the horse's reins in one hand, he kneed his own mount, and they galloped away from the bank.

He soon urged the horses into a loping run, and, in due time, they had left the river far behind.

Back at camp, Karen put away her journal and went downstream to find Marsha and Laura. She soon came upon their discarded clothes. Looking through them, she realized that two sets were missing. Laura's riding boots and Marsha's shoes were also gone. She wondered if they had taken a stroll farther down the bank. She walked onward, unalarmed. She hadn't gotten very far, though, before getting worried. Zeb had warned the women not too venture too far from camp, and she was sure they wouldn't have disobeyed.

She called their names anxiously. When she didn't receive an answer, she tried again. Silence!

Now alarmed, she raced back to camp and told Zeb the women were gone.

Together they hurried to the spot where Karen had found their clothes. Zeb's experienced eye scanned the area. Noticing the heavily indented grass — some blades bent more than others — he remarked, "It looks like there were two horses. One had a rider, but it appears that Laura and Mrs. Donaldson mounted the other one."

Karen was about to ask him how he knew such a thing, but she didn't have time, for he was already on his way back to camp. She hastily gathered up the clothes and followed.

Zeb got his shotgun, pointed it into the air and emptied both barrels. "Craig and Jim oughta hear that," he said, reloading his weapon.

A short time later, the men came racing into camp. Reining in, Craig asked, "What's wrong?"

Zeb quickly told him what had happened.

The men dismounted and began packing a few supplies, plus extra ammunition. Craig was indeed concerned for Laura's safety, as well as Marsha's.

As Craig was preparing to leave, Zeb went to him and asked, "You reckon Laura was abducted by a bounty hunter?"

"It's a distinct possibility."

"If she was, why do you suppose Mrs. Donaldson was taken?"

"I don't know. Maybe he didn't want to leave anyone behind to warn the rest of us. Taking her, gave him extra time. Also, if we catch up to him, he can use her as a pawn."

Zeb understood. "You mean, he'll threaten to kill Mrs. Donaldson, if you don't turn back?"

"Yeah, that's my guess."

"You got any idea who he is?"

"Neosha!" He said the name as though he were referring to the devil himself. "He's a full-blooded Cherokee, and he makes his living collecting bounties. I caught a glimpse of him in Peaceful. But we were arriving, and he was leaving, so I didn't give it much thought."

"Is this Neosha dangerous?"

"He's dangerous, all right."

Laura and Marsha had indeed been abducted by Neosha, and he set an exhausting pace, for he wanted to put several miles between himself and Craig Branston. The day he had ridden out of Peaceful, he had seen Craig and the others arriving. Branston's presence had aroused his curiosity, for he knew he was a successful bounty hunter. That night, Neosha sneaked back into Peaceful. His store of wanted posters were out of date, and hoping Branston might have newer ones, he slipped into the stables and went through Craig's saddlebags. His search didn't come up empty; he found the poster on Laura. As he was about to leave, he detected voices and hid in an unoccupied stall. There, he overheard Laura's and Jim's conversation. Taking a cautious peek at the couple, he recognized Laura as the face on the poster. He waited until they were gone, then stealing a horse and an extra saddle, he left as furtively as he had arrived.

He found a place to hole up, and the next morning, he followed Craig and the others as they left Peaceful to set out on their journey. He had been hoping an opportunity to snatch Laura would present itself, and when he spied her and Marsha alone in the river, he could barely believe his good luck. He had had a purpose for stealing the horse; he needed it for his captive. However, he hadn't counted on Marsha, but Craig's guess that he would use her as bargaining power was right on target. Neosha didn't doubt that Branston would follow, nor did he doubt that he'd steadily shorten the distance between them. The women, riding double, would certainly slow down their progress.

The horses had been galloping at a relentless pace for over an hour, before Neosha allowed them to slow down. He knew if he didn't, the horses would drop in their tracks from fatigue.

Now, moving at a more leisurely speed, Laura made the effort to talk to her captor. "Who are you, and why did you abduct us?"

"My name is Neosha." He delved into his pocket and brought out the wanted poster that he had stolen from Craig's saddlebags. "This is why I took you. You are worth five hundred dollars."

Jim had told Marsha about Laura, and the poster came as no surprise. She was, however, dismayed that the man had taken her as well. After all, it was Laura he wanted! Suddenly, her heart lurched. Had Carson City distributed wanted posters on her and Jerry? Was Neosha planning to collect a reward on her, too? This she had to know!

"Mr. Neosha," she began, her voice quivering slightly. "What is your reason for abducting *me?*"

He laughed aloud. No one had ever referred to him as "Mr. Neosha."

"Why are you laughing?" Marsha asked. The tremble hadn't left her voice.

He skipped that question and answered the first one. "I brought you along for insurance. When Branston catches up to us, I'll threaten to kill you if he doesn't turn back."

Marsha's gasp was filled with terror. "Surely you don't mean that!"

"I never say anything I don't mean." A deep sneer curled his lips, as his black eyes flitted from Marsha to Laura. "It is in your best interest to keep that in mind."

"You mentioned Craig Branston, so you must know him," Laura remarked.

"We are not friends, but I know much about Branston." He was through conversing. "No more talk!" he ordered abruptly.

Laura was willing to cooperate, for now, she had nothing more to say.

Marsha wasn't quite so cooperative, she intended to plead for her life. "Please, Mr. Neosha! Set me free! Don't you realize there's a federal marshal riding with Mr. Branston? His name is Jim Slade, and he's in love with me. If you let me go, I'll ask him not to hunt you down. But if you keep me prisoner or harm me in any way, he'll arrest you and see to it personally that you hang!"

Neosha was evidently bothered. He had heard of Jim

Slade, but had never seen him, thus, he hadn't recognized Jim in Peaceful. Abducting Laura was not against the law, for she was a fugitive; the other woman was an entirely different matter.

He brought the horses to a stop and sat quietly, immersed in thought. The marshal's reputation was widely known, and Neosha didn't relish having him as a stalker. He was the kind of law officer who always got his man— one way or another! He quickly decided it would be in his best interest to let the woman go free.

"Dismount!" he told Marsha tersely.

With Laura's help, she managed to slide off the horse's back.

"Head straight west," he said to Marsha. "Slade and Branston will be coming from that direction. You will soon meet up with them."

Dusk was descending rapidly, and Marsha eyed her surroundings with misgivings. "It'll soon be dark!" she said, her voice quaking pathetically. "I'll get lost!"

Neosha chuckled, looked at Laura, and said disdainfully, "You white women are scared of your own shadows."

"Don't judge all white women by her!" Laura snapped. "I'm not scared of the dark!"

His expression turned watchful. "Are you scared of me?"

"Yes!" she answered unhesitantly. "Only a fool wouldn't be afraid of you, and I'm no fool!" However, there was a slight, defiant tilt to her chin. Unknowingly, she had gained a measure of Neosha's respect. That, in itself, was quite a feat, for Neosha had no use for white women. In his opinion, they were worthless!

He looked back at Marsha, and said, "Stay here, and the men will find you." With that, he galloped away, taking Laura with him.

Alone, Marsha's fear intensified. She wondered if she should stay put, or start walking westward. She looked

150

down at her shoes, they certainly weren't made for trek-king through the wilderness. She glanced about, hoping to find a good place to hole up. Spotting a small opening bordered on all sides by shrubbery, she headed toward it. She was wearing a long, gingham gown, and the flowing skirt snagged on a bush. She jerked it loose, went to the patch of open ground, and sat down.

She watched the dark come on, her heart pounding fear-fully. She waited for the moonlight that never came, for the sky had turned cloudy. Gradually, full blackness cov-ered the land like a dark cowl. Marsha grew more fright-ened, and despite the warm night, she shivered as though she were chilled to the bone. Nocturnal creatures began to emerge from their resting places, and their many sounds filled the air. Overhead, a lone owl hooted, and his yellow eyes, gleaming in the dark, stared down at Marsha.

Now, panic-stricken, she was on the verge of hysterics when she heard horses approaching. She bounded to her feet, and without waiting first to see if they were friends or foes, she called out loudly.

Craig and Jim, due to the dark night, were almost upon her before she recognized them. Lobo was trailing behind.

The moment Jim dismounted, Marsha flung herself into his arms. "Thank God, you're here!" she cried.

"Where's Laura?" Craig asked anxiously.

"That awful man took her with him."

"Why did he set you free?" Jim questioned, holding her at arms' length.

"Because of you. When he heard that you were traveling with us, he decided to let me go. I'm not sure why, but I think he was afraid you'd arrest him."

"Is the man an Indian?" Craig asked.

"Yes, he said his name was Neosha."

Craig grimaced; he had been hoping it wasn't Neosha. The man was sly and experienced. Trailing him wouldn't be easy. He glanced down at Lobo, who was sitting at his feet. The wolf, however, would make his task a little easier, for Lobo would certainly follow Laura's scent.

"Jim, you take Marsha back to camp. If Laura and I don't return in four days, go on to San Francisco without us." Giving Lobo the signal to follow, Craig mounted and rode quickly away.

Jim took Marsha's arm and started to lead her to his horse, but she drew back. "Jim, let's stay here for a few minutes. This has been a trying ordeal, and I need a short rest." Seduction, and not resting, was on her mind. She had been too long without a man and was sexually starved.

"Of course, we can stay," Jim said considerately. "I know your ordeal was trying, but I'm sure you handled yourself very bravely."

"Well, I was a little frightened," she murmured modestly, putting emphasis on the word little.

Jim got a blanket from his horse, unrolled it, and spread it on the ground. Taking Marsha's hand, he helped her sit beside him.

She went immediately into his arms and clung tightly. "Jim, I'm falling in love with you," she murmured, the fib crossing her lips easily.

Her declaration delighted Jim, for he had already fallen in love with Marsha, and he kissed her deeply.

Marsha's passion was aroused instantly, and she responded wantonly.

"My darling," Jim whispered, his warm lips traveling to her neck, covering her throat with feather-light kisses.

He eased her back onto the blanket, drawing her body flush to his. Jim's hardness was so stiff that her skirt and petticoat didn't prevent her from feeling his pulsating desire.

With blazing passion, Jim rained fiery kisses upon her

lips as, together, they stimulated the other's need with heavy fondling that drove them both wild with aching torment.

Jim, wanting to possess her totally, raised up on his knees, removed his holster, and laid it aside. He then released his trousers, and to Marsha's joy, the moon coming out from behind a cloud revealed that Jim Slade's manhood was indeed the perfect size to please a woman.

He drew the long folds of her skirt and petticoat up to her waist, then slipped her pantalets down her legs and past her ankles.

The moonlight hadn't disappeared, and Jim's eyes raked her hungrily. Gently, he ran his fingers over the smooth texture of her stomach, then downward to caress her fully. She was moist, ready for him, and hovering above her, he told her to wrap her legs about his waist.

She did so gladly, and when his hardness plunged into her enveloping heat, she moaned aloud with pleasure. As they surrendered to their union, Jim made love to Marsha with all his heart; Marsha, however, simply responded with animal-like passion.

Steadily, they climbed gloriously to the peak of excitement, causing their thrusting to grow more aggressive. Then, reaching passion's ultimate thrill, they found breathless, satisfying fulfillment.

Jim, now even more in love, kissed Marsha tenderly. "Will you marry me?" he asked huskily.

The moon had lost its dominance to a large cloud, and Jim didn't see the frown on Marsha's face. She thought him such a fool! A good lover perhaps, but a fool nonetheless. She certainly had no intention of marrying him. A federal marshal didn't make nearly enough money. She wanted to laugh in his face, but refrained from doing so.

"Darling, let's not discuss marriage just yet," she said

sweetly. "I wouldn't feel right about marrying so soon after Jerry's death."

"But you didn't love him."

"That's true. But, Jim, please give me a little more time. Darling, I *do* love you, isn't that enough for now?"

He moved away, drew up his trousers, and buckled on his holster. "All right, I'll give you more time. But, Marsha, I don't play games. The next time I ask you to marry me, I'll expect a definite answer. And remember, darlin', the next time I ask will be the last."

Marsha couldn't have cared less. "I understand," she murmured, smiling at him as though he meant the world to her.

Jim rolled up the blanket. As they headed toward the horse, Marsha's skirt once again got tangled on a prickly bush. Jim drew it loose, but cut his hand on a thorn in the process.

"Damn!" he cursed. A stream of blood was oozing from his finger. He removed his neckerchief, wrapped it about the wound, and thought no more about it.

Thirteen

Craig, following Lobo's lead, had been pursing Laura and Neosha for over an hour, when it began to drizzle. Dark clouds swirled overhead, and Craig knew a downpour was imminent. Angry, he cursed the blasted weather; the rain would wash away any tracks, and would also make it more difficult for Lobo to pick up Laura's scent.

The rain grew steadily harder until it was falling in heavy, blinding sheets. No lightning was involved, so Craig took shelter beneath a wide-branched tree. He tied his horse to one of the limbs, and as he sat down, Lobo came to his side. The wolf whined forlornly, and Craig supposed he was missing Laura.

"I know how you feel, boy," he said, drawing Lobo closer. "I miss her, too."

Craig was gravely worried about Laura, and hoped she was holding up all right. There was an intimidating aura about Neosha that could make a man quake in his boots; Craig could well imagine how badly the Cherokee could frighten a woman. But, then, he told himself, Laura's no ordinary woman! She was brave, and had a cool head. She'd certainly keep her wits about her.

Craig's thoughts went to the knife Laura kept hidden; he hoped she wouldn't try to use it. Neosha was too experienced and acute to be bested by such a weapon. If Laura tried anything, it might result in Neosha harming her—or even worse!

The rain continued to fall; it looked as though it was set for the night. With an impatient sigh, Craig leaned back against the tree's trunk to make himself more comfortable. He'd undoubtedly be here for a while. He didn't think the weather would delay Neosha, and with each passing minute, he was sure Laura was getting farther away.

For a moment, Craig considered continuing, but the thought was brought on by desperation. He quickly discarded it. Tracking Laura and Neosha at night in the middle of a rainstorm would be impossible. He might as well blindfold himself, take off on horseback, and hope he would head in the right direction. No, he had no choice but to wait until the rain let up, or dawn broke, whichever came first. Then, with luck, he might be able to find their tracks, or better yet, maybe Lobo would pick up Laura's scent.

Forcing himself to remain patient, Craig relaxed, drew the brim of his hat over his eyes, and made a futile effort to get some sleep.

Craig's speculation was right, the weather didn't stop Neosha. He and Laura moved onward, drenched, the rain blowing in their faces. The Cherokee still held the reins to Laura's horse, and she rode behind. She wondered how he could see, for the night was pitch-black and the rain was blinding. Also, there was no lightning to light the way even intermittently.

Laura was miserable. Despite the warm night, her wet clothes had brought on a slight chill. Shivering, she huddled over her horse, and turned her face away from the pelting rain.

She didn't doubt that Craig was tracking them, and she

wondered how close he was. Would this rain force him to hole up? She hoped not, for that would put him miles behind. Certain that Lobo was with him, she thanked God that the wolf hadn't been with her at the river. After the rain, she figured Neosha would start covering their tracks, but that was man's cunning trick—it wouldn't keep the wolf from finding her.

The night wore on, and the passing hours seemed interminable. By morning, Laura was chilled to the bone, and so fatigued that she could barely stay in the saddle. She was also hungry. But even more pressing, she needed to relieve herself.

The rain had stopped, and it looked as though the day would be sunny and pleasant. For that, Laura was grateful.

Suddenly, Neosha brought the horses to a halt, dismounted, then said gruffly to Laura, "Get down."

She did so with discomfort, for it seemed every bone in her body was stiff, and every muscle was drawn as tight as an arrow's bow.

Neosha pointed at a patch of thick foliage. "Use it if you need to, but either talk to me the whole time, or keep a bush shaking. That way, I'll know you're not trying to run."

She moved into the shrubbery; having nothing to say, she grabbed a bush and kept it wiggling. When she returned, Neosha handed her a strip of dried jerky. She accepted it without comment, and took a good-sized bite. It was tough, and she had to tear it with her teeth. After several chews, she was able to swallow what she had in her mouth.

Neosha, eating his own jerky, had been watching her intently. He now nodded toward the canteen on her horse. "You have water."

"Yes, I know," she replied. She uncapped it and helped

herself to a drink. The Cherokee's eyes remained on her, and she began to grow uncomfortable under his steady perusal. "Why do you keep staring at me? " she finally asked.

"You interest me," he answered.

"Why is that?"

"Your clothes are wet, you're hungry and cold. Why haven't you complained?"

"Would it have done any good?" Her sky blue eyes were shining rebelliously.

"You will be easy to travel with; you have the grit of a Cherokee woman. You are not like other white women, who are always whining and complaining."

"If I start being a nag, will you turn me loose?"

He couldn't help but laugh. "I see you have a sense of humor. I hope you will still have it when I turn you over to the sheriff in Silver Star." He waved a hand toward her horse. "Mount up, it's time to leave."

She was surprised when he handed her the reins. "I plan to ride behind and cover our tracks. If you try to run, I'll shoot your horse, for it makes a target too big to miss. Then you will be forced to walk."

Laura didn't say anything. She had no intentions of running; she didn't doubt that Neosha would carry out his threat.

Harry and Joshua stopped at sunset to make camp; they were now two days from Seclusion. Joshua prepared a good supper, but having no appetite, Harry merely toyed with his food.

"You better eat, Mista Harry. You needs your strength. This trip ain't gonna get any easier."

"I know, Joshua. But I have too much on my mind to think about food."

"Is you thinkin' 'bout Miss Laura?"

"Among other things."

"For instance?"

"You've made it quite clear that you don't believe Laura shot Lee. If you're right, then why did Lee write down her name? Also, who actually killed him?"

"I ain't got no idea. But maybe Mista Lee didn't write Miss Laura's name. The real killer could've wrote it. I mean, it was wrote kinda scribbled. There was no way to recognize it as Mista Lee's handwriting."

Harry agreed. "Yes, I've considered that."

"Is you gonna try to get Miss Laura to come back home?"

"Maybe. I hope I can convince her to tell me exactly what happened between her and Lee."

"She'll tell you what happened, and it'll be the truth. Miss Laura ain't no liar."

Harry regarded Joshua closely. "You're quite an admirer of hers, aren't you?"

"I reckon I'm a good judge of character, and Miss Laura is a fine, honest lady."

"Exactly how well do you know her?"

"I see her in town a lot, and she always stops and talks to me. She don't act like all them other white folks, who think just 'cause I's colored, I ain't worth talkin' to. No, suh, Miss Laura treats me like . . . like I got feelin's."

"Apparently, she has her mother's compassion." Harry sounded impressed.

"I cain't understand why you never got to know Miss Laura. She's a daughter to be proud of."

"It wasn't easy for me to turn my back on her."

Joshua's brow wrinkled thoughtfully. "Mista Harry, I reckon I knows you better than anybody, but I never suspected that you and Miss Beth was in love. I still find it hard to believe that I didn't catch on. I's known you all your life, we was both born on your pappy's plantation.

159

He gave me to you when you was six, and I was eight. I know you like the back of my hand. How come I didn't catch on 'bout you and Miss Beth?"

"We kept our love well guarded," Harry sighed deeply. "But not well enough. Beth's husband found out."

Joshua's eyes lit up. "So that's why there was a rift between you all! I always wondered what caused it. When they first bought their ranch, all of you got along real good. Then, all at once, you started avoidin' one another like the plague."

"John, Beth's husband, was a sorry excuse for a man. He was weak, selfish, and a coward. But he needed Beth, and he wasn't about to let her go. He said if she left him, he'd take the ranch and their son, and accuse her as an adulteress. The law would certainly have been on his side. Beth was a good and loving mother, and she could not have borne losing her son. At the time, I was also married, and I couldn't leave Charlene. My God, she was a cripple and wholly dependent on me! Beth and I stopped seeing each other. A few months later, I came across her in town. I could see that she was pregnant. She swore that the child was John's. I knew it could very well be mine, but I respected her wishes. Apparently, that was what she wanted. So, as far as I was concerned, the child belonged to her and John."

Joshua shook his head with wonder. "You makes it all sound so cut and dried."

A small, bitter laugh escaped Harry's lips. "Well, it wasn't that simple, believe me!"

It was late, and Joshua set about cleaning the dishes and putting everything away. Harry, sitting at the fire, sank into his own thoughts. He smiled sentimentally. Considering he and Beth had gotten off on the wrong foot, it was a wonder that they grew to be so close. His mind, journeying into the past, brought that day back vividly . . .

160

The slap Beth delivered across Harry's face was severe, and it turned his cheek scarlet-red. Startled, he stepped back, and with mocking eyes, said, "Ma'am, I know there's a war going on, but I didn't know it had reached Nevada. The last I heard it was between the North and South."

"Don't be impertinent!" she spat. "How dare you spy on me!"

"If you don't want to be seen this way, then I suggest the next time you bathe, you do so indoors."

Beth's blue eyes stared defiantly into a pair of eyes that were as azure as her own. She was embarrassed, and felt like a fool standing there wearing nothing but a towel before this handsome stranger! However, there was something about him that she instinctively liked; she also thought him disturbingly attractive. She found herself wishing she wasn't married.

Harry's feelings were the same as Beth's, and the need to reach out and touch her was almost palpable. He longed to run his fingers through her long, auburn tresses, and gently trace her high, delicate cheekbones, before kissing the most sensually shaped lips he had ever beheld. He gazed deeply into her clear cobalt-blue eyes, which, fringed with thick ashen lashes, were indeed bewitching.

Harry and Beth, lonely and unloved, were overpowered by their feelings, and they shared an instant, total attraction. It was love at first sight . . .

Harry, clearing his mind of Beth, left the fire and retired to his bedroll. His thoughts were now on Laura, and guilt squeezed his heart in a viselike grip. She was his daughter—he didn't doubt it for a moment—and he had failed her terribly.

He prayed that God would give him a second chance to make it up to her. When he found her, he'd tell her the truth, and hope that she would forgive him. He wanted desperately to be a father to Laura, but was worried that he had waited too long.

It was after midnight before Neosha decided to stop for the night. Again, their meal consisted of dried jerky.

Laura took the strip of meat, moved to a tree, sat down, and leaned back against the wide trunk. She was almost too tired to chew, but knowing she needed nourishment, she forced herself to eat.

Tonight the sky was clear, and luminous moonlight fell across the land like a golden beam. She watched as Neosha watered and tethered the horses. She wasn't as frightened of Neosha as she had been in the beginning. She didn't take him lightly, and knew he wasn't a man to cross. Laura also knew he was determined to take her to Silver Star and collect the reward, and would surely kill anyone who tried to stop him. Thus, she was more worried for Craig's safety than her own. Craig was a professional, true, and he knew what he was doing, but Laura had a feeling that Neosha was his equal.

Finishing his task, the Indian began walking slowly toward Laura. He carried a rope in his hand, and Laura grimaced. He was undoubtedly planning to tie her for the night.

She figured he would do so immediately, and was startled when he simply sat down beside her. Toying with the rope, he said, "I cannot go any longer without sleep, so I must make sure you do not escape."

"I'm surprised you bothered to explain."

"Why do you say that?"

162

"Such consideration doesn't square with your disdain for white women."

He chuckled tersely. "You are not like other white women."

"Do you hate all whites, Neosha? Men as well as women?"

"A few white men have earned my respect." He turned to Laura, and watching her hawklike, asked, "Why did you commit murder?"

"I didn't kill anyone. I was falsely accused."

Neosha instinctively believed her, but it didn't change anything. He was still bent on collecting the five hundred dollars. "Turn around," he told her.

She did so, he tied her hands together, then ordered her to lie down. He cut the rope and used the second strip to bind her feet. He left, got three blankets, returned, put one on the ground, lifted Laura onto it, then used another one to cover her. He spread the third blanket close to Laura, and took it for his own bed.

She didn't like having him sleep in such proximity. But she knew there was nothing she could do about it, so she didn't say anything. Keeping her back turned, she tried to put her mind to rest. She needed sleep! To her dismay, however, thoughts kept swirling about her head, keeping her wide-awake. She hadn't forgotten the knife hidden in her boot, but tied in such a fashion, it was impossible to reach it. She knew the concealed weapon was her best chance for escape, but, so far, the right opportunity to use it hadn't arisen. Last night, though, she had considered throwing the knife into Neosha's back. The darkness plus the rain made a clear target impossible, but she might have inflicted a fatal wound. She had discarded the plan for two reasons: if she merely wounded him, he would take away her knife and most likely keep her tied; the second reason, and the more influential, the thought of killing someone sickened her. Today, she hadn't been tempted to use the knife, for Neosha had either kept her horse abreast of his, or was trailing behind covering their tracks.

Laura closed her eyes, and willfully routed all thoughts from her mind. A short time later, she drifted into slumber.

Jim had his pallet beneath the wagon. He had been asleep, but was awakened by a throbbing in his hand. Zeb, sleeping close by, was snoring softly. Moving quietly, Jim crawled out from under the wagon, and looking through his belongings, he found a first aid kit. He took it to the campfire, built up the flames, then removed the bandage that he had earlier wrapped hastily about his finger. The thorn bush had pricked his flesh deeply, and the cut was now infected.

He was opening the kit when, Karen, unable to sleep, left the wagon. "I thought I heard someone moving about," she said, joining him. Noticing the medicine kit, she asked, "What's wrong?"

"I cut my finger on a thorn."

"Let me see," she said, concerned. The wound was red and puffy. She quickly covered it with an antiseptic ointment. "You should have put salve on this sooner."

"I know," he admitted a little sheepishly. "But I didn't think it'd become infected."

She looked at him as though he were an irresponsible child. "Honestly, Jim! Don't you realize some thorns are poisonous?"

"Yeah, but I guess I just didn't think."

She wanted to tell him he was very proficient at that! Only a man who didn't think would fall in love with Marsha Donaldson. It hadn't taken Karen very long to see through Marsha. The woman was obviously shallow, insensitive, and totally involved in herself. Jim's love for the woman was evident, for he fawned over her at every opportunity. Karen almost wished she hadn't asked to come along on this trip, for watching Jim fall more and more in love with Marsha was torture.

Jim closed up the medicine kit. "Couldn't you sleep?" he asked.

"No, I'm too worried about Laura. I pray Craig will save her."

"I feel the same way. But I have a lot of confidence in Branston, and if anyone can save her from Neosha, he can."

"Is this Neosha as terrible as Marsha claims?"

"I don't know. I've never seen the man, but I have heard of him. He used to be an Army scout, then he got into some kind of trouble over a white woman, and the Army let him go. That's when he became a bounty hunter."

Karen, her expression frightened, asked haltingly, "Do you . . . do you think . . . he'll harm Laura?"

"Sexually?"

The direct question made her blush profusely. Embarrassed, she dropped her gaze to her lap.

"Neosha has quite a notorious reputation, but, as far as I know, he's no rapist."

"I'm glad to hear that," Karen murmured weakly, still embarrassed. She stood up. "Well, I think I'll try and get some sleep. You should do the same."

"I will in a few minutes."

There was still coffee in the pot, and Jim placed it on the fire to heat it. He didn't think he'd be able to sleep, for the pain in his finger was now spreading beyond his hand and up into his arm.

Fourteen

The next day, Neosha continued his relentless pace. He and Laura traveled practically nonstop; their diet consisting of dried jerky and water. Laura, exhausted, wasn't sure how much longer she could hold up.

It was well past noon when Neosha veered their course and headed into the desert. Although Laura had been hoping he would skirt the barren region, she wasn't at all surprised, for this was the shortest route to Silver Star.

The weather was warm, but as they journeyed farther into the desert, the temperature rose steadily until it was uncomfortably hot. Laura, perspiring, was glad the mercantile in Seclusion had stocked riding clothes designed for summer wear. The clothes she had purchased there were plain but practical. The blouse, though long-sleeved, was made of lightweight cotton. The skirt was a shade darker, and divided so the wearer could ride western-style. She had on her wide-brimmed hat, and, now, as the sun's scorching rays bathed the land with dazzling light, she drew the brim forward to shade her face.

Neosha was no longer attempting to cover their tracks. For that, Laura was grateful. Craig would certainly map out Neosha's route; once he and Lobo were in the open desert, the wolf would undoubtedly find her!

The day wore on, and Laura traveled without uttering a complaint; not that she didn't feel like complaining, she simply knew it wouldn't do any good.

She and Neosha covered the miles mostly in silence, for the Cherokee didn't seem interested in talking. Laura didn't mind, she didn't have anything to say to him.

The sun was setting when Neosha stopped to water the horses from the extra canteens he had packed. An underground spring was only a few miles away; there, he planned to replenish his water supply.

Laura, dismounting, took her canteen, moved to a small boulder, and sat down. Her throat was dry, and she helped herself to a large drink. Meanwhile, Neosha was busy tending to the thirsty horses. Finishing, he grabbed his own canteen, then walked over to Laura.

"We will rest a few minutes," he said. "There's a spring about three hours from here, we'll make camp there." He took a long drink, closed the canteen, lay on the ground, and drew his hat's brim over his eyes.

He was vulnerable, and Laura thought about the knife hidden in her boot. There might never be a better time to use it! But she would have to inflict a fatal wound, or face Neosha's wrath! The thought of killing increased her perspiration, and she rubbed a hand over her brow. Dear God, could she take a person's life? Maybe, if it was in self-defense! She supposed in a way this was self-defense, however, Neosha wasn't really life-threatening! But what about Craig's life? If he caught up to them, would Neosha try to kill him?

Laura's heart began to pound erratically. She had never killed, and she wasn't sure if she could. At least, not this way—cold and premeditated!

As Laura's debate with her conscience continued, dusk set in and the landscape darkened. She turned toward

Neosha, she could still see him fairly well; sending her knife into his heart wouldn't be a problem. But time was of the essence, for it was getting darker by the minute. Stealthily, inch by inch, she lowered her hand to her boot—her pulse racing madly—but, suddenly, she stopped. She couldn't do it! She wasn't capable of murder!

Her eyes were still on Neosha. He was lying very still, and she wondered if he was asleep. Should she make a dash for her horse and try to escape? She instantly discarded the notion, she'd never make it. Most likely Neosha would shoot her horse out from under her.

She was about to look away from Neosha when, all at once, she spotted a scorpion crawling dangerously close to his head. The creature was mere inches from Neosha's face, and, Laura, momentarily stunned, looked on as the scorpion curled its tail, ready to deliver its poisonous sting.

Laura, her movements now instinctive, drew her knife, took perfect aim, and sent the sharp weapon into the deadly scorpion.

Neosha actually heard the knife cut through the air as it whizzed past his head. He sat up quickly, looked at the dead scorpion for a moment, then drew the knife out of its body. He got to his feet, tucked the knife into his belt, turned to Laura, and asked, "Why didn't you let it sting me? A scorpion's sting is not always fatal, but it can make a man very sick. If I was ill, I couldn't stop you from escaping."

"The scorpion was getting ready to strike, I didn't have time to consider such things."

He rubbed a hand over the knife's handle. "Why didn't you use this on me, instead of the scorpion?"

"I thought about it," she replied honestly. "But I couldn't go through with it."

He gestured toward the horses. "It is time to leave."

168

She was perturbed, but she wasn't sure why. Had she been expecting Neosha to thank her? Considering she had chosen to kill the scorpion over him, he probably thought her God's greatest fool!

Laura's thoughts couldn't have been more wrong. Quite the contrary, Neosha's admiration for Laura had grown. He found her phenomenal, she was in stark contrast to his opinion of white women. So far, her every action had surprised him.

Karen, with Zeb's help, had just finished washing the supper dishes when Jim, who had been resting in his bed under the wagon, came to the campfire.

"You missed a good meal," Zeb told him. "But you were asleep, and we didn't want to wake you. But don't worry, we saved back a plate for you."

Jim sat down heavily, as though he were too weary to stay on his feet. "Thanks, but I'm not hungry."

"Are you feelin' all right?" Zeb asked.

"I'm okay," he mumbled offhandedly. "Where's Marsha?"

"Inside the wagon," Karen replied. Jim didn't look well, and she placed a hand on his brow. "You're burning up with fever!" she exclaimed, alarmed.

His shoulders were slumped, but he raised his head and gazed up at Karen. He was bleary-eyed.

"Zeb," she said briskly. "Get the medicine kit." She sat beside Jim, took his hand, and removed the bandage wrapped about his finger. The wound was pus-infected, but she was more alarmed to see a red streak running from his hand up his arm.

Zeb returned, and together they cleaned and bandaged Jim's finger, then Zeb helped him to his feet. He was now very weak, and had to lean against Zeb to keep from col-

169

lapsing. Jim couldn't have made it to the wagon without his friend's support.

Marsha was climbing over the backboard as they arrived. "What's wrong with Jim?" she asked, worried that he might have a contagious disease.

As Zeb helped Jim inside, Karen told Marsha that his cut finger was badly infected.

"Oh, is that all?" she remarked, disinterested.

"The infection has spread. I'm afraid Jim's condition is serious."

Marsha was aghast. "But how can that be? He merely pricked his finger on a thorn!"

"Apparently, the thorn was poisonous." Karen waved a hand toward the wagon. "I suppose you'd like to take care of him."

"I don't know anything about taking care of sick people," she was quick to reply. "Karen, I'm sure you can do so much better. You don't mind, do you?"

She didn't mind at all! She wanted to be with Jim! Marsha's actions didn't surprise Karen, she never once believed that the woman returned Jim's love. Karen suspected that Marsha Donaldson wasn't capable of loving anyone but herself.

Karen went inside the wagon, where Zeb had Jim resting on a pallet. She checked Jim's brow and was startled to find that his fever was escalating.

"We need to get his clothes off," Zeb said, the statement taking Karen off guard.

She blushed. "Why . . . why must we undress him?"

"You'll need to keep washing him in cool water. It'll keep his fever down. After we get him undressed, I'll bring in a bucket of water. Then, I'll have to leave, but I hope I won't be gone too long."

"Leave!" Karen exclaimed. "But where are you going?"

170

"To look for some medicinal plants. I know an Indian remedy that might help pull Jim through this. I just gotta find the right ones."

"These plants grow in this area?"

"They're kinda scarce, but they're out there." He began taking off Jim's boots. "Can you manage his shirt?"

"Yes, I think so," she answered. She sat beside Jim, he had sunk into a feverish state and was no longer coherent. Somewhat awkwardly, she was able to take off his shirt. Zeb, taking over, removed the rest of his clothes, then covered him with a blanket. Karen, embarrassed, kept her eyes turned away.

"Ma'am," Zeb began, "this is no time for modesty. I realize you're an unmarried lady, and this is awkward for you, but you gotta set those kind of feelin's aside. Jim's gonna need constant care; you're the only one who can give it to him. I know his naked body wouldn't embarrass Mrs. Donaldson, 'cause I bet she's seen plenty of naked men in her time. I'd tell her to come in here and tend to Jim, if I thought she'd do a good job. But she'd probably let him die, 'fore tirin' herself out keepin' him washed."

"You're absolutely right," Karen said, ridding herself of embarrassment. "And please don't worry, I won't let anything interfere with what I must do."

Zeb smiled warmly. "Jim's a dadblasted fool to choose Mrs. Donaldson over you. Why, she ain't good enough to wipe your shoes."

Karen's astonishment was evident.

"You needn't look so surprised, young lady. I'd have to be as blind as a bat not to see that you're in love with him. It's written all over your face, every time you look at him."

"Do you suppose Jim knows?" she asked, hoping he didn't. She certainly didn't want him feeling sorry for her.

"Nope, I don't think he knows. But don't give up on

171

him, ma'am. Eventually, he's gonna see Mrs. Donaldson for what she really is, and then once those blinders are removed, he'll see what a treasure you are."

"I'm not a treasure," she replied softly. "I'm not even pretty."

"Beauty lies in the eyes of the beholder, and I think you're very beautiful."

"Thank you, Zeb. That's the nicest compliment I've ever had. And do you know what makes it extra special?"

"What's that?"

"You meant it sincerely."

"One of these days, Jim's gonna know you're beautiful, too. Just wait and see if he don't." Zeb gave her an encouraging wink, then left the wagon to fetch the water.

Now that Karen could no longer see him, a grave expression fell across his face. He was very worried about Jim, for his condition was serious. Even if he found the medicinal plants he needed, it might be too late to save Jim's life.

It was well into the night before Laura and Neosha stopped to make camp. Tired, Laura dismounted lethargically, found a patch of grass beside the small, gushing spring, spread her blanket, and lay down. She couldn't recall ever being so worn out, these last two days had sapped her strength. If Neosha continued setting such an exhausting tempo, she wasn't sure if she would be physically able to go on.

A few minutes later, Neosha joined her. He carried both strips of rope, and Laura knew he was going to tie her again. She was too fatigued to care!

He put his blanket beside hers, and sat down Indian-style. He gazed thoughtfully into the darkness.

Laura, wondering why he hadn't bound her hands and feet, sat up to see what he was doing. She was surprised to find him gazing at nothing in particular.

"I once loved a white woman," he said. The remark was casual, as though they had been discussing it. "It was years ago, I was an Army scout at Fort Sill. She was the daughter of a major. I thought she loved me, too. But she was merely toying with me. You see, she was curious about Indians, and wanted to know what it was like to make love to a warrior. At the time, I didn't know that. I was young and gullible. But I wanted more than her body, I wanted to marry her. We had to see each other secretly, for her father would never have allowed it. One night, he caught us together. She was in my arms, and we were kissing. She spotted her father before I did, and she started screaming and fighting, so he would think I was forcing myself on her. She swore before him, and before the fort's commander, that I had tried to molest her. I was put on trial and found guilty. The major wanted me to hang from a rope, but the commander thought the penalty too strong. After all, he believed it was only attempted rape. The young woman's virtue was still intact. I was lashed, and barred from all Army posts."

Neosha gently ran his fingers over the long scar on his cheek. "The major did this to me. He said it would always remind me to stay away from white women."

"Neosha, why are you telling me this?"

"I don't know. I have never talked about it to anyone else."

"Is the major's daughter the reason you dislike white women?"

"She is a big part of the reason. All white women I have encountered are like her, or that woman who was in the river with you. She is not to be trusted, and there is much evil in her."

"That's quite a statement, considering you were with her only a short time."

"Her kind are easy to spot. I saw you save her from drowning. The foolish woman tried to drown you both. She would have, if you hadn't slapped her." He chuckled softly. "You should have hit her twice, she deserved it."

"I thought about it," Laura replied, smiling. The smile faded instantly, however. This man was her enemy, and she shouldn't forget it—not for a moment!

"I stole that wanted poster from Branston's saddlebags."

Laura looked at him uncertainly. Why, all of a sudden, was he confiding in her?

"I slipped into the stables," he continued. "I had found the poster when you arrived with your friend. I hid in an open stall and listened to your conversation." He turned his head, and met her eyes. "You and Branston are in love, but he is engaged to another woman."

"That's right," she murmured.

"Why is there a problem? He must tell this other woman that he has found someone else."

"It's not that simple. Besides, it no longer matters. I won't be marrying Craig or anyone else. If I don't hang, I'll spend the rest of my life in prison." She wanted to add "thanks to you," but refrained from doing so.

"You are worth five hundred dollars. That is a lot of money."

"Yes, it is. But is it enough to buy your conscience? You know I'm not a murderer. If I was, I would have killed you."

An inscrutable mask suddenly fell over his face. "Enough talk! Do you want something to eat?"

174

"No," she replied, knowing he'd offer her dried jerky. She was sick of the diet.

"It is time to get some sleep." He quickly bound her hands and feet, then helped her lie down.

She rolled to her side, turning her face away from his. She was so exhausted that she fell asleep almost instantly.

The sun shining on Laura's face brought her slowly awake. She sat up groggily, and, at first, wasn't even aware that she was no longer tied.

Then, as her mind cleared, she got hastily to her feet. Her eyes scanned her surroundings, but Neosha was nowhere in sight. She looked about with amazement, her horse was tethered, but his was gone. She took a step forward, and stumbled over the rifle Neosha had left next to her blanket. Her bowie knife was beside it. A burlap bag was close by, she hurried over and opened it. He had left her a supply of food.

A large, happy smile brightened Laura's face. "Thank you, Neosha!" she cried, even though she knew he was probably miles away.

She wondered what she should do. Should she start back toward the wagon, or wait here for Craig and Lobo to find her? If she headed back, she might miss them. There was no guarantee that their paths would cross. Also, she wasn't too sure she could find her way back, she might become lost. She quickly decided it would be better to stay put. At least, for a couple of days. Surely, by then, Craig would be here! If not, she would start back and try to keep on the same trail that she and Neosha had traveled.

For a few minutes, Laura basked in her happiness—Neosha had actually set her free! The glorious feeling didn't last long, however, stark reality soon set in. She was alone in the desert, she didn't even have Lobo to warn her of possible danger.

She went to her rifle and checked to make sure it was loaded. The open land was somewhat comforting, no one could possibly sneak up on her.

The horse neighed softly, and Laura walked over to it and patted its neck. She stood by it for a long time; its presence was comforting. She and the horse seemed to be the only living creatures for miles around. The desert was quiet, eerie, and appeared totally devoid of life.

Laura had never felt so alone!

Fifteen

Karen was so weary, every muscle in her body seemed to ache. She had stayed awake all night, assiduously nursing Jim. To keep down his temperature, she had continuously sponged his fevered flesh. Although her patient often moaned and groaned, he remained unconscious. However, she felt that he somehow knew she was there tending to him, for when she was bathing his warm brow, several times his hand sought her free one and held on tightly.

The wagon was roomy, and Marsha's bed was across from Jim's. Now, as she came awake, she pushed off the top blanket, and stretched catlike. She sat up slowly, looked over at Karen, and asked, "How's Jim?"

"He's not any better. I do wish Zeb would hurry back."

Marsha frowned. "You mean, he hasn't returned?"

"I'm afraid not."

Getting up, Marsha took off her gown and began dressing. Her mood was indeed foul. Zeb wasn't here, and Karen was taking care of Jim, which meant *she'd* have to build up the fire and make her own breakfast! That was a chore Zeb and Karen had been handling. Marsha wasn't even sure she could manage the task, her journey from Carson City hadn't made her an experienced camper. First, she'd had her husband to take care of all the chores, then, later, the others had taken charge.

Marsha left the wagon; the fire had burned down to glowing embers. Zeb had stacked kindling close by, so she threw on a few branches. She was pleased when the flames took hold. Sitting, she filled the pot with water from a canteen, then haphazardly dropped in coffee grounds. As she set the pot on the fire, she wondered if she should attempt breakfast. She decided not to bother, after all, she wasn't all that hungry.

Her thoughts went to Jim Slade. She liked him well enough, and he was most certainly a virile lover, but he was nevertheless a problem. She knew it would be in her best interest if he didn't live. The fool was apparently in love with her, but she had no intentions of marrying him. Which, she was sure, would lead to problems. After all, the man was a federal marshal, and if she angered him, he could get even by taking her back to Carson City to stand trial. Scorned lovers could be very vindictive!

The sound of an approaching horse caught Marsha's attention, and she looked on as Zeb arrived. She was glad to see him, for she didn't like not having a man's protection. He might be getting on in years, but she had a feeling he was still good with a gun.

Dismounting, he asked, "How's Jim?"

"He isn't any better," she replied, repeating Karen's prognosis.

Zeb, carrying a burlap bag, hurried to the wagon and climbed inside.

Marsha waited a few minutes longer, then deciding the coffee was ready, she poured herself a cup. She took a drink, frowned distastefully, and shivered. The coffee was entirely too strong, and she set the cup aside.

A short time later, Zeb reappeared. Joining Marsha, he reached toward the pot.

"It's too strong," she told him.

"I like my coffee that way," he replied, pouring a cup. He took a drink, but quickly spit it onto the ground. "Damn! That's strong enough to walk by itself!"

"I wasn't sure how many grounds to put in."

"Mrs. Donaldson, didn't you ever fix your husband any coffee?"

"Jerry did all the cooking."

"I can see why," he mumbled.

She let the remark pass. "Did you find the plants?"

"Yep, I sure did. Karen and I managed to get a good dose down Jim. Speakin' of Karen, she's about to keel over from fatigue. She also needs a few hours of sleep. I want you to relieve her."

"But I don't know how to take care of sick people."

"All you gotta do is keep Jim sponged off so his fever won't rise too high." He regarded her impatiently. "You can do that, can't you?"

She was beginning to dislike Zeb by the minute. How dare the uncouth man speak to her in such a way! She got to her feet, lifted her chin smugly, and replied, "Yes, I'm sure I can manage."

"Good!" he remarked tersely. "I'll make another pot of coffee, and bring you a cup."

She started toward the wagon, but turned and asked, "Do you mind making breakfast? If I'm going to nurse Jim, I'll need nourishment."

"Yep, I reckon I can fix something to eat."

Marsha went inside the wagon. Karen was sitting beside Jim, washing his brow.

"Zeb wants me to take over for a while. He thinks you need some sleep."

Karen agreed reluctantly. She did indeed need sleep, but she didn't want to leave Jim's side—not even for a moment! Hesitantly, she moved over to her own pallet, which was at the foot of Marsha's.

"Don't worry," Marsha told her. "I'll take good care of him."

"If there's a change in his condition, you'll wake me, won't you?"

"Of course," she replied. She hid an amused smile. Until this moment, she hadn't realized that Karen was in love with Jim. But only a woman in love could be so concerned! Marsha found Karen's infatuation humorous, for she saw her as plain and mousy; a man as handsome as Jim wouldn't look twice at her!

Marsha sat beside Jim, took the cloth from the water basin, and rubbed it across his brow. She studied his face closely; yes, he was indeed attractive, but she still wanted him dead! The country was full of handsome men, and replacing him would be easy.

Murder suddenly popped into Marsha's head. It was so unexpected that, for a moment, it gave her a jolt. Why not? she thought. She had killed before, why not again? Furthermore, it would be so simple! Her eyes went to the pillow beneath Jim's head. She could slip it out from under him, then place it over his face. Unconscious, he couldn't even put up a struggle. After smothering him, she could yell out to Zeb as though panic-stricken, he would rush into the wagon, check Jim, then assume that he had simply died. He and Karen would never suspect that she had murdered him!

Yes, the plan was perfect! She cast Karen a cautious glance, and was relieved to see that her back was turned. She was lying very still, and Marsha was certain that she was asleep. Now, to get rid of Jim once and for all! Her hand moved carefully to the pillow, she was about to slip it from under his head when, all at once, his eyes opened.

She gasped, and drew her hand away.

"Marsha," he whispered weakly.

Marsha had been wrong to assume that Karen was asleep, and she heard Jim's whisper. Delighted that he had regained consciousness, she was about to rush over, but his next words stopped her.

"Darling," he said feebly to Marsha. "I've been awfully sick, I know that. But somehow, I knew you were with me. Your hands nursed me . . . washed my brow." He managed to take her hand into his. "Your gentle, loving touch gave me the strength to stay alive."

At that moment, Zeb came inside. Marsha's heart lurched, but she nonetheless breathed a relieved sigh. Thank goodness Jim had awakened, otherwise, Zeb would have caught her in the act of suffocating him!

A large smile crossed Zeb's face. "I see you're awake," he said to Jim. "That's a mighty good sign."

Karen got out of bed. She was thankful that Jim was better, but, despite her joy, she was disheartened. She, and not Marsha, had taken care of him! It had been her hands that had nursed him through the night! She was tempted to tell Jim the truth, but decided against it. What good would it do? She'd merely gain his gratitude, not his love!

Laura had never known a day to drag by so interminably. Alone in the desert, with nothing to do but worry, had made the hours move by slowly. However, as the sun began to set, she almost wished the day wasn't ending. She dreaded the approaching night, for it brought out nocturnal creatures such as scorpions and the poisonous Gila monster! She was understandably frightened, but she had no patience with her fear, for it made her feel like a child who was afraid of the dark.

With a somewhat brave tilt to her chin, she sat down, squared her shoulders, and mentally prepared herself to face the upcoming night.

Her back was turned toward the open desert, but a sudden sound caught her attention. She bounded to her feet and whirled around, just as Lobo jumped to greet his mistress. His large paws landed soundly on her shoulders, and his lapping tongue tried vainly to reach her face.

Dropping to her knees, Laura hugged her pet eagerly. She had never been so happy to see him. A horse's hooves were pounding across the desert, she got up and rushed to meet Craig, who was racing to her side.

He swung from the saddle before the horse had come to a complete stop. Laura flung herself into his arms, and he lifted her into the air, whirling her about. Then, lowering her feet to the ground, he drew her close and kissed her deeply.

"Laura!" he uttered gratefully. "Thank God, you're all right!"

"Oh Craig, hold me closer! I need you so much!"

He embraced her tightly. "Where's Neosha?"

"I woke up this morning to find him gone."

"I don't understand. Why did he leave?"

"I'm not sure, but I think Neosha has more compassion than he realizes. Craig, I'll tell you about him later, but now I just want to feel your arms about me."

He kissed her again, and she clung desperately.

"We're only a couple hours away from Seclusion. I think we should spend the night there."

Laura stepped back, gazing at him with surprise. "I had no idea the town was so close! This desert is so confusing. Apparently, I've lost all sense of direction."

"The desert has that effect on a lot of people." His lips brushed against hers softly. "Are you ready to get out of

182

here? I imagine a hot bath, a warm meal, and a bed sounds mighty inviting."

"It sounds heavenly, but only if . . ."

"If what?"

She smiled saucily. "If you'll share my bed with me."

He faked a grimace. "Well, since you twisted my arm . . ." He drew her body flush to his, told her he loved her, then kissed her long and hard.

Harry sat alone in the hotel dining room. He and Joshua had ridden into Seclusion over an hour ago. They had stabled their horses, and rented rooms at the hotel. Harry had asked Joshua to join him for dinner, but the man refused. He knew how a lot of people reacted to eating in the same room with a Negro. To avoid a possible scene, he had chosen to have his meal upstairs.

Harry had finished and was relaxing with a second cup of coffee. His thoughts were on Laura. Upon his arrival, he had questioned the desk clerk about her. The man had remembered her well, and had talked about her quite freely. Harry had been surprised to learn that she was now traveling with so many people—including her uncle. The clerk let him know that she and the others were going to San Francisco.

It was late, and the dining room wasn't very crowded; thus, the atmosphere was quiet and cozy, causing Harry's musings to drift dreamily. In his mind, the years melted away, and his thoughts were on Beth when Laura and Craig came into the room.

Harry caught a vague glimpse of them out of the corner of his eye. He glanced up with little interest, and, at first, he failed to realize it was Laura. But, then, he was suddenly dumbstruck to find her so unexpectedly. Incredulous, he got somewhat awkwardly to his feet.

Laura had also seen Harry, and she was staring at him with disbelief. Harry, his mouth agape, watched as she spoke to the man at her side, then together they approached his table.

"Mr. Talbert, what are you doing here?" she asked.

"I've been looking for you. But I thought you were on your way to San Francisco."

"I was, but I was detained."

Harry gestured toward two extra chairs. "Please sit down."

As they complied, Laura introduced Craig.

"I'm glad to meet you, Mr. Branston," Harry said cordially.

"Mr. Talbert," Laura began, "why are you looking for me?"

"The first wanted posters on you states that you're to be brought in alive, but a second batch was run off, and they read dead or alive. I wanted to find you, because I was worried that someone might try to kill you for the reward."

Craig was visibly upset. "Dead or alive!" he exclaimed. "I thought Ed Talbert was determined that she be delivered alive!"

"He is! It was a mistake! Sheriff Longley is trying to call back as many of the posters as possible."

At that moment, the waiter came to their table. As Craig ordered dinner for himself and Laura, Harry took time to study Laura closely. Her face certainly wasn't unfamiliar, for he had seen her often, but he had never really looked at her. He had tried a few times, but her resemblance to Beth had always caused him to turn away. Seeing her mother in her face was always too heartbreaking. Now, however, he searched for a resemblance to himself. Yes, she was indeed a Talbert; it was there in the shape of her nose, the high forehead, and the color of her hair. Harry remembered that his mother's hair had been full, wavy, and the color of spun honey.

Harry sighed remorsefully. God, why had he ignored his own daughter all these years? How could he have been so unfeeling? Even when Laura was a child, he had intentionally avoided her! What compulsion had driven him to go to such lengths? Deep in his heart, Harry knew the answer; he had always known! Now, he had to face his own failure. Like an ostrich, he had hidden his face in the sand, believing what he didn't know wouldn't hurt him.

"Mr. Talbert," Laura said. "Why did you give me money? Why, if you believe I killed Lee, did you help me?"

"Did you shoot him?"

"No, of course not. When I left your home, he was very much alive."

"Joshua believes it was the murderer, and not Lee, who wrote down your name."

"What do *you* believe?" Laura asked intensely.

"I believe, as usual, Joshua is right. By the way, he's traveling with me. He's upstairs in his room."

Laura smiled warmly. "I'm looking forward to seeing him."

"He's quite an admirer of yours."

"Who's Joshua?" Craig asked.

Laura answered the question. She then spoke to Harry, "Is Sheriff Longley recalling all the posters, or only the ones that read dead or alive?"

"All of them."

Laura was puzzled. "But why?"

"Because I asked him to, that's why."

She shook her head with wonder. "I don't understand why you are helping me."

185

"I think you're innocent."

Craig had been watching Harry thoughtfully, and he now asked, "You must have some kind of evidence. I can't believe you think she's innocent on faith alone."

"I'm afraid I have no evidence."

Craig didn't say anything, but he knew the pieces to the puzzle didn't fit. It was obvious that Harry Talbert was hiding something.

"If you have no objections," Harry began, "I'd like to travel with you to San Francisco."

Laura was now even more perplexed. "Why do you want to go there?"

"I have a good friend in San Francisco," he lied. "Since I'm this close, I'd like to visit him." Harry's true reason, of course, was to spend more time with Laura. Then, when he believed the time was right, he'd tell her that she was his daughter.

"We'd be glad to have you join us," Craig replied. "We'll be leaving at dawn. Can you be ready?"

"Yes, I can. Joshua will come along, too, that is, if you don't mind."

"Of course not," Craig said. "The more the merrier."

Harry got to his feet. "I won't impose any longer. Good night, and I'll see you bright and early."

Laura didn't say anything as Harry walked away from the table, but the moment he was out of the room, she turned to Craig. "Do you think it's wise to let him travel with us? After all, he's a Talbert, and I don't trust any of them."

"But that's exactly why I said he could come along. If he's an enemy, it's in our best interest to keep him in sight."

"I suppose you're right." She frowned thoughtfully. "Harry Talbert certainly is a mystery. I've known him all my life, and he's never been very friendly. Now, all at once, he acts as though he wants to be my protector." She mulled it over, then dismissed it with a shrug. "Maybe he always wanted to be friendly, but the rift between him and my parents put a stop to it."

"A rift? What caused it?"

"I have no idea."

The waiter brought their dinner, and over the meal, they discussed Harry Talbert in length. Nothing was settled, however, the man's motives remained a total mystery.

Following dinner, Laura and Craig went to the stables and checked on Lobo. They fed him and gave him fresh water, then returned to the hotel. Craig, for appearance's sake, had rented two rooms; they climbed the stairs, and went to their separate quarters. Laura had requested a bath, and after the tub had been brought in and filled, she moved quietly down the hall and knocked on Craig's door. It was opened at once.

"Grab a change of clothes and come with me," Laura told him, her eyes sparkling merrily.

Doing so, he accompanied her back to her room, where he was immediately confronted by the filled tub. It was quite large, and filled the center of the floor.

Laura smiled enticingly. "Would you care to join me, Mr. Branston?"

"I'd be delighted, Miss Mills. However, as a gentleman, I feel I must warn you that I'll consider this bath sensual foreplay."

"Promise?" she said pertly.

"Ma'am, I'm always a man of my word."

"Well, in this case, I hope your actions will be as good

as your words."

"You provocative little vixen," he uttered, taking her into his arms. His lips seized hers demandingly, and she responded by moving her body against his suggestively.

Now, anxious to share the tub, they helped each other undress, both openly admiring the other's naked flesh. Craig lifted Laura into his arms, and placed her gently in the warm water. He was quick to join her. The tub was large, still, it was a tight fit. However, they wouldn't have had it any other way, they relished such intimate closeness.

Craig was true to his word, and their bath did indeed turn into glorious foreplay. They took turns washing each other, their ministrations sensual and erotic.

Their desire eventually became overpowering, and Craig lifted her from the tub. He dried her with a towel, and she returned the favor. Hand in hand, they moved to the bed, stood beside it, and went into each other's arms. Craig's mouth smothered Laura's in a wild, hungry caress that sent her senses reeling. He drew her naked body tightly to his, and she felt wonderfully crushed by his masculine strength. His manhood, stiff and throbbing, was pressed against her stomach, and her breasts were flush against his chest; she could actually feel the rhythmic drumbeat of his heart. She trembled with need, and leaned against his sinewy length for support.

He then lifted her onto the bed, and went into her awaiting arms. They expressed their love through intimate, stimulating gestures, and passionate, fiery kisses that left them breathless with wonder.

Craig, his loins on fire, moved over her, and she slid her legs about his waist, waiting anxiously for his exciting entry. His impaling hardness filled her with rapture; she arched strongly, and accepted him fully.

They made love with a feverish intensity, both giving

and receiving fervent desire. Wrapped in splendid ecstasy, the lovers surrendered totally to their wondrous union.

Later, they slept, awoke, and made love again; the second time as beautiful, and as breathtaking, as the first!

Sixteen

Craig set a fast pace traveling back to the wagon, because he wanted to get there before the others pulled out. Laura kept up without complaining, she was used to traveling in such a way; Harry and Joshua, despite their age, managed very well.

Harry did wish Craig wasn't in such a hurry, for he craved leisure time with Laura, but he soon realized he wouldn't get his wish, at least, not until they reached the wagon.

They made the journey in a day and a half, and arrived in the late afternoon. Craig was indeed relieved to find Zeb and the others hadn't broken camp and moved onward.

Zeb, along with Karen and Marsha, were eating dinner when Craig and the others rode up. Zeb was happy to see Laura, and the moment she dismounted, he took her into his arms and gave her a big bear hug. She was then embraced by Karen.

Marsha, remaining at the campfire, had hoped Craig would return alone. Losing Laura would have upset him, but she had planned to ease his aching heart. She had confidence in her charms, and was sure that once he bedded her, he would forget all about Laura Mills. She was finding Craig Branston a challenge, for she rarely met a man who wasn't immediately smitten by her beauty.

Now, as she watched Craig talking to Zeb, she compared him to Jim Slade. Both men were dashingly handsome, and it was impossible to say one was better-looking than the other. She supposed only a woman's personal taste could set one above the other. Jim was muscular and blond, whereas, Craig was lean and dark. As her eyes continued measuring Craig, she decided that she preferred his swarthy good looks. A disappointed sigh escaped her lips, for she knew Craig was unavailable—he was too much in love with Laura.

Clearing Branston from her mind, she next looked at the two men accompanying Craig and Laura. She wondered who they were and why they were here. She simply glanced at Joshua, for he didn't interest her. Harry, on the other hand, aroused her curiosity.

She watched as Zeb, followed by Laura and Craig, went inside the wagon to see Jim. Karen brought the two men over, and introduced them to Marsha.

As Karen served their guests dinner, Marsha's thoughts were concentrated on Harry Talbert. Jim had told her about the man, and she knew that he was very rich. She was still determined to marry a wealthy man, and Talbert was a perfect candidate—except for his sons! When it came time for her to marry, she didn't want to share her fortune with anyone else. She shrugged the sons aside. If Harry Talbert should prove to be the man of her choice, she'd find a way to eliminate his offsprings. A professional killer was not that hard to find—if one had the right price!

Harry, eating his dinner, was sitting on her right. She turned to him, smiled brightly, and asked, "Are you going to San Francisco, Mr. Talbert?"

"Yes, I am," he replied.

"How long do you plan to stay?"

191

"Only a few days. My ranch is very demanding, and I can't afford to stay away much longer."

"I heard your ranch is a prosperous one."

He smiled a little self-consciously. "Well, I don't like to brag, but, yes, it's prosperous. I'm very proud of my home."

"Tell me about your house."

"Well, it's two stories, and is colonial in style. You see, I was raised in the South, and I designed my home to look a lot like the one I grew up in. My father had a plantation in Georgia, and our house was very grand."

"Why did you leave Georgia to move to Nevada?"

"I left home at eighteen. I didn't get along too well with my father, and we had a falling out. I traveled westward, and eventually ended up in Nevada, where, with luck and hard work, I built the Circle T."

"Did you ever go back home?"

"No, but I did visit the South again. I took a trip to New Orleans. That's where I met my wife."

"I understand you're a widower."

"Yes, I am."

"I'm sorry."

"Thank you, Mrs. Donaldson, but I lost my wife several years ago."

She smiled sweetly. "Please call me Marsha, and if you don't mind, I'll call you Harry. After all, if we're going to be traveling together, we shouldn't be so formal, should we?"

Talbert was inwardly amused. He had seen through Marsha from the beginning. He had come across her kind more than once. A young, beautiful woman wanting to marry him for his money was nothing new. He laughed to himself. Why did women like Marsha Donaldson think maturity made him a fool?

4 FREE BOOKS

TO GET YOUR 4 FREE BOOKS WORTH $18.00 —MAIL IN THE FREE BOOK CERTIFICATE T O D A Y

Fill in the Free Book Certificate below, and we'll send your FREE BOOKS to you as soon as we receive it.

If the certificate is missing below, write to: Zebra Home Subscription Service, Inc., P.O. Box 5214, 120 Brighton Road, Clifton, New Jersey 07015-5214.

FREE BOOK CERTIFICATE

4 FREE BOOKS

ZEBRA HOME SUBSCRIPTION SERVICE, INC.

YES! Please start my subscription to Zebra Historical Romances and send me my first 4 books absolutely FREE. I understand that each month I may preview four new Zebra Historical Romances free for 10 days. If I'm not satisfied with them, I may return the four books within 10 days and owe nothing. Otherwise, I will pay the low preferred subscriber's price of just $3.75 each; a total of $15.00, *a savings off the publisher's price of $3.00.* I may return any shipment and I may cancel this subscription at any time. There is no obligation to buy any shipment and there are no shipping, handling or other hidden charges. Regardless of what I decide, the four free books are mine to keep.

NAME	
ADDRESS	APT
CITY	STATE ZIP
TELEPHONE ( )	
SIGNATURE	(if under 18, parent or guardian must sign)

Terms, offer and prices subject to change without notice. Subscription subject to acceptance by Zebra Books. Zebra Books reserves the right to reject any order or cancel any subscription.

"I'd be honored to call you Marsha," he said politely. He saw no reason to be rude, he'd simply let her play her game, then when she made her move, he'd put her firmly in her place.

Marsha got up and began washing the dishes. She wanted to impress upon Harry that she was a woman willing to do her share of work.

Karen, astonished, looked on wide-eyed. Marsha Donaldson working? She shook her head with wonder; she never thought she'd live to see the day!

The campsite was quiet, everyone—except Zeb who was taking the first watch—had gone to bed. Jim was again sleeping outdoors, and the women had the wagon to themselves.

Harry had placed his blankets beside the fire, he had tried to fall asleep, but despite his fatigue, sleep eluded him. He stared thoughtfully into the dying flames. He was disappointed, for his relationship with Laura seemed to be getting nowhere. He wanted so desperately to tell her the truth, but how could he confront her with such astounding news, without first cushioning the shock with friendship?

His thoughts drifted to Beth. Would she have wanted him to do this? Telling Laura that he was her father would undoubtedly disrupt her life. What would such a shock do to her? He wondered if she could handle it. But, damn it! he thought, angry with himself. She should be made aware that she's a Talbert! Not that being a Talbert elevated her above anyone else, it was simply her birthright to know.

Harry closed his eyes and allowed his mind to float backward over the years. His Beth, his darling Beth . . . he remembered the day he found her crying . . .

* * *

Harry Talbert hadn't seen Beth Mills since the day he'd encountered her at the river. Considering the awkwardness of the situation, he didn't accompany her home to meet her husband. Four days later, however, he decided to pay another visit to the Diamond Cross. This time, he figured he'd see John Mills; he still intended to welcome him to the community.

John Mills had purchased his ranch at a low price, for the place was badly rundown, the former owners had neglected the upkeep. As Harry rode up to the house, which was in need of repair, he was surprised to see Beth, hammer in hand, nailing the porch's loose planks. He considered that a man's job!

Beth, putting the hammer aside, watched as he dismounted, flung the reins over the hitching rail, and stood at the bottom of the steps. She had been crying, and she quickly wiped at her eyes.

Harry, however, had glimpsed her tears. He had an overwhelming urge to take her in his arms. She obviously needed comforting.

"What's wrong, Mrs. Mills?"

"Nothing," she murmured, but her expression told him otherwise.

"Where's your husband? I'd like to meet him."

"He's in town." Anger sparked in her eyes. "You'll probably find him in the saloon playing cards."

"Why isn't he here helping you?"

"Work and my husband are incompatible." She picked up the hammer, intending to go on with her job.

Harry moved up the steps, reached out a hand for the hammer, and said, "Here, let me."

"Thank you, Mr. Talbert, but I wouldn't feel right about letting you do this."

"I don't mind," he replied, taking the tool. "I have a

couple of free hours, so I might as well be neighborly and pitch in."

A baby's cry sounded from inside the house.

"That's my son Johnny," Beth said. "Will you excuse me?"

"Yes, of course."

She went inside, a few minutes passed, and she returned with the child in her arms.

"How old is he?" Harry asked.

"He'll be a year next month."

"I have three sons myself."

"What are their ages?"

"Six, three, and the youngest one just had his first birthday."

She looked on as Harry returned to mending the porch. She couldn't help but envy his wife. If only she had been blessed with a husband like Harry Talbert!

Beth would have been shocked to know that her feelings coincided with Harry's. He, too, was wishing for what he couldn't have—a woman like Beth Mills . . .

Harry, locking the memory safely away, returned to the present. He supposed it wasn't healthy to spend so much time reliving the past, but he treasured his memories of Beth. He could no more cast them aside than he could stop breathing: they were too precious.

A movement caught his eye, and seeing Laura leaving the wagon prompted him to sit up. She came to the fire, and said with a friendly smile, "Mr. Talbert, I was hoping you'd be awake. I need to talk to you."

"Yes, of course," he replied, gesturing for her to sit beside him. He added more wood to the fire, and the flames, sparking back to life, illuminated Laura; Harry could see

195

her clearly. She was wearing a gown and robe, their color as blue as her eyes, and her silky blond hair fell past her shoulders in lustrous waves. Harry thought her very beautiful, and his heart swelled with pride.

"Mr. Talbert," Laura began, somewhat hesitantly. "Will you please be totally honest with me?"

"I'll try," he answered.

"Why did you give me money? I realize I asked you that before, but you never truly gave me an answer."

"I didn't want you to stand trial for Lee's murder."

"I'm sorry, Mr. Talbert, but I don't accept that answer. You thought I was guilty. I know, because Joshua told me."

"Laura, soon I hope to explain my motives in detail." His eyes beseeched hers. "Will you give me a little more time?"

She didn't see where she had any other choice.

"You know, my dear, you look very much like your mother."

"Yes, there's a resemblance. But I also have a look that's all my own."

"What do you mean?"

"Well, I certainly don't resemble my mother completely, and I don't look anything like my father, so there's a part that's just me."

He wanted so badly to tell her that it was her Talbert blood that she couldn't define! He suppressed the urge; it was still too soon!

Laura sighed sadly. "I miss Mama so much." The words had come without forethought. She was surprised that she had expressed such an emotion before Harry Talbert. After all, her mother had always avoided the man. Apparently, there was something about him that she hadn't liked.

"Your mother was a wonderful woman," Harry murmured.

Laura, perplexed, asked, "Why do you say that?"

"Well, don't you agree?"

"Yes, of course, I do. But I didn't think you thought of her in that way."

"I admired Beth. She was strong, willful, and independent. She was also very loving and compassionate." His eyes sought hers, and taking her hand, he said softly, "You're very much like your mother."

A strange sensation came over Laura; it was the same feeling she experienced the night she gazed at Harry Talbert's portrait. The incident came vividly to mind. Lee had shown her into the study, where she had seen the painting. She had stood before it, sensing that she was seeing someone she had once known or dreamt about. At the time, she shook the feeling aside; she did so again!

She drew her hand away, she didn't completely trust Talbert, and thought it prudent to keep their relationship casual.

Her rejection hurt Harry, but he understood her reserve. He decided it would be best if he steered their conversation away from Beth. It was impossible for him to discuss her without revealing his true feelings, and Laura wasn't ready for that yet.

"The night Lee was murdered," he began, "why did you want to see him?"

"I didn't. I wanted to see you."

"Me?" he questioned, surprised. "But why?"

"I planned to ask you for a loan. I wasn't after charity, however, I intended to put up my home and land as collateral. And pay you back with interest, of course. Lee said you'd never agree, because you wanted my land. Earlier, I tried to get a loan from the bank, but Mr. Richardson turned me down. I told Lee that you Talberts probably paid him off. Lee didn't deny it."

197

"I can assure you none of us paid off Mr. Richardson, and I never wanted your ranch. I wish I had been home, I would have agreed to your loan, and Lee—"

"Would never have been murdered."

"Laura, when you left the house that night, did you see anyone lurking about?"

"No, I didn't." It was getting late, and Laura stood up. "We'd better get some sleep, Craig will want to get an early start in the morning." She made a half-turn to leave, but turned back, and asked with intensity, "Mr. Talbert, why did my parents dislike you?"

Harry wasn't prepared for the question. "Wh . . . what?"

"Why did they dislike you? My mother avoided you, and my father spoke your name with contempt. Why?"

"I'm sorry, Laura, but I can't answer that. Maybe . . . in time . . ."

"You're as secretive as they were." She spoke testily, for Harry's hedging tried her patience. However, she let the matter rest. "Good night, Mr. Talbert."

"Good night, Laura," he replied. He watched, his eyes moist, as she went back to the wagon.

"Is you all right, Mista Harry?" Joshua suddenly asked.

Harry was startled, for he thought Joshua was asleep. The man's pallet was on the other side of the fire, and glancing over at him, he asked, "How long have you been awake?"

"I ain't never been asleep."

"Then you heard everything Laura and I said?"

"Yes, suh. Mista Harry, you gots to be more careful when you talkin' 'bout Miss Beth. Don't you realize you do so with love in your voice?"

"Yes, I know, but I can't speak about her in any other way. I loved her too much." He bowed his head in his

198

hands, and moaned heartbrokenly, "God, how deeply I loved her!"

The next morning, Jim was still too weak to drive the wagon, and Marsha went out of her way to ask Harry to take over. She was very disappointed when he handed the chore over to Joshua. She wasn't about to share the seat with a Negro, so she rode in the back of the wagon.

Jim was there, resting on a bed of blankets. He erroneously assumed Marsha had chosen to be at his side. The day was sunny and pleasant, and he encouraged her to ride outside.

"I'd just as soon stay in here," she replied firmly.

"Darling, I know you're doing this for my sake. But I honestly don't mind being alone."

She almost laughed in his face. He was such a fool! Did he really think she couldn't bear being away from him? At the moment, there was nothing she wanted more! Jim Slade was getting on her nerves!

"I have a headache," she fibbed, going to her bed across from his. "I think I'll try and get some sleep."

"Are you sure you're all right?" He was concerned.

"I have these headaches often. All I need is rest and quiet. So, darling, you will be silent, won't you?"

"If that's what you want."

It was indeed! "Thank you," she said sweetly. "You're such a dear." She rolled to her side, presenting her back to Jim. She thought about her money hidden in the secret compartment. She was anxious to spend it, but knew that would be impossible as long as Jim Slade was around. San Francisco was full of expensive dress shops, fine restaurants, and elaborate hotels. She could hardly wait to enjoy them all to the fullest. She couldn't, however, until she got

199

rid of Jim. If she started spending a lot of money, he'd certainly guess where it came from. Damn Jim Slade! He was ruining everything! She was also very anxious to use her feminine wiles on Harry Talbert, but, again, Jim was in the way! Well, she'd not let him deter her, she'd simply use caution.

Earlier, when Karen had learned that Marsha was planning to ride in the back with Jim, she had decided to share the wagon's seat with Joshua. She was tired of riding horseback.

Now, as she and Joshua were discussing San Francisco, she was surprised when Jim suddenly climbed over the back of the seat and joined them.

"You should be lying down," she said sternly.

"I'm tired of being an invalid. Besides, the sun feels good."

"Well, I suppose it's all right. But you mustn't do too much too soon."

"Yes, ma'am," he said, grinning disarmingly. Karen's concern was flattering. He wasn't used to having a woman fuss over him.

"I'm surprised you left Marsha alone."

"She has a headache, and is resting."

"That's too bad," Karen replied, holding back a smile. She couldn't help but be pleased. The seat wasn't all that wide, which meant Jim was sitting very close to her. She supposed she could move over a little toward Joshua, but she wasn't about to do so. Jim's closeness was too thrilling, and she was perfectly happy squeezed against him.

They made camp at sunset, and following dinner, Marsha again started washing the dishes, as though it were a chore she always took upon herself. She was delighted when Harry offered to take the first watch.

She retired early, and searching through her cedar chest, she took out a silky, revealing dressing gown. She slipped it on, then brushed her hair until the tresses gleamed with reddish highlights. Getting into bed, she drew the top blanket up to her chin, and turned to lie on her side.

Later, faking sleep, she heard Laura and Karen come inside. They talked in low voices as they undressed for bed. The lantern was soon extinguished, and shortly thereafter, the wagon was silent.

Marsha forced herself to stay put, for she wanted everyone to be asleep before she ventured outside. She waited at least an hour, then stealthily left the wagon.

She looked about the campsite, the men were ensconced in their bedrolls, she hoped they were sound asleep. She certainly didn't want Jim to know what she was doing. Harry had taken a position a short distance away, but from where Marsha was standing, she could see him.

Smiling inwardly and confident of success, she moved furtively away from the wagon, and over to Harry.

Her clandestine visit didn't surprise him. In fact, he had been expecting it.

"I couldn't sleep," she told him. "I thought some fresh air might help." She stood poised with the moon at her back, for she knew its light would sift through her thin dressing gown.

Her voluptuous curves were indeed seductively defined, and, Harry, amused, but nonetheless a man, raked her with his eyes. She was striking and quite beautiful, but as deadly as a black widow spider. He waited for her to spin her web, in which he didn't plan to become entangled.

She moved closer until her body was mere inches from his. She hadn't missed his eyes raking her, and it elevated her confidence even more. "Harry," she murmured throatily, "you're a very handsome man. And you look so much younger than your age."

"Thank you," he replied, trying not to laugh. The woman's ploy was far from unique.

Suddenly, she swayed and put a hand to her brow. "My goodness, I feel a little faint." She leaned gracefully toward him.

He was holding his rifle, but he quickly put it on the ground, and took her into his arms.

"That's much better," she whispered, her tone undeniably seductive. She raised her face, and her lips were almost touching his. "Harry, please don't think I'm forward, but I want you to kiss me. I find myself terribly attracted to you. Nothing like this has ever happened before. But, for some reason, I'm completely drawn to you."

"Maybe the reason's because I'm rich," he said, pushing her gently out of his arms. "Marsha, you might as well go back to the wagon and get some sleep. Your charms are wasted on me. I've come across your kind before, and I can spot you a mile away. There are plenty of rich men in San Francisco, and I'm sure you'll find one."

"Well!" she huffed. "I've never been so insulted!"

"Neither have I," he replied, grinning. "That I would fall for your seductive ploy is an insult to my intelligence."

"Mr. Talbert, you are very rude!"

"And you, Mrs. Donaldson, are a tramp!"

She slapped his face, then with a petulant toss of her head, she whirled about and went back to the wagon. She got into bed and pulled the blanket over her. She was fuming. However, she was also very upset. Nothing was going the way she planned! Burying her face into her pillow, she gave in to her misery and cried.

202

Seventeen

San Francisco! Laura found the bustling city fascinating. She was overwhelmed by the theaters, gambling casinos, businesses, and magnificent homes. A city sitting on the hill above a shimmering bay, it was cut off from the westward expansion by miles of empty plains and towering mountains. Facing the ocean, it was America's primary contact with the Far East. San Francisco was completely dependent on imports from the outside: lumber came from Maine, agricultural products from Latin America, oranges from Tahiti, and coffee from Java.

Chinese and Australian immigrants provided the much needed labor in the rapidly growing urban economy, for they were willing to work for low wages. They lived and multiplied in the poor sections of the city; however, a few managed to prosper and move on to better neighborhoods. The harbor area, its streets lined with shabby barrooms, was known as the notorious Barbary Coast. In contrast, Nob Hill, overlooking the city, was entrenched with millionaires who were comfortably ensconced in their majestic mansions. The majority of these millionaires had obtained their fortunes from the Comstock Lode — a gold and silver vein discovered in 1859 in western Nevada. Discovered by an American prospector, Henry Comstock, it yielded over five hundred million dollars.

Laura had never heard of the Comstock Lode, and when Craig told her about it, such a rich find seemed beyond one's imagination. No wonder prospectors searched so relentlessly for that big strike!

The group found rooms at the Winston Hotel, named after its original owner. The establishment wasn't the grandest in San Francisco, but Laura suspected it was nonetheless one of the finest. A red, plush carpet covered the floor of the lobby, and its walls were embellished with expensive paintings. The desk clerk, dressed in a black linen suit with a white ruffled shirt, eyed the hotel's new patrons with misgivings. The long, arduous journey had taken its toll on the group, and they looked unkempt and travel-worn. The clerk, judging by their appearance, doubted if they could afford to stay at the Winston. However, when the men, refusing to let the ladies pay, flashed their money, the clerk's welcome was more cordial indeed.

Laura was very impressed with her room; it had blue velvet drapes, a carpet of the exact same shade, and a huge, four-poster bed. Two overstuffed chairs, a glossy mahogany table between them, sat facing french doors that led out to a terrace. She was taken with such grandeur, however, she also felt a little guilty. After all, this room was terribly expensive, and she didn't think Craig could afford such luxury. She had listened when the men paid in advance, and she knew that Craig, over Talbert's objections, had insisted on paying her expenses, as well as Zeb's. Harry had agreed reluctantly, but had taken it upon himself to pay for Karen's and Marsha's rooms. Laura could see that Jim had been a little bothered by Talbert's gesture, but a federal marshal certainly couldn't afford to be as generous. In fact, Laura supposed paying for even one room was a strain on Jim's finances. She liked Jim, but was finding him hard to understand. How in the world did he think he could afford Marsha Donaldson? Or was he too blinded by love to see her objectively?

A knock sounded at the door, and Laura opened it to Karen. The young woman stepped inside, saying, "I just talked to Zeb. He and Craig have gone to the stables. They plan to leave Lobo there, and also the wagon. Then they're going to ask about town and see if they can learn anything about my father." Her large eyes shining brightly, she looked about Laura's room. "Isn't this hotel grand?" she asked excitedly. "I've never been in an establishment as elegant as this."

"Neither have I," Laura admitted. "Karen, let's go shopping. We'll both need a nice dress for dinner tonight."

"Oh, I wish I could!" she exclaimed, sounding disappointed. "But I'm afraid I can't afford it. I need to watch my money closely, I may need it to get back to Boston."

"I have enough for both of us," Laura told her. She had spent very little of the five hundred dollars Talbert had given her. She had tried to give the money back, but he had flatly refused to accept it.

"I wouldn't feel right about letting you buy my clothes," Karen replied.

"Then consider it a loan. Someday, you can pay me back." She could see that Karen was still uncertain: the woman had her pride. "Please let me do this!" Laura continued. "Besides, the money isn't truly mine. Harry Talbert gave it to me, and he won't take it back."

Karen could no longer refuse, a new dress was too tempting! "All right, let's go!"

"Why don't we really splurge, and have lunch, too?"

"Yes, why not?"

Laura got the money, put it in her skirt pocket, then she and Karen set out eagerly to enjoy the afternoon.

Laura had barely returned from shopping when Craig and Zeb stopped by. Seeing the packages on the bed, Craig asked with a smile, "Did you buy something nice to wear to dinner tonight?"

"Yes, I did. I can hardly wait for you to see me in something besides riding clothes."

Only Zeb's presence prevented Craig from saying he'd rather see her in nothing at all. "What color is your gown?" he said instead.

"White and dark blue," she replied, wondering why he had asked. She started to question him, but decided it wasn't important. "Did you find out anything about Karen's father?" Laura inquired, looking from Craig to her uncle.

"Nope," Zeb answered. "I kinda doubt if he was ever here. I hate to say this, but I suspect the man perished in the desert."

"I wonder if Karen will ever know exactly what happened to him," Laura said.

"Maybe not," Zeb replied. "By the way, I found Johnny."

"Where is he?" she asked at once.

"He used the money from our claim to buy a gambling casino. Craig and I paid him a visit, and I told him 'bout his Pa dyin'. He said he'd stop by and see you this evenin'. The casino's real fancy, and I reckon it'll turn quite a profit for Johnny."

"I'm glad he's doing so well."

"Yeah?" Zeb remarked. "Just remember, he wouldn't be doin' so good, if he hadn't used *your* money. When I gave him my part of the sale, I made it perfectly clear that he was supposed to send it to you. When I talked to him, he didn't say nothin' 'bout payin' it back."

"You know how Johnny is."

"Yep, he's just like his father."

Laura agreed wholeheartedly. She had often wondered why she hadn't inherited any of her father's traits. She was nothing like him — physically or otherwise. Now, as she thought about Johnny's likeness to their father, she wondered again why she was so different.

Laura was dressed for dinner and waiting for Craig to call, when her brother knocked on the door. She was happy to see him, and accepted his warm hug.

Johnny's gaze swept admiringly over his sister. He had never seen her look so stunning. Laura's new gown was white muslin with an embroidered flounce, and a silk blue ribbon was arranged to simulate the dress's lace-trimmed overskirt. The neckline was cut low, but tastefully so, and barely revealed the fullness of Laura's breasts. A pair of dainty blue slippers peeked out beneath the gown's flowing hemline. She had left her blond tresses unbound, and the long, silky curls cascaded radiantly past her bare shoulders.

Johnny was indeed impressed, and as he took her hands into his, he looked her over from head to foot. "Laura, you're absolutely beautiful!"

"Thank you," she murmured, returning his perusal. Johnny was very handsome, his thick, wavy hair was the color of chestnuts. He had grown a moustache since Laura had last seen him; it was well groomed, and perfectly matched the shade of his hair. He was of average height, and his frame was attractively trim. His fawn-colored dress jacket, complimented by tan trousers, and a beige, ruffled shirt, were apparently tailor-made and quite expensive.

"Zeb told me about Lee Talbert," Johnny said. "But I'm sure everything will be all right. If old man Talbert thinks you're innocent, then he'll see to it that the charges against you are dropped."

"Maybe," she agreed. "However, I'm determined to find out who *did* kill Lee Talbert. If I don't, there will always be a doubt in people's minds. I must clear my name." She paused, hoping Johnny would offer to go home with her and help her prove her innocence. Not that she thought he would be all that much help; she simply wanted him to care enough to offer.

He didn't!

Disappointment mingled with hurt fell across her face. Johnny, misreading the reason behind her expression, was quick to say, "Laura, I know what you're thinking. You're perturbed because I didn't send you your part of the money. But I needed it all to buy my casino. It's called The Lucky Lady, and it's a thriving business. Of course, I haven't made a profit yet. But that's because I had to sink so much money into it. I not only had to buy it, but I had to redecorate. I also had to purchase myself a new wardrobe, a proprietor should look prosperous. Soon, though, I'll start making a profit, and I promise you'll get your share of the money, plus interest."

"Johnny, keep the money. I don't want it."

"Sis, you can't be serious!"

"I'm not like you, Johnny. Money doesn't mean everything to me. Love, compassion, and loyalty mean so much more."

He frowned testily. "You wanted the money for the Diamond Cross, didn't you?"

"I could have used it, yes."

"Laura, I know how much you love that miserable ranch. But I always hated it. Papa hated it, too. He only stayed there because Mama wouldn't leave. After she died, Papa felt it was too late for him to start over. He remained at the Diamond Cross because he didn't have any place to go. Well, I was determined not to get in the same rut as Papa! That's why I left with Uncle Zeb. I knew it was a chance for me to get somewhere. And, by God, I did! I love this city, and I've never been happier. That damned ranch is yours to do with as you please."

Laura smiled wistfully. "Johnny, we're so different. We always have been."

"Yes, I know," he murmured, sounding a little sad. The feeling passed quickly though, and with a bright smile, he said, "Good luck, Laura. I'm sure you'll clear your name, and even find a way to get the Diamond Cross operating again. You're just like Mama, when you set your mind to something, you do it. By the way, I was shocked to hear Papa's dead. But considering how much he drank, I guess it's not too surprising."

He placed his hands on Laura's shoulders, drew her close, and kissed her forehead. "Well, I have to run. If you get a chance, stop by and see me before you leave."

He opened the door and stepped into the hall, where he bumped into Marsha. She had gone downstairs for a moment and was on her way back to her room. Dressed for dinner, she was wearing a green silk gown, the dress cut daringly low. Marsha's ample breasts seemed about to burst free of their confinement.

Johnny, taken aback, could hardly believe that he had stumbled onto such a gorgeous woman. The expression in his hazel eyes was starkly sexual.

"Excuse me, Miss," he said. "I didn't mean to be so clumsy. Are you all right?"

"Yes, I'm fine," she replied somewhat breathlessly. Bumping into such a handsome man so unexpectedly had rendered her speechless. Her sole purpose for venturing downstairs had been to scrutinize the lobby for rich bachelors, or any young, attractive man to use her flirtatious charms on. Now, to find such a good-looking gentleman coming out of Laura's room, had Marsha flabbergasted. He was not only handsome, but looked rich as well!

However, before Marsha could collect herself, Johnny had already started down the hall and was heading for the stairway.

"Who is that gentleman?" she asked Laura.

"My brother Johnny. But there's no reason for you to be interested in him, he isn't rich by any means."

"Well!" Marsha said, sounding greatly offended. "That remark was totally unwarranted!"

"Was it?" Laura challenged. "Aren't you interested in money?"

"No more than anyone else."

"In that case, you and Johnny might get along famously." With that, Laura moved back into her room, closing the door. Yes, she thought, Marsha and Johnny might be a good match—neither of them was capable of loving anyone but themselves!

A short time later, Craig came to Laura's room to escort her to dinner. She thought him dashingly handsome, for he was wearing a dark linen suit, matching vest, and a pale blue shirt, which was set off elegantly by a black silk cravat.

Craig's eyes, glinting with admiration, thoroughly examined Laura. He found her so breathtakingly beautiful that his voice was a rasping whisper, "Darling, you're more lovely than words can describe."

"Thank you," she replied. "You're very handsome, yourself."

He carried a small, gift-wrapped present, which he now

handed to her. "This is for you."

"My goodness! What is it?"

"Why don't you open it and find out?"

She did so somewhat awkwardly, for her hands were slightly trembling. It was a jewelry case, she opened it to find a gold chain with a sapphire pendant, there was also a pair of matching earrings. "Craig!" she cried joyously.

"Do you approve?"

"Approve? she exclaimed. "I've never seen anything more elegant."

"That's why I wanted to know the color of your dress, so I could buy jewelry to match."

"But, darling, these must be terribly expensive!"

"Don't worry about the price, I can afford it." He took the necklace, and as he stepped behind her, she lifted her long tresses. He clasped the chain, then kissed the back of her neck.

She hurried to the mirror, and put on the earrings. Then, turned to Craig, she asked, "How do I look?"

"Like an angel," he replied.

She rushed into his arms, and their lips came together in a long, passionate exchange. "I love you, Craig. And thank you very much for such a wonderful gift. I'll treasure it for a lifetime."

"I'll treasure you for a lifetime," he added, before kissing her again.

Later, when Laura and Craig entered the hotel dining room, they found Zeb, Jim, and Marsha sitting at the long table that had been reserved earlier. The men looked very debonair in their dress jackets and slacks. They stood at Laura's approach, and showered her with compliments.

Marsha was bitterly jealous, for Zeb and Jim certainly hadn't carried on so much about *her* appearance.

Actually, the men had kept their praises at a minimum,

211

for they had found her dress too flashy and revealing. It reminded them both of an affluent prostitute's gown — expensive, but not in good taste.

Laura and Craig were barely seated when Harry, escorting Karen, came into the room. Everyone, except Laura, stared at Karen with wonder. Laura had helped her friend choose and try on her new dress, so she already knew that Karen was much lovelier than anybody had imagined.

The ladies had visited several shops before finding the perfect gown for Karen. The evening dress was pink silk, trimmed in a darker pink velvet. It fit her tiny waist snugly before billowing into graceful, draping folds that touched the tops of her slippers. Laura had advised her to wear her hair down, and the golden brown tresses softly framed her heart-shaped face. Karen wasn't strikingly beautiful, but she was lovely indeed.

Jim's chair was next to Marsha's, but the one on the other side was empty. He pulled it out, and invited Karen to sit beside him. She was more than glad to do so.

It became a joyful evening, a delicious, four-course dinner was served. After eating around a campfire for so long, the food tasted especially appetizing.

Laura, anxious to be alone with Craig, pleaded fatigue and asked to be excused early. The others bid her a pleasant good night, and with Craig accompanying her, she left the room.

Harry was disappointed to see her leave so soon, for he had been hoping to find an opportunity to ask her if they could talk in private. A warm friendship had developed between them, and he knew the time had come to tell her the truth.

Meanwhile, as Laura was ascending the stairway, she was beginning to feel apprehensive. They had been in San Francisco since this morning, and, so far, Craig hadn't mentioned Deborah. His engagement was not a topic they could continue to avoid, and she was determined to bring the matter into the open. However, it made her uneasy, and she dreaded talking about it.

Craig unlocked her door, then stood back for her to precede him. Following her inside, he put the key into the lock and turned it.

Laura gestured toward the two chairs. "Craig, let's sit down. We need to talk."

The patio doors were open, and a gentle breeze cooled the room. They sat facing the terrace, feeling the pleasant air on their faces. Sounds of the bustling city drifted inside.

"When do you plan to see Deborah?" Laura asked, wringing her hands somewhat nervously.

"In the morning," he replied.

"And?" Her eyes looked anxiously into his.

A troubled expression wrinkled his brow. "I'm not exactly sure how I plan to handle the situation. God, I've had plenty of time to figure it out, but every angle I come up with comes back to the same thing—Deborah's going to be hurt." He ran his fingers distractedly through his hair. "Damn it! I feel sorry for Deborah! First, her blindness— and now this! How much can she take?"

Laura, responding to his apparent desperation, left her chair and knelt at his feet. She gazed sadly into his face. "Darling, I hate this as much as you do! But you have no other choice but to tell her the truth! That is, if you truly love me as much as you say you do."

"Love you?" he groaned. "Laura, you're my whole life!"

Fighting back tears, she laid her head in his lap. She, too, didn't want Deborah to be hurt. "Craig?" she said softly.

"Yes?"

213

"What kind of person is Deborah? You've never really told me what she's like. Is she nice?"

He smiled ruefully. "Yes, she's a very nice young lady. Growing up, she had a somewhat hard life, and had to do without a lot. Her father was a reverend, and didn't make much money. He never remarried after his wife's death, and as soon as Deborah was old enough, she had to take care of the household chores. She didn't have much of a social life. Maybe that's why she never got over the childhood crush she had on me, she didn't have any beaux to help her forget."

"Perhaps. But, then, maybe she loved you too much to find someone else."

"I never encouraged her; at least, not intentionally."

"Except when you asked her to marry you."

Craig sighed heavily. "You're right, as always."

She lifted her head, and gazed into his eyes. "I didn't mean that the way it sounded."

Standing, he drew her to her feet and into his arms. "I know, darling." He kissed her with deep longing, then murmured intensely, "I'll never let you go, Laura."

"If I were to lose you, I'd die inside." She meant it so sincerely that tears gushed from her eyes.

He brushed his lips across one tear-stained cheek, then the other. "We'll always be together, I promise you."

Eighteen

The waiter served coffee soon after Laura and Craig had left. Zeb, telling prospecting stories, had Harry's and Karen's rapt attention; Jim took this opportunity to lean toward Marsha and whisper discreetly, "May I come to your room tonight?" His eyes were filled with desire and anticipation. He hadn't made love to her since that first night.

Marsha was annoyed, but she hid it well. Jim was a virile lover, true, but it was important that she discourage his affections. She wasn't sure how to go about it without arousing his anger. If he were to become enraged, he might get even by arresting her. The man was such a nuisance!

She rubbed her temples as though she were in pain. "Darling, not tonight. I have one of my horrid headaches." She forced a loving smile. "Maybe tomorrow we can manage to be alone."

Jim watched her uncertainly. "Marsha, have your feelings for me changed?"

"Whatever makes you think that?" she asked innocently.

"You've been very cold. Marsha, if you don't want anything to do with me, just say so. As I told you before, I don't play games."

Marsha was suddenly hopeful. If she were to admit that

215

she had lost interest, would he bow out like a gentleman? Had she been wrong to assume that he'd react angrily and with spite?

"Jim," she began sweetly, patting his hand. "I'm not sure how I feel. It's still too soon after Jerry's death. I didn't love him, that's true. However, his death was still very devastating. Darling, I need more time."

"You've got it," he replied. He sounded more resigned than angry. "Tomorrow, though, I want to take you about the city. Maybe you'll spot the three men who killed your husband and stole the money."

"Perhaps, but it's a big city with lots of people. The odds are certainly not in our favor."

"We'll give it a try anyhow."

"Jim," she began with calculated intent, "during dinner, Laura mentioned that her brother bought a gambling casino. Maybe we should start by looking there. Do you know where this casino is, and what it's called?"

"It's not far from here, and it's called The Lucky Lady."

Marsha beamed inwardly. She had gotten the information so easily. The Lucky Lady. She'd pay Johnny Mills a visit, all right. But she'd do so tonight, and without Jim Slade!

Pleading a throbbing headache, she quickly told everyone good night, and asked to be excused. Jim offered to escort her upstairs, but she insisted that he stay and drink his coffee.

Jim watched her closely as she moved gracefully from the room. He had never made a fool of himself over a woman, but he knew with Marsha he was doing just that. She had totally bewitched him.

"Jim, is everything all right?" Karen asked, breaking into his thoughts.

"Yes, of course," he replied.

"Are you sure? You seem troubled."

He smiled with warm spontaneity. "Karen, you're very kind to worry about me. But I can take care of myself, believe me."

"It's Marsha, isn't it?" she persisted. "She's such a fool not to appreciate you." Karen blushed at her own words. She hadn't meant to go quite so far.

Jim found himself responding to her concern. "Apparently, Marsha isn't ready to commit herself. Maybe it's best. I'm not sure she'd be happy living in my home. It's small and far from elaborate. Also, the closest town is Winding Creek, and compared to Carson City, it isn't much. My job, of course, demands that I travel a lot. Marsha isn't the type to sit at home and wait for a husband."

Karen said with an amused smile, "No, I can't quite picture Marsha sitting in a rocking chair, knitting away the hours until her husband came back. Nor can I imagine her being a mother."

Jim sighed deeply. "Marsha and I aren't really compatible, I've always known that. But, nevertheless, I fell in love with her."

It was time to leave, the dining room was practically empty. Jim stood, and as Karen got to her feet, he drew out her chair. "Karen," he said, his gaze measuring her. "You look very lovely tonight." He touched a lock of her hair, curling the tendril about his finger. "You should always wear your hair down, it makes you look . . ."

"Less severe?" she asked.

"Softer and more feminine."

His compliment was thrilling, and she dared to hope that he would offer to escort her upstairs. She was disappointed, however, for he told everyone good night, said he was going to the saloon down the street, and left.

217

Harry's quarters included a servant's room, for several patrons who frequented the Winston traveled with their domestic help. Joshua's small bedroom was adjacent to Harry's; it was clean, neat, but severely plain. The white walls lacked pictures, and the lone window was covered with a nondescript curtain. A cot had been installed in lieu of a bed, however, it was spread with freshly starched sheets, a soft feather pillow, and a clean blanket.

Earlier, Joshua had eaten dinner in the hotel kitchen, and was now lying on his cot, reading. That afternoon, he and Talbert had visited several shops; and, Harry, knowing how much Joshua loved to read, had bought him some books.

Hearing the door open, Joshua put his book aside, leapt from the cot, and hurried into the master bedroom. "Mista Harry, did you tell her?" he burst out.

"No," he replied regretfully. "Laura retired early, and I didn't get the chance."

"You gots to tell her real soon. If need be, you gots to make the time."

"I'll tell her tomorrow."

"Mista Harry, you look mighty tired."

"I am," he said, stifling a yawn. "After sleeping on the hard ground for so long, that bed's going to feel very good."

"You needs any help?"

Harry's sudden chuckle was tinged with impatience. "Joshua, have I ever needed help getting ready for bed?"

"No, suh."

"Well, I don't need any help now! Go on back to bed, and I'll see you in the morning."

"Yes, suh. Good night, Mista Harry."

Talbert went to the washbasin, sponged his hands and face, undressed, then drew back the covers, and got into bed.

He extinguished the bedside lamp, and waited for sleep to overtake him. It didn't work, however, for insomnia set in, and he was soon tossing restlessly. Thoughts of Laura and Beth swirled turbulently through his mind. He was anxious to tell Laura the truth; still, he was plagued with misgivings. During the last few days, he had managed to build a good relationship with her, would the truth destroy that friendship? She might very well turn on him with a vengeance. If she did, he certainly wouldn't blame her.

Harry sighed deeply. In the beginning, his love for Beth had been so innocent . . . he had merely loved her from afar. That he might someday express his feelings verbally or even physically seemed very far removed. After all, Beth was a lady, a loving mother, and a faithful wife.

Harry's mind traveled back in time, and he relived the day he had accidentally come across Beth in town. He was walking past the bank as she was coming out . . .

They came very close to colliding, and Harry grabbed her shoulders to steady her, for she was carrying Johnny, who was sound asleep. He had come to know Beth very well, and could see that she was troubled.

"Is something wrong?" he asked.

Beth wasn't one to talk about her troubles, but, for some reason, she didn't feel that way with Harry. He had become her closest friend, and it seemed so natural to confide in him. "I just asked Mr. Richardson for a loan, and he turned me down. At first, I thought it was because *I* had asked and not John. I told him I'd send John to see him, but he said not to bother. He considers us a bad investment. Apparently, he knows that John is a compulsive gambler. I offered to put up my home and land as collateral, but Mr. Richardson said they're not worth much. I suppose he's right." A bright sparkle suddenly lit up her eyes. "But, Harry, the Diamond Cross could be very prosperous if only . . . if only I had money to invest in it."

"I agree," he replied. "It's perfect grazing land. And don't worry, Beth, you'll get your chance to make the ranch successful. I'll gladly loan you as much as you need."

She was taken aback. "Harry, are you sure you're willing to take such a risk?"

"I don't consider it a risk. The Diamond Cross has good potential."

Her buckboard was in front of the bank, she moved over and placed Johnny in the back on a blanket. He stirred, but didn't awaken.

"Harry, will you accept my land and house as collateral?"

"That won't be necessary, I'll loan you the money as one friend to another."

Her chin lifted proudly. "I must insist that you let me pay you back with interest."

"Beth, you don't have to do that."

"Please, Harry. I have my pride. I can't accept handouts." A soft expression came to her eyes, it was akin to love. "I can't take charity; not even from you."

He knew she meant what she said. "All right, have it your way."

"Thank you, Harry." She smiled beautifully. "What would I do without you?"

He dared to take her hand and squeeze it gently. He spoke from the heart, "Beth, you're my best friend."

At the moment, Beth wasn't feeling friendly, she was too physically aware of his touch, and a trembling thrill raced through her. But she felt she must fight such forbidden desire, and she drew away her hand.

Harry had experienced the same awareness, and it had sent his heart slamming into his ribs. No woman had ever affected him so powerfully.

At that moment, Beth Mills and Harry Talbert knew that they were in love. They hadn't set out to fall in love, it had come about naturally and without premeditation. But they believed in conforming to one's own sense of right and wrong. Beth's conscience, as well as Harry's, fought back righteously. They were both married to someone else, not happily perhaps, but bound just as strongly by their marriage vows.

Harry, speaking as though nothing had transpired between them, told her to come to the Circle T in the morning, and he'd have the money for her.

Beth thanked him cordially, got into the buckboard, and started for home. There were tears in her eyes, but she quickly wiped them away. It was terribly wrong to covet another woman's husband, and she must clear her mind of such fantasies. But clearing such feelings from her heart would prove to be impossible.

Harry, watching her ride out of town, was battling the same inner conflict. Beth could never be his. If only they had met at another time . . . another place. His heart ached with regret.

Marsha left her room, scurried down the hall, descended the marble stairway, and went outside where she hailed a public conveyance. She told the driver to take her to The Lucky Lady.

She wasn't sure how to explain her presence to Johnny. She worried about it for a moment, then shrugged it aside.

When it came time, she'd think of something.

She considered her stolen funds, which were still hidden in the bottom of the wagon. She wondered if she should get the money and stash it somewhere else. For the moment, it was safe, but she didn't want to leave it there too long.

The journey to the casino was short, and before Marsha had time to figure out what to do with her money, the enclosed carriage had stopped in front of The Lucky Lady. The driver leapt from his perch seat, and opened the door for her.

She delved into her purse, paid him, then took a close look at the gambling establishment. She was impressed, for it was grand indeed. Evidently, The Lucky Lady could make its owner very rich. Her shrewd mind raced fluidly. If she were to marry Johnny Mills, then he suffered a fatal accident, The Lucky Lady would be hers. Yes, what a convenient scenario! she thought merrily.

Her spirits soaring, she stepped up to the front door, expecting the doorman to open it for her.

"I'm sorry, Miss," he told her. "But unescorted ladies are not allowed inside."

She wasn't about to be turned away. "I'm here to see Johnny Mills. He's the owner."

"Yes, I know," he replied, perfectly aware of who paid his wages. He opened the door, spotted an employee, and asked him to get Mr. Mills.

As Marsha waited, she took close note of the people who went inside. Most of the clientele were gentlemen, and to her delight, they looked very rich. Once she owned The Lucky Lady, she'd be hobnobbing with these wealthy patrons. She might climb to greater heights than she had ever imagined!

Johnny, stepping outside, recognized her immediately. A

man didn't forget bumping into so stunning a woman.

Marsha smiled charmingly. "Mr. Mills, allow me to introduce myself. My name is Marsha Donaldson, and I'm a friend of your sister's." She managed to look a little embarrassed. "You'll probably think I'm very foolish, but I've never been inside a casino. I'm simply dying of curiosity. Since you're Laura's brother, I knew it would be safe to come here." She cast him a most pleading expression. "May I please have the grand tour?"

He was more than happy to oblige. "I'd consider it an honor, Miss Donaldson."

"Call me Marsha," she was quick to say. "And it's not Miss, but Mrs."

She was pleased to see that he was disappointed.

"I'm a widow," she continued.

His mood was instantly uplifted. Smiling, he took her arm and escorted her into his place of business.

Marsha had weaved her web, and was certain that Johnny Mills would soon become hopelessly entangled.

Dawn was minutes away when Marsha returned to the hotel. She moved quickly through the lobby, and went upstairs. Her mood was optimistic, for she was confident that Johnny had fallen prey to her charms. She thought about The Lucky Lady. She had been overawed by the establishment, and could hardly wait to own it. Johnny had told her that the casino was showing signs of wear when he purchased it, but that he had restored it to its original splendor. She didn't find that hard to believe, for the place was magnificent. It had a saloon area, complete with a stocked supply of liquor. The gambling rooms were separate from the bar, and they were filled to capacity with rich patrons. Drinking and gambling, however, were not all The Lucky Lady had to offer. Upstairs there was a secluded room decorated to resemble a parlor, except it also had a bar complete with a bartender. Here, the customers could choose a lady for the evening.

Marsha was indeed pleased with The Lucky Lady. Gambling, drinking, and sex: the three vices that tempted a man to part with his money.

She was sure her evening with Johnny would prove to be very profitable. She had even gone to bed with him. That, however, had been disappointing. Johnny wasn't a very good lover. Yes, she had been let down, but certainly not deterred. She'd marry Johnny Mills, and soon thereafter, The Lucky Lady would have a new proprietor. She hadn't decided yet how she'd kill her new husband, but she'd find a way when the time came.

As she passed Laura's room on her way to her own, she smiled nastily at the closed door. She couldn't stand Laura Mills, and would relish making her life miserable. Her smile broadened considerably. Well, soon, she would do just that. Johnny had mentioned that the Diamond Cross was in his name, which meant, it would also belong to his wife. When she became Johnny's widow, she'd sell the Diamond Cross out from under Laura, and take great delight in doing so.

Well-pleased with herself, Marsha unlocked her door and went into her room. She was tired and knew she'd sleep like a baby.

Craig, sleeping with Laura in his arms, came awake as the morning sun cast its light through the open patio doors. He awoke with a heavy dullness in his heart, for he dreaded his visit to Deborah. The thought of hurting her was tearing him to pieces.

Without realizing it, he groaned aloud.

The sound, though soft, awakened Laura. She didn't ask Craig what was wrong, she already knew. She snuggled closer, nestled her head on his shoulder, and whispered, "Please try not to worry. Deborah will understand."

"I hope so."

"I love you, darling," she murmured, pressing her naked flesh to his.

They were nude, for they had made love last night, then fallen asleep wrapped in each other's embrace.

Her body, flush against his, sparked Craig's passion. He rolled over, drawing her beneath him. His mouth swooped down on hers, she parted her lips, and his tongue thrust inside. He ravaged her sweetness, and she clung to him tightly as his kiss sent fire pulsing through her.

His fingers were soon caressing her body, and he gloried in the feel of her silken flesh. His touch etched a heated path over every inch of her; and she responded in kind. Exultant sensations wafted through them as they gave and received such wondrous pleasure.

Craig, his manhood now demanding release, moved over her. Laura's passion was burning fiercely, and wrapping her legs about him, she pulled him into her.

They made love with intensity, each kiss and thrust adding more fuel to their already blazing desire. Their passion fanned heatedly until, ultimately, firebolts of ecstasy arced through their bodies, bringing them love's explosive fulfillment.

Craig kissed her tenderly, then moved to lie at her side. She cuddled close, wishing he didn't have to leave. She could well imagine how much he dreaded facing Deborah, he had her full sympathy and understanding.

"Well, I don't suppose there's any reason to procrastinate," he said, sounding as though he wished he could do

225

just that. "The sooner I see Deborah, the sooner I get it over with."

"My thoughts will be with you. I know that isn't much consolation, but there's nothing more I can do."

He placed a light kiss on her brow. "Your thoughts are greatly appreciated." He got up and slipped into his trousers and shirt. He sat on the edge of the bed to put on his shoes. He started to reach for one, stopped, and looked closely at Laura. "Deborah has no money or kin. I plan to offer her financial help for as long as she needs it. You don't mind, do you?"

"No, of course not. It's the least you can do."

"You're very understanding. No wonder I love you so much." He slipped on his shoes, then rose to leave.

Laura, craving his arms, bounded from the bed. Standing before him nude and unashamed, she said, "Darling, please hold me!"

He did so at once. He relished her closeness, and drew her body tightly against his. "I'll go to my room, change into appropriate clothes, then leave. I don't know how long I'll be gone, but I should be back by this afternoon at the latest."

"You will come back to me, won't you?"

He moved her so that he could see into her face. "Sweetheart, why would you ask such a thing? Of course, I'll come back."

She smiled shakily. "I don't know why I asked something so foolish. I guess, I'm just a little frightened."

"Frightened?"

"Yes, of losing you. Maybe I'm afraid our love is too good to be true."

He kissed the tip of her nose, winked tolerantly, and said, "Stop having such silly thoughts. Laura Mills, I'm all yours—heart, body, and soul."

226

"Forever?" she asked, her smile now saucy.

"Forever, and then some." He kissed her long and passionately, released her reluctantly, grabbed his dress jacket, and went to the door.

"I'll see you later," Craig said. He opened the door and left.

Laura knew she wouldn't draw an easy breath until he returned.

Nineteen

When Laura finished breakfast with Talbert, Karen, and Jim, Harry asked her if they could talk in private. She said they could talk in her room, and he accompanied her upstairs.

Laura slipped her hand into her skirt pocket and took out the key, Talbert reached for it, unlocked the door, and gave it back. They went inside, and Laura suggested they sit on the terrace. The day was already warm, and she knew it would be cooler outside. She sat on a small, wrought iron bench. Harry, taking the matching chair, pulled it around so that he faced Laura.

He could tell that she was somewhat upset, and wondered if it had anything to do with Branston. "At breakfast, you said Craig had some business to take care of this morning. You seem worried, is anything wrong? Craig isn't in trouble, is he?"

"No, it's nothing like that," she replied.

"Would you care to talk about it?"

Harry's concern was obviously genuine, and Laura found herself telling him about Craig's engagement to Deborah.

He listened intently, fully empathizing with Laura's and Craig's situation. It wasn't the same as his and Beth's, but there were similarities: he and Beth hadn't been free to love without hurting others. Now Laura and Craig had fallen in love, and their love was destined to break Deborah's heart.

Laura, finishing her explanation, said sadly, "I feel sorry for Deborah, I really do. But it would be wrong for Craig to marry her, he doesn't love her, he loves me! I just hope Deborah will understand."

"Maybe she's much stronger than you and Craig realize. Furthermore, she might not be in love with Craig, you said she had a childhood crush on him. Well, most childhood crushes are just that—a crush."

Laura wasn't so sure, but discussing the matter wouldn't bring any answers. She'd simply have to wait until Craig returned. Dropping the subject, she asked, "Why did you want to see me in private?"

Harry tensed, and nervous perspiration suddenly dampened his brow. A gnawing uneasiness, settling at the bottom of his heart, ate away at his confidence. He had waited days for this moment, and now that it was here, he wasn't sure if he could go through with it.

Harry's anxiety was evident. Laura reached over and touched his arm. "Mr. Talbert, what is it? Aren't you feeling well?"

His smile wavered. "I'm fine, dear. But there's something I must tell you. I'm not sure if I can get up the nerve."

"Of course, you can tell me. We're friends, aren't we?"

"We're more than friends, Laura."

She was puzzled. "What do you mean?"

He rubbed a hand across his brow, sighed uneasily, and said, "My God, how do I say this?"

"Please, Mr. Talbert, what is it?"

He drew a long, calming breath, leaned back in his chair, and tried to relax. "Laura," he began, "I once loved a woman with all my heart." He spoke evenly, his tone belying his inner tension. "We met too late, we were both already married to someone else. I had fallen out of love with my wife. I suppose I was never that much in love with her to begin with, and her feelings for me were the same. But we stayed together because of our sons."

"I remember your wife," Laura cut in. "I was very young when she died, but I saw her at the barbecues you gave. She was in a wheelchair. Mama told me that she got hurt in a carriage accident."

"Yes, she did. But our love had died years before her accident."

"Did she know you were in love with another woman?"

"No, I don't think she ever knew." He paused, gathered his courage, and continued, "Laura, I know you've always wondered why your parents and I were never very friendly. John Mills despised me, and your mother . . . Well, I suppose you could say she avoided me as much as possible."

"Yes, except for your yearly barbecues. As I grew older, though, I realized my parents attended to curb any gossip. For some reason, the three of you never wanted anyone to know that a rift existed."

"What happened between us was too personal; it had to be kept secret, for all of our sakes."

Laura placed her hands in her lap, clasping them together. Her palms were clammy; she had suddenly started to perspire. A staggering rush of apprehension and dread whirled inside her, and her heart pounded rapidly. She felt threatened, and sensed that her life as she now knew it was about to crumble. Her eyes met Harry's, he was watching her warily. He reminded her of a condemned criminal facing the judge, waiting contritely for his sentence.

Her mouth went dry, and she wished for a drink of water. She swallowed nervously, and asked in a quivering voice, "You were in love with my mother, weren't you?"

"Yes, I was," he replied.

He wanted to say more, but Laura's face had gone deathly pale. He bounded from his chair, hurried into her room, and got her a glass of water.

He handed it to her, then returned to his chair.

She tilted the glass to her lips and emptied it. Strangely, she was still thirsty. Her mouth felt as dry as cotton.

"Laura, believe me, your mother and I didn't plan to fall in love. It just happened. Now, as I think back, I realize that she and I fell in love at first sight, but we didn't admit this to each other or even to ourselves. Beth and I became friends, very good friends. We found a companionship that we didn't have at home."

"But eventually you became lovers, didn't you?" Laura sounded stricken.

"Yes, we did."

"How long were you lovers?"

"Not very long. John found out about us. He threatened to take Johnny away from Beth, if she left him. Also, at the time, I was still married. Beth and I never really had any choice but to let go of each other."

"Why are you telling me this?" she demanded, her tone tinged with anger. "It happened years ago! What difference does it make now? Why have you found it necessary to slander my mother's memory?"

"Slander?" he questioned sharply. "Beth was a wonderful, compassionate woman. I would never say anything slanderous about her, and I would kill any man who did!"

"Oh?" she remarked. "You just told me she was an unfaithful wife, is that or is that not slanderous?"

"I suppose that would depend on who I was saying it to; telling it to you isn't the same. I had hoped you would understand, and even sympathize with Beth. You know John

Mills was a weak, selfish, and worthless husband. How can you fault Beth for falling in love with another man? Surely, your feelings for Craig have taught you that love is a very strong emotion. When you met Craig, he was engaged to another woman. But despite that commitment, you two surrendered to your feelings. Well, in a way, it was like that with Beth and me. Our love overpowered us. We knew it was socially and religiously wrong, but, God, in our hearts, it was so right!"

Laura rose and moved to stand at the railing. She remained noncommittal as she stared vacantly down at the busy street below. She had always believed her mother above reproach, and she wasn't about to sit in judgment on her now. Furthermore, she could understand why Beth fell in love with Harry. He had all the good qualities that had been lacking in John Mills. Had their love really been so wrong? Laura didn't think so.

She turned and faced Talbert. "I can understand why my mother fell in love with you, I truly can. What I don't understand is why you felt you had to tell me."

Harry's heart thumped against his ribs. Should he continue? Now that he had opened the door to his and Beth's past, should he open it all the way, or should he slam it closed? He felt that would be cowardly, but he was nevertheless tempted to close the door to the past, then lock it away for good. But taking the easy way out went against Talbert's grain, and he couldn't do it. Moreover, he still believed Laura had a right to know the whole truth.

He started talking, and his voice was edged with desperation and agony, "A few months after Beth and I stopped seeing each other, I came across her in town. It was obvious that she was with child. I asked her if the baby was mine, she swore to me that it was John's. I pretended to believe her, because I knew that was the way she wanted it. But deep down in my heart, I knew Beth wasn't telling the truth. The child she carried was mine."

A look of abject misery fell across Harry's face. "You're my daughter, Laura. If you have any doubts, just take a good look at yourself in the mirror. The resemblance between us cannot be denied."

Laura's knees weakened, and she grasped the railing for support. She wanted to lash out at him—to call him a liar! But if she did, she would only be lying to herself! She had always known she had nothing in common with John Mills, and the quandary had mystified her. Well, it was no longer a mystery!

Anger and bitterness stirred within her, it was a normal reaction, and Harry was expecting it. "You're my father, yet all my life you ignored me! How could you be so cold-hearted, so damned unfeeling?"

"In the beginning, I told myself I was doing it for Beth's sake. But that wasn't true, not really. I shut you out of my life, because I was too weak to take the pain. You see, I had no choice but to cast Beth from my life, so I cast you out along with her. It was the only way I could live with it. I'm not trying to make excuses for myself, Laura. What I did to you is unforgivable, and I'm not expecting you to forgive me. I only hope that someday you'll understand."

"Why, after all these years, did you decide to tell me? Why didn't you just leave it alone?"

"I can't give you a logical reason, because I'm not sure myself. But I do believe you have a right to know who you really are."

"Do you expect me to rejoice because I'm a Talbert?" Her words had a terrible bite to them. "Don't you realize I have always despised you Talberts? Lee was totally unlikable, Doyce is despicable, and you and Ed have always been arrogantly distant!"

233

He got up from his chair, went to her, and placed a hand on her arm. "Laura, please—"

She shook off his hand. "Don't touch me! I want to be alone! Will you please leave?"

"Yes, I'll leave," he replied. He sounded tormented. There was still more to say, the whole truth hadn't been revealed. But he knew the rest had to wait, for Laura couldn't take any more.

She waited until he was gone, then she rushed to the bed and fell across it. She hoped Craig would hurry back, for she needed him desperately! She felt as though her whole world had been turned upside down. Harry Talbert was her father! God, what a shock! She wanted Craig's arms about her, for she wasn't sure if she could deal with the situation alone!

Joshua was waiting for Harry, and the moment he stepped into his room, he asked anxiously, "Did you tell Miss Laura?"

"Yes, I did," Talbert answered heavily.

"And?" the servant encouraged.

"She took it very well. Laura's a very emotionally strong young lady."

"But, Mista Harry, how does she feel 'bout you?"

"I'm not sure. She's somewhat bitter and angry, but that's to be expected. However, I'm hopeful. I think with a little more time she'll adjust, and might even accept me as a father." Harry sighed wearily. "Joshua, would you mind going downstairs to the kitchen and ordering a pot of coffee? I could sure use a cup."

"No, suh, Mista Harry, I don't mind."

When Joshua was gone, Harry went to the bed and sat on the edge. His shoulders were slumped as he stared

234

down blankly at the floor. Was he being too optimistic? Would Laura really adjust and even see him as a father? Or did he just want it so badly that he was fooling himself?

Anxiety gnawed at him. He supposed there was indeed a chance that she might understand, and even find it in her heart to accept him. But would she be as lenient if he revealed the whole truth? God, should he tell her the rest? He wasn't sure!

He got up, walked out onto the balcony, and sat in a chair. At the moment there was no reason to make a final decision. Later, he would decide whether or not to tell Laura everything.

His thoughts drifted to Beth. Laura was very much like her mother. She had Beth's strength, independence, and compassion. A reflective smile flickered across his lips. He could well understand why Branston had fallen in love with Laura. He hoped they would marry, have children, and spend the rest of their lives together. He prayed earnestly that Craig and Laura would achieve the happiness that had been denied him and Beth.

Harry leaned back in his chair, the morning sun fell across his face, and its warmth was soothing. He closed his eyes, and his mind skimmed back over the years, plucking at the strings of time . . .

Beth Mills was on Harry Talbert's mind as he rode across his land. He had been working with his wranglers and was now on his way back to his house. He had labored as hard as his crew, and was tired, yet, somewhat exhilarated. He was proud of the Circle T, and although the work was tiring, it was nonetheless rewarding—for it never failed to fill him with pride. The prosperous ranch was a reflection of his own success.

He thought about the Diamond Cross, it was now on its way to prosperity, for Beth was determined that it succeed. He was very impressed with the way she was running her ranch; a man couldn't do any better. At first, of course, she hadn't known anything about operating a ranch, and when he offered to teach her, she accepted without hesitation. She was an astute student and learned quickly. Now she was managing the Diamond Cross superbly, and very seldom needed to ask his advice. Although Harry was happy for her success, he missed helping her, for during that period, they had spent a great deal of time together.

Harry was deeply in love with Beth, but, so far, he had managed to keep his feelings suppressed. They were friends—very good friends—but that was all. As much as it pained him to be away from her, he knew it was best that they not see too much of each other; otherwise, his tenuous composure might crumble like a broken dam and release his emotions in a nonstop flood.

Harry glanced up at the sky, a storm was brewing and he knew it wasn't very far away. He doubted if he had time to reach the house before it hit. A streak of lightning flashed overhead, followed closely by roaring thunder. The advancing storm didn't bother Harry, quite the opposite, his land needed lots of rain.

A mote on the horizon caught his attention, and as it drew closer he could see that it was a lone rider. He slowed his horse and watched. Then, recognizing Beth, he galloped over to meet her halfway.

"Hello, Harry," she said with a smile, reining in.

He stopped alongside her. Her vibrant beauty was overwhelming, and he tried vainly to still the wild pounding of his heart. Beth was dressed in a suede riding skirt, which hugged her delicate hips. She wore a matching vest, and beneath it she had donned a powder-blue blouse that perfectly matched the color of her eyes. Her wide-brimmed hat, attached by a leather thong beneath her chin, was hanging at the back of her neck. Her shiny auburn tresses, windblown, fell about her face in provocative disarray. She was beautiful beyond measure.

"I stopped by your house," Beth began, "and Joshua told me where I could find you." Her smiled brightened considerably. "Harry, I want to start paying back my debt to you. I have my first installment."

He grinned happily. "Beth, is the Diamond Cross doing that well?"

"Yes! Oh, isn't it wonderful? I feel so successful and secure! And I owe it all to you!"

"You did it yourself, Beth. I just gave you advice, that's all."

Another flash of lightning, accompanied by thunder, zigzagged ominously across the sky, but Beth and Harry didn't even seem to be aware that the weather was threatening.

Beth's smile faded, and her countenance turned very serious. "Harry, I know what happened between you and John. The scene attracted quite a crowd, and people are gossiping about it. When I was in town this morning, Mrs. Brown at the mercantile gave me a full account."

"Exactly what did she tell you?"

"That you found John at the saloon gambling. You grabbed him by his shirt collar, drew him to his feet, and told him if you ever again found him gambling with the Diamond Cross's money, you'd break both his legs."

Harry chuckled easily. "Mrs. Brown's information is accurate. Beth, if I don't put a stop to John's gambling, he'll lose every cent you have."

"I know," she replied softly. "And I do appreciate your

help. Gossip has it that you're worried about your investment. If John was to lose all our money, we couldn't pay you back."

"Then let's just leave it like that, shall we?"

"For gossip's sake, and for John's sake, we'll leave it as it is. But, Harry, I know you aren't worried about your money, you're worried about me."

"Well, what I said to John is true. If he wants to gamble, then let him find some way to earn the money. He'd better keep his grubby hands off the Diamond Cross's profits. That's yours and Johnny's security."

"Apparently, you put the fear of God in John, for he's acting very strangely. He's on edge, and . . . and . . . I think he's scared."

Harry could tell that it bothered Beth to admit such a weak trait in her husband.

"John's a coward, and he isn't worth a grain of salt. That you ever married him astounds me."

"I didn't know John was like that when I married him. I guess I was blinded by his good looks and charm."

Harry could empathize with that, he had married Charlene for the same reasons. He had loved her, though, and his love had endured several unhappy years before it finally died. He was sure it was the same way with Beth. She had undoubtedly loved John when she married him, but he didn't think she loved him now.

Dark clouds had formed overhead, and as drops of rain began to fall, Beth and Harry suddenly paid attention to the threatening storm.

As the rain fell steadily harder, Harry said, "I have a storage shed not far from here. We'd better take shelter until this passes. It looks like it might get severe."

With Harry leading the way, they galloped over a distant hill, which took them to the shed. By now, the rain was falling in pelting sheets, and their clothes were soaking wet.

They hurried into the shelter, the wind was gusting, and Harry had to use both hands to close the door. Bags of oats, branding irons, and other ranching paraphernalia were stored inside. Going to a stack of blankets, Harry took one and offered it to Beth.

"Here, you'd better get out of those wet clothes before you catch a cold. I'll keep my back turned."

"You should take your own advice. You're also soaking wet."

"I intend to, but ladies first."

She moved to him to take the blanket. As she reached for it, their hands touched, and the contact was like an electrical shock, sending sparks through every nerve in their bodies. Harry's eyes, filled with a scorching intent, stared fervently into hers.

Beth's gaze was as fiery as his, and her lips trembled as she suddenly murmured, "Harry, I love you." She hadn't meant to reveal her true feelings, the words had simply poured forth.

Harry groaned raspingly. "God, help us! I love you, my darling Beth! I'll always love you!"

At that moment, lightning flashed brightly, ensued immediately by an earth-shattering clap of thunder. The violent storm, its winds swirling, resorbed reality into its powerful force. Inside the small shed, surrounded by nature's turbulence, Harry and Beth felt as though they had been transported to a different world . . . another lifetime.

Suddenly, they were in each other's arms, and their lips came together in an urgent, passionate exchange that left them breathless with wonder, but hungry for more. Their love, suppressed for so long, demanded to be set free, and

239

they could no longer keep it constrained.

As the storm climbed toward its zenith, Harry and Beth surrendered to their feelings. They made love with an intensity that surpassed the tempestuous storm raging about them.

Twenty

Laura was still lying on her bed, trying to deal with Harry Talbert's being her father, when a rapid knocking sounded at the door. Hoping Craig had returned, she sprang from the bed, and swung the door open. She was disappointed to find Johnny instead of Craig.

Her expression gave away her feelings. "Were you expecting someone else?" her brother asked, quirking an eyebrow.

She motioned him inside. "Yes, I was."

"Sorry to disappoint you."

"Don't be silly. I'm glad you stopped by."

He reached into his waistcoat pocket, brought out a sealed envelope, and handed it to her. "Here. I brought you something."

"What is it?"

"It's a notarized letter; I've given up all claim on the Diamond Cross."

Laura was obviously perplexed.

"After Mama died," Johnny explained, "Papa made me the sole heir. I don't know why."

Laura suddenly suspected the reason why — had John Mills known she wasn't really his daughter?

"Anyway," Johnny continued, "that miserable ranch is all yours — lock, stock, and barrel."

She smiled tolerantly. "Johnny, why do you say it's miserable? The Diamond Cross is a home to be proud of, and it's worth holding on to."

"Then hold on to it, Sis. I want no part of it."

Determination shone in her eyes. "Oh, I intend to hold on to it, all right! And someday soon it's going to be prosperous again."

"I don't doubt it. You're just like Mama, she loved that ranch something fierce. But Papa wasn't a rancher, and neither am I."

"Johnny, let's not lose touch. I know we're very different, but we are brother and sister — and I do love you."

He hugged her briefly. "Sure, we'll keep in touch. By the way, when are you leaving?"

"I'm not sure, but soon."

"Well, if I don't see you before you leave, you can write to me in care of The Lucky Lady."

"Good luck with your casino."

"Thanks, and good luck with the Diamond Cross."

With that, he left the room.

Laura stared dismally at the closed door. Johnny had left as suddenly as he had arrived. She wished her brother felt more warmth toward her, after all, he was the only family she had left.

Suddenly, her body tensed. No, Johnny wasn't her sole family! Dear God, she still had a father and two half brothers! Knowing she was kin to Doyce made her feel a little sick, she couldn't stand him! She didn't really know Ed, and wasn't sure how she felt about him. She thought about Harry Talbert, a warmhearted friendship had developed between them, and he had come to mean a great deal to her. She couldn't deny that he had found a special place in her heart.

She felt confused, and her emotions were jumbled. She moved back to the bed and sat down. She wished Craig would hurry back, she needed him desperately!

Johnny had gotten Marsha's room number from the desk clerk, and after leaving Laura, he went down the hall and knocked on Marsha's door.

She was delighted to see him, and taking his arm, she drew him inside. Thank goodness he hadn't come an hour earlier, for he would have found her still in her night clothes, her hair tangled, and her face devoid of rouge. But she had bathed, dressed, and was looking her best.

"Johnny, what a pleasant surprise!" she exclaimed, gazing at him with adoring eyes. She was exultant! Apparently, he was so smitten with her that he couldn't wait to see her again! Yes, manipulating him into marriage would be a breeze!

"I apologize for stopping by uninvited, but I had to come to the Winston to see Laura, and since I was already here . . ."

"Johnny, there's no reason to apologize! I'm delighted to see you." She regarded him cautiously. Had he said anything to Laura about their relationship? If so, Laura probably tried to turn him against her. "How was your visit with Laura?" she asked, sounding as though she were only slightly interested.

"I had a letter notarized this morning, giving Laura full rights to the Diamond Cross. I wanted to give it to her before she left."

Marsha hid her annoyance. Damn the luck! Once she had become Johnny's widow, she had planned to take the Diamond Cross away from Laura! Now, thanks to Johnny's generosity, she had been robbed of the pleasure.

"Did you say anything to Laura about us?" She managed to ask the question casually.

"No, I didn't."

She breathed an inner sigh of relief, then cast him one of her most glamorous smiles. "Johnny, do you have a special reason for stopping by?"

"Yes, I certainly do."

Her smile widened expansively.

"Marsha, last night you told me that you plan to stay in San Francisco, and since you'll need employment, I'm offering you a job. I have only five . . . hostesses working for me, and I could sure use one more. You're a beautiful woman, and my clientele will pay a bundle for you."

Marsha's smile vanished. She could hardly believe what she was hearing. "Johnny, you can't be serious!"

"Of course, I am. Don't worry, Marsha. You'll make good money."

"How dare you insult me so horridly!"

He chuckled amusedly. "Marsha, let's not play games. I know you're a whore. I've bedded enough of them to know when I'm being entertained by a professional."

"Get out!" she hissed. "Leave, before I lose my temper!"

He headed toward the door, saying over his shoulder, "If you should change your mind, the job will be waiting for you." He started to leave, but pausing at the threshold, he asked with a sly grin, "Marsha, did you think I would fall in love with you, and ask you to marry me? Did you really take me for a complete fool?"

"Get out!" she screeched, reaching for the water pitcher to throw it at him.

Laughing, he closed the door with a solid bang.

Marsha was beside herself with fury, and she slammed the ceramic pitcher against the floor, breaking it into several pieces. Rage flamed in her so fiercely that her face turned red and blotchy. She wished Johnny would come back so she could attack him, she wanted to rake her long fingernails down his face until she drew blood. How dare he take such unfair advantage of her! Last night, he had been so considerate, and had showered her with compliments. The damned cad! He had never intended to court her!

A knock came at the door, and Marsha tried to compose herself. As she went to answer it, she hoped it was Johnny, coming back to tell her he'd had a change of heart.

She was disgruntled to find Jim instead.

"Are you ready?" he asked, stepping inside.

Marsha didn't understand. "Ready? What do you mean?"

"I want to take you around town. Maybe you'll spot the men who killed your husband. We can start by going to The Lucky Lady."

Marsha was not about to visit The Lucky Lady and face Johnny Mills. The man had humiliated her enough for one day! "I'm sorry, Jim," she said, massaging her temples. "I don't feel well, and I'm not up to traveling about the city."

Jim's patience snapped. "Marsha, what the hell's wrong with you? Do you have headaches morning, noon, and night?"

"Jim, please don't be so nasty. I really do have a split-

245

ting headache." It wasn't a fib, her head was indeed throbbing.

He gave up, and waving his arms in exasperation, he grumbled, "To hell with it, and to hell with you!" He stormed out of the room, slamming the door behind him.

Marsha wasn't upset, quite the opposite, maybe she was now rid of Jim Slade once and for all!

Zeb, sitting on the terrace with Laura, listened attentively as she told him about her mother and Harry Talbert. Although Zeb was surprised to learn that Beth had fallen in love with Talbert, he wasn't all that shocked. John Mills had been a sorry excuse for a husband, and he certainly could understand why Beth had turned to another man. Actually, Zeb was pleased to find out that Laura was Talbert's daughter; he had despised John Mills and was glad Laura didn't belong to him.

"Now I know why I'm nothing like Papa," Laura sighed, finishing her story. "Papa? I mean the man I thought was my father."

"Well, if I were you, it wouldn't make me unhappy to learn I wasn't kin to John Mills. You're better off not havin' his blood runnin' through your veins. If you did, you might be as useless as Johnny."

"Zeb, you shouldn't be so hard on Johnny. He isn't that bad, he's just wrapped up in himself. He's always been that way."

"Yeah, I reckon you're right." He watched her closely. "Tell me, how do you feel about Talbert bein' your father?"

"I'm not sure. It's still too soon. The shock hasn't worn off yet."

"It's gonna take time for you to adjust. I just hope you don't let this turn you bitter. Maybe Talbert was wrong not to claim you all these years, but I suppose he had his reasons. I ain't gonna try and judge him."

"Do you like him?"

"Yep, I sure do. I don't know him all that well, but, so far, he ain't done nothin' to keep me from likin' him."

"It doesn't bother you to know that he had an affair with your niece?"

"Laura, when you get to be my age, you understand how things like that can happen. Beth and Talbert met and fell in love too late. I don't think it was a bad situation, just a sad one."

Her uncle's words brought an ache to her heart. For the first time, she put herself in her mother's place. What if she were married to a man like John Mills, and had met Craig too late? Would she have had the strength to fight her feelings? No, she didn't think so. Like her mother, she would certainly have surrendered.

"It must've been very hard for Mama to stop seeing Mr. Talbert. No wonder she always went out of her way to avoid him. I used to think it was because she didn't like him." Laura groaned sadly. "But she avoided him because she loved him. Poor Mama, how difficult it must have been."

"Yep, I'm sure it was." Zeb reached into his pocket, drew out a cigar, and lit it. "Shouldn't Craig be back by now?"

"Yes, he should have been here over an hour ago. I'm getting a little worried."

"I'm sure he'll show up any minute." Zeb got to his feet. "I'm gonna go to my room and wash up for dinner."

"Craig and I will meet you in the dining room."

He leaned over Laura's chair and gave her a kiss on the forehead. "Try not to worry. I'm sure Craig worked everything out between him and Deborah. Also, don't get down in the dumps over Talbert. Give yourself a little more time, and you'll probably be glad he's your father. It's never too late, you know. You two still have plenty of time to make up for lost years."

With those words of advice, Zeb left for his room.

Despite Marsha's foul mood, hunger had convinced her to join the others for dinner. She was seated next to Jim, but he ignored her and acted as though she wasn't even there. Marsha couldn't have cared less!

The diners waited awhile for Laura and Craig to arrive, but then decided to go ahead and order. Karen offered to go upstairs and check on them, but, Zeb, suspecting they might be discussing Deborah, suggested that Karen not interrupt.

However, when dinner had been served and eaten without Laura and Craig making an appearance, Zeb was concerned. He was considering checking on them, but Talbert beat him to it.

Pushing back his chair and getting to his feet, Harry said, "I'm going to see what's keeping Laura and Craig."

Zeb stayed put. After all, Talbert was Laura's father, and Zeb felt it was time he started acting like one.

Harry went up the stairs, down the hall, and to Laura's room. He raised a hand to knock at the same moment the door opened.

Laura, bursting from her room, almost ran smack into him.

"What's the hurry?" he asked.

"Craig hasn't returned, and I'm going to the school to check on him."

Harry was immediately concerned. "He hasn't returned? But he's been gone all day."

"Something has happened to him! I just know it!" She was obviously very upset.

"If you don't mind, I'll go with you."

She had no objections, in fact, she welcomed his company. She was worried and needed a friend's support.

"Thank you, Mr. Talbert. I'd be glad to have you come with me."

He took her arm, and escorted her downstairs. They stopped at the dining room to let the others know where they were going, then hurried outside where they hailed a public conveyance.

Laura told the driver to take them to Mrs. Meredith's School for the Blind. Harry assisted her into the enclosed carriage, sat beside her, and closed the door.

As they started their journey to the school, Laura was filled with dread. Dusk had already fallen, and it would soon be full dark. Craig had expected to be back by this afternoon at the latest. Something terrible must have happened to him! Laura could think of no other reason to explain his absence. Fear knotted in the pit of her stomach. Craig had a lot of enemies from his days as a bounty hunter. Had he met up with one or more of them? Was he hurt or . . . or . . . ? A shudder ran through her, that he might be dead was too horrible to even consider.

Harry, aware of her anxieties, tried to calm her with comforting words. His kindness was appreciated, but it failed to assuage her apprehensions.

It was a good thirty-minute drive to the school, but to

Laura it seemed much longer. By the time the carriage stopped in front of the three-story building, Laura was a bundle of nerves.

Harry told the driver to wait, then with a hand on Laura's arm, he helped her up the flight of steps leading to the front door. He lifted the brass knocker and announced their presence.

As they waited to be admitted, Laura glanced about with vacant interest. A large sign, posted in the yard, proclaimed the building as Mrs. Meredith's School for the Blind. The walkway was lined with rose bushes, their colors a mixture of reds, pinks, and yellows. The establishment was located at the city's outskirts, and the area was quiet and peaceful.

The door was finally opened, and they were greeted by an elderly woman dressed in a maid's uniform. "Good evening," she said cordially.

"You have a student here by the name of Deborah," Laura replied. "I don't know her last name. But we need to see her."

"You must mean Deborah Kent." She laughed lightly. "But, of course, you do. This school has been here ten years, and we've had only one Deborah."

"I know it's late, but may we see her? I need to ask her about someone."

"She isn't here," the woman replied, smiling widely. "She got married this afternoon."

"Married!" Laura exclaimed.

"Yes, bless her heart! She waited so long for her fiance to come back to her. He arrived this morning, and he was so anxious to marry that he whisked her away to the nearest chapel."

Laura was too shocked to say a word.

"Where are they now?" Harry asked.

"They left for Seattle. That's where they plan to spend their honeymoon. I understand the country there is breathtaking. Miss Deborah was so happy, and she's so much in love. I hope her new husband loves her as much as she loves him."

"What makes you think he doesn't?" Harry wanted to know.

"Well, the man stayed away a long time, and Deborah was beginning to worry that he had jilted her. She adores him so much, and he means everything to her."

Laura tugged weakly at Harry's arm. "Come on; let's leave. I've heard all I can take."

As they were walking down the steps, the maid called out to them, "Deborah and her husband are expected to return in a couple of weeks, if you want to come back."

Harry mumbled that they probably wouldn't bother, then he helped Laura into the carriage. Sitting beside her, he slipped an arm about her shoulders, and drew her close.

He waited for Laura to say something, to pour out her heart, or even to vent her rage. Nothing! She remained perfectly silent.

Harry longed to comfort her, but, at a time like this, words seemed so useless. Nonetheless, he made the effort. "Laura, we both know that Craig's very compassionate and caring. Obviously, when he saw Deborah again, he couldn't bring himself to break her heart."

"He might be compassionate and caring," she said, her voice tinged with anger, "but he's also a damned coward! He didn't have the courage to face me! How could he do this to me? How could he let me find out like this? Damn him! Damn him!"

251

Laura was miserable, she wanted to cry until she ran out of tears. But she kept a tenuous hold on her emotions. Bawling like a baby wouldn't change anything; Craig had chosen loyalty over their love! A strange numbness came over her, and, for now, she could feel no emotions at all.

When they reached the hotel, Harry wasn't surprised to find everyone sitting in the lobby, waiting for them; even Marsha was present.

Talbert told them that Craig had married Deborah.

"How do you know it was Craig she married?" Zeb burst out. "Did you ask her husband's name?"

"Craig was her fiance," Laura replied firmly. "How many men do you think she was engaged to?"

"I don't know, but I'm gonna find out. What's the name of this school?"

Harry told him.

Zeb went to Laura. "Come on, hon. I'm gonna take you to your room, sit with you a spell, then pay a visit to that school."

Marsha, listening, stood back inconspicuously. Now, as she slipped outside, no one seemed to notice. Flagging a carriage, she told the driver to take her to the stables where her wagon was stored. As the driver waited, she climbed inside the wagon, grabbed a tool, and pried open the loose planks. She delved into the hidden compartment, took out a tidy sum, then pressed the planks back into place.

Returning to the carriage, she said she wanted to be taken to Mrs. Meredith's School for the Blind. Her mind swirled wickedly, for she relished getting even with Laura Mills. She hated her, as well as her brother! The carriage seemed to be moving at a snail's pace, and Marsha grew apprehensive. It was imperative that she reach the school before Zeb.

The moment the driver brought the carriage to a stop, Marsha dashed outside. Ordering him to wait, she hurried to the front door and rapped the knocker loudly.

Again, the maid answered the door.

Marsha smiled brightly. "Excuse me, but are you the same woman who talked to a couple of friends of mine? They were here earlier, looking for Deborah."

"Yes, ma'am. I talked to them."

"Tell me, who did Deborah marry? Do you know his name?"

"Yes, of course I do. She married Dr. James Stevenson."

Marsha wasn't surprised. Craig wasn't the type to leave Laura for another woman, regardless of the circumstances.

"Do you remember if Deborah had a visitor named Craig Branston?"

The woman thought a moment. "Yes, she did. Mr. Branston was here this morning. He talked to Deborah and Doctor Stevenson for a couple of hours, then left."

Marsha wondered what had happened to Craig, but she didn't ponder very long, right now she had a more pressing matter to complete.

Marsha plastered a jovial smile on her face. "You're probably going to think I'm very silly, but my friends and I are playing a harmless prank. In a few minutes, a man named Zeb Douglas will be here, and he'll ask you who Deborah married." She opened her purse, and took out some bills. "This hundred dollars is yours, if you tell him that she married Craig Branston."

The maid ogled the money hungrily. A hundred dol-

253

lars was more than she had ever had at one time. She figured this woman, as well as her friends, were wealthy. Apparently, the idle rich had nothing better to do than throw their money around and play ridiculous games. She would be a fool not to cooperate.

"I'd be only too glad to tell him she married Mr. Branston."

Marsha gave her the bills. "Here. Go ahead and take the money. You have an honest face, and I'm sure I can trust you."

As Marsha returned to the carriage, she was actually beaming. She told the driver to take her to the hospital, it was merely a wild hunch, but she had a feeling she might find Craig there — or else at the morgue! She could think of no other reason why he hadn't returned to Laura.

Twenty-one

At the hospital, Marsha was greeted by an attendant, a young man with a handlebar moustache. He was surprised to find a woman visiting so late at night; visiting hours had long since ended.

"Can I help you, ma'am?" he asked.

"Yes," Marsha replied. "A friend of mine is missing. Did you have any new patients admitted today?"

"Are you looking for a gentleman?"

"Yes, I am."

"An unidentified man was brought in early today."

"Unidentified?" Marsha questioned, not quite understanding.

"Yes, ma'am, he's unconscious. He didn't have any identification on him. It appears he was beaten and robbed."

"May I see him?"

"Come with me," he said, motioning for her to follow.

He took her down a long, narrow hallway that led to an isolated room. Marsha was somewhat uncomfortable, for she disliked hospitals. The lingering odors of chloroform, ether, and antiseptics filled the corridor, and Marsha found the smells nauseating.

The attendant showed her into the brightly lit room; there were five beds inside, three of them occupied with seriously ill patients. Two nurses were on duty, their stiffly starched uniforms as white as the barren walls. Marsha followed her guide to the last bed on their left.

"This is him," the man said, gesturing toward the patient.

Marsha took a close look, and despite the patient's badly bruised and battered face, she recognized Craig. "Good Lord!" she gasped. "I've never seen anyone so horribly battered! Will he live?"

"The doctors aren't sure. He has a concussion, and with head injuries, you never can tell. He also has two broken ribs, but of course, that's not serious. Is this the man you're looking for?"

Marsha shook her head. "No, I've never seen this person before."

"That's too bad, I was hoping you could identify him."

The attendant escorted Marsha from the room and to the front door. She hurried outside and filled her lungs with fresh air. Her carriage was waiting; she started to climb inside, changed her mind, and asked the driver, "Where can I find someone to run a couple of errands for me? I'll pay handsomely."

"I'll take care of the errands for you."

"Good," she replied. "I want you to go to Johnson's Livery and tell the owner that you have a message from Craig Branston."

"What's the message?"

"That he's on his honeymoon and must leave his horse there for another two weeks. Then I want you to go to the Winston, and tell the desk clerk that Mr. Branston wants his belongings stored. I'll give you money for your troubles, plus enough to pay the livery to hold Mr. Branston's horse."

The driver agreed, and, Marsha, feeling exultant, said she wanted to return to the Winston. She was smiling like the proverbial cat who had swallowed the canary. She wasn't exactly sure why she had taken such lengths to destroy Laura's happiness. She didn't like her, true, but it was more than that. In her opinion, Laura was as arrogant as her brother. By hurting Laura, she felt as though she were getting even with Johnny at the same time. It wasn't logical thinking, but Marsha was nonetheless pleased with herself.

Laura paced her bedroom restlessly. Karen, sitting on the edge of the bed, watched her friend anxiously. Zeb, accompanied by Jim and Harry, had gone to the school, but they had left Joshua with the ladies. He was perched at the end of his chair, wishing he could think of comforting words for Laura. It bothered him to see her so tormented; she was a kind, wonderful lady, and didn't deserve such heartache.

Karen's feelings were similar to Joshua's. Laura was a good friend, and she thought the world of her. It pained Karen to see Laura so troubled.

"Laura," she said. "Please try to relax. I just know Zeb and the others are going to return with good news. Craig loves you; he wouldn't marry another woman."

Laura stopped her pacing, turned to Karen, and replied with apprehension, "If he didn't marry Deborah, then where is he? Something terrible must have happened to him!"

Karen wished she could think of a plausible excuse for Craig's disappearance without alarming her friend. But Laura was right. If Craig wasn't married

257

to Deborah, then he was in some kind of trouble.

At that moment, a short rap sounded at the door. It was opened, and, Zeb, along with Jim and Harry, came inside. Their expressions were dour.

Zeb went to Laura, and said regrettably, "We went to the school, and talked to the same woman you and Mr. Talbert saw. She said that Deborah married Craig Branston."

Her uncle's words were heartbreaking, yet, at the same time, Laura was relieved to learn that nothing terrible had befallen Craig. Her feeling of relief, however, was short-lived; and it was soon overtaken by sadness. She had lost Craig, and she felt as though she could literally feel her heart breaking in two. She moved to a chair, and sat down feebly, her emotions totally wrecked. Despair threatened to consume her, but Laura's pride fought back furiously. She'd not give in to depression! She had believed in Craig, but he had failed her! Somehow, she'd learn to deal with it! But how? How? Craig had been her life, and without him, she felt so empty inside! She must find a way to fill her life again, something to keep her mind active and her hours occupied. The Diamond Cross, of course! She wanted to go home! There she would find the will to go on, and the solace to heal her broken heart.

She looked about the room to find that everyone was watching her. She was deeply touched to see such concern in their eyes. She had true friends, and she had the Diamond Cross! With them, she'd muster the strength to get through this. But she knew it wouldn't be easy, she loved Craig with all her heart, and his betrayal was excruciating. She had never known such heartrending pain!

"I want to go home," Laura said suddenly, her gaze

sweeping over the others. "Without delay. Can all of you be ready to leave in the morning?"

Except for Karen, they all said they could.

"Is there a problem?" Laura asked her.

"I guess not, if you don't mind taking me to Peaceful. From there, I'll make arrangements to travel to Boston. I've given up on finding my father."

"I know you don't want to go back to Boston," Laura said. "Why don't you come with me? Consider the Diamond Cross your home for as long as you wish. Please, Karen! I truly need your company."

Karen was delighted! "Thank you, Laura! And I gratefully accept your invitation!"

"Then it's settled," Laura replied firmly, getting to her feet. "Now, I think we should all get a good night's sleep. I want to get an early start in the morning."

They began to pile out of her room, but Harry held back. When the others were gone, he moved to Laura, took her hands, and asked, "Are you going to be all right? Do you want me to stay for a while?"

She lifted her chin proudly. "I'll be fine. I don't intend to let Craig Branston destroy my life!" *Only my heart,* her thoughts butted in.

Harry studied her admiringly. She had never reminded him more of Beth. Like her mother, she was a survivor. She would find the strength to pick up the pieces of her life and go forward. He had an overwhelming urge to take her in his arms and give her a fatherly kiss, but fearing rejection, he simply told her good night and left.

Alone, Laura surrendered to her sorrow, fell across the bed, and cried until there were no tears left to shed.

The next morning, Jim was awake when dawn began to lighten the sky. He was already dressed and packed. He left his room, went down the hall, and knocked on Marsha's door. He had stopped by last night, but Marsha hadn't been in her room.

"Who's there?" she called out drowsily.

"Jim," he replied. "I need to talk to you."

"Go away," she moaned testily. "It's too early! We'll talk later!"

"Open up, Marsha!" he said firmly. "I wouldn't bother you if it wasn't important."

"Just a minute," she replied crankily. She got out of bed, slipped on her dressing robe and went to the door. Waving Jim inside, she remarked petulantly, "This had better be damned important. My God, it's just dawn!"

Jim delved into his shirt pocket, removed some bills, and handed them to Marsha. "Here, this is from Mr. Talbert. He gave me the money last night, and said for me to make sure you get it."

"I don't understand," she replied, puzzled. "Why is Mr. Talbert giving me money?" She quickly counted the bills, and was pleased at the tidy sum.

"He's buying your wagon, the supplies stored inside it, and your horses. As you can see, he paid you at least twice what they're worth."

Marsha's body tensed, and she drew a deep breath as though she were about to plunge into icy water. "No!" she cried desperately. "My wagon isn't for sale!"

Jim was naturally confused. "You can't be serious. He's paying you a lot more than it's worth."

Marsha didn't know what to say. If she acted upset, Jim might start asking too many questions. She had to find an excuse to go to her wagon and secretly remove her money, without arousing Jim's suspicions.

She forced a smile. "Of course, I'll sell my wagon, supplies, and horses. This is all so sudden that I was taken off guard. But I don't understand why Mr. Talbert is anxious to buy everything so quickly."

"The others and I are leaving in a couple of hours. I stopped by your room last night to let you know, but you weren't here." He paused, wondering if she'd explain her absence, but she didn't offer an explanation. "Laura is eager to start for home, and I plan to accompany her. I once promised that I'd help her find out who killed Lee Talbert."

"I have a few things in my wagon that I'd like to keep." She managed to speak as though it were merely a trivial matter. "I'll get dressed, hurry to the livery, and get my things."

"I'll wait for you."

"There's no need." She couldn't very well get her money with Jim looking over her shoulder!

"I'm going to the livery anyhow, so we might as well go together. Zeb's probably already there, and he'll need help hitching the wagon and saddling the horses."

Marsha's heart sank! She was at a dead end! How could she retrieve her stolen funds without getting caught? Her money might as well be on the moon! Damn! Why had she left it in the wagon? If only she had gotten it out and deposited it in a bank! But she had foolishly believed her money was safe, at least for a couple of days!

She turned away from Jim's watching eyes, and set her mind to thinking. She plotted quickly but thoroughly. She whirled about, her dressing gown flowing gently about her legs. As she met Jim's gaze, a sad mask fell across her face. "I don't want you to leave me," she murmured.

Her confession took him by surprise. "You certainly haven't acted like you cared whether or not I left."

"I know I've behaved very coldly, but I had my reasons."

"For instance?"

Her expression was imploring. "Jim, I lost my husband so tragically! I didn't love Jerry, true, but I was very fond of him. Then you came into my life so unexpectedly, and I just couldn't cope with Jerry's death and your love happening so close together! Also, we barely know each other! I love you, but . . . but . . . I'm terribly afraid!" Real tears came to her eyes, for she was very upset. If she failed to win Jim back, he and the others would leave with her money! If her money left, she intended to leave with it! Later, she would figure out a way to keep her money and get rid of Jim Slade!

"Why are you afraid?" Jim asked, watching her closely.

"I'm afraid I'll fall even more in love with you, and you'll jilt me. I mean, look at Craig and Laura. She believed in him, and he betrayed her."

"Yes, he did," Jim replied heavily. "Zeb, Mr. Talbert, and I went back to the school last night. We found out that Craig did marry Deborah."

"Poor Laura. She must be devastated."

"I'm sure she is, but she's holding up remarkably well."

Marsha wasn't too pleased to hear that. However, at the moment, she was concerned with a more important matter—her stolen funds!

She moved closer to Jim. "I want to leave with you and the others. We need time to get to know each other better." She slipped her arms about his neck, and leaned into his embrace. "Please give me another chance to show you how much I care. I love you, Jim. I really do!" She lifted her lips to his, and kissed him passionately.

He drew her body flush to his, and responded ardently. He believed she did indeed care, otherwise, why would she leave San Francisco just to be with him?

Jim swooped her up into his arms, carried her to the bed, and laid her down gently. "Marsha!" he groaned huskily. "I still want you."

"Yes, my darling," she purred. "Make love to me!"

He kissed her again, then as he doffed his clothes, she hastily removed her dressing robe and gown. She lay before him unclad, and his eyes drank in her luscious curves. She boldly returned his admiring perusal. She didn't love Jim, but she did like his masculine body. She thought about Johnny Mills, his love-making had been limpid and too quick, but she knew Jim would take her to fulfilling heights.

He stretched out beside her, and as his mouth took hers in a wild, urgent caress, his hand traveled up and down her body, exploring her silken flesh. Moaning with pleasure, she thrust her breasts toward him, and he kissed one erect nipple, then the other. His lips flickered downward, past her stomach and beyond, where he relished her with hot desire.

Marsha's passion was burning as fiercely as Jim's, and hunger flared in her with savagelike lust. Jim's mouth and tongue were driving her wild, causing her head to toss and turn on the pillow, as she was engulfed in sexual ecstasy.

Jim, his loins on fire, moved his body over hers, and claimed her completely. At first, his strokes were slow and measured, but as his desire intensified, he began to thrust more rapidly.

Marsha's hips met his in perfect timing, and abandoning herself to a spiraling climax, she cried aloud with breathtaking satisfaction.

Simultaneously, Jim reached his own peak of excitement, and uncontrollable tremors shook his body. He kissed her softly, then moved to lie at her side.

Marsha snuggled close. "Jim, you aren't going to leave me behind, are you?"

"No, I could never do that. I love you too much."

Marsha smiled, it wasn't a sign of happiness, but relief. She wasn't pleased about leaving San Francisco, however, her money was much more important.

Well, she thought, there are more cities than this one. She considered St. Louis; it had its share of millionaires. Yes, maybe she'd go there. A small frown crossed her face. First, she had to endure another trip with Jim and the others, but then she'd find a way to leave them behind and go to St. Louis.

"Marsha?" Jim said softly.

"Yes, darling?"

"Will you marry me?"

"Of course, I will. Just as soon as this trip is over."

"We can be married in Silver Star."

"That's a marvelous idea, darling." Marsha had heard of the town, and knew it was close to Laura's ranch. Once they reached Silver Star, she'd get her money, tell Jim Slade goodbye, and leave on the first available stagecoach!

A little later, Jim and Marsha made love again, then

he helped her pack. He offered to carry her luggage downstairs, his hands were full, and she opened the door for him. He stepped into the hall, where he encountered Karen and Laura. They had their carpetbags, and were on their way to the lobby.

They were stunned to find Jim coming out of Marsha's room with a packed suitcase.

Marsha, poised in the open doorway, saw the surprise on their faces. She grinned spitefully. She was sure Laura and Karen resented her coming along. Especially Karen, for she was obviously in love with Jim.

"I thought you were staying in San Francisco," Laura said curtly to Marsha.

"I was, but I changed my mind." She turned to Jim, favored him with a loving smile, then looked back at Laura. "Jim and I plan to be married."

Laura didn't express congratulations, for it would have been a lie. Actually, she wanted to tell Jim that he was a fool!

Karen continued on to the lobby. Watching Jim and Marsha together was more than she could stand. She had believed that with Marsha out of the picture, she might have a chance with Jim. But now she knew her love was hopeless, and she was crestfallen.

Meanwhile, Marsha intentionally cut Laura with words as sharp as a knife, "By the way, Laura, I was sorry to hear that Craig jilted you." She twisted the blade even deeper. "Who would ever have thought that he was a two-timing cad? He was probably in love with Deborah all along."

"Marsha, if we're going to travel together, let's get one thing straight right now."

"What's that?"

"Don't mention Craig's name to me."

"Of course, my dear. I can understand why his name upsets you."

"It doesn't. It's your false sympathy that upsets me." With that, Laura started down the hall.

Jim quickly caught up to her. "Laura, did you have to be so rude? Marsha was trying to be nice."

She sighed impatiently. "Jim, that woman has completely pulled the wool over your eyes."

"How can you say that? She's here with me, isn't she? That's more than we can say for Craig. Apparently, you're the one who had the wool pulled over your eyes." Jim was immediately sorry, he hadn't meant to be cruel. "Forgive me, Laura. I shouldn't have said that."

She accepted his apology. Furthermore, as much as it hurt to admit it, he was right. Craig had indeed deceived her!

Karen greeted them as they entered the lobby. "I just talked to the desk clerk, and he said a man stopped by this morning with a message from Craig."

"A message?" Laura questioned.

"Yes, he wants the hotel to store his belongings until he returns from his honeymoon."

"There wasn't a message for me?"

"No, I'm afraid not."

"Damn Craig!" she swore softly. She was still finding it hard to believe that he had so coldly double-crossed her.

"The wagon's out front," Karen said. "Everyone's ready to leave."

They left the hotel. Jim placed Marsha's suitcase in the wagon, then hurried back inside to get her.

Harry was on his horse, and, Joshua, planning to drive the team, was sitting on the wagon seat with Lobo perched beside him. Zeb was holding the reins to Karen's and Laura's horses. He helped them mount, then said to Laura, "I learned at the livery that Craig sent a message. He wants them to keep his horse there for two more weeks."

"He tied up all his loose strings very neatly!" Laura remarked, fuming. "Except for one, that is! He seems to have forgotten my very existence! I hope I never see that damned, cowardly skunk for as long as I live! I despise him!" But even as she spouted the words, she knew they weren't really true. She wanted to hate Craig, but she couldn't; deep in her heart, she still loved him. She had a disheartening feeling that she always would.

Twenty-two

It seemed strange to Laura to ride without Craig at her side, to sit about the campfire and not have him with her, and, most of all, she longed for his tender gestures and heartwarming smiles. But Laura knew she had to force herself to remain strong, if not, she'd certainly sink into a state of depression.

Laura had the support of her friends, and their concern helped carry her through this most difficult time in her life. Karen was more like a sister than a friend; and, despite Marsha's influence, Laura knew she could still depend on Jim. Zeb was indeed a comfort, and she didn't know what she would do without him. He had decided to stay at the Diamond Cross for as long as she needed him, and for that Laura was very grateful. Her friendship with Joshua had deepened, she liked and respected him very much. A warm bond was developing between Laura and Harry Talbert, and with each passing day, Laura's feelings for him grew stronger.

It was now the third day of their journey, and they stopped at sunset and made camp in an area surrounded by trees and shrubbery. Laura and Karen were starting supper when the sounds of approaching horses alerted the camp. Lobo, poised beside his mistress, sensed possible danger and growled deeply. Meanwhile, Zeb grabbed his shotgun and Jim drew his pistol.

Four men rode into view; Harry, recognizing the two riding in front, smiled broadly and told Zeb and Jim to put away their weapons.

Laura recognized them at the same time—Ed and Doyce Talbert! The sight of Doyce, however, placed a testy frown on her face, for she disliked him immensely. The other two men looked familiar, and, at first, she couldn't place them. Then, all at once, she remembered where she had seen them. They were the same two snakes who had tried to attack her!

As Ed and Doyce dismounted, Harry stepped forward, shook their hands, and gave them a fatherly hug. "What are you two doing here?" he asked, very much surprised.

"We were worried," Ed answered. "I heard that Branston was riding with Laura, and I was afraid he might kill you."

Harry laughed warmly. "Well, as you can see, I'm alive and well." He gestured toward Laura. "She's coming back home, and I'm going to see that the charges against her are dropped."

Ed was bewildered, but he decided not to question his father until they could talk privately.

Harry introduced his sons; Ed and Doyce were both quite taken with Marsha's provocative beauty, however, Doyce was disgruntled to learn that Jim Slade was a federal marshal. He still planned to get rid of his father and Ed, and the lawman's presence might complicate matters. Also, he wasn't too sure about Zeb, the man looked like he could pose a threat. Doyce's mood turned sour. Damn it! He hadn't counted on finding his father traveling with this many people! To get rid of Ed and Harry, he'd have to eliminate the others as well! He wasn't sure such a feat was possible, and decided not to attempt it.

Ed motioned for Morgan and Elias to come over and meet Harry Talbert and the others. Laura didn't let on

269

that she had once encountered the two men; they, in turn, made no mention of it. Later, however, Laura intended to tell Harry about their attempted assault. But she didn't consider this the right time.

Laura moved to the wagon, sat down, and leaned back against one of the large wheels. Lobo, following, took his place beside her. She reached over and wrapped an arm about his neck, drawing him closer. Encouraged, he lay down and put his head in her lap. The wolf whined softly, it sounded forlorn, and Laura wondered if he missed Craig.

Karen was watching Laura, and noticing that her friend seemed troubled, she went over and sat beside her. "Is something wrong?"

"I don't want Doyce Talbert and his two friends traveling with us."

"Why not?"

"I don't like Doyce. He's trouble, and so are those men he hired."

"Do you know them?"

"I came across them once. They tried to rape me."

Karen's mouth dropped open. "Good Lord!"

"They didn't hurt me, in fact, they never even touched me. Lobo and I handled the situation." Wistfully, she remembered that Craig had also been there; she hadn't needed his help, but if she had, he certainly would have come through for her.

Suddenly, Lobo leapt to his feet, and a low, vicious growl emanated from deep in his throat. Laura and Karen, wondering what had alerted the wolf, got quickly to their feet.

"Hello in the camp!" a man's voice rang out strongly. It came from somewhere in the dense shrubbery. "I'm comin' in, but I don't mean you no harm!"

"You're more than welcome!" Zeb called back.

The man had been squatting, but as he stood upright, his hat popped above a bush and into view, then the rest of him materialized. Instead of coming toward camp, however, he turned about and walked the other way. He soon reappeared, leading his pack mule, which he had left out of sight.

The stranger looked as though he were in his late fifties. He was dressed in fringed buckskins, and his face was covered with a full red beard streaked with gray. The mule was toting prospecting equipment.

"Howdy, folks," he said, his smile friendly. He nodded toward the campfire. "That coffee sure smells good. Mind if I have a cup?"

Zeb filled a cup and handed it to him.

"I'll just drink this and be on my way," the prospector replied. He took a tentative sip, for the coffee was hot. "My name's Rufas," he said, "and I appreciate your hospitality. By the way, where are you folks headed?"

"Silver Star, Nevada," Zeb replied.

"Well, if you're a-headed in that direction, you better take precaution. There's a small band of Paiutes on the prowl, and they're up to no good. Spotted 'em myself a few days back. But they didn't see me, if they had, I'd lost my mule and gun—maybe even my life."

"Thanks for the warning," Jim spoke up.

"Well, more than likely, you ain't got nothin' to worry about. Them Paiutes ain't gonna attack a party that's got seven able-bodied men in it." His gaze swept fleetingly over the women. Rufas certainly hoped they wouldn't attack, for he hated to think what might happen to the ladies should the Indians win.

Although Laura and Karen had remained by the wagon, they had heard everything Rufas said. "Karen," Laura re-

271

marked softly, "regardless of how I feel about Doyce and his friends, it's good that they're traveling with us. There's safety in numbers, and we'll need their guns if we're confronted by those Paiutes."

Karen agreed. "You're right. For now, I don't think you should tell anyone what happened between you and those two men. It'll only cause trouble, and they'll be forced to leave."

"They sicken me, but they certainly don't pose a threat, so I guess I can stomach their presence."

Karen, somewhat frightened, reached over and grasped her companion's arm. "Laura, do you think we'll be attacked by Indians?"

"I doubt it. You heard what Rufas said, the band is too small to attack seven armed men."

Karen prayed that Rufas was right.

Rufas, true to his word, left after he drank his coffee. He said he was on his way to San Francisco, where he intended to spend the summer months. He reminded Zeb to make sure both wagon barrels were filled with water before starting through the desert. Summer had arrived early, and the weather was already uncomfortably warm.

Following supper, Harry drew his sons aside and told them that Laura was his daughter. Ed, honoring his mother's memory, was a little embittered to learn of his father's infidelity. Doyce, however, was enraged. Not only did he persuade himself that he despised Harry for cheating on his mother, but, more importantly, now he might have to share his inheritance with Laura, as well as Ed! Well, he'd be damned if he'd do any such thing! His plan to murder Harry and Ed was quickly reborn. He'd find a way to get rid of them and the others at the same time.

Talbert and his sons had walked to the edge of camp. Laura, sitting at the campfire, wondered if Harry was telling them that he was her father. She turned so that she could see the threesome, and recognizing shock on the sons' faces, she was certain that Harry was making a full confession.

She was sitting alone, and when Ed and Doyce left their father, neither stopped to say anything to her. They went straight to their bedrolls, which, due to the heat, had been placed a distance from the fire.

Harry soon joined her, and sat down with a heavy sigh. "I told Ed and Doyce everything. I'm not sure how they took it."

"Right now, they're in shock. You'll have to give them time to adjust."

"Ed's anger I can understand, but Doyce's . . . ?"

"What about Doyce?"

"His anger was so intense that it was frightening. I saw a murderous glare in his eyes that chilled me to the bone." Harry shook it aside, Doyce was his own flesh and blood, how could he be capable of such wrath against his own father? He wondered if he had misread his son's rage.

"Was Doyce close to his mother?"

"More so than the others. He was Charlene's favorite."

"That probably explains his anger. He might never forgive you for being unfaithful to her."

"He'll get over it in time." But Harry didn't sound too certain.

"I remember Mama telling me that your wife was in the carriage alone when she had her accident. Exactly what happened?"

"She was leaving me. For years, we held our marriage together because of the boys. I wouldn't let them go, and she wouldn't leave them. The night before her accident, we

273

had a heated argument. The next day, I came in from the range to find she had left me a note. She said I could have our sons. She packed only one suitcase, saying she would send for the rest of her things. She took the carriage into town, where she planned to catch the stagecoach. She was running late, raced the horses recklessly, and the carriage overturned. She was trapped beneath it, and her legs were crushed." He paused, gathered his somber thoughts, and continued, "After that, she sank into a state of depression. Her health slowly deteriorated, she caught pneumonia and died."

"I'm sorry," Laura murmured ruefully. "I'm sorry for you, Charlene, Mama, and John Mills. What a sad life all of you had."

"It wasn't as unhappy as it sounds. I can only speak for myself, of course, but I learned to adjust to life without Beth. I never stopped loving her, but I was able to put our past relationship in its correct perspective. I had the Circle T, my sons, and several good friends. My life wasn't empty, believe me."

"That night I went to your home and talked to Lee, he showed me into the study. I'd never been in that room before, and when I saw the portrait of you, it had a strange effect on me. You're still a young man in the painting. For some reason, which I couldn't understand at the time, I felt as though you were someone I had once known or dreamt about. It's hard to explain exactly how I felt, but it was very weird. Now, of course, I know why you seemed so familiar. I was seeing myself in your portrait. Your youth caused the resemblance between us to be more pronounced."

Harry reached over and patted her hand. "You're my daughter, Laura. There's no doubt in my mind."

"Or in mine," she replied. She smiled affectionately.

Talbert's hopes soared. "We're going to make it, Laura. I really believe that. In time, we'll build a solid daughter and father relationship. And I'll never again deny you. When we get back to Silver Star, I'll publicly claim you as my daughter."

"No!" she exclaimed. "You can't do that!"

"Why not?"

"I don't want my mother branded an adulteress."

"You're right, of course. I'm just so damned proud of you that I wasn't thinking. Beth's memory and your reputation are more important than my pride."

"My reputation?"

He smiled tenderly. "Don't you understand?"

All at once, she did. She would certainly become the center of malicious gossip.

"You told Zeb the truth, but have you told anyone else?"

"Karen."

"You didn't tell Jim?"

"I thought about it, but I was afraid he'd let it slip to Marsha, and I don't want that woman knowing my business."

"We can trust Karen and Zeb, and we don't have to worry that Ed or Doyce will say anything."

It was very late, and Laura decided she might as well try to get some sleep. She knew it would be difficult, for thoughts of Craig would surely keep her awake.

She said good night to Harry, and went to the wagon. She got undressed, and laid down on her pallet. She tried to erase Craig from her thoughts, but the effort was futile. Against her will, she imagined him lying beside his bride . . . holding her in his arms . . . and making love to her. The vision was heartbreaking, but somehow she managed to forcefully thrust it from her mind.

Tears threatened, but she refused to give in to them.

275

Craig Branston wasn't worth one teardrop! A deep-buried anger of fire burned inside her, it flared to life and consumed her sorrow, leaving resentment blazing through her heart and mind. As far as she was concerned, Craig Branston could go to the devil!

Her anger, however, burned out much too quickly, and sadness emerged victoriously. She still loved Craig as deeply as ever! She wondered how long it would take for her love to die. Depression pressed down upon her, for she had a sinking feeling that she would always love him.

The next few days passed uneventfully, and, making good time, they covered many miles. Emotionally, however, the trip was very strained. Ed and Doyce avoided Laura as much as possible, Ed with cold indifference, and Doyce with disdain. Laura, taking their rudeness in stride, responded perfunctorily. It wasn't quite as easy for her to be unconcerned with Morgan's and Elias's presence, for she despised them. However, the Paiutes' threat was still imminent, and she knew she mustn't let her personal feelings interfere with safety.

Meanwhile, Marsha was playing havoc with Jim's emotions, for she was paying a lot of attention to Ed. Slowly, but surely, Jim was beginning to see the woman behind the pretty face, and he didn't like what he was forced to see. It was obvious to him that her interest in Talbert stemmed from money; someday he would inherit his father's empire. Still, Marsha was a puzzle, and he couldn't make the pieces fit. If all she craved was riches, then what did she want with *him?* It was a mystery he couldn't solve. Regardless, his love for Marsha was starting to fade.

Karen, on the other hand, found Marsha's interest in

Ed Talbert a hopeful sign. Surely Jim would now realize that Marsha was heartless and insensitive, and unworthy of his love. She hoped desperately that he would then notice her, but even if he didn't, she would be glad to see his relationship with Marsha come to an end. She loved Jim unselfishly and wanted him to be happy; she knew Marsha Donaldson would make his life miserable.

The travelers stopped in Seclusion, and the thriving settlement was a welcome sight, for they were looking forward to spending the night at the hotel and enjoying hot baths and soft beds.

Laura and Karen, sharing a room, retired early, for they were fatigued. The others, except for Doyce and his two companions, followed suit.

Seclusion had one saloon, called The Lost Mine. It was small, and like most of the settlement's buildings, it was constructed from logs. Going there, Doyce and his friends got a bottle of whiskey, found a back table, and sat down to talk.

Traveling with the others in such close proximity had made it impossible for them to plot murder, but now they had the privacy they needed.

"In order to get rid of Pa and Ed, we're gonna have to kill all of 'em." Doyce remarked. He sounded troubled, not about killing, but getting away with it.

"I got an idea," Morgan replied. "The shortest route to Silver Star will take us through part of the desert. There's no danger travelin' that way *if* you stay on the right trail. But what if we were to take over by gunpoint, and force them to travel farther into the desert, then empty their water, take their horses, and leave. There's no way any of 'em could survive. We'll head straight for Silver Star, and you can tell anyone who asks that your Pa was worried about the Circle T, so he sent us on ahead. Later, when their bones are discovered, people will take for granted that they took a wrong turn and got lost. It happens! Even experienced prospectors get lost in that desert, and go in circles until finally their water runs out and they die of thirst."

Doyce was impressed with Morgan's idea. This way, no one would ever suspect him of murder. Suddenly, though, he was plagued with doubt. What if one or more of them were to survive . . . ?

"Are you sure this will work?" Doyce asked. "What if all of 'em don't die?"

"I know that valley inside and out. A few years back, I did a lot of prospectin'. Where I aim to take 'em, there's no water for miles in any direction. Believe me, they'll die. You know how warm it's been the last couple of days, I can guarantee you that the desert is as hot as the fires of hell."

Doyce was almost convinced. "Are you sure they won't find any water?"

"You can count on it." Morgan didn't admit that he couldn't be totally sure, there were underground springs in the valley that he knew nothing about. But he was fairly certain there weren't any such springs in the area he had mentioned.

"All right," Doyce decided. "We'll wait until we get into the desert, then we'll take over. They won't be suspecting anything, so getting their guns should be easy. But we have to be careful, and remember Slade's a federal marshal, so use caution when you take his gun. He's a fast draw if I ever saw one."

Elias chuckled. "Doyce, you ain't thinkin' like a professional. All we gotta do is grab one of the women, and threaten to blow her brains out if he don't surrender his gun."

Morgan, smiling coldly, added, "Yeah, and let's grab

278

Laura Mills. I got a score to settle with her, and I wouldn't mind puttin' a bullet in her head."

"It's important that we don't shoot any of them," Doyce said impatiently. "We don't want any of their deaths to look like murder. If you need to grab Laura to get Slade's gun, then do so. But, for God's sake, don't shoot her! If he's hesitant to hand over his gun, knock her around a bit. That'll convince him."

Morgan concurred. "Yeah, you're right." He hoped Slade wouldn't surrender his gun too agreeably, for he was looking forward to hitting Laura. He'd teach the bitch a lesson or two! He rubbed his shoulder where Laura's knife had penetrated. The injury hadn't healed correctly, and, at times, it still pained him.

Doyce gulped down his whiskey, then refilled the glass. Plotting multiple deaths didn't touch his conscience, for he was an unfeeling and heartless individual. An icy smile curled his lips, soon now the Circle T and all its profits would belong solely to him. As soon as he got home, he'd take enough money from his father's safe to pay his gambling debt to Ganey. Then, when sufficient time had lapsed, he'd hire a search party to look for Harry, Ed, and the others. He hoped the searchers would find their bleached bones, but he knew that in the desert human remains weren't always discovered. But that wouldn't make any difference, if they weren't found, then they would be assumed dead, and he'd still get his inheritance.

Doyce was well pleased with himself, and with Morgan's plan.

Twenty-three

Laura was dreaming about Craig. In her dream, they were together again, and he had asked her to marry him. All of that faded abruptly, and Laura awoke. Melancholy tried to overpower her, and with tears threatening, she got quickly out of bed. Her resolve to avoid depression was still holding firm. She simply would not let Craig do that to her! He had taken her innocence and her heart, then had thrown them aside as though they were of no value! She was determined not to lose her own self-esteem! Somehow, she'd get through Craig's betrayal with her dignity intact!

Laura went to the washbasin and splashed water on her face. It was refreshing; the sun hadn't cleared the horizon yet, and the weather was already extremely warm.

She was getting dressed when Karen came awake. "My goodness, you're up early," she said drowsily.

"I couldn't sleep. I'm going downstairs and have a cup of coffee. I'll meet you in the dining room."

Karen watched her leave, and her heart ached for Laura, she knew losing Craig had to be tearing her to pieces. She admired Laura, though, for she was holding up remarkably well. Still, she couldn't help but wonder if Laura was as stalwart as she appeared. She was afraid that eventually such a facade was destined to crumble, and then Laura would be forced to confront her heartbreak. When that happened, Karen intended to be there for her, and to give her as much support as possible.

As Laura entered the hotel dining room, she was a little surprised to see Ed Talbert. She had expected to find Zeb, for he was usually up at the crack of dawn. Except for Ed, the room was empty.

Laura wasn't looking forward to a tête-à-tête with Ed Talbert, but she couldn't very well sit at another table. After all, they were traveling together. She squared her shoulders, lifted her chin proudly, and started her approach.

Ed pushed back his chair and got to his feet. "Good morning," he said, his tone not especially friendly.

"It seems we're the first ones up," she replied, sitting. A pot of coffee and several cups were on the table. She was about to serve herself; but, Ed, his manners impeccable, filled a cup and put it in front of her.

Laura wished one of the others would come down, being alone with Ed was an uncomfortable situation. She was certain that he didn't like her, however, she wasn't sure how she felt about him. Unlike his brothers, he had never done anything to warrant her disfavor. She had known him all her life, and he had always treated her with indifference.

Laura took a sip of her coffee, then put the cup back on the saucer. The room was so quiet that the china's making contact seemed unusually loud. Wondering if she should start a conversation, she looked at Ed, and was unsettled to find that he was staring at her.

"There's a resemblance between us," he said. "It's small, and isn't really noticeable unless one's looking for it."

She hadn't really thought about it before, but she now searched for a likeness. Yes, she could see that they shared the same blood. But, as Ed had pointed out, the resemblance wasn't striking.

"You look more like your mother than my father," he remarked.

"Our father," she corrected.

A humorless grin crossed his lips. "Yes, of course, our father. I suppose you were pleased to learn that you're his daughter."

"Why would you think that?"

"Pa's a very wealthy man, and I'm sure you plan to worm your way into his will."

Laura's anger was instantly piqued. "Well, you're wrong! I don't want his money! I want nothing from him except what I already have!"

"What's that?"

"His love and respect!"

Ed studied her thoughtfully. Could he be wrong about her? Doyce was certain she was after their father's money, but what if she wasn't? He decided to give her the benefit of the doubt.

"Pa doesn't believe you killed Lee," he said, changing the subject.

"I didn't!" she replied forcefully. "Whoever killed him wrote my name on that paper. I was framed."

"But why was the blame put on you?"

"I don't know. Maybe the murderer saw me leaving the house, and knew I would make a prime suspect."

"It's possible," Ed concurred.

"I hope to find out who did kill Lee, and clear my name once and for all. Jim Slade has offered to help me."

"You have my father and a federal marshal on your side, you're either very manipulative, or else—?"

"Or else, what?" she asked sharply.

"You're everything Pa claims you are—honest, compassionate, and innocent."

She looked him directly in the eyes. "I didn't kill Lee! I didn't like him, but I certainly had no reason to shoot him!"

Ed leaned toward believing her. He considered himself a fairly good judge of character, and he had a feeling she was telling the truth. "If you didn't shoot him, then who did?"

She shrugged. "Lee wasn't very likeable, I'm sure he had his share of enemies."

Ed took a drink of his coffee, his eyes watching her over the rim. For the first time, he tried to see her as a sister. It was hard to think of her in that way, he wasn't sure if he ever could. "Laura," he began, "when Pa told you the truth, how did it make you feel?"

"Angry, and a little bitter. I was also shocked, of course. But I'm learning to deal with it."

"Pa and your mother. Who would ever have thought it? Now I understand why there was a rift between Pa and your folks. I used to plead with him to tell me what had caused their feud, but he always refused to explain."

"I know what you mean," she said. "I always questioned Mama and Papa, but I never got any answers."

"And those yearly barbecues," Ed put in. "It was so obvious that your parents attended just to stop gossip."

"Well, things are now very clear." She sounded disheartened.

Ed picked up on her mood. "I'm sorry, Laura. I've been so wrapped up in my own feelings, that I haven't considered yours. Learning the truth about yourself couldn't have been easy."

His kindness surprised her as much as it pleased her.

She smiled warmly. "My goodness, you are human after all."

"Did you think I wasn't?"

"I've never known you to be anything but coldly distant."

"But that's where you're wrong. Believe it or not, I used to dream about courting you. You're very lovely, and I was quite attracted to you. I never did anything about it, because I knew Pa would disapprove. Also, you never gave me any encouragement."

"I never knew you felt that way. If I had known . . ."

"Ah, but it's a good thing we didn't get together, can you imagine the predicament we'd be in now?"

"Heaven forbid!" she exclaimed, her cheeks turning scarlet red. Suddenly, though, she found herself laughing.

Ed's mood turned as jovial as Laura's, and his deep laughter, mingling with hers, filled the room.

It was at this moment that Harry arrived. Poised in the open portal, he watched, pleased, as Ed and Laura laughed together. It did his heart good to see them getting along so well.

Zeb, coming up behind him, said, "That's a positive sign, ain't it?"

"Yes," Harry answered. "It certainly is."

"Well, you know what they say—blood's thicker than water."

Harry, glowing with happiness, walked over to their table, and asked, "What's so funny?"

Laura's blush deepened, she couldn't imagine telling him why they were laughing.

Ed, hiding a smile behind his hand, replied, "We were just speculating, Pa. That's all." He looked at Laura and winked.

Nurse Woodhouse had worked at the hospital in San Francisco for fifteen years, during which time she had seen several cases like Craig's. Sometimes the patient would slip in and out of unconsciousness for days, then awaken and make a complete recovery. Other times, however, the patient would sink into a coma and die.

Woodhouse, standing beside Craig's bed, hoped such a tragedy wasn't about to happen again. Her gaze, motherly in its affection, skimmed over Craig. Now that his facial bruises were healing, she could see that he was very handsome. She wondered if he had a family somewhere. She was certain that if he did, they weren't in San Francisco, for no one had come looking for him. She puzzled over who he was, and why he was evidently alone. Surely, he must have a sweetheart or a wife!

Suddenly, Craig moaned softly, it was almost inaudible, but the nurse's trained ear picked it up immediately. She leaned over the bed, saying clearly, "Sir, can you hear me?"

He moaned again, and placing a hand firmly on his shoulder, she said authoritatively, "Try to open your eyes. You must make yourself wake up." She was worried that he might sink permanently into an unconscious state.

Craig, responding to the commanding voice, opened his eyes. At first, his vision was blurry, but as it cleared he could make out a large, strapping woman looking down at him. She was dressed all in white, a nurse's uniform!

"Am I . . . am I in a hospital?" he asked weakly.

"Yes, sir, you certainly are." A water pitcher was beside his bed, she filled a glass, elevated his head, and offered him a drink.

He drank thirstily, for his mouth and throat were terribly dry.

"How long have I been here?"

"For days," she replied.

Craig was astounded.

"I was beginning to fear that we were going to lose you."

"Why am I here? What happened to me?"

"Don't you remember?"

He shook his head.

"Well, it'll come back to you." She smiled cheerfully, told him she would get the doctor, and hurried away.

Craig's head throbbed, but despite the pain, he forced himself to concentrate. Initially, his mind refused to cooperate, but slowly his memories returned. He remembered visiting the school, and how delighted he had been to learn that Deborah planned to marry another man. He met her fiance, and at their insistence, he joined them for an early brunch. Then, anxious to tell Laura the wonderful news, he offered the couple his best wishes, and left as quickly as possible.

At this point, Craig drew a blank, and he had to concentrate even harder. Then, suddenly, as though a dark curtain had been ripped aside, his mind saw and remembered. Leaving the school, he had ridden into the center of the city. As he rode past an alleyway, he detected a woman's feeble cry for help. Dismounting, he rushed to her aid. She was lying sprawled, her clothes crumpled, she wasn't moving, and Craig wondered if she was dead.

He knelt beside her, but, at that moment, two huge men grabbed him from behind. The woman, unharmed, leapt to her feet and took his wallet. Craig was totally disgusted with himself; my God, he had been taken by one of the oldest scams around.

He thought the men would let him go, then flee with the woman and his money, but Craig had thought wrong. Violence was their goal, and they beat him unmercifully. As one held him, the other one delivered pile-driving blows to his stomach and ribs, then finishing him off, he smashed his fist more than once across Craig's jaw.

The man holding Craig released him, and as Craig toppled to the ground, he drew back his foot and kicked him in the head. The vicious blow knocked him unconscious.

Now, recalling the scene in detail sparked Branston's anger, however, his anger was aimed mostly at himself. He could hardly believe that he had foolishly walked into such a trap!

He started to sit up, but a sharp pain shooting through his ribs changed his mind. He groaned testily, he hated being flat on his back like this!

Nurse Woodhouse returned with the doctor. The physician was middle-aged, sported a goatee, and wore spectacles. A warm smile was on his face; he was dedicated to his profession, and was pleased that his patient had regained consciousness.

"I am Doctor Anderson," he said. He leaned over the bed, checked Craig's eyes, then had him follow his finger as he moved it back and forth in front of his face. Then, with a stethoscope, he listened to Craig's heartbeat, it was strong and regular.

"What's your name, young man?"

"Craig Branston."

"Do you remember what happened to you?"

"I was beaten and robbed."

"You were beaten unconscious, Mr. Branston. I was afraid you were going to slip into a coma. But it seems you'll make a complete recovery. However, you do have a couple of broken ribs, and they'll keep you in bed for a few more days." He gave Craig a drink of water, then asked, "Is San Francisco your home?"

"No, I'm from Abilene."

"I see. You're traveling alone then?"

"No, I'm not. I have friends staying at the Winston."

287

"I've been in contact with the authorities, and they don't have a Craig Branston listed as a missing person. You've been here for days, why haven't your friends tried to find you?"

"I don't know," he replied. It didn't make sense. He couldn't imagine Laura not scouring the city for him.

Doctor Anderson turned and motioned to an attendant, who hurried over. It was the same man who had talked to Marsha.

"Jack," the doctor began, "I want you to go to the Winston. Mr. Branston says he has friends staying there. Let them know that Craig Branston is here." Anderson looked at Craig. "For whom should he ask?"

"Laura Mills. If for some reason she's not available, ask for anyone in her party. The desk clerk will know who they are."

The attendant went on his way, and shortly thereafter, Doctor Anderson and the nurse left. Alone, Craig tried to figure out why Laura hadn't gone to the authorities, but he couldn't come up with a logical explanation.

The nurse brought him a bowl of soup; although he was hungry, he was too worried to eat very much. He did manage to finish half of it, and the nurse took away the tray.

Time crawled by as Craig waited for Jack's return. He wondered if Laura would arrive with the attendant; surely she would!

Jack was gone close to an hour, and when he came back, Craig was disappointed to find he was alone. He went to Craig's bed, pulled up a chair, and sat down.

"I talked to the desk clerk," he began. "Laura Mills and her party checked out days ago."

"What?" Craig exclaimed. "But that can't be!"

288

"I'm sorry, sir, but it seems they checked out the day after you were admitted to the hospital."

"Laura wouldn't leave town without finding out what happened to me!" Craig was visibly upset.

"Try not to get excited, Mr. Branston. It isn't good for your condition."

"To hell with my condition!" Craig mumbled. Intending to go to the Winston himself, he threw back the covers and attempted to get out of bed. Excruciating pain cut into his rib cage; with a grimace, he sat up, and gingerly put his feet on the floor.

"Mr. Branston, you're too weak to stand up!" Jack remarked firmly, moving to help him lie back down.

Craig flung off the man's hand, but as he got to his feet, dizziness overtook him, and he had to grab the attendant's arm to keep from falling.

Gently, Jack assisted him back onto the bed, and drew the covers up. "Mr. Branston, it's going to be a few more days before you're able to move around."

"But I've got to find out what's going on. I tell you, Laura wouldn't leave town without me! I can't believe she didn't look for me."

"Only one woman came here looking for a missing person. She was a real pretty lady. She didn't give her name, but I brought her in here to see you. But you weren't the man she was trying to find. As far as I know, she's the only person who's been here looking for someone."

"Do you know where The Lucky Lady is?"

"Sure, I've been there a few times."

"Will you please go there and ask Johnny Mills to come see me? He's the proprietor."

"You want me to go now?"

"If you don't mind."

Jack was more than willing to help, and he left at once.

Again, Craig was alone to ponder Laura's actions. That she and the others had checked out of the hotel was more than he could grasp. Laura loved him, Slade was his friend, and Talbert and Zeb seemed to like him; that they would leave like this didn't make any sense. There had to be an explanation! But what? What? He couldn't think of one!

This time Jack was gone more than an hour, but when he returned, Johnny Mills was with him. He showed Johnny to the bed, then left.

"Hello, Mr. Branston," Johnny said, drawing up a chair and sitting. He had only seen Craig once, the day he had stopped at The Lucky Lady with Zeb.

"Call me Craig."

Johnny responded in kind, then asked Craig why he was in the hospital.

He quickly told him what had happened. "Is it true that Laura and the others checked out of the Winston?"

"Yes, they left days ago. Zeb stopped by to see me the night before they planned to leave. He wanted to say good-bye."

"Did he say anything about me?"

"No, not that I can remember."

"Damn it! This whole thing is crazy! Laura and I were supposed to get married. She wouldn't leave town this way!"

"Married!" Johnny remarked, surprised. "She didn't tell me she was getting married."

"I hadn't exactly asked her, but we had an understanding."

"Well, I'm sorry, but she's gone."

Craig was starting to fume. Had Laura betrayed him? God, no! He couldn't believe such a thing! She loved him! But, damn it, if she loved him, how could she leave town?

Didn't she even bother to look for him? Well, he'd be out of here in a couple of days, then he'd head for Silver Star, find Laura, and demand some answers!

"Johnny," he began, "I need your help."

"I'll help you if I can."

"Will you go to the Winston, get my belongings, and keep them until I get out of here? Although I was robbed, I still have some money hidden in my carpetbag. It's sewn into the lining. Take out enough to cover my horse's keep. It's at Johnson's Livery."

"Sure, I'll do that for you. But there's no reason to leave your horse at the livery. I have private stables behind my casino. I'll put your horse there."

"Thanks, Johnny. I appreciate your kindness."

They talked a few minutes more, then Johnny took his leave. First, he stopped at the hotel. The usual clerk was on duty, he got Craig's belongings from the storage room, and handed them over, explaining to Johnny that he'd received a message to keep them for two weeks. Such a message puzzled Johnny, but he didn't say anything about it.

After that, he went to the stables, Johnson was in charge, and he told Johnny that he had received two week's keep for Branston's horse. He said a cabbie had brought the money; in fact, the man was due at any moment. He came for his own horse this time every day.

Johnny decided to wait and question him. A few minutes later, the man arrived. He talked freely, explaining that a woman had paid him to run the errands. He didn't know her name, but he gave Johnny a good description.

Johnny was certain that the woman in question was Marsha Donaldson.

Returning to the casino, Johnny put Craig's horse in his private stables, then stored his belongings in his own room. He went down to the bar, ordered a brandy, and pondered Marsha's actions. He decided she and Craig had once been in love, and Marsha was now acting like a woman scorned.

He shrugged the puzzle aside, took a big drink of brandy, and thought no more about it.

Twenty-four

Laura dreaded traveling through the desert, she didn't like the barren region and knew it would be terribly hot. Thank goodness, they had two filled water barrels! The verdant tableau thinned out, and began to look more desertlike. Grassy areas disappeared . . . trees were supplanted by sagebrush . . . and the soil became dry and sandy. To Laura, the landscape was depressing, the valley seemed shunned by nature, and even by God, who had created it.

They stopped and made camp at dusk. The day had been extremely warm, but full darkness brought a cool breeze that drifted in gusts across the land.

Following supper, Marsha, sitting at the fire beside Ed, touched his arm, and asked, "Will you take a walk with me?"

Harry had talked to Ed about Marsha, and he was forewarned. Nevertheless, he saw no reason to refuse. He got up, took her hand, and helped her to her feet.

Zeb, watching them, warned, "Don't wander too far, or you might find your scalps hangin' from a Paiute's belt."

Ed wasn't too concerned; Marsha, however, shuddered at the thought.

Jim was tending to the horses, but he caught sight of the pair as they strolled away from the fire. He had an impulse to go after them and confront Marsha once and for all! He thought about it, then decided not to bother. The realization that he no longer cared about Marsha struck without warning, and it gave him quite a jolt. He recovered quickly, and with an inner smile, went back to watering the horses. Thank God, he was over Marsha Donaldson! He didn't know love could die so suddenly, but, then, perhaps he had never truly been in love. More than likely, he had simply been infatuated!

Marsha and Ed didn't walk very far before stopping. Marsha wasn't about to leave herself vulnerable to an Indian attack! The cloudless sky was dominated by a half-moon, and its saffron glow cloaked the land with a romantic hue. Marsha watched as Ed reached into his pocket, removed a cheroot, and lit it. She was quite impressed with Harry's oldest son, and thought him notably handsome. She had decided to become Mrs. Ed Talbert, and knew it was time to start weaving her web. This time, however, she wasn't planning to marry and then become a widow; quite the contrary, she intended to hold on to Ed Talbert for a lifetime. He was the kind of man she had always dreamed of marrying—young, rich, distinguished, and handsome. She knew it was important that she tread carefully, for Harry Talbert had no doubt taken his sons aside and talked against her. That, however, was not a deterrent; she'd simply find a way to convince Ed that his father was wrong.

Now, favoring Ed with a glamorous smile, she said, "I heard Silver Star is a very nice place, and I'm considering staying there." It was merely an excuse to live in Ed's hometown so she could entrap him.

He looked at her somewhat questioningly. "Aren't you and Jim Slade supposed to get married?"

Marsha was prepared for the query. "Jim and I aren't exactly engaged," she fibbed. "He asked me to marry him, and I told him I'd think about it."

"And?" He watched her closely.

"I'm very fond of Jim, but I'm not in love with him. I don't plan to marry him, but I haven't told him yet, because I want to let him down gently. So you won't say anything, will you?"

"No, I won't betray your confidence. But I advise you to be perfectly honest with Slade. You should tell him how you feel."

"Oh, I intend to do just that." She spoke truthfully, she did plan to cast Jim out of her life, she just hadn't decided yet how to go about it. She was still wary about angering him.

Ed, puffing on his cheroot, wondered if his father had been right about Marsha. Was she as conniving as he claimed, and was she about to use her seductive charms on him? Well, he wasn't one to play games, and hoped she'd hurry and make a move so he could dissuade her.

But Marsha was wise and had other tactics in mind. The best way to prove that Harry had misjudged her, was to behave in a demure fashion. She would use her feminine wiles on Ed Talbert, but she'd do so subtly and with seductive undertones.

"It's a beautiful night, isn't it?" she asked, gazing up at the myriad of stars dotting the heavens. "The weather in the desert is so strange, the days are hot but the nights are cool."

"Yes, but we can't get out of this desert any too soon for me. I don't like this place."

"I know what you mean," she replied. She drew him into an easy conversation, and Ed found himself talking about the Circle T, his family, and his ambitions. Marsha, in turn, told Ed the same fabricated story that she had related to others. With eyes brimming, she told him that after her first husband's death she had come westward to start a new life. She spoke of her made-up husband in such detail that Ed had no reason to doubt the man's existence. She also talked about Jerry Donaldson, and swore that she had known nothing about the embezzlement.

Marsha played her cards wisely, but she knew it was now time to fold her hand and call it a night, so she suggested they go back to camp. She was proud of herself, for her behavior had certainly been above reproach. She was also sure that Ed had fallen for her ploy—hook, line, and sinker. Now Harry Talbert would have a difficult time persuading his son that she was—as Harry had put it—a tramp! She intended to continue her ladylike facade until Ed was totally smitten, then she would tempt him, inveigle him, but withhold her body until she had a wedding ring on her finger!

As they returned, Jim was placing his bedroll beside the wagon, but Marsha didn't see him—she only had eyes for Ed Talbert. She bid him a pleasant good night; he gave her a hand up into the wagon, and went to the fire.

Karen, alone, was inside sitting on her pallet. She had seen Marsha leave with Talbert, and the woman's insensitivity angered her. How could she hurt a man as kind as Jim Slade?

Marsha, aware that Karen's expression was far from genial, asked, "What's wrong with you?"

Outside, Jim could hear their conversation. He wasn't the type to eavesdrop, and he started to move away, but Karen's reply held him riveted.

"How dare you treat Jim so horridly! I've never known anyone so brazen! When you left with Ed Talbert, did you stop to think what that did to Jim? He must be terribly upset!"

Marsha, hands on hips, eyed Karen haughtily. "I'm not interested in Jim, and if you want him, he's all yours." Her sudden laugh was derisive. "But, of course, he wouldn't look twice at a mousy little nobody like you. You're pathetic, Karen! When Jim was sick, you stayed by his side, nursing him through the night! What did it get you? He thinks I was the one who took care of him! You didn't even have the gumption to tell him it was you! Why, you silly little fool, he doesn't even know you exist!"

Karen leapt to her feet. "That's not true! Jim and I are good friends. And just for the record, I didn't tell him I was the one who nursed him because I want his love, not his gratitude!"

Jim, listening, was taken aback. Marsha's words didn't surprise him, for he was no longer blindly in love. Karen, on the other hand, amazed him. He'd had no idea that she felt that way about him.

Meanwhile, inside the wagon, the discussion continued.

"Marsha," Karen was saying, "I don't understand why you keep leading Jim on! What do you want from him?"

"Nothing!" she replied tersely. Furtively, her gaze dropped to the compartment hidden beneath the wagon. She wanted Slade out of her life so she could start spending her stolen funds!

"Why did you tell Jim that you'd marry him?" Karen demanded. "Apparently, you never intended to go through with it!"

Marsha was losing patience. "That's my business, and you keep your nose out of it! Who do you think you are to question me like this?"

Karen's large eyes were flashing with fury. "Marsha, someday you're going to get what's coming to you!" With that, Karen went to the backboard. She was wearing a riding skirt, and had no difficulty climbing to the ground. She was fuming, and her heart was pounding. She despised Marsha Donaldson!

When Jim suddenly stepped around the corner of the wagon, his presence took her by surprise. That surprise, however, was mild compared to the shock she felt when he took her arm, said they were going to take a walk, and led her away from the campsite.

When they were out of sight of the others, Jim stopped, turned to her, and said, "I overheard your conversation with Marsha."

She blushed profusely.

"Karen, please don't be embarrassed. And you don't have to worry about me. I no longer love Marsha. I don't suppose I ever did, not really. I was just infatuated with a beautiful woman. I could never truly love someone like her. She's selfish, insensitive, and totally involved with herself. That's not the kind of woman I intend to marry." He placed his hands on her shoulders, and gazed tenderly down into her eyes. "Why didn't you tell me you were the one who took care of me when I was sick?"

"If you overheard our conversation, then you already know the answer."

"You want my love, and not my gratitude?"

Her shyness made her look away.

Jim put a hand beneath her chin, and tilted her face up to his. "Look at me," he said gently. She did as he asked. "You have my gratitude whether you want it or not."

Karen's heart sank, she had been hoping for more encouraging words.

"And, as for my love," he continued, "I can't give you any guarantees; not yet. But, maybe, in time . . . ?"

Happiness suddenly sprang up in her heart, and overcoming her shyness, she murmured, "We have plenty of time, Jim."

He studied her face in the moonlight. Her delicate features were finely sculpted, and her dark eyes were huge and loving. Her hair was unbound, and the cool breeze ruffled the long tresses, causing a tendril to fall across her cheek. He reached out and brushed the silky lock aside. His perusal continued; he was finding Karen desirable.

In the meantime, Karen was mesmerized by Jim's closeness, and her heart was hammering. Her eyes filled with admiration as she studied his arresting good looks. He had a sensuous face, direct and serious, yet, it had a boyish quality that was irresistible. He was impressively tall, and very masculine. Excitement mounted within her as she dreamed of being held in his strong, powerful arms. She knew she would not only feel wonderfully crushed by his strength, but also safe and secure!

Slowly, Jim drew her against him, bent his head, and touched his lips to hers. It was a light kiss, but a tender, lingering one. The sensation brought a warm tingle to his depths, as well as to Karen's.

Jim, somewhat stunned by the warm feelings coursing through his heart, released her reluctantly. He regarded her with something much deeper than physical desire.

His expression confused her. "What are you thinking about?" Had he found her kiss disappointing? Was he wishing she was Marsha Donaldson?

He smiled tenderly. "When I was sick, a caring, gentle angel washing my fever-racked body helped keep me alive." He took her hands into his, and turned them so her palms were facing upwards. "But it was the love in these hands that pulled me through. I could feel that love, I could sense it. Your love, Karen, gave me the strength to fight off death." Gently, he lifted her hands to his lips, and kissed both palms. Then, suddenly, he brought her into his arms, and this time his mouth claimed hers demandingly.

With a small gasp of wonder, she leaned against his firm body and surrendered breathlessly. When he finally released her, she was trembling, for his kiss had awakened her deepest passion. She had never known such primitive excitement, her heart was racing, and desire was pulsing through her.

Jim's need was also burning, but he forcefully controlled

299

his longing. He wanted very much to make love to Karen, but not now and not here—she deserved much better than that! She also had a right to expect a firm commitment, and he'd not make love to her until he could do so with no reservations, and from the bottom of his heart.

He took her hand, and suggested they return to camp. Karen, walking beside him, had never been happier, for she was certain that Jim was falling in love!

When Karen returned to the wagon, Marsha and Laura were in their beds, and thinking they were asleep, she undressed quietly and retired. Laura, however, was wide-awake. She knew Karen had taken a walk with Jim, and she was pleased. That Karen was in love with Jim was obvious to Laura, and she was hopeful that Jim would come to his senses and cast Marsha aside for Karen.

Laura tried vainly to fall asleep, but, as always, thoughts of Craig kept her awake. Finally, giving up, she vacated her bed, dressed quickly, and went outside. Due to the Indian threat, the men were now standing guard in pairs. She looked about the campsite, Harry and Zeb weren't in sight, and she figured they were taking the first watch. She glanced around for Lobo, she didn't see him and wondered if he was with Zeb. She was concerned that the wolf might wander and stay away through the night. If he wasn't back by morning, she'd hesitate to break camp and leave without him. Chances were good that he would catch up to her, but what if he didn't? She hated the thought of losing Lobo, he meant too much to her.

Deciding to find Zeb and see if Lobo was with him, she gazed into the distance. The barren region made it possible for her to make out a man's silhouette. From here, though, she couldn't be sure if it was Harry or Zeb. The men had apparently taken up separate positions.

She started forth when a movement at her side caught her attention. She paused, turned about, and was unnerved to find Morgan standing beside her. He seemed to materialize out of thin air.

His bearded face was grinning, but the expression in his eyes was hard and cruel. "How come you ain't said nothin' to the others 'bout me and Elias? If old man Talbert knew what we tried to do to you, he'd send us packin'."

Laura took a step backwards, the man was so close she could actually smell his fetid breath. "The Paiutes is the reason I haven't said anything. Right now, we need your gun and Elias's."

"You're a real level-headed lady, ain't you? Tell me, you still carry that knife in your boot?"

"Believe me, you don't want to find out."

"Is that a threat?"

"Stay away from me, Morgan, or the next time you'll find my knife plunged in your heart!" With that, she whirled about and walked away.

Doyce came up quietly behind Morgan. He touched the man's shoulder, and, startled, Morgan swung around. His first instinct was to strike out, and his fists were doubled.

"Goddamn!" Morgan uttered. "Don't sneak up on me like that!"

"Keep your voice down," Doyce warned. "Why were you talking to Laura? You didn't say anything to make her suspicious, did you?"

"Naw, of course not. I only talked to her for minute or so, and we didn't say much of anything."

Doyce breathed a relieved sigh. He knew Morgan detested Laura, and when he saw them talking, he had been afraid Morgan might cause a scene. Keeping his voice low, he said, "I just talked to Elias, and it's on for the morning. You and Elias have the last watch, that will make it easy for you to take over the camp. Everyone will be asleep."

Morgan smiled. "All these sonsofbitches will wake up lookin' down a gun barrel."

"Good!" Doyce whispered. "Now, let's get some sleep, tomorrow's gonna be quite a day."

Meanwhile, Laura had found Zeb, and was relieved to see that Lobo was with him. She stood with her uncle, conversing quietly. Zeb was worried about her, he knew she was having trouble sleeping. Also, her appetite was poor, she merely picked at her food.

Now, out of concern, he murmured, "You know, they say nobody ever died of a broken heart, but that ain't always true. Not that I think you're gonna give up, wilt away, and die. You got too much spunk for that. But, Laura, you gotta start takin' better care of yourself. A body needs sleep and food."

She watched him speculatively. "Why do I get this feeling that you knew someone who died of a broken heart?"

"I don't know," he answered, his tone evasive.

"Well, I *do* know. It was the way you said it. Mama told me that you were once married, but your wife died. Were you thinking about her?"

Zeb didn't say anything for a long moment, then with a heavy sigh, he replied, "I was in my early twenties when I got married. Lord, that was years before you were born. In fact, your Ma was only a youngster. My wife's name was Maggie. I reckon you know that I was raised on a farm in Ohio. Maggie and her folks were our neighbors. I was still a sapling when I knew that someday I'd marry Maggie Whitney. We fell in love at a young age, and neither of us ever looked at anyone else. When the time was right, we got married. But I didn't see where there was any future for us in Ohio. I had a hankerin' to go westward. Maggie was kinda reluctant, but I talked her into it. Hell, she loved me enough to follow me to the ends of the earth. We ended up in Texas, where we built a homestead by the Brazos River. We were there 'bout a year when the Comanches got in an uproar. One of their villages had been attacked by a group of scalp hunters. Back then, the government paid money for Indian scalps. The warriors were away hunting, and only women, children, and old men were in the village. It didn't make any difference, the scalp hunters massacred every last one of them. The warriors, when they returned, wanted revenge, and they left burning homes and dead bodies in their wake. I took Maggie to the fort, left her there, and rode with the Texas Rangers. The Comanches surrounded us; we were outnumbered and didn't stand a chance. I was shot, fell off my horse, and lost consciousness. When I came to, I saw that the Comanches had hacked the Rangers' bodies into pieces, and were burnin' their remains in one big pile. I've never seen a more God-awful sight. Apparently, I was the only one left alive. For some reason, which I never learned, I was taken prisoner. For two years, I was a captive slave. I've never told anyone about the degradation I suffered at the hands of the Comanches, and I don't intend to talk about it now. There are some things so horrible that a man has to keep them to himself. Well, to shorten a long story, I managed to escape, and make my way back to the fort. I'd been gone for two years, so I didn't expect to find Maggie there. I figured she went back to Ohio. There was no reason for her to wait, she and everyone else thought I died along with the others. After the Comanches finished with those bodies, there was no way to identify them, or even to know how many there were."

Zeb paused, collected his thoughts, and continued, "I learned that Maggie had died and was buried in the cemetery behind the fort. At the time of my capture, she was pregnant with our first child, but when she heard I was dead, she became so ill that she lost the baby. After that, she simply pined away. I was told she died of a broken heart."

Laura moved close and slipped her arm around Zeb's waist. "Mama never told me anything about this."

"I never gave her any details." He placed an arm about her shoulders.

"I'm sorry, Uncle Zeb. If only Maggie had remained strong. Dear God, you would have come back to her!"

"Maggie never had your kind of strength. I lost her over thirty years ago, and I still haven't forgiven myself for takin' her to Texas. Maybe if we had stayed in Ohio . . . ?"

"Why didn't you ever remarry?"

"Never fell in love again. I guess I just didn't have the heart."

Laura kissed his bearded cheek. "I love you, Uncle Zeb."

His mood brightened. "Have I ever told you that you're my favorite niece?"

"I'm your only niece," she said, punching his arm playfully.

"Well, if I had a dozen of 'em, you'd no doubt be my favorite."

Twenty-five

Morgan and Elias, having stood the last watch, waited for dawn to break before slipping back to the campsite. The other men were asleep with their weapons close beside their bedrolls. Moving furtively, Morgan and Elias began to gather the guns. Doyce, now awake, gave them a hand. They went last to Jim Slade; and, Elias, his pistol drawn, watched cautiously as Morgan reached down to pick up the marshal's rifle.

Although Jim was asleep, his instincts were uncannily attuned to danger, and he was suddenly awake. He made a grab for his rifle at the same moment Morgan's hand touched it.

"Don't try it, Marshal!" Elias warned, cocking his pistol.

Jim froze.

Chuckling, Morgan took the rifle, then gestured for Jim to get up.

Carefully, he got to his feet.

Jim was using his saddle as a pillow, and Morgan found his holster and pistol beneath it. He then glanced at the other men, who were now awake. Only Slade wore a holster, the others carried rifles, except for Zeb, who toted a shotgun. Unarming them had been as easy as taking candy from a baby!

Doyce fired a shot in the air and brought the camp awake. The men were shocked and befuddled to find their weapons gone, and the camp taken over by Doyce, Morgan, and Elias. Doyce's gun was not aimed at anyone in particular, he simply moved it back and forth from one man to the other, as though he expected one of them to lurch at any moment.

"What the hell's going on?" Harry demanded.

"Shut up, old man!" Morgan uttered. He went to the back of the wagon, and called loudly, "You women get out here! Now, on the double!"

The man's bellowing moved them to dress more quickly; the shot had already awakened them.

"We'll be right there!" Laura called back.

The ladies quickly threw on their clothes; that something was wrong was obvious. Were there Paiutes in the vicinity? Fearing an Indian attack, the women hurried outside with their clothes still partially unbuttoned. Their hair, unbrushed, was in disarray. They were completely taken aback to find Doyce and his two companions holding the others at gunpoint.

"My God!" Laura burst out, staring wide-eyed at Morgan. "Why are you doing this?"

A threatening smile crawled to his lips, curling itself like a rattlesnake about to strike. "Don't ask questions! Just do as I say! Have you got that knife stuck in your boot?"

She cast him a look of contempt, then bent over, removed her knife, and handed it to him.

He took it and stuck it in his belt. He was itching to get even with Laura, and with revenge in his eyes, he took a step toward her.

But Doyce's commanding voice suddenly halted him. "Morgan, get everyone into one group. That way, it'll be easier to watch them."

"Later, I got a score to settle with you!" he mumbled to

Laura. Then doing as Doyce ordered, he told the ladies to get over by the men.

"Damn it, Doyce!" Harry raged. "Tell me what the hell's going on!"

"Are you blind, Pa? What's happening is quite obvious! For once, I'm taking charge! And there's not a damned thing you or Ed can do about it!"

"I don't understand why!" he replied angrily.

Doyce had always despised his father, and now with a lifetime of hate simmering within him, he moved over and stood before Harry.

Laura, watching, was appalled at the awful loathing she saw on Doyce's face.

"I'll tell you why I'm doing this, Pa! I want the Circle T! I thought about waiting around for you to die, but, hell, as healthy as you are, you'll probably live another twenty years or so! Besides, I bet you plan to leave the ranch to Ed! After all, he's always been your favorite!" Doyce, now glowering at Ed, continued, "You arrogant ass! I've hated you since we were boys! You've always bossed me around, and you find fault with everything I do!"

"You crazy bastard!" Ed said, gritting his teeth.

"Yeah? We'll see whether I'm crazy or not!"

"Doyce!" Harry demanded. "What do you plan to do with us?"

He laughed hideously. "You're gonna die, every last one of you!"

"Dear God!" Harry groaned. "Kill me, if you want! But let the others go!"

"Pa, you know I can't do that! I mean, I sure can't let Ed live. These others are witnesses, that means they gotta be eliminated." He cast Laura a murderous look. "Especially you, dear sister!"

Harry, his instincts protective, slipped an arm about Laura's shoulders, drawing her close.

Doyce found the impotent gesture humorous, and he laughed tersely. "Your arm around her ain't gonna keep her alive, Pa. You know, even if she *had* killed Lee, I think you'd still try to save your love-child."

"If she *had* killed Lee? How do you know she didn't?"

"Because I killed him, that's why."

"God in heaven!" Harry moaned wretchedly.

"I was in town that night, remember? When I left, you and Ed were still at the saloon. I rode straight home, and was puttin' my horse in the corral when I saw Laura riding away. She never looked in my direction, so she didn't even know I was there. I went into the house and to the study. It was empty. I guess Lee had gone to his room. I was plannin' on having a nightcap, but then that big safe of yours caught my eye. I knew if I just helped myself to the money, you'd probably get mad enough to throw me out. So I decided to make it look like robbery. I ran to the toolshed, got what I needed, and returned. I planned to use the combination to unlock it, take out the money, then use my tools to make it look like the door was forced open. I was just startin' to turn the lock, when Lee caught me. The goddamned bastard said he was going to tell you what I was up to! We got into a scuffle, I took his gun, and shot him just as a clap of thunder hit. Otherwise, Joshua would have heard the shot. Thinkin' fast, I scribbled Laura's name on a piece of paper, and dropped it next to Lee's body. I was planning to blame her for the murder, as well as the robbery. But before I could open the safe, I heard you and Ed come into the house. I grabbed the tools, and crept up the back stairs." Doyce turned to Laura. "You know, I didn't give a damn whether or not you were caught. All I wanted was for everyone to think you killed Lee. That's why, unlike Ed, I wasn't all hell-bent on pursuin' you."

"Doyce," Harry began, his voice terribly strained,

"why did you need money so badly?"

"I owe Ganey."

"My God, how many times have I told you not to gamble with that man?"

"Don't preach me to me, Pa! Those days are over!" A demonic, spine-chilling laugh came from deep within. "I don't ever have to listen to one of your lectures again!"

Laura looked into Harry's face. His initial shock had waned, and now disillusionment and heartbreaking pain took over. It seemed to Laura that the man aged before her very eyes.

"Doyce, you're my son!" he groaned pathetically. "I've always loved you! You've disappointed me, angered me, and tried my patience. But through it all, I loved you! Dear God, you're my own flesh and blood!"

"If you love me, then that's your problem, because I sure as hell don't give a damn about you!"

"Doyce," Morgan spoke up. "We ain't got time for family gripes! We gotta get movin'!"

"How do you intend to kill us?" Ed asked his brother.

"I ain't gonna kill you," he replied. "The desert's gonna do it for me. We're going to take you farther into the desert, empty your water, take the horses, and leave all of you there to rot."

"Why, you murdering sonofabitch!" Jim bellowed, taking a step toward Doyce.

Elias, moving quickly, slammed the butt of his rifle across Slade's head, the powerful blow knocking him to his knees.

Karen and Zeb helped him back up. "Keep a lid on your temper," Zeb warned Jim quietly. "For now, just do as these bastards say, 'fore you get yourself killed."

Jim's head was bleeding, he removed his neckerchief and blotted the flow.

Doyce, taking charge, told Morgan and Elias to leave

Joshua unbound, but to tie the other men, then saddle their horses and help them mount. He planned for the women to ride inside the wagon with Joshua driving the team.

When his comrades had completed their tasks, Doyce sent Elias to the wagon to search for weapons. He returned with Jerry Donaldson's shotgun.

They packed the extra weapons on Laura's mare, then ordered the women inside the wagon, and Joshua onto the driver's seat.

Doyce, ready to pull out, swung up onto his horse. Suddenly his stomach growled, reminding him that breakfast had been forgotten. He rode to the back of the wagon, and asked the women, "You got anything in there to eat?"

Marsha, intending to get on Doyce's good side, quickly found a couple of biscuits left over from last night's supper. "Will these do?" she asked, handing them to him.

"I guess cold biscuits are better than nothing at all."

She smiled invitingly. "Is there anything else I can do for you?"

Doyce, reading the invitation behind her smile, answered with a lustful grin, "Later, baby doll." He left to ride to the front of the wagon.

Marsha watched until he was out of sight, then she turned warily around to face Laura and Karen. Their angry expressions came as no surprise.

"You make me sick!" Laura uttered furiously.

"Is that right?" Marsha responded huffily. "Well, you're going to be a lot worse than sick, you're going to be dead! But I intend to survive, and if that means playing up to Doyce Talbert, then that's exactly what I'll do!"

"You stupid fool!" Laura remarked. "Doyce won't spare your life! He doesn't intend to leave any witnesses. He'll bed you, but that won't stop him from killing you!"

"We'll see about that!" she retorted.

"Laura," Karen said, "don't try to dissuade her. I hope when Doyce leaves, he takes her with him. I don't want to spend the last days of my life with someone like her."

Marsha eyed Karen bitterly. "My goodness, you certainly have changed. You used to be such a prim, quiet little mouse. What brought on such a transformation? Did Jim do this to you? Did he ram you with his magic wand and turn you into a real woman?"

Joshua, driving the team, couldn't help but overhear their conversation. He turned, glanced over his shoulder, and said strongly, "You women bickerin' like that ain't gonna make things any better. At a time like this, we gotta stick together."

"Joshua's right," Laura remarked. "Let's cool our tempers, and put our personal feelings aside."

Karen, agreeing, nodded tersely.

Marsha cast both women a resentful glare, but she didn't say anything.

Laura moved so she could gaze out the back of the wagon. Elias was riding behind. Doyce had no doubt placed him there to make sure she or one of the others didn't jump to the ground and try to escape. Laura snickered—in the desert—on foot—there was no escape!

She wiped at her perspiring brow; the temperature was climbing steadily. The morning sun, rising higher in the cloudless sky, would soon hang over the desert like a seething, burnished ball of brass. Laura watched vacantly as the wagon slowly made its way across the barren region. The scenery consisted of clumps of dried sagebrush and intermittent flowering cactus. Laura kept one such cactus in her vision as long as possible, for its colorful red flower made the landscape seem less dreary.

The wagon took a wide turn, and Laura could now see the distant mountain range. It loomed majestically over the desert, and its tall peaks were filled with a purple mist, but the scorching sun had bleached the highest tips to white. This godforsaken land had managed to deface its beauty.

Laura turned her back to the passing scenery as, against her will, Craig came to mind. She supposed he was in Seattle, enjoying his honeymoon. Inside, she laughed bitterly. Fate had certainly led Craig and her onto different roads—he was having the time of his life—and she was about to lose hers!

The Lucky Lady didn't open for business until after the noon hour, however, Craig, explaining that he needed to see Mr. Mills, was taken to Johnny's office. The employee knocked on the door, announced Branston, then left to go about his business.

Johnny was surprised to see Craig, he thought he'd be in the hospital for another couple of days. He showed Branston to a chair, then sitting at his desk, asked, "How do you feel?"

"I'm all right," Craig answered. Grimacing somewhat, he added, "My ribs are wrapped so tightly that I can barely catch my breath, otherwise, I'm as good as new."

"I'm glad to hear that. I suppose you're here to get your things and your horse."

"Yes, I am. And I want to thank you again for your help."

"You're more than welcome." Johnny regarded him curiously. "Will you tell me about yourself and Laura?"

Craig had no objections, and he explained how they had met, and that despite his engagement to Deborah, he and Laura had fallen in love. Continuing, he said, "The morning I went to the school, I didn't know how I was going to tell Deborah that I was in love with another woman. But I was determined to find a way. I was shown into the parlor, a few minutes later Deborah joined me. Before I could tell her about Laura, she told me she was going to marry a doctor! I was surprised, of course, but I was also very pleased. The doctor is young, and moved to San Francisco to start his practice. A few weeks back, Deborah wasn't feeling well and was taken to Doctor Stevenson. It seems he fell in love with Deborah at first sight. He started calling on her, and eventually asked her to marry him. She was also in love, and said yes to his proposal. His mother suddenly took ill—his family lives in Seattle—and he returned home. He was gone longer than he had planned, and Deborah was beginning to worry that she had been jilted. Well, the morning I visited her was the same morning Doctor Stevenson returned. They decided to get married that very afternoon, and leave immediately to visit his family. Over a month ago, Deborah had written me a letter, telling me about the doctor, but I never received it. She wrote to my address in Abilene, but I haven't been home in a long time."

Johnny shook his head. "Everything would have worked out perfectly, if Laura hadn't left."

"It doesn't make sense. Laura wouldn't leave me like that."

Johnny studied Craig closely. "Are you sure you've told me everything?"

"I don't understand"

"What about Marsha Donaldson?"

"What about her?"

"Was there anything between you and Marsha?"

"Hell, no!" Craig's reply was abrupt.

A bemused frown creased Johnny's brow. "In that case, her actions are certainly strange."

"What are you talking about?"

Johnny explained that Marsha had visited the school,

313

then had sent the cabby to the hotel and the livery to run her errands.

Listening, Craig could hardly believe what he was hearing. Why the hell did Marsha want to destroy his relationship with Laura? His puzzlement, however, was quickly supplanted with rage.

"Damn that woman!" he cursed. "If I ever see her again—!" He cooled his anger, pushed back his chair, and got to his feet. "I'd like to get my things. I need to stop at the hospital, take care of my bill, and be on my way."

"Are you going to Silver Star?"

"As fast as I can get there."

Johnny, standing, offered Craig his hand. "I hope things work out between you and Laura."

Branston shook his hand. "Thanks."

"By the way, you'll never get her to leave the Diamond Cross. She loves that ranch."

"Yes, I know. But that's fine with me. Together, we can make it prosperous again." Together? He wondered if he and Laura would ever be together again. The thought was too painful to consider, and he thrust it aside. He couldn't imagine life without her!

Camp was set up at sunset, Doyce kept the men tied and ordered Joshua bound for the night. He had the women prepare supper, serve it, then put everything away.

When their chores were finished, Laura and Karen went to the men and sat with them. Marsha, preferring to be alone, was about to climb inside the wagon, but Doyce's hand was suddenly on her arm, halting her.

"Let's take a walk, doll," he said. A lewd grin was on his lips, and a folded blanket was beneath his arm.

314

She agreed readily, for she was more than willing to oblige. Regardless of Laura's warning, she still believed she could win Doyce's affections.

Doyce, wanting privacy, led her a good distance away before stopping and spreading the blanket on the ground. He turned to her, and said abruptly, "Get your clothes off, baby doll!"

His brusqueness was unsettling. "I . . . I don't understand why you are treating me this way. I'm not a tart, Mr. Talbert!" She tried to look very offended. This wasn't going the way she had planned, she had thought Doyce would be flattered.

He chuckled coldly. "Don't get uppity with me, woman. I know you're a tramp." Moving quickly, he reached out and grasped her shoulders, jerking her close. "You want to trade, don't you? Your body for your life? Well, show me you're worth it! Get undressed and on the blanket."

It didn't take Marsha long to make up her mind. Self-preservation was more important than pride. Her days as a prostitute had prepared her for moments such as this one, and modesty played no part as she removed her clothes. She was pleased with her body, and was glad that the moon's golden rays highlighted her voluptuous attributes. She lay down, and a smile was on her face as she saw the hunger in Doyce's eyes. He wanted her; that was obvious! She must make sure he continued to hunger for her!

Doyce unbuckled his gun belt, placed it aside, then leaning over Marsha, he drew his pants down past his thighs. He dove into her without preliminaries, and his entry was painful, causing her to cry out. Her pain whetted his desire, and his hips pounded ruthlessly. He climaxed quickly, stood, and drew up his trousers.

Marsha could hardly believe it was already over! How could she entrap him with her seductive charms, when he made love like an animal?

315

"Get dressed!" he ordered tersely, buckling on his gun belt.

She did as she was told, then stood numbly, wondering if he would now show a little tenderness.

Doyce grabbed the blanket, then motioned toward camp. "Well, why are you just standin' there? Let's go!"

Depression weighed heavily in Marsha's heart as she accompanied Doyce back to camp. Evidently, Doyce Talbert was too cold and cruel to be softened by seduction. She was now afraid that her death was as imminent as the others'. Tears filled her eyes and rolled copiously down her face.

God, she didn't want to die!

Twenty-six

Another day's journey was completed before reaching the area that Morgan had in mind. He told Doyce it was the ideal place to leave the others, for there was no water for several miles in any direction.

Camp was set up for the night. Doyce and his companions planned to leave at dawn. Again, the women cooked supper. Morgan and Elias, along with Doyce, had ravenous appetites; the others, however, merely picked at their food.

When their chores were finished, Laura and Karen joined the men, who were sitting together, their hands and feet bound securely. Laura sat between Harry and Zeb, as Karen squeezed in between Jim and Joshua. Ed, his expression grim, was sitting on his father's other side. Lobo had followed Laura, and, now, looking for a place to settle, he curled up at Ed's feet. Ed reached down and distractedly rubbed the wolf behind its ears.

Meanwhile, Marsha chose the solitude of her wagon over their company, but no one cared enough to comment on it.

Jim, however, was seething, but his anger was directed solely at himself. That Marsha Donaldson had made such a fool of him was infuriating. How could he have been so blind? He had always considered himself level-headed and reasonably intelligent, but he had certainly been taken in by a beautiful face. He cooled his temper; he supposed every man was entitled to such a mistake at least once in his life. He turned to Karen, who was gazing at him with loving eyes. If only he had come to his senses sooner, at least he and Karen could have fully expressed their feelings before dying. He was now certain that he loved Karen, he was also certain that they would perish in this desolate desert. It was apparent to Jim that Morgan knew what he was doing, for he had led them into the heart of the valley, from which, without water, there was no escape! They were surrounded by a trackless waste of sand, and hemmed in on all sides by titanic rocks and majestic mountains. A deathly silence, so thick that it could almost be felt, hung over the region. Such an eerie quietness was enough to appall the stoutest heart, and drive one over the brink of sanity!

"Jim," Karen said, her tone worried. "What are you thinking about? You look so . . . so troubled."

"This damned desert, that's where my thoughts are."

"It'd be more merciful if they just shot us, wouldn't it?"

He tried to encourage her. "As long as we're alive, there's hope."

The men's hands were tied in front of them, and Karen reached over, placed her hand on Jim's, and murmured, "I know there's no hope. I'm not scared to die, but I am afraid of dying in this valley. I've heard so many horrible stories of people going raving mad in the desert, before they finally die."

He wished for comforting words, but he couldn't think of any. Instead, he said softly, "Karen, I love you."

Unbeknownst to Jim, those words were by far the most comforting. Karen, resting her head on his shoulder, whispered, "I love you, Jim Slade. I love you with all my heart."

In the meantime, Harry was trying to ease Laura's terrible apprehensions; his encouraging words, though appreciated, were nonetheless a failure. Laura knew that the odds of survival were not in their favor, in fact, their death was almost a certainty.

That Harry wanted to lighten her worries warmed her heart; he had so much on his mind, still, he was trying to console her. She felt he needed consolation more than she did. She could only imagine what he must be feeling. Learning Doyce had killed Lee, and was now planning to kill all of then, had to be ripping him apart inside!

She smiled kindly. "Mr. Talbert, you don't have to try and make me feel better. I know we probably won't come out of this alive."

"You're very brave, Laura." He returned her smile. "I wish you wouldn't call me Mr. Talbert. It sounds so formal. I don't expect you to call me father, papa, or anything like that. But Harry would be nice."

At that moment, Morgan walked up to them, grabbed Laura's arm, and jerked her roughly to her feet. "You're comin' with me!" he uttered gruffly.

"Let me go!" she cried furiously, trying to pull free.

Lobo, his instincts protective, leapt to his feet. The hairs on the back of his neck bristled, and a vicious snarl, curling his mouth, bared his long, sharp fangs.

Morgan, aware of the wolf's threat, shoved Laura aside and reached for his holstered pistol. Before he could draw it, Laura pounced on him and made a futile effort to get his gun. Jim, realizing she had no chance, managed to get to his knees, then heave his body into Morgan's. His bound hands and feet kept him from inflicting any harm, but he was hopeful that his interference might give Laura the edge she needed to grab Morgan's pistol.

Her reaching fingers had barely grazed the gun when, Doyce, coming up behind her, seized her by the shoulders and flung her aside. Lobo made a lurch for Doyce, but Laura moved quickly, grabbed her pet, and held him back. She didn't doubt that Doyce would shoot him.

"Goddamn it, Morgan!" Doyce raged. "What the hell do you think you're doin'?"

"I just want to have a little fun with the woman. After all, I got a score to settle with her!"

"The desert will take care of that." He made a terse wave in the direction of the wagon. "Hell, if you're horny, go see the Donaldson woman, she'll open her legs for anyone!"

Morgan wasn't interested in Marsha, he knew she would be too easy. He liked a woman with fight in her—like Laura Mills! "I want her!" he said firmly, pointing a finger at Laura.

"All right," Doyce relented. "But take her away from camp."

"Doyce!" Harry bellowed. "For God's sake—"

"Stay out of this, Pa!"

"You cold-hearted demon! I curse the day you were born!"

Doyce, his eyes filled with hate, doubled his fists and took a step toward his father.

"Wait!" Laura called. "There's no reason for more violence." She turned to Morgan. "I'll leave with you, but I'll do so without a struggle. You can have your way with me, I won't even fight you. I'll be very submissive and cooperative."

Morgan had been looking forward to forcing himself on Laura, her thrashing arms and legs would certainly intensify his sexual hunger. He wanted to strike her, degrade her, hear her beg, then leave her weeping with despair. Now, damn her to hell, she had intentionally spoiled his plans! Her subservience caused the hardness in his pants to go flaccid.

"To hell with it!" he mumbled, walking away.

Laura smiled. She had summed up Morgan correctly, he didn't want her without a fight.

The next morning everyone was up at the crack of dawn. Laura, sitting with the others, looked on as Morgan and Elias filled several canteens before emptying the two water barrels. They poured the water onto the ground, and the dry sand immediately absorbed the liquid. Then they unloaded the rifles, the shotgun, and Jim's pistol, and left the weapons beside the wagon.

Laura's eyes blurred with tears as she watched the two men gather the horses and her spirited mare. She was very fond of her horse, and was sure she would never see it again. Lobo was at her side, she put an arm about his neck, and his closeness brought her a measure of comfort.

When they were ready to leave, Doyce approached his father. He stood before him, his countenance stoical. "Well, Pa, I guess this is goodbye. Maybe good riddance is more like it."

Laura, listening, looked closely at Harry. She was worried, for his health seemed to be deteriorating rapidly. His shoulders were drooped, his face was drawn and etched with pain. It seemed to Laura that the man had aged years within the last forty-eight hours. Doyce had destroyed his father's vim and vigor, and had shattered his heart. Even if by some miracle they were to come out of this alive, she was afraid Harry Talbert would never be the same. He was a broken man!

Doyce, now smiling spitefully, spoke to Ed. "How come you aren't actin' so high and mighty, huh? Where's all that arrogance?"

"Go to hell, Doyce!" he muttered.

"I'm not the one who's goin' to hell! You are!" He waved a gesturing hand toward the others. "You and the rest of

321

'em! You're in hell right now! And as soon as that sun climbs a little higher, you're gonna know you're smack in the middle of it!"

Marsha was nearby, she now rushed to Doyce, clutched his arm, and pleaded desperately, "Don't leave me here! Please take me with you! I'll never tell anyone what happened to the others! I don't care if they die! I really don't!"

"Why should I burden myself with you, when I can buy all the whores I want?" He pried her fingers from his arm, then pushed her away.

For a moment, Marsha considered trying to buy her life, but she quickly discarded the notion. Doyce would simply take her money, and would still leave her behind! No, she would hold on to her money, in case she came out of this alive!

Doyce turned back to his father. "Well, Pa, aren't you going to tell me goodbye?"

"Goodbye, son. May God have mercy on your soul!"

"You'll see God in a couple of days, Pa. Put in a good word for me, will you?" With that, he walked away laughing.

Morgan and Elias were mounted, holding the lead rein to the other horses. Doyce swung into the saddle, and without bothering to look back, he spurred his horse into a fast gallop.

Elias quickly followed. Morgan, however, rode over to Laura, and drew her knife from his belt. He sent it soaring strongly through the air. It landed at her feet, and the sharp blade embedded itself into the hard-crusted sand. Then, turning his horse about, he caught up to Doyce and Elias.

Taking the knife, Laura cut the ropes binding the men's hands and feet.

No one said anything, and the silence quickly got on Marsha's nerves. "Well?" she screeched. "What are we going to do?" Her gaze flew to Zeb. "You're familiar with this region, where can we find water?"

He pointed toward the distant mountains. "There's plenty of water up there."

"Then why are we just standing here? Let's start for the mountains!"

"Ma'am, if you want to start walkin' toward the mountains, then go right ahead. But you'll never make it on foot and without water. I realize from here the mountains don't appear that far away, but it's an illusion. This desert's full of them kind of illusions."

"But if we stay here, we'll die!" she cried.

"We'll die if we leave, and we'll die if we stay. In other words, we're damned if we do, and we're damned if we don't."

Jim spoke up. "I'd rather die heading for the mountains, than give up and sit here waiting for death. Even if we don't make it, at least we'll go down fighting."

No one had noticed that Karen went inside the wagon, and, now, as she reappeared, they were shocked to see that she carried a canteen.

"I filled this last night when we were cooking supper," she explained. "I hid it in the wagon. Thank God, they didn't find it!"

"Good thinking!" Jim told her.

The others, except for Zeb, praised Karen as well.

"What's wrong, Uncle Zeb?" Laura asked.

"We got eight people and one canteen of water. Even with rationin', it ain't gonna last very long." Zeb turned to Harry and Joshua. "I need to talk to you two — alone."

He motioned for them to follow, and they walked a short distance away. The three men stood huddled, conversing in low tones. A few minutes later, they returned.

Zeb looked at Jim, and said, "You were right, it's better to head for the mountains than to stay here. With one canteen of water, you might make it. The odds are heavily against you, but it's worth a try. But, remember, you gotta ration the water, and be damned stingy about it."

"Uncle Zeb," Laura interrupted. "You're talking as though you won't be with us."

"I won't. And neither will Harry and Joshua. With five of you drinkin' from one canteen, you got a slim chance of survival. Don't you understand, hon? Eight people are just too damned many. We're the oldest, so we stay behind."

"No!" Laura exclaimed. "Either we all leave, or none of us leave!"

"Speak for yourself!" Marsha butted in. "Zeb's right! He and the others are old, they *should* be left behind! They'll only drag us down, drink our water, and cause all of us to die!"

Laura, fuming, took a step toward Marsha, and was about to slap her face, but Ed suddenly intervened.

He grabbed Marsha's arm, his grip so tight it was painful. "You cold-hearted witch! Open your mouth again, and I'll shut it permanently." It now amazed him that he had once questioned his father's opinion of her!

He released her, and she backed away. Anger, however, radiated in her eyes. How dare he treat her so ruthlessly!

Ed, forgetting Marsha, looked at Zeb, then at Joshua, his gaze settling on his father. "If you stay behind, I'm staying also." His expression pained, he added in a voice that choked, "I won't leave you, Pa!"

"I'm not leaving either!" Laura said emphatically.

"Neither will I," Karen chipped in.

"Then, except for Marsha," Jim remarked, "that makes it unanimous, because I won't agree to leave anyone behind."

"For God's sake!" Harry pleaded. "Don't you realize what this means? It means we're all going to die!"

No one backed down. Marsha wanted to speak her

324

mind, but she was too afraid Ed might carry out his threat.

"Well?" Jim remarked, eyeing the three men unwaveringly, "Are we leaving or staying?"

"We might as well start for the mountains," Zeb mumbled. "I don't think any of us will make it across the desert alive, but it'll give us something to do while we're waitin' to die. We gotta travel light, so take only what you're willin' to carry."

Marsha hurried to the wagon and climbed inside. Moving with haste, she pried open the loose planks, grabbed her carpetbag, and put her money inside it. Zeb had said, "take only what you're willing to carry." Well, Marsha was quite willing to carry her carpetbag.

Meanwhile, Laura, intending to get her wide-brimmed hat, made a half-turn to leave, but was halted by Jim's hand on her arm.

His expression was dismal. "We have only one canteen and eight people. We don't have enough water to give any to Lobo. It's not right to let the wolf suffer. If you want, I'll destroy him as quickly and as painlessly as possible."

Laura gasped. "Kill Lobo? No, I won't let you do that!"

Jim was gentle. "It's better than letting him die of thirst. Furthermore, when the canteen is passed around, how do you think you'll feel drinking water while your pet is begging you for a drop?"

"I'll share my ration of water with Lobo."

"Your ration!" Jim said sternly. "Good God, Laura, don't you realize your ration will only be a cap full?"

"What difference will it make in the end? We'll never reach those mountains! You know that as well as I do!" She placed her hands on her hips, and her eyes flashed defiantly. "Lobo is my responsibility, and he's coming with us!"

"Don't argue with her, Jim," Zeb said. "She's right. In the long run, it's not gonna make any difference."

Marsha, returning, couldn't hold her tongue any longer. "Why must everyone keep saying that we won't reach the mountains?" She looked at Zeb. "You talk as though it's impossible!"

"Under these circumstances, it is impossible."

The finality in his words sent a horrifying chill up Marsha's spine.

They set out in a westerly direction, the sand beneath their feet was dry and gritty. The only vegetation that seemed to luxuriate in the arid region was the ever-present sagebrush, accompanied here and there by a cactus, some of them quite large in size.

As the day wore on, the desert baked under the sun's scorching rays, and the heat rose considerably. A grim, awful silence, unbroken by the scurrying of an insect or a rodent, hovered over the valley so thickly that it was almost tangible.

Early summer, however, made the trek more bearable, in a another two weeks or so, the temperature would be much hotter.

The group moved slowly, exhaustion would call for more water. Harry, his vitality gone, kept lagging behind. The others, except for Marsha, would stop and wait patiently for him to catch up.

Finally, Laura decided to walk beside Harry and try to keep him in step. She was worried, for he seemed so dispirited. She cursed Doyce for what he had done to his father.

"Harry," she said, "you can't let Doyce destroy you like this."

"God, Laura!" he groaned. "Where did I go wrong?"

"It's not your fault that Doyce turned out the way he did."

He shook his head. "No, somehow I failed him."

Laura wanted to convince him that he was wrong, but talking only intensified her thirst. She slipped her arm into his, and despite the dryness in her mouth, she murmured, "You still have Ed and me, and we'll help you through this."

Her kindness was touching, but Harry was dying inside, and not even Laura could save him.

The sun, fading to a deep, fiery red, tinted the distant mountain range with glorious color. It dipped gradually behind the tall peaks until, at last, only a dusting of ash-orange fell across the open, desolate land.

The weary travelers carried blankets, which they now spread out on the ground. Ed, in charge of the food, handed everyone a strip of jerky. Their throats were so dry that eating the dried meat was difficult, but knowing nourishment was essential, they somehow managed. Jim then rationed the water—one capful per person. When he gave Laura hers, she drank half of it, poured the remainder in the palm of her hand, and offered it to Lobo. The wolf lapped it up greedily.

"In the morning," Harry told her, "I want you to drink all your water, I'll give Lobo half of mine."

"Miss Laura," Joshua spoke up, "I'll share my water with him tomorrow at noon."

"And I'll share mine in the evening," Ed put in.

Karen started to make the same offer, but Laura held up a quieting hand. "I know you all are doing this for my sake, and not Lobo's. I understand, and I appreciate your concern. But it was my decision to bring Lobo, and I will pay the price."

327

Zeb went to his blanket, sat down, and said heavily, "In less than two days, that canteen's gonna be empty. Sharing a rationed capful with Lobo ain't gonna drain it any sooner. Besides, we oughta try and keep that wolf alive, if there's any water closer than those mountains, his instincts will find it. More than one prospector has been saved from death by his mule sniffin' out water."

"Then it's settled," Harry remarked. "We share our water with Lobo."

"Ha!" Marsha declared sharply. "I certainly don't intend to give that wolf part of my water!"

Zeb chuckled bitterly. "Don't worry, Mrs. Donaldson, 'fore it comes your time to share, the water will be gone."

"We might as well try and get some sleep," Jim said.

Everyone agreed, but sleep wasn't easy to come by. They lay on their blankets, where they were plagued by their own thoughts and fears.

Twenty-seven

The next day, the sun again baked the region, and wind hot as the devil's breath swept across the endless sand. Thirst became a constant companion, and when the rationed water was passed around, dry lips clung to their capful, draining every last drop of the precious life-giving liquid. Joshua, keeping his word, shared his pittance of water with Lobo.

The mountains didn't seem any closer, quite the contrary, the more they walked toward them, the farther away they appeared. Nevertheless, they continued their slow, weary march, keeping the highest peak in sight, as though it were a candle in the window, guiding them home.

The sun hung in the cloudless sky, the shifting sand palpitated with heat, and the landscape was one shimmering mass, now unbroken by so much as a rock or a cactus stump. They had indeed been transported into hell upon earth; the parched and arid region offered no shade, nor even a stray cloud to intercept the sun's scorching rays. The godforsaken area, as if presided over by cunning devils, tortured the travelers with delusive mirages — pastoral plains and sparkling springs appeared suddenly in their paths, only to vanish as magically as they had popped up.

By late afternoon, they were all so tired, thirsty, and drained, that it was a chore to put one foot in front of the other. Through sheer willpower alone, they managed to trudge onward. It soon became obvious, however, that Harry Talbert was on the verge of collapse. Jim and Ed took turns supporting him, and helping him to stay on his feet.

Laura was very worried, she had a feeling that Harry had lost the will to fight. Doyce had destroyed him as surely as if he had taken a gun and shot him in the heart.

When they stopped for the night, everyone sank wearily to their blankets, too fatigued to even hold up their heads. They rested for an hour or so, then Ed handed out strips of jerky, after which, Jim rationed the water. The canteen was now less than half-full—they had another twelve hours of water at the most!

Harry refused to eat, but he did drink his water. He lay on his blanket, almost too weak to move.

Laura sat beside him, and her eyes swept over him with concern. "Harry, I'm worried about you."

He managed to summon a tender smile. "I know you are, hon. And your concern means a lot to me. But, Laura, I haven't been all that well for a long time. The boys weren't aware of it, and neither was Joshua. I didn't want them to worry."

"If you weren't well, then why did you take this trip? You should have stayed home!"

"I had to try and find you. Those wanted posters had me very upset, and then . . ." He paused a moment. "I wanted to tell you that you were my daughter."

Sudden tears smarted her eyes. "You must make it through this! We all must survive! You and I have a lot of years to catch up on!"

He sat up wearily, took her hand, and held it gently. "Laura, I haven't told you everything."

"About you and Mama?" she asked.

He lowered his voice so only Laura could hear. "I loved Beth, but my love killed her."

"I don't understand. Mama died in childbirth." She spoke softly, like Harry, she didn't want anyone to overhear their conversation.

"Your mother and I managed to avoid each other for years. We put our love behind us, and went on with our lives. Then one afternoon, a fierce storm hit. I had been in town, and was on my way home. The closest shelter was a tack shed on the Diamond Cross. I reached the shed at the same moment that Beth did. She had also been caught in the rain, and had decided to take shelter. I considered riding away, but, by now, the storm was raging. We shared the shed, and once again we shared our love. The years had failed to dim our passion, it was as strong as ever. The storm passed, and we again went our separate ways. That afternoon was like a dream that was too wonderful to be true. I held onto it, treasured it, and relived it in my mind over and over again. But the dream soon became stark reality. Beth was with child. John came to the ranch and told me she was pregnant. He knew the child wasn't his, for he and Beth hadn't been together in that way for several months. He said if I tried to claim the child, he would divorce Beth and take you and Johnny away from her. Later, Beth sent me a letter, begging me to cooperate. She also made it quite clear that she didn't want to talk to me or see me. She was willing to make any sacrifice to keep you and Johnny. I did as Beth wanted."

Harry's eyes, staring into Laura's, were filled with despair. "When I learned that Beth died giving birth to our son, I nearly went out of my mind. I hated myself for what I had done to her. I also blamed myself for her death."

Silence pressed down upon them, and it was a long moment before Laura replied, "Mama's death wasn't your fault. That afternoon in the shed, I'm sure she wanted your love as much as you wanted to give it."

"You're very understanding, Laura. I was afraid you might turn against me." He sighed deeply. "God, I wouldn't blame you if you hated me!"

"I could never hate you!" Tears suddenly spilled down her cheeks. "If only things could have been different for you and Mama!"

He brought her into his embrace. "Laura, I love you. There's nothing I wouldn't do for you. Very soon now, you'll understand what I mean."

She dried her eyes with the back of her hand. "You don't have to prove your love. I know how much you care. It's written on your face every time you look at me."

At that moment, Ed and Zeb decided to join them. They talked for a while, then as full darkness set in, everyone went to their blanket to try and get some sleep. Zeb, however, went to Laura, knelt, kissed her cheek, and told her that he loved her. Then giving her a wink that seemed to say, "keep your chin up," he went to his own bed. She was deeply touched by his token of affection.

A dry wind whispered ominously over the desolate tableau, it was the only sound in the otherwise silent valley. Laura, listening to the eerie quietness, wished for the sounds of nocturnal creatures; a nightingale's chirp would be music to her ears. But not a vestige of night life interrupted the grim, awful silence.

As sleep continued to elude her, thoughts of Craig came to mind. She tried not to imagine him in his bride's arms, but the picture stubbornly appeared. She wished she could hate Craig, maybe then this terrible pain in her heart would go away.

She laughed softly, bitterly. Why was she worrying? Death would soon take away the pain! The chances of their survival were growing slimmer by the hour—she didn't think any of them would ever leave Death Valley— it would most likely become their eternal tomb!

Laura was awakened by a pair of hands shaking her shoulders. She opened her eyes to find Ed kneeling beside her. She sat up, it was still dark, but dawn's light was edging the horizon.

"Is something wrong?" she asked Ed.

"Pa's gone."

"Gone!" she exclaimed.

"Yes, and so are Joshua and Zeb."

She stared at him blankly, she didn't want to believe what he was saying.

"They left so the rest of us could have their share of the water."

"Where do you think they went?"

"I don't know, but they probably headed back in the direction we came from."

"We have to go after them!" Laura declared, bounding to her feet. She called to Jim, and her voice awakened everyone.

Ed quickly told the others what had happened.

"Jim, we must find them!" Laura said desperately.

Slade and Talbert exchanged somber glances—they knew such a search was hopeless!

Ed placed his hands on Laura's shoulders, gazed solemnly into her eyes, and said, "We can't go after them. They most likely planned this sometime yesterday, and left during the night. By now, there's no telling how far they are."

"But we can't just let them go off into the desert to die!"

"Laura," Jim said gently. "We can try to find them, but we'll run out of water. Even if we did catch up to them, we couldn't save them or ourselves. We'd all perish." He groaned wretchedly. "God knows I hate to say this, but we have to accept their decision! They chose to sacrifice their lives to give us a chance, and if we don't take that chance, their sacrifice will be for nothing. They'll die, and so will we!"

Laura turned to Ed. "Is that how you feel?"

Tears were in his eyes. "It's not a question of feeling, but reasoning."

Suddenly, she remembered Harry telling her that he would soon prove his love. Pain, as sharp as a razor's edge, cut into her heart. "Dear God!" she moaned pathetically. "This is more than I can bear!"

Ed drew her into his arms, and needing his comfort, she clung tightly.

Marsha, watching the couple's embrace, was filled with bitterness. Well, she had certainly misjudged Laura! She had believed the woman was truly in love with Craig, but, apparently, she had been wrong. Marsha, forming her own opinion, was certain Laura was making a play for Ed Talbert—she undoubtedly planned to marry him for his money! She looked away, after all, what difference did it make to her? She had already ruined any chance she had with Talbert! God, if only she could get out of this desert alive, go to St. Louis, and start all over again!

In such a thriving city, she'd certainly find a rich husband! A selfish smile crossed her lips, at least now there were three less people to drink from the canteen! That Zeb, Joshua, and Harry were gallantly forfeiting their lives to help save hers, didn't faze her conscience; quite the contrary, she was glad to be rid of them!

Laura moved gently out of Ed's arms. All her life she had been a fighter, but she now felt as though every ounce of strength had been drained from her body. She would go forward—toward the mountains—but her mind and heart would remain behind with Zeb, Joshua, and Harry.

Slowly, Laura moved to her blanket, sat down, and drew Lobo close. She felt as though he was all she had left. Sorrowfully, she recalled Zeb kissing her good night, and telling her that he loved her. God, it had been his way of saying goodbye! Laura leaned her head against the wolf's neck, gave in to her grief, and wept sadly.

Karen rushed over, and with her own tears flowing, she put an arm about Laura's shoulders.

The men's eyes were also misty. Jim's grief wasn't as deep as Ed's, but it was still painful.

There was only one pair of dry eyes in the group. Marsha had remained untouched by the three men's sacrifice.

The sun, reaching its meridian, beat down upon the desert, turning the sand white-hot. The barren land seemed to stretch to the ends of the earth, but the towering mountains, banked on the horizon, kept beckoning the travelers onward. The burning desert wind, dry as an oven blast, breathed into their lungs, and unspeakable thirst tortured them.

They came upon sand dunes, and stopped there to rest. The water was rationed, but it did little to quench their parched throats.

Karen's strength was ebbing quickly, and she begged to rest a moment longer. Jim didn't have the heart to insist she go onward. She was so small and frail, he knew she would succumb before the others. He lay beside her, holding her hand, for it was too hot to hold her in his arms.

Ed and Laura were totally fatigued, and they collapsed on their blankets and stayed there, for they were too physically and emotionally drained to move.

Marsha spread her blanket on the hard bed of sand, and dropped down upon it wearily. The sun was blinding, and through a fuzzy haze, she watched as Lobo, his legs barely carrying him, managed to make his way over a high sand dune. Remembering Zeb had said the wolf might find water, Marsha was suddenly hopeful. She started to alert the others, but then decided to check this out on her own.

She got up quietly, and forced her tired legs to climb the sandy dune. She spotted Lobo immediately. The wolf was pawing at the sand, as though he were trying to dig a hole. Marsha had heard of underground springs, and praying Lobo had found such a miracle, she rushed forth with renewed strength.

Falling to her knees beside the wolf, she dug at the sand with her hands, and cried joyously as liquid oozed from beneath the earth. She dug more vigorously, her efforts bringing forth more of the liquid. It was clear, and dripped through her fingers like sparkling diamonds.

Marsha, so enthralled with her glorious discovery, failed to notice that Lobo, whining forlornly, had turned away. Taking no note of the wolf's warning, she cupped her hands, filled them with what she believed was life-sustaining water, and drank thirstily. The taste was strange, but it was wet, and she swallowed even more.

She heard the others coming up behind her, and without bothering to turn around, she exclaimed proudly, "I found water! Just look at all this beautiful water!"

Jim, grasping her shoulders, pulled her roughly to her feet. He dipped his hand into the oozing liquid, and cupping a handful, he took the tiniest taste, then spit it onto the ground. "Good God, Marsha!" he gasped. "This isn't water!"

"Of course, it is!" she argued.

"It's an underground liquid coming from a lava bed. That's why Lobo isn't drinking it."

"Well, I don't care! It's wet, isn't it?"

"Yes, but it's also poisonous!"

Marsha paled. "You . . . you're lying!"

"I wish I were."

"No!" she screamed, terror slamming into her heart. "I don't believe you! You're making this up just to scare me!" But even as she spouted the accusation, her stomach began to cramp. The pain was so severe that it doubled her over. She dropped to her knees, leaned over, and retched violently until only dry heaves remained.

Jim lifted her into his arms, carried her back to her blanket, and laid her down gently. The sand dune, affording a narrow margin of shade, did little to ease Marsha's discomfort. Her stomach, now bloated, was seized with one agonizing cramp after another.

Jim moved to the others, who were standing close by.

"Will she die?" Ed asked quietly.

"I don't know. She threw up a lot of the liquid, she might make it. But I don't think so."

"What do we do now?" Ed questioned. "Do we stay

here and wait for her to die, consuming our water in the interim? Or do we leave her behind?"

Jim was undecided. "I guess we'll have to take a vote. The mountains are still at least three or four days away, but I don't think we have enough water to make it. Still, our only hope to survive is to keep pushing onward. If we stay, death is certain."

"We're going to die regardless," Laura remarked. "I vote we stay here. Heaven knows, I can't stand Marsha Donaldson, but I can't bring myself to leave her. It just seems too inhuman."

"Laura's right," Karen said. "I also vote we stay. Besides, I'm too worn out to go any farther. There's no possible way I can make it to those mountains."

"Then I'm staying, too," Jim replied. "I won't leave you and Laura."

"Neither will I," Ed murmured, sounding totally resigned to his fate.

Marsha, tossing and turning, was begging for water.

"Should I give her a drink?" Laura asked the others.

"Why not?" Jim said wearily.

Marsha clung tenaciously to life, and she was still alive at sunset. The water was gone, they had given most of it to Marsha, for none of them had the heart to turn a deaf ear to her pitiful cries for a drop of water.

Tired, emotionally beaten, and knowing they could do no more for Marsha, they finally lay down on their blankets. Gradually, the descending night shrouded the desert in blackness.

They succumbed willingly to sleep, for it was their only escape from this purgatorial valley.

Hours later, Lobo, lying beside Laura, got wearily to

his feet. He pricked his ears, and a weak growl sounded in his throat. His warning, however, was too faint to awaken anyone.

The wolf watched cautiously as a man, leading two horses, rode into view. He dismounted, grabbed his canteen, and approached Laura. Lobo's instincts were to protect his mistress, but he was too feeble to launch an attack.

The man, speaking gently to the wolf, watched carefully as Lobo, whining softly, stood back and allowed him to advance. He opened the canteen, removed his hat, and poured water into it. He then placed the hat in front of the wolf, who lapped at it thirstily.

The man then knelt beside Laura, elevated her head, and put the canteen to her lips. The water, dripping down onto her chin, brought her awake.

For a moment, her eyes stared incredulously into his, but her thirst was more powerful than her shock, and grabbing at the canteen, she tried to drink greedily.

"Easy," the man said soothingly. "Only a little at first." He allowed her two swallows.

The amount, though not a lot, revitalized her. She sat up, looked at the man with wonder, and gasped, "Neosha! My God, what are you doing here?"

"I'll explain later. First, let's awaken the others and give them some water."

They roused them quickly, and after their thirsts had been appeased, Jim, taking the canteen with him, went over to Marsha. He soon returned to the others, the canteen had remained capped.

"Marsha's dead," he said softly. Then, speaking to Neosha, he told him that she had drunk the poisonous liquid.

"We have no tools to dig a grave," Neosha said. "We'll

have to cover her body with sand. There's no wildlife in this region, her body will not be violated."

Laura and the others hadn't liked Marsha Donaldson, but that didn't make her death any less tragic, and a grim sadness came over them.

"How did you know we were here?" Jim asked Neosha. "I can't believe you just happened to pass by."

"I found your friends."

"Zeb and the others?" Laura exclaimed.

"Yes, I gave them water and two horses. They plan to return to the wagon, then go to Peaceful. I told them I would bring you there."

"Then they're all right?" Ed wanted to know.

"The man called Harry Talbert is very ill."

"God!" Ed groaned.

Laura hadn't paid any attention to the extra horses with Neosha, but, now, as she happened to glance toward them, she was astounded to see her mare. "How did you get my horse?" she asked suddenly.

"I came across a small band of Paiutes, they had several horses, your mare among them. I saw the brand on the mare and knew it was from the Diamond Cross. I also remembered that when I was following you, I had seen you ride a mare very much like this one. The warrior leading the band owed me a favor—I once saved his life. He let me pick four horses, then told me that we were now even. I went looking for you, I found the wagon, and then later I found your friends."

"But how did the Indians get the horses?" Ed asked. "When my brother left us in this desert to die, he took the horses with him."

"The Paiutes attacked the three white men, killed them, and stole their horses and weapons."

"Are you sure they killed all three?" Ed questioned.

340

"I'm very sure. After I left the Paiutes, I came across the three bodies. Two men were heavy-set and bearded, but the third man was slender, young, and had a strong resemblance to you."

"That was Doyce," he mumbled. Despite his brother's cold-blooded treachery, his death made him feel sick inside. However, he knew Doyce had gotten what he deserved.

"It will soon be dawn," Neosha said. "We'll leave at the first sign of light." He gestured toward the horses. "The gelding is strong and can carry two men, the ladies can ride the mare. Now, we need to cover the woman's body."

Laura and Karen looked on as the men scooped handfuls of sand from the dune, and dropped the gritty particles on top of Marsha's lifeless body. The sight, however, was too ghastly to watch, and they turned away.

It took a long time for the men to finish, and by the time their chore was completed, dawn had arrived. No one paid any attention to Marsha's carpetbag, which was resting close to her grave.

They mounted their horses, and anxious to leave the wretched area behind, they rode quickly away.

The sounds of the horses' hooves soon faded into the distance, and the area was again cloaked in deathly silence. The wind, gusting across Marsha's grave, stirred the sand, sending it raining down upon her carpetbag. In time, the withering winds and the shifting sands would bury the bag, along with its rich contents.

Marsha and her money would spend eternity in the Valley of Death!

Twenty-eight

The village of Peaceful, its homes and buildings nestled among tall, billowing trees, was indeed a welcome sight to Laura and the others. As they rode past the babbling brook, which was colorfully bordered by summer flowers, Laura remembered her first trip to the settlement—she had been with Craig and Jim. It was hard for her to imagine that only a matter of weeks had passed; considering everything that had happened, it seemed so much longer.

They rode to Mrs. Nelson's rooming house, where they expected to find Harry, Zeb, and Joshua. Laura ordered Lobo to stay, then she and the others went to the door and were greeted by Mrs. Nelson. She knew Karen well, and was happy to see her. She also remembered Laura and Jim. Neosha was a regular visitor to Peaceful, and although Mrs. Nelson was somewhat in awe of him, she greeted him pleasantly. She wasn't acquainted with Ed, but she welcomed him into her home.

She showed her guests into the parlor, which was furnished with pieces she had brought with her from San Francisco. Embroidered doilies adorned the chairs and sofa, and were also placed on the tables to protect the glossy finish. Mrs. Nelson had lived in Peaceful for ten years; she had come with her husband who had dreamed of staking a rich claim. Six years ago, the desert had taken his life, and, Mrs. Nelson, having no wish to leave, had turned her home into a boardinghouse.

Now, as Karen dropped wearily into a chair, she asked Mrs. Nelson, "Will you please tell Harry Talbert and Zeb Douglas that we're here?"

The woman was evidently puzzled. "I don't have any boarders."

Laura exclaimed, "But they were supposed to meet us here! They should have arrived at least two days ago!"

"I'm sorry," Mrs. Nelson said. "But I haven't seen them."

Ed bounded to his feet. "Neosha, will you go with me to look for them? I'll pay you for your trouble."

The Cherokee nodded. "We'll borrow fresh horses and leave immediately."

"I'll come with you," Jim remarked.

"Maybe you should stay here with the ladies," Ed replied. "If for some reason we don't come back, they'll need you to get them to Silver Star."

Jim concurred. "All right, I'll stay."

Ed started to follow Neosha out the door, but was stopped by Laura's hand grasping his arm. "What do you think could have happened to them?" She was obviously distraught.

"I don't know," he replied grimly. He summoned an encouraging smile, patted her hand, and said, "Try not to worry."

She watched, her heart gripped with apprehension, as he and Neosha hurried outside. She prayed desperately that Ed and Neosha would find the others, and that they would be alive and well!

Mrs. Nelson took her guests upstairs, gave Jim a

room, showed him inside, then took the ladies to the same room they had shared before.

She followed them through the door, closing it behind her. "Karen," she said, her tone suddenly sad. "I'm afraid I have bad news."

"Is it about my father?" she asked.

"Yes, it is. Last week two prospectors stopped here. They found your father and his friends. I'm sorry, honey, but your father is dead. These men had some of his things, among them was his journal. He had written that you were staying here, and had requested that you be notified of his death should someone come upon his journal. Apparently, toward the last, he knew he was going to die. I have his journal and the other things the prospectors brought. They're in my room. I'll get them for you."

As Mrs. Nelson left, Laura took Karen in her arms in a consoling gesture. "Karen, I'm so sorry."

"I knew he was gone," she murmured. "I've felt it in my heart for a long time."

Karen burst into tears, and Laura held her as she cried.

The day went by slowly for Laura, for with each passing hour she hoped Ed and Neosha would return with the others. Night finally fell, and following dinner, she and Karen retired.

Despite Laura's state of mind, her fatigue was overpowering, and she drifted into a sound sleep.

Karen, however, was plagued with insomnia. She was tired, and the soft feather mattress felt good to her weary body, yet, she was too upset over her father's death to fall asleep. Earlier, Jim had tried to console her with caring words and tender gestures, but she needed more from him. She longed to feel his arms wrapped tightly about her, with his lips pressed passionately to hers. Coming westward had taught her a valuable lesson: life was too uncertain not to grab at happiness. Jim Slade was her happiness, and she wanted to love him completely. Now! Not after they were married, but right this very minute, for tragedy could strike tomorrow!

Moving quietly, she got out of bed, slipped on her robe, and left the room. She went down the hall, and rapped lightly on Jim's door.

He was surprised to find Karen, and taking her hand, he drew her inside. He was still dressed, but his shirt was unbuttoned, and he had taken off his boots.

"Is something wrong?" he asked.

"No, not really. I just want to be with you."

Jim brought her into his arms, holding her close. "I love you, Karen," he whispered. His lips found hers in a fiery kiss that sparked a sensuous flame.

Karen clung tightly, as thoughts of making love to him raced through her mind. A few days ago, such ideas would have made her blush, but Jim's love, and the dangers she had faced in the desert, had changed her. She was no longer painfully shy and naive as a schoolgirl.

Holding her close, his body pressed to hers, Jim uttered thickly, "Karen, I want to make love to you."

"Yes," she murmured, her heart hammering with anticipation.

Draping an arm about her shoulders, he guided her to the bed. He adjusted the lamp's wick down to a romantic hue, then drew Karen into his embrace and kissed her fervently.

His mouth, claiming hers demandingly, courted her senses with commanding persuasion. She leaned against his sinewy strength, and responded completely.

Jim's hands trembled with desire as he helped her remove her robe and gown. His eyes raked her slender frame hungrily, then he swept her off her feet, and laid her on the bed. He doffed his clothes hastily, for he was indeed anxious to love Karen fully.

She boldly admired his muscular body as he took his place beside her. He drew her close, and as his lips seized hers in a deep emotional commitment, her searching fingers skimmed over his hard-muscled ridges.

Her exploring touch added fuel to his already burning desire, and his hand etched a heated path over her silken flesh, igniting their passion into a leaping, all-consuming flame.

Engulfed in their own erotic paradise, they expressed their love through stimulating gestures and heart-stopping kisses. Jim, his need reaching a crucial juncture, moved over her.

Karen laced her arms about his neck, and waited breathlessly for him to claim her completely. With one driving thrust, he made them one. A soft moan escaped her lips as she lost her innocence, but the discomfort was short-lived, and she was soon immersed in ecstasy.

The couple, lost in total rapture, consummated their love and united their hearts forever.

The next morning, everyone was at the breakfast table when Ed suddenly appeared.

Laura, leaping to her feet, asked with bated breath, "Did you find them?"

"Yes, we did." He spoke to Mrs. Nelson. "Will you please prepare a room for my father? He's very ill. Is there a doctor here?"

"I'm sorry, but no doctor has settled in Peaceful."

Ed was gravely disappointed.

"I already have a room ready," Mrs. Nelson told him. "I'll hurry upstairs and turn down the covers."

Laura, along with Jim and Karen, followed Ed outside. The covered wagon was parked out front.

Zeb was talking to Neosha, but seeing Laura, he walked over to her, and said, "Harry insisted on findin' Doyce's body. He wanted to make sure he was dead, that's why we're late gettin' here."

"Did you find him?"

"Yep, him and his buddies. We buried the three of 'em. Harry's not well at all. I'm really worried about him."

"Let's get him into the house," Laura said, hurrying to the back of the wagon.

Joshua and Ed were with Harry, they lifted him over the backboard and handed him to Zeb and Jim, who carried him inside. Laura and the others followed.

Mrs. Nelson had the bed ready, and the men put him down gently. Laura's heart lurched with fear when she saw that Harry's face was pallid and pinched. She knew with terrible certainty that he was dying.

Talbert was barely conscious, but he managed to murmur weakly, "Laura . . . Laura . . ."

She took his hand, holding it firmly. "Yes, I'm here."

"I'm sorry . . . for all those . . . wasted years."

"Please don't talk, you must save your strength."

"I . . . I don't have . . . any strength left." His eyes closed.

347

Zeb, checking him, was relieved to report that he was sleeping.

Laura pulled a chair up close to the bed, she wasn't about to leave Harry's side. Ed, feeling the same way, drew up his own chair. The others left quietly.

"I'm going to lose him," Ed groaned hoarsely. "I love him . . . very much."

"Doyce did this to him," Laura remarked angrily.

Ed agreed. "He was my brother, but I hope he burns in hell!"

Laura and Ed remained by their father as the clock on the wall ticked away the hours. Mrs. Nelson came in to invite them downstairs for lunch, but they refused to leave Harry's bedside. The others stopped by periodically to check Talbert's condition, especially Joshua. The prognosis was always the same: Harry was sleeping, but his breathing was shallow and rasping.

Late afternoon shadows were falling across the room before Harry finally opened his eyes. His vision was blurred, but he could make out Laura and Ed watching over him.

"Laura," he whispered feebly. "I dreamt about Beth . . . she's waiting for me."

A sob caught in Laura's throat.

"Because of you," Harry continued, his voice terribly weak, "the love Beth and I shared will never truly die, it'll live through our grandchildren, their children and . . . and until the end of time."

Laura broke into tears.

A faint smile touched his lips. "You must be brave, Laura."

She controlled her grief, but her throat ached with torment.

Harry's strength was ebbing, and it took much effort for him to continue, "You and Ed are family. For God's sake, love each other."

"We will, Pa," Ed answered. "That, I can guarantee you."

Laura turned to Ed, her expression amazed. She hadn't realized that he felt that way about her. She touched his arm, and he placed his hand over hers. Neither of them had ever shared a warm and strong sibling relationship, but she knew they would now.

"Ed," Harry murmured. "I love you, son . . . You have been a blessing. Tell Joshua . . . tell him I said . . . Goodbye, dear friend."

He closed his eyes, and a few moments later, Harry Talbert drew his last breath and died peacefully.

As Ed went to the parlor to tell the others that Harry had passed away, Laura slipped through the kitchen and out the back door. She felt she needed a moment alone before seeing anyone; Talbert's death had her very upset. She certainly didn't expect to find Joshua sitting on the back stoop, and his presence startled her.

He got hesitantly to his feet, and looked closely at Laura. Her sorrowful expression sent his heart sinking. "Mista Harry's gone, ain't he?"

"Yes, he is," she whispered sadly.

Joshua dropped back onto the stoop, bowed his head, and sobbed. His shoulders shook with each rasping sob that tore from his throat.

Laura went quickly to his side and sat down. She placed a hand on his arm, and with tears brimming, she murmured, "Harry said to tell you . . ." She paused,

349

fought back the need to break down and cry, then continued, "He said to tell you—goodbye, dear friend."

It took a moment for Joshua to get a tenuous hold on his emotions. "Mista Harry was a wonderful man. He had his faults . . . don't we all? But he was kind, generous, and always fair. He was like that from the time he was a boy."

"Harry told me that you grew up with him on his father's plantation."

"Yes'm, I sure did. Masta Talbert gave me to Mista Harry when we was still youngsters. I had a happy life growin' up with Mista Harry. We wasn't masta and slave; we was friends."

"What about your parents? Did they live on the plantation?"

"My pappy died 'fore I was born. Mama died givin' me birth."

"Joshua, why did Harry have a falling out with his father? What caused him to leave home and not return?"

"Mista Harry had a older brother, and he was as mean as the devil. I reckon you could say Mista Doyce was just like 'im. Mista Harry and his brother—his name was William—was always disagreein'. Masta Talbert always took William's side; they was alike as two peas in a pod. Mista Harry took more after his mother. She was a real kind and gentle lady. She died when Harry was seventeen. Along about this time, I fell in love with a little gal who worked in the kitchen. Her name was Clara. She loved me, too. We was about to ask Masta Talbert's permission to marry, when Masta William suddenly began to notice that Clara had filled out and was now a young woman. He wanted her for himself, and one night he ordered her to his room. She despised Masta William

350

somethin' awful, and she fought 'im. A slave girl fightin' her masta was almost unheard of. Mista William turned on her with a fury, and beat her so unmercifully that he killed her."

Joshua fell silent for a spell as a rush of bitter remembrance rippled across his mind. "I was gonna kill Masta William, I was aimin' to wrap my fingers 'bout his throat and squeeze until he was dead. But 'fore I could, Mista Harry confronted 'im, and they got into a real bad fight. It was so violent that Mista William challenged him to a duel. Without the Masta knowin' nothin' 'bout it, they met at sunrise. I was with Mista Harry that mornin', he won the duel, then helped carry his wounded brother back to the house. William didn't die, but the Masta was so angry that he disowned Mista Harry. That was why Mista Harry packed up and moved westward. I belonged to 'im, so the Masta didn't say nothin' 'bout me goin' with 'im."

"God!" Laura sighed. "It's hard for me to imagine that those people were my grandfather and uncle!"

"Don't you worry none 'bout that. You didn't take after them, you got Mista Harry's and his mother's nature. You're a lot like Miss Beth, too. She was a real nice lady."

Again, tears flooded Laura's eyes. "I suddenly feel so alone! Mama's gone, and now Harry! Craig ran out on me, and Johnny's wrapped up in his own life!"

"You aren't alone," a voice sounded from behind her.

Laura turned to find Ed standing outside the back door. He came to her side, sat down, and took her hand into his. "We're family, Laura. And we promised Pa that we'd love each other. I'll have no problem keeping that promise, for you're a very easy person to love."

351

"So are you," she replied, smiling warmly. "That is, now that I know you. I used to think you were cold and arrogant, but I was very wrong."

The threesome, discussing Harry Talbert, remained on the back porch a long time. Ed and Joshua did most of the talking, for they had so many more memories to share. Laura listened with rapt attention, for she wanted to learn as much as possible about the man who had been her father.

The next morning, Ed purchased a buckboard to carry Harry's coffin. He wanted his father buried in the cemetery in Silver Star. Everyone was anxious to get the journey behind them, and they planned to leave Peaceful immediately. Jim and Karen had decided to accompany Laura back to the Diamond Cross, get married in Silver Star, then travel to Jim's home outside Winding Creek.

Before departing, Laura went in search of Neosha. Considering everything that had happened, she hadn't had a chance to truly thank him for his help.

She found him in the stables, saddling his horse. He seemed surprised to see her.

"Neosha," she said, "I want you to know how grateful I am. The others and I would have died in that desert, if it hadn't been for you."

"I knew you were worth saving."

She smiled. "So were the others."

He shrugged. "Maybe."

"Neosha, there are a lot of decent white people, you know."

"Yes, I have met a few."

352

"Well, if you ever find yourself in Silver Star, stop by the Diamond Cross and see me."

"I will." He was finished saddling his horse, and he led it from the stall. He paused before Laura. "Jim Slade told me what happened between you and Branston. I am sorry."

"He chose Deborah over me, and I have to learn to live with it." She spoke wistfully.

"Branston is a fool. If you were my woman, I would never let you go."

"Apparently, Craig didn't feel that way." She told him goodbye, then impulsively went to him, reached up, and kissed his cheek. She turned about and hurried outside.

Neosha's eyes, filled with unrequited love, followed her. If he thought he could win her love, he'd go after her and sweep her off her feet. But he was certain she could never feel that way about him.

He mounted his horse and rode out of Peaceful. He would always remember Laura Mills with love and respect.

Twenty-nine

Laura had been home only a few days, and the Diamond Cross was already showing prosperous signs. Ed loaned her money to buy cattle; he wanted to just give it to her, but she insisted on a loan with interest. With Ed's help, she managed to find most of the wranglers who used to work for her. They were glad to return, and the bunkhouse was again filled. The married couple Harry had hired as caretakers had done their job well, and, Laura, taking an instant liking to them, kept them on. They in turn took her under their wings, as though she were their own daughter. Wed for over thirty years, their children were married and lived in different parts of the country. The Diamond Cross had become home to Mary and Charlie Goller, and they were grateful to Laura for letting them remain.

Jim and Karen were staying at the ranch, but they planned to be married in a few days and leave for Jim's home. Although Laura was sincerely happy for them, she dreaded their departure, for she knew she would miss them a lot. She wasn't sure how long Zeb intended to stay, but she was certain he would soon move on. Zeb never lingered in one place very long.

Laura submerged herself in work, and stayed busy from sunup to sundown, which left her little time to think about Craig. At night, however, before falling asleep, he was always there with her, filling her mind and piercing her heart. Not even slumber brought her peace, for Craig haunted her dreams.

Now, as Laura rode across her land, heading for Silver Star, her thoughts were occupied with Craig. She wondered if he was happy, or was he wishing he hadn't married Deborah? Did he lie awake at night, longing for Laura in the same way she longed for him? Probably not! Craig wasn't the type to marry one woman, then crave another. Laura was certain he had chosen Deborah over her because that was the way he wanted it. Apparently, seeing Deborah again had made him realize that, despite his feelings for Laura, Deborah was the one he truly wanted to marry.

She forcefully routed Craig from her mind, thinking about him only depressed her. He was no longer a part of her life, and the sooner she learned to accept that, the better off she'd be! Somehow, she would find a way to cast him out of her heart forever!

Laura slapped the reins across her horse's neck, and urged it into a faster gallop. She was anxious to reach town. Earlier, she had gone to the Circle T to see Ed. He wasn't home, and Joshua had told her he was in town. She had some ranch business to discuss with Ed, so she cut back across her land, and headed for Silver Star.

Meanwhile, as Laura was riding across the pastoral countryside, Craig was riding into Silver Star. Sheriff Longley, sitting in front of his office, caught sight of Branston and waved.

Craig rode over, and asked, "Did Laura make it back to the Diamond Cross?"

"She sure did—been back for quite a few days."

"Thanks," Craig replied. He kneed his horse, and started toward the hotel. He was relieved to hear that Laura had returned safely. If Craig had stopped in Peaceful, Mrs. Nelson would have told him a great deal about Laura's trip, but he had bypassed the settlement.

He stopped in front of the hotel and dismounted. Although he was anxious to see Laura, he nonetheless needed a bath and shave. He didn't want to visit Laura in clothes coated with trail dust, and sporting a ragged three-day beard.

As Craig went inside the two-story hotel, he was not aware of the four men standing across the street, watching him. The foursome could hardly believe their own eyes. Craig Branston in Silver Star! What luck!

It was the three Mitchell brothers, along with their father, who was now out of prison. The sons had told their father about their encounter with Branston in Smoky Gulch. They had given him a full account, explaining how they had Craig at gunpoint, but that he was saved by a woman shooting from the hotel's second-floor window.

Actually, Gus Mitchell had been glad to learn that his sons' attempt to kill Branston had been thwarted. In his opinion, a quick death was too easy for the bounty hunter! He wanted Branston to die all right, but he wanted him to die slowly and painfully!

His lips twisted into a cruel smile. "Boys . . ." he began, "I got an idea. I think we oughta take Branston home with us, and show him some Mitchell hospitality."

"How are we gonna grab him?" the oldest son asked.

"We'll take him by surprise, Ryan. He most likely went into the hotel to get a room, so I reckon we'll just give him a little room service. What do you think?"

"Sounds good to me," he replied.

The others readily agreed.

The Mitchells sauntered across the street, went into the hotel, and speaking to the desk clerk, Gus learned Craig's room number. They climbed the stairs, moved quietly down the hall, then stopped in front of Craig's door.

Gus rapped lightly, saying, "Mr. Branston, this is the desk clerk. I need to see you for a moment."

Craig, planning to go down the hall for a bath, was laying out a clean set of clothes. If his thoughts hadn't been on Laura—anticipating their reunion—he might have sensed danger. But Craig had waited a long time for this day, and peril was the farthest thing from his mind as he went to the door and opened it—to suddenly find himself held at gunpoint.

Gus shoved Branston backwards, then he and his sons barged inside. Ryan quickly took Craig's pistol, and stuck it in his belt.

"Gus Mitchell," Craig said, as though the name left a foul taste in his mouth. "How the hell did you get out of prison?"

"They let me out. You see, I was never convicted of murder, 'cause the law didn't have enough evidence against me. So I was tried for robbery and got five years. I only served three of them years, but they were the longest three years of my life. You know how I got through it, Branston? I kept thinkin' 'bout how I was goin' to find you, and make you pay for turnin' me over to the law. I had planned to kill you real quick-like and get it over with. But that was 'fore I learned that my woman left me. I had me a young, pretty gal, but, thanks to you, when I went to prison, she ran out on me. Losin' Anna almost drove me crazy! I really did love that gal! I've looked everywhere for her, but I can't find

357

her. You got any idea, Branston, what it's like to lose the woman you love? I just wish to hell you had a woman, so I could show you what it's like! I'd kill her right before your eyes!"

"Pa," the youngest son butted in. "Branston had him a woman in Smoky Gulch!"

"She isn't my woman," Craig was quick to say. "We just happened to be traveling together. She means nothing to me."

"Now that we got Branston," Ryan said to his father, "how are we gonna get him out of town?"

"We'll wait until dark." He drew up a hard-backed chair and sat down. "Ryan, you stay here with me." He glanced at his other sons. "You two don't have to hang around all afternoon, go get a couple of drinks if you want."

Their father's suggestion met with their approval, and they left the room, saying they'd be back later.

Gus, using his revolver, gestured toward the bed, and told Craig to be seated.

He did as he was told.

"Make any fast moves," Gus warned, "and I'll kill you here and now!"

Craig didn't doubt it. He sat silently, and tried to figure out a way to save his life.

Laura, riding into town, was passing the sheriff's office when the lawman waved her down. She reined in, and waited as he hurried over to talk to her.

"Branston's in town," Longley said.

"Craig?" she gasped.

"I saw him ride in a short time ago. Didn't he travel to San Francisco with you and the others?"

"Yes, he did. But I certainly didn't expect him to come back here."

"He's at the hotel, if you want to see him."

She wanted to see him, all right! The damned cad! Oh, he had his nerve coming to Silver Star! She could hardly believe he had such gall!

Laura cantered to the hotel, tied her mare beside Craig's stallion, and hastened inside. The clerk gave her Branston's room number, he was about to comment on Craig's having so many visitors, but, Laura, hurrying up the stairs, didn't give him time.

She knocked soundly on the door, calling angrily, "Craig, let me in!"

Inside, Gus leapt to his feet, looked at Branston, and asked quietly, "Who's here?"

Laura's presence caused a hard fist of fear to knot in Craig's stomach. Somehow, he had to keep Mitchell from guessing his feelings for Laura. The murdering sonofabitch would no doubt kill her!

"Who the hell's here?" Gus asked again, his voice soft but determined.

"Just a woman I used to know. She's of no importance."

"Damn you, Craig!" Laura shouted, her patience snapping. "Open this door!"

Gus, keeping his voice low, told Ryan to empty Branston's pistol. He then handed the gun over, warning Craig not to try and reload it. He headed for the closet, motioning for Ryan to follow.

"I'm gonna leave this door cracked," he said to Craig. "I'll be watchin' you real close. You make one wrong move, and I'll kill the woman! And don't open that door, just tell her to come in."

Craig dreaded the scene about to take place, but for

359

Laura's sake, he had no choice but to act like the heel she undoubtedly believed him to be.

"The door's unlocked," he called out.

She stormed inside, slamming the door closed behind her.

Craig, seated on the bed, got slowly to his feet. He drew an inscrutable mask over his face, and it hid his feelings well. However, he loved Laura so much that seeing her again hit him with a powerful force. God, she was beautiful! She was wearing riding clothes, and the suede trousers adhered smoothly across her feminine hips and down her long, shapely legs. Her blouse, its color as blue as her eyes, fit snugly, emphasizing the fullness of her breasts. Her western-style hat was hanging halfway down her back, held in place by a leather thong tied beneath her chin. Laura's blond tresses, windblown, fell about her face in seductive disarray. Craig, fighting back the need to hold her close, unconsciously doubled his hands into fists, keeping them flat against his sides.

In spite of Laura's anger, she couldn't help but be physically aware of him. His clothes were flecked with dust, and he badly needed a shave, yet, he was still strikingly handsome. A wayward lock of coal-black hair had fallen across his brow, and Laura controlled the desire to reach up and lovingly brush it back into place. She gazed into his dark eyes, hoping to find a trace of remorse, but they were studying her with an expression so stoical that it rekindled her rage.

"You damned coward!" she said furiously. "Why didn't you come back to the Winston and tell me you wanted to marry Deborah? How could you let me find out the way I did?"

God, how desperately Craig longed to tell her the truth, but he couldn't, not with Gus eavesdropping.

Laura's life depended on him convincing Gus that she meant nothing to him!

In a flat voice, he replied, "I figured you'd make a scene, and I didn't want to listen to your hysterics."

"A scene? Hysterics?" she flared. "Oh, you contemptible snake! How could I have been so wrong about you?"

"Laura, I'm married to Deborah now, and I love her very much. I admit that we had something for a while, but it was only that. Deborah always has been, and always will be, the only woman for me."

His words cut into her heart ruthlessly, but she kept the pain well concealed. She'd not give him the satisfaction of seeing her break down. "If you love Deborah so much, then why isn't she with you?"

"As soon as I find a place for us to live, I intend to go back for her."

Suddenly, she turned on him with blazing fury. "I hate you, Craig Branston! You damned, despicable, two-timing skunk!" She drew back a hand and slapped his cheek harshly.

The forceful whack resounded throughout the room. Craig, playing his role to the hilt, said threateningly, "If you were a man, I'd kill you for that!"

Her eyes, glazed with tears, stared intensely into Craig's. She felt as though she were staring into the eyes of a stranger—a cold, heartless stranger!

"Get out of my town!" she raged. "Get out of here before I kill you!" With that, she whirled about, and with her head held high, she walked out of the room.

Once in the hall, and out of Craig's sight, she gave in to her true feelings, and tears flowed from her eyes as she rushed down the stairs, through the lobby, and outside.

She caught sight of Ed, he was in front of the general

store. She called out to him, got his attention, then fled down the wooden sidewalk, flung herself into his arms, and told him what had happened with Craig.

There was only one saloon in Silver Star, and it was located across the street from the general store. The two youngest Mitchells were there, sitting at a table by the front window. A saloon girl had joined the brothers, and was keeping them company.

Glancing out the window, one of the Mitchells happened to see Laura with Talbert. "Joe," he said, "isn't that the same gal who was with Branston in Smoky Gulch?"

"It sure looks like her," Joe agreed. He turned to the woman at their table, pointed toward Laura, and asked, "Do you know who she is?"

"Sure I do. Her name's Laura Mills, and that man with her is Ed Talbert. His father died recently, and now he's the richest man in these parts. Since he and Laura came back from San Francisco, they've been practically inseparable. Those two are the talk of the town, and everyone's wagering when they'll announce their engagement. As chummy as they are, it's quite obvious they're gonna get married." She sighed loudly. "I sure do envy Laura Mills! Just imagine marrying a man as wealthy as Ed Talbert! Some women have all the luck!"

"Get lost!" Joe told her tersely.

"Wh—what?" she stammered.

"You heard me! Go away!"

His abruptness was infuriating, but swallowing back a retort, she left, taking her filled glass with her.

"Why did you send her away?" his brother whined. "I was just gettin' ready to take her upstairs."

"Hell, Dave! Your brains have always been in your

362

pants. Don't you realize what we got goin' for us?"

Dave was totally confused.

"Ain't you ever heard of the Talberts?"

"Yeah, I reckon I have."

"That gal didn't tell me anything I don't already know. The Talberts are rich as sin! I didn't know, though, that the old man was dead."

"What are you gettin' at?" Dave asked impatiently.

"Ed Talbert's in love with the Mills woman. Let's keep an eye on her, and if she leaves town alone, we'll follow. Then, when we know it's safe, we'll grab her. Talbert will pay a lot of money to get her back."

"Don't you think we should talk this over with Pa?"

"Hell, if we go back to the hotel, we might lose the woman."

"Yeah, I see what you mean."

"Besides, if we pull this off, Pa will be pleased. We need money, don't we? Once we collect the ransom, we can take off for Texas or someplace. Who knows, maybe we'll go to Mexico. I understand them señoritas are hot little ladies!" He winked conspiratorially. *"Comprendo, amigo?"*

Dave laughed heartily. "You bet, I do!"

Ed felt sorry for Laura, losing Craig to Deborah had hurt her deeply, but, now, for Branston to treat her so coldly, was like kicking her when she was already down. He was tempted to go to the hotel and give Branston a piece of his mind. He mentioned doing just that to Laura, but she quickly asked him to stay out of it.

"But Laura—" he began.

"Please, Ed! I don't want you to fight my battles. Besides, Craig's not worth the trouble."

"I suppose you're right," he agreed, albeit reluctantly. "I'll try to avoid Branston."

Suddenly, Laura felt totally drained, and she said wearily, "Ed, I need to talk to you about business, but right now I don't feel up to it. Can you come to the Diamond Cross this evening?"

"Yes, of course, I can."

"Good. I'll see you then."

She started to leave, but Ed caught her arm. "Wait, and I'll ride home with you. At a time like this, you shouldn't be alone."

"Thanks, Ed. But you're wrong. I need desperately to be alone. I'll be all right, I promise."

"Are you sure you don't want me to come with you?"

"Yes, I'm sure," she replied. She mustered a smile, reached up, and kissed his cheek. "I'll see you tonight."

Across the street, the Mitchells, staring out the window, watched as Laura gave Ed a parting kiss. They got up quickly, left the saloon, and hastened to their horses, tied close by.

As Laura rode down the street, her bitter thoughts were on Craig, and she was unaware of the danger that lurked behind.

The Mitchells followed at a good distance, for now they hoped to remain undetected. Keeping Laura in their sights, they trailed her out of town.

"Where do you intend to take me?" Craig asked Gus. He was lying on the bed, his arms folded beneath his head, and was staring up at the ceiling.

Gus's voice came from the nearby chair, "I'm takin' you to my cabin. It's farther north. Once there, I'm gonna kill ya. Not real fast, though, I'm gonna let you suffer!

By the time I get through with you, you'll be beggin' me to kill you and get you out of your misery."

"You're a real likable guy," Craig murmured flippantly.

"Yeah? You bet your ass, I am!" He guffawed huskily. "Tell me, Branston, did you ever see an Indian skin a man alive?"

"Can't say I have."

"It ain't no pretty sight."

"Is that what you have in store for me?"

"What do you think?" He slipped his sharp knife from its scabbard, and ran a finger across the shiny edge. "Yep, this-here knife could sure peel the skin off a man's body. Too bad your wife ain't with you, I could tie her to a stake and you could watch me skin her like a deer. Then, when I was finished with her, I could start on you."

Craig didn't say anything, but he winced slightly, as though he could already feel the knife slicing into his flesh. He could think of better ways to die. Well, at least he had saved Laura from Gus's savagery. His thoughts turned wistful, if he didn't find a way to escape, death was certain—and Laura would never learn how deeply he loved her, but would spend the rest of her life believing he had betrayed her.

Thirty

"How are we gonna grab her?" Dave asked Joe. They were now a couple of miles out of town, and Laura was still a good distance ahead. "She's got a rifle with her," Dave continued. He remembered Smoky Gulch. "She knows how to use that damned gun, too!"

Joe thought for a moment, then said, "There's only one way to take her. I'll shoot her horse out from under her."

"Good thinkin'!" Dave remarked with a smile.

The area was open grazing land, and Joe scanned the surroundings to make sure they were alone. As he drew his Winchester from its scabbard, he said to Dave, "There's an old abandoned cabin north of here. I'll take the woman there, you ride back to town and tell Pa what happened."

Dave wasn't sure about breaking the news to his father. "Why do I have to be the one to face Pa? This was your idea; *you* oughta tell 'im!"

"Hell, Dave! He's gonna be pleased!"

"You reckon?"

"You act like you're scared of the old man."

He was, but he didn't want to admit it. After all, he was twenty-one years old, at his age he shouldn't fear parental authority—but Gus Mitchell was meaner than a grizzly, and twice as dangerous!

Joe reined in, hefted his rifle to his shoulder, and took careful aim through its rear sight for greater accuracy. He was a good shot, and he knew he wouldn't miss.

Tears were in Laura's eyes, she wiped at them with the back of her hand, and silently chastised herself for crying over Craig. The heartless devil wasn't worth it!

Laura's emotions were jumbled, she was not only hurt and angry, but was also stunned. Craig's personality had changed completely, and she felt as though he were someone she didn't know.

The bullet from Joe's Winchester suddenly slammed into the mare, and as the gunshot reverberated across the vast plains, Laura's horse plunged headfirst onto the ground.

Laura was thrown forward, and her body landed solidly beside her horse's. The hard jolt knocked the breath from her lungs, and she came close to losing consciousness. Getting to her hands and knees, she crawled to the mare. Tears were streaming, for she was very fond of her horse. She had owned the animal for a long time, and they had been through a lot together. The stalwart mare had carried her across the desert, to San Francisco, and back home.

The mare was still alive, but the sounds of approaching riders sent Laura reaching for her rifle. She strove to free it from its encasement, but it was lodged beneath the horse's body.

Arriving abruptly, the Mitchells swung down from their mounts. Going to Laura, Joe clutched her arm and roughly jerked her to her feet. "Do you remember me?" he asked, leering down into her face.

He looked familiar, but she couldn't place him.

"Me and my brothers kinda met you in Smoky Gulch."

She now realized who he was. "What do you want with me?" she demanded, trying vainly to wrest free.

His grip tightened. "If you do as you're told, you won't get hurt. We don't aim to harm you, doll. All we want is some money from Talbert. If he pays your ransom, we'll set you free."

"You're kidnapping me?" she exclaimed.

He smiled greedily. "Your boyfriend's rich, and he can afford to part with some of his money. And I just bet he'll pay plenty to get you back." His gaze traveled lewdly over her slender form. "A pretty woman like you is worth a lot."

He started to hand her over to his brother, but she drew back, looked down at the mare, and said desperately, "What about my horse? I don't want her to suffer!"

Joe gave the mare a passing glance. "Hell, it's dead!"

A sob caught in Laura's throat, aching for release, but she wasn't about to let these men see her cry.

Dave now grabbed her arm and held her firmly, as Joe went to his horse, removed a strand of rope from his saddlebags, returned, and tied Laura's hands.

"I'll take her to the cabin," he said to Dave. "It's almost sunset; Pa said he'd leave town when it was dark. So I'll be expectin' you all to show up 'fore too much longer."

Dave moved to his horse, mounted, and started back to Silver Star. In the meantime, Joe lifted Laura and placed her on his saddle. He swung up behind her, and his arms encircled her as he reached for the reins. Her back was pinned against his hard chest, and he was so close that she could feel his breath falling on the back of her neck.

He urged his horse into a fast gallop, and headed in the direction of the cabin.

"Where the hell are those boys?" Gus complained, pacing the room restlessly. Dusk had fallen, and he was anxious to leave. Damn it! He had given them permission to have a couple of drinks, he hadn't told them to stay gone this long!

"They'll be here, Pa," Ryan said, trying to pacify him. He was well acquainted with his father's violent temper, and he hoped it wasn't about to erupt.

"Go get our horses and Branston's, and take 'em to the back of the hotel. We'll leave by the rear door."

"Ain't you gonna wait for Joe and Dave?"

"If they ain't here when I'm ready to leave, then they get left behind."

Craig, lying on the bed listening, hoped the others wouldn't show up. That way, the odds would narrow down—two against one. It bettered his chance for escape.

At that moment, however, a light knock sounded on the door, followed by Dave's voice. "It's me, Pa. Let me in."

Gus nodded at Ryan, who hurried to the door and opened it. "Where have you been?" he asked. "And where's Joe?"

Dave swallowed nervously. He still wasn't convinced that his father would approve of the kidnapping.

"Well?" his father bellowed. "Answer your brother! Where's Joe, and where the hell have you been?"

Dave's weight shifted anxiously from one foot to the other. "Well, you see Joe got this idea—a way for us to make some good money. We was at the saloon, when we seen this woman out the window. It was the same woman who shot at us in Smoky Gulch . . ."

Craig's body tensed.

"She was talkin' to one of them Talberts. I think his

name's Ed, anyway, he's the one with all the money. We learned that him and the woman's gonna get married . . ."

Married! The word thundered through Craig's mind.

"So Joe got this real good idea. He said that we should kidnap the woman and hold her for ransom. She left town alone, we followed her, and Joe captured her by shootin' her horse out from under her. He took her to an abandoned cabin north of here. He's waitin' there for us."

"He's talkin' 'bout the same woman who was here," Ryan said to Gus. Earlier he had told his father that Laura was the one who had helped Branston in Smoky Gulch.

Gus looked at Craig. "Well, it seems you toyin' with her affections didn't prevent her from hookin' herself a wealthy boyfriend. I've heard of the Circle T, it's the richest spread in these parts."

Craig kept his expression impassive, but he was stunned inside. Laura engaged to Ed Talbert? He couldn't help but feel a stirring of anger, it certainly hadn't taken very long for her to get over him!

The hotel furnished paper and pen, they were on the dresser. Gus went over, dipped the pen into the inkwell, and began to write. The ransom note was badly spelled, and the penmanship was terrible. At the bottom of the page, he drew a crude map. Finishing, Gus handed the note to Ryan, saying, "Pay someone to deliver this to the Circle T, then hurry back. We gotta get goin'."

Then, stepping to Dave, Gus slapped him proudly on the back. "You and Joe did real good!"

Ed stayed in town until sunset. He went to the saloon, had a few drinks, then had dinner in the hotel dining room. He planned to stop by the Diamond Cross on his way home.

Now, riding across the vast countryside, the moon lighting his way, Ed caught sight of something up ahead. He slowed his horse, and peered into the distance. The object was large, and was apparently alive, for it was moving. He galloped forward, and as he drew closer, he recognized Laura's mare. The animal was on the ground, and was trying vainly to get on its feet.

Reining in, Ed leapt from the saddle and hurried to the injured horse. He looked about, hoping to spot Laura. Had the mare taken a fall? Probably. But, then, where was Laura? He couldn't imagine her leaving her horse like this.

He knelt beside the mare, and, at first, failed to notice that Laura's rifle was in its scabbard, for it was hidden beneath the horse's body. Again, the mare tried to get its wobbly legs to hold its weight, and Ed suddenly saw Laura's Winchester. None of this made any sense. Laura wouldn't take off on foot without her rifle!

Ed grasped the mare's harness and encouraged her to get to her feet. He knew that if she didn't find the strength to stand, she'd certainly die.

She whinnied, and the sound was filled with agony, but with Ed's prompting, she managed to get up. He ran a hand over her trembling legs; there were no broken bones. Continuing his examination, he found blood caked on her flank. He looked closely at the wound, and was alarmed to see that it was caused by a bullet. Had someone shot the mare in order to abduct Laura? It was the most logical explanation!

Ed got back on his horse, took the mare's reins, and started toward the Diamond Cross. He had to hold his horse to a slow walk, so the wounded mare could keep up. His concern for Laura, however, almost convinced him to shoot the mare, then race to the Diamond Cross as quickly as possible. But he couldn't bring himself to destroy Laura's horse. Like Lobo, it meant the world to her. He would try to save the mare, but if her strength gave out, he'd have no choice but to shoot her.

Laura sat in a corner of the dilapidated cabin. Her hands were still tied, and now her feet had been bound as well. It was dark inside, but the pale moonlight sifting through the windows and cracks, gave off enough light for Laura to see fairly well. Joe was standing by a window, watching for his father and brothers.

Laura thought about the knife hidden in her boot. Tied in such a fashion, reaching it was impossible. Still, she was glad it was there. Maybe later she'd get the opportunity to use it to escape.

A deep frown creased her brow. That she had been kidnapped for ransom was shocking. Furthermore, where in the world had the Mitchells gotten the notion that she and Ed were lovers? She decided to question Joe.

"What makes you so sure Ed Talbert will pay my ransom?"

He turned away from the window. "I heard all about you and Talbert. It seems you two are the talk of the town. Everyone's wagerin' when you'll announce your engagement."

Laura was amazed. But as she thought about it, her surprise waned. She and Ed had been spending a lot of time together, and they openly expressed affection. Yes, she supposed an onlooker could misconstrue their closeness. They had decided not to publicly reveal their kinship. They didn't want their parents' memories slandered, nor did they want to become the center of malicious gossip.

The sounds of horses' hooves suddenly carried into the cabin, and, Joe, drawing his pistol, stepped to the door and cracked it open. Recognizing his family, he holstered his gun and moved outside.

"Is the woman with you?" Gus asked.

"Yeah, Pa."

"Get her out here, we gotta get movin'!"

Joe hesitated. "Are you glad I grabbed her, Pa?"

"Sure, I am. I'm real proud of you, son!"

Joe swelled with pride. His father's approval was important. He hurried inside the cabin, went to Laura, and drew her upright. Then, bending over, he unsheathed his knife and cut the rope binding her feet. Grasping her arm tightly, he led her outside.

Laura scanned the group, but as her eyes fell across Craig, she stepped back, stung! "What are you doing here?" she burst out.

His dark eyes, staring into hers, gave nothing away. He was sure Laura's life was depending on him. If Gus even suspected that Craig was in love with her, he'd kill her out of revenge.

"The woman can ride with me," Gus said, motioning for Joe to bring her over.

Joe picked Laura up, and placed her on his father's horse. She was sitting in front of Gus, and his brawny arms went about her. "You sure are a pretty little gal," he whispered in her ear.

She stiffened, and thoughts of this man and his sons touching her sent fear coursing through her like a hot swift current.

Gus, chuckling, said, "Relax, sweetie. I ain't gonna hurt you."

"Where are you taking me?" She tried to discipline her voice, but, despite her effort, it quavered.

"I got a cabin north of here. We'll be there in a few hours. It ain't all that far."

As Gus turned his horse about, Laura glanced over her shoulder and caught a quick glimpse of Craig. For a fleeting moment, their gazes met and held. Then Laura quickly looked away from his granite eyes. Craig's indifference cut her painfully to the core.

"Why do you have Branston?" she asked Gus. She had seen that Craig's hands were tied, and knew he was also a prisoner.

"I got some business to take care of with him. But don't you worry 'bout that. It don't concern you. As soon as Talbert brings me the money, I'll let you go. After that, I'll tend to Branston." Suspicion flickered in his mind. "You still got feelings for him?"

The damned scoundrel! She despised him! "He's nothing to me!" she spat.

"Reckon maybe he cares 'bout you?"

"He doesn't care whether I'm alive or dead!" She believed what she said, and the words tore into her heart. Tears threatened, but she fought them back. Her pride demanded that she not cry in front of Craig and the Mitchells. Later, when she was home . . . alone in her room . . . she would give in to her torment, and cry until she ran out of tears! Then, once she had a good cry, she would never again weep over Craig! She would put him out of her heart and mind . . . forever!

Jim and Zeb were sitting on the front veranda when Ed rode up, leading Laura's mare. The men had been discussing Laura, she should have been home hours ago, and they were considering searching for her. Ed's arrival with the mare was a bad omen, and they exchanged worried glances before hurrying down the porch steps to greet Talbert.

"I found Laura's horse a couple miles from town," Ed said, dismounting. "The horse has been shot."

"What?" they exclaimed in unison.

"I think she was abducted, and whoever took her, shot the horse out from under her."

At that moment, Karen stepped outside with Laura's hired couple, the Gollers. They had heard what Ed said, and Charlie hurried to check the mare. He had doctored animals before, and he gave the horse a quick examination.

"I'll take Miss Laura's horse to the barn. I can get the bullet out, but I'll need a couple of wranglers to give me a hand."

Zeb's permission was a quick nod of the head. He turned back to Ed. "Jim and I will mount up and go look for her. You wanna come along?"

"Of course, I do."

Before Zeb could head for the stables, a rider galloping toward the house caught everyone's immediate interest.

As the visitor rode in closer, Ed saw that it was one of his wranglers.

Reining in, the man swung from the saddle, went to his boss, and handed him a folded piece of paper. "Joshua figured you might be here. He told me to give you this. He seemed real upset, I guess he read it."

It was too dark outside to read, so Ed took the note into the house. The others followed close behind.

Going to the parlor, Ed stood beside a lamp, unfolded the paper, and scanned it quickly. "My God!" he gasped. "Laura's been kidnapped for ransom!"

"Ransom!" Zeb remarked. "But she ain't got any money!"

"The kidnappers are demanding that *I* pay the money. I'll read it to you: 'Talbert, we have your woman. If you don't bring us two thousand dollars, she will die. I drawed you a map at the bottom of the page, showing where we'll be waiting for you. Bring the money before Thursday noon. Come alone. You will be watched, so don't try nothing.' "

"Is that all?" Jim asked.

He handed him the note. "That's it."

Jim looked closely at the map. "I'm familiar with this area, it's smack in the wilderness. I also know who has a cabin somewhere in that vicinity. The Mitchells! I was in town earlier, and I saw them. Old man Mitchell was sent to prison, but he got out after serving three years. He and his sons are cold-blooded murderers!"

"I intend to pay the ransom," Ed said firmly. "They'll let Laura go, won't they?"

Jim's expression was grave. "I don't know."

"But what do you think?" Ed persisted.

He answered soberly, "I think after you deliver the money, they'll kill you and Laura both."

"Then we'll have to follow Ed," Zeb remarked.

"That'll never work," Ed replied. "The note said I'll be watched."

"He's right," Jim said. "The Mitchells might be crazy, but they're sly. I'm sure when they meet you at the spot indicated on the map, one will stay behind to make sure you weren't followed."

"But he can't stay behind too long," Ed remarked. "You've seen the map, you know where we're going to meet. Just stay about an hour behind me."

"That'll get us to *that* spot," Jim said, "but how do we

follow you from there? The Mitchells aren't going to leave a trail."

"That's right," Zeb declared, his eyes gleaming. "They won't leave a trail *we* can follow—but what about Lobo?"

Ed and Jim looked at him questioningly.

"Laura trained that wolf to track, he's as good as a bloodhound. All we gotta do is have a piece of Ed's clothing, give Lobo a whiff, and he'll track him."

"Are you sure?" Jim asked.

"You're damned right I'm sure!"

"I'll go home, get the money, and be back in a couple of hours," Ed said. "I'll also bring a few of my wranglers with me. We might need their guns."

"Should I get the sheriff?" Zeb asked.

"There's no need for that," Jim replied. "Where we're headed is out of his jurisdiction. But it's not out of mine." Jim's badge was in his shirt pocket, he took it out and pinned it on.

Ed turned to leave, but, pausing, he looked back at the others, "By the way, Branston's in town." He quickly told them what had transpired between Craig and Laura.

That Craig had treated Laura so coldly surprised Jim, he had never known Craig to be cruel. He couldn't help but feel anger. Nevertheless, he knew they could use Branston's skill for this job. "Maybe I should go to town and ask Craig to ride with us."

"Over my dead body!" Zeb exclaimed furiously. "After what he's done to Laura, if I ever see him again, I'll knock his teeth down his throat!"

Jim knew Zeb was merely letting off steam. In a fight, he wouldn't stand a chance against Craig.

"I don't want Branston along either," Ed said. "We can handle this job without him."

Ed left, and Zeb went into the kitchen to see about packing food for the journey ahead.

Karen was in the parlor, and had heard the men's discussion. She had remained noncommittal, but, now, stepping over to Jim, she said ruefully, "Poor Laura. She loves Craig so much, and then to have him treat her so terribly! It must've broken her heart." Tears welled up in her eyes. "Now she's been kidnapped! Oh, Jim, I'm so worried about her!"

He drew her into his arms, holding her close. "We'll get her out of this alive . . . somehow."

Thirty-one

The Mitchells' cabin was falling to ruin, the front porch was partially caved in, and the door was hanging obliquely on its rusty hinges. The inside was as dilapidated as the exterior, a few pieces of chipped furniture were placed here and there in a disorderly fashion. The lingering odors of cooking grease and unwashed dishes hung heavily in the air.

Gus and Ryan led their prisoners to a storage room off the kitchen; a lantern was lit and placed in the corner. A row of shelves, nailed to one wall, held a few canned goods and a burlap bag filled with potatoes. The room had a window, but it was much too narrow for a person to slip through.

The Mitchells forced Laura and Craig to the floor, made sure their hands were tied securely, then, as a precautionary measure, they decided to bind their feet.

Gus removed three cans of beans and a few potatoes, told Laura and Craig that they'd get some grub later, then he and Ryan left, closing the door behind them.

Laura tensed, she was sitting so close to Craig that their shoulders touched. She managed to move over a little.

Craig felt sick inside, he wished he could tell Laura the truth. It was on the tip of his tongue to do so, but he swallowed back the words. If he told her he wasn't

379

married to Deborah, and that they had been tricked by Marsha, her feelings toward him would soften. She might show too much emotion in front of Gus, and that could make him suspicious. He could try explaining to Laura that her life might depend on them acting as though they cared nothing for each other. But could Laura pull it off? He wasn't sure. He decided—at least for now—to continue his charade.

"Do you still carry that knife in your boot?" he suddenly asked.

Laura glared at him. "Why do you want to know? One lone knife against the Mitchells won't get you out of here."

"Just tell me if you have it."

"I have it. But I don't intend to give it to you." She frowned harshly. "I'd give it to you straight in your heart, if you had one!"

That she hated him so much hurt him deeply, but he didn't let on. "Do you think Talbert will pay your ransom?"

"Of course, he will."

Craig raised an eyebrow. "His feelings toward you have changed drastically. The last time I saw Talbert, he had placed a five-hundred-dollar reward on your head."

"Yes, but he thought I killed Lee. Now he knows I didn't."

"Oh? What changed his mind?"

"I don't owe you any explanations!" she muttered testily. Why should she tell him about Doyce, or that he had left them in the desert to die? He didn't care!

"Is it true that you and Talbert are getting married?"

"Yes, it's true!" she spat, the lie passing her lips before she could stop it. But she didn't retract it—let him think she and Ed were engaged! The lie did wonders for her pride! The two-timing skunk probably thought she was pining away for him! Well, she just shattered his conceited arrogance!

"Do you love him?" Craig watched her face closely.

A tiny smile flickered across Laura's mouth. Did she love Ed? Yes, she certainly did! Not in the way Craig had in mind, but it was still love. Her eyes met his, and she answered without hesitation, "Yes, I love Ed Talbert. He's kind, generous, and means the world to me."

Craig flinched, as though her words had struck him physically. He knew Laura very well, and could see that she was telling the truth. He had lost her to Talbert! A spark of anger burned within him. If she had truly loved him, she couldn't have fallen in love with another man so quickly!

He spoke bitterly, "It didn't take you long to get over me, did it?"

"Oh, you have your nerve!" she retorted.

A tense silence wedged itself between them, and it hung on for several minutes. It was finally broken by Craig, "If we get a chance to escape, we'll have to take it. I'm not sure Gus will let you go, even if Talbert delivers the money. He might decide to kill you both."

"He plans to kill you, too, doesn't he?"

"Without a doubt."

Laura sighed hopelessly. "How can we possibly escape?"

"Are Jim and Zeb still with you?"

"Yes, they're at the Diamond Cross."

"Slade knows all about the Mitchells. He'll figure they might kill you and Talbert. He'll come up with a plan to try and save you two."

"Jim and Karen are getting married in a few days."

Laura wondered why she had bothered to tell him such a thing, but she had said it without thinking. For a moment, Craig's betrayal had ducked behind the shadows of her mind, and she had slipped naturally into the old habit of sharing everything with him. She berated herself. She must not let that happen again. Craig Branston was a heartless cad! It would be in her best interest not to forget it, even for a moment!

"That's good news," Craig replied. "I'm glad he got rid of Marsha Donaldson. By the way, where is she?" If he got out of this alive, he had a score to settle with her!

"She's dead," Laura answered.

"How did she die?" he asked, surprised.

"What difference does it make?" she mumbled.

"Tell me what happened."

She shrugged; she might as well tell him the whole story, if she didn't, he'd keep questioning her. Laura drew a deep breath, then gave Craig a detailed account. She explained why Doyce and his friends had left them in the desert to die, how they were finally saved by Neosha, and the way in which Marsha had died. Then, with tears glistening, she told him that Harry had passed away in Peaceful. She didn't, however, reveal that Harry Talbert was her father. For one thing, she despised Craig too much to confide something so personal, also, she wanted him to believe that she was in love with Ed.

Craig, digesting her story, didn't say anything for a minute or so. He was sorry to hear Harry had died, he had liked and respected him. He thought about Laura and the horror she had faced in the desert. God, when she had needed him the most, he hadn't been there for her! Determination shone in his eyes, and his expression grew grim. Well, he'd not fail her this time! Somehow, he'd get her out of this alive! Tender emotions suddenly weaved their way around his heart. Maybe he should give in to his feelings, and tell Laura that he hadn't betrayed her. Such a confession wouldn't guarantee her love, but she would no longer detest him. Apparently, he had lost her to Ed Talbert, he supposed he could live with that, but he didn't feel he could live with her hating him. All at once, he laughed inwardly. Live with it? Die with it was more like it! His death was almost a certainty! Unless, he thought, his hopes rising, Slade got here in time! He had confidence in Jim, as well as Zeb. He knew they weren't sitting idly at the ranch, waiting for Talbert to return with Laura.

Craig looked thoughtfully at Laura, his gaze admiring her delicate profile. He noticed how her jawline was strong yet exquisitely feminine, and the sensual way her long eyelashes curled upwards. She had removed her hat, and her blond hair flowed past her shoulders like spun gold. His eyes, filled with hunger, raked her slender form, if his hands weren't tied he would have impulsively taken her into his arms.

Laura, feeling the power of his gaze, turned her face to his. The lantern's saffron glow fell across his masculine features, and she studied him closely. He hadn't shaved in days, and his dark beard reminded her of pirates she had read about—their black beards always made them devilishly handsome. His brown eyes, widely set beneath prominent brows, were staring intensely into hers. She thought she saw desire in their fathomless depths, but she wasn't sure. Suddenly, Laura looked away. His closeness had touched a loving chord deep inside her; she knew she was still vulnerable! If only . . . if only she could truly stop loving him! She had no patience with such weakness, and she silently chastised herself, making a mental note not to forget, even for a second, that he was a two-timing cad!

Craig had caught a glimpse of love in her eyes, before she had abruptly turned away. It gave him reason to hope. Maybe she didn't love Talbert as much as she claimed. Could it be possible that she still carried a torch for him? He knew there was one sure way to find out. He'd tell her the truth. If she still loved him, she would certainly tell him so!

"Laura," he began, his heart thumping apprehensively, "there's something I must tell you. Now, before it's too late."

She didn't look at him. "What is it?" she asked, sounding indifferent.

"I need to talk to you about what happened in San Francisco—"

Craig didn't finish; at that moment, Joe opened the door.

" 'Fore Pa and my brothers left, Pa told me to leave this open, so I can keep a close eye on you two."

"Where did they go?" Craig asked.

"To meet Talbert." Joe went to the wood-burning stove to dish up his prisoners' dinner.

The stove was in Craig's line of vision; it wasn't very far from the storage room. He knew Joe would hear every word he and Laura said.

"What about San Francisco?" Laura asked, watching him curiously. What could he possibly tell her that she didn't already know?

"Never mind," Craig murmured. He wasn't about to discuss their personal relationship with Joe eavesdropping. For now, his love for Laura must remain hidden!

A testy frown furrowed her brow. "What do you mean—never mind?"

"We'll talk about it later," he said softly, hoping there would indeed be a later time.

"Don't bother!" she remarked tartly. "There's nothing you can tell me about San Francisco that I want to hear!"

She withdrew into a simmering silence. Craig had a feeling she intended to remain there a long time. He didn't try to convince her to talk to him; right now, silence was best!

As Gus and his sons rode to meet Talbert, the eastern horizon was turning a burnt orange. The sun's climbing rays shone faintly through interlocking clouds, but the western sky was still a dark, vast mass. The countryside was interspersed with indigenous evergreens, most of them piñon and juniper, and a family of mountain bluebirds, welcoming the morning, shrilled musically. The landscape gradually grew lighter, and the clouds, now a fluffy white, skimmed weightlessly across the pewter sky.

The Mitchells, unimpressed with nature's painting, rode steadily toward their destination. Shortly before the noon hour, they reached the area where they were supposed to meet Talbert.

A few minutes later, he arrived.

"You alone?" Gus mumbled tersely.

"Yes, I am," Ed replied. He was perspiring, more from nerves than heat, and he distractedly rubbed a finger between his shirt collar and neck, as though the garment was choking him. The shirt was in dire need of a good washing, he had worn it since yesterday morning. Zeb had told him not to change, the stronger his scent, the better chance Lobo had of tracking him.

Gus spoke to his sons. "You two make sure he wasn't followed, then come on to the cabin, but make damned sure you cover our tracks."

They assured him that they would.

"You got the money?" Gus asked Ed.

He nodded.

"Where is it?"

He pointed at his saddlebags.

Gus started to tell him to hand it over, but he decided to let Talbert hold onto it until they reached the cabin. That way, the man would think he was going to honor his half of the deal. It tickled Gus to know that the rich sonofabitch would think he and his woman were going to come out of this alive.

Ryan and Dave lingered behind for over thirty minutes, then, certain that Talbert was alone, they started toward the cabin, carefully covering their tracks.

A short time later, Zeb, Jim, and five of Talbert's wranglers rode into view. Lobo was trotting in the lead, but he wasn't sniffing a trail, for Zeb hadn't yet put him on Ed's scent. The map had shown them how to get to this area.

Reining in, Zeb dismounted, reached into his saddlebags, and removed a shirt belonging to Ed. He went to Lobo, waved the shirt under the wolf's nose, and said, "Find him, boy!"

Lobo took a good whiff, then whined excitedly. His wild instincts were prompting him to chase down his prey.

Zeb swung back into the saddle, and with Lobo leading the way, the riders headed in the right direction.

Laura, overcome with fatigue, had fallen asleep. She was sitting, her back against the wall, and her head on Craig's shoulder.

Craig had also dozed, and as he came awake, he was surprised to find Laura's head nestled on his shoulder. While they had been asleep, she had snuggled against him. Craig took time to relish her closeness, for he knew that when she woke up, she would move away.

After a time, Craig grew uncomfortable and needed to stretch, but he didn't dare move a muscle, for he didn't want to disturb Laura. She needed rest, furthermore, he was still enjoying having her so close.

A few minutes later, Laura opened her eyes. At first, her sleep-drugged mind was too drowsy to think clearly. But, suddenly, reality hit with startling force. Her nerves grew taut, and her body stiffened. Then, as she became aware that she was nestled against Craig, she moved so that their bodies no longer touched.

Branston impetuously lost his patience. "Will you please stop acting like I'm something to shrink away from?"

"You are!" she spat, anger bursting in her. "You're a two-timing skunk!"

"Two-timing?" he came back. "Look who's calling the kettle black. It didn't take you very long to find another man, did it? And a rich one, I might add!"

"Rich? Are you implying that I'm only interested in his money?"

"Are you?" he quipped.

"How dare you think such a thing!" Her temper ran amuck. "I hate you, Craig Branston! I never want to see you again as long as I live!"

"Which might not be very long." He had spoken the words quietly, but their cold seriousness cooled Laura's tirade like a frigid wind.

"You're right," she murmured calmly. "It's foolish for us to spend our last minutes on this earth arguing."

"Maybe Gus will let you go." Craig prayed his words would come true.

"He isn't the type," she replied, her composure collected. "He'll kill me, and he'll kill Ed, too, if he brings the money."

"If? Are you doubting him?"

"No, of course not. I didn't mean that the way it sounded. Instead of delivering the ransom, Ed and the others might be planning a way to rescue me."

Craig's voice dropped to a whisper. "Keep those ideas to yourself. Joe might be listening. I can't see him, but that doesn't mean he isn't close by."

"What about my knife?" she whispered back. "Now's the time to use it, before the others return."

"I've been thinking about that," he replied, keeping his voice hushed. "Can you get it out of your boot?"

She reached down to give it a try, but with her hands tied together, retrieving the knife might be impossible. She tried several times, but she couldn't get a grasp on the knife's handle.

"Let me try," Craig said.

She moved around so that he could reach her boot, but his fingers, thicker than hers, wouldn't slip inside.

"Damn!" Craig cursed softly, giving up.

Laura sighed with exasperation. "I might as well have left the knife at home, for all the good it's doing."

Suddenly, Joe's tall frame materialized in the open doorway. "What do you two keep whisperin' 'bout?" he demanded gruffly. "No more talkin' in low voices. If I hear one more whisper, I'll gag both of you! You understand?" He glowered at them, then went to the stove, and poured himself a cup of coffee.

Craig and Laura exchanged hopeless glances, then they both withdrew into silence. If they couldn't plot an escape, there was nothing left to talk about . . . anything else would only lead to another argument.

As the day wore on, the small storage room grew uncomfortably hot, the narrow window afforded only a minimum of circulation. Laura was tired, miserable, and couldn't help but imagine how wonderful a cool bath would feel. Earlier, Joe had untied her feet, taken her outside, shown her a clump of bushes, and had given her permission to use them for privacy. As Neosha had once done, he ordered her to keep a bush wiggling the whole time. Joe then returned her to the room, retied her feet, and took Craig outdoors for the same purpose. That was the last she and Craig had seen of Joe, but they knew he was nearby, for they could hear him moving about in the next room.

The sounds of arriving riders suddenly drifted in through the open window, followed by Gus calling out a greeting to Joe.

"They're back," Laura murmured. Her heart had started pounding. Was Ed with them?

She didn't have long to wonder; Gus, holding Talbert at gunpoint, shoved him into the storage room. Joe, following close behind, drew Ed's arms behind him and tied his wrists. He then pushed him roughly to the floor.

Laura's hands were bound in front of her, which made

it possible for her to kneel beside Ed, grasp his arm, and help him to sit upright.

Gus, looking on, laughed cruelly. "You two lovebirds better make the most of the time you got. As soon as my boys get here, I'm gonna kill you both." He turned his evil gaze to Craig. "While them lovebirds are kissin' and a-huggin' each other for the last time, you can be thinkin' 'bout how them Indians skin a man alive!" With that, he motioned for Joe to leave, then followed him, closing the door with a solid bang.

"Are you all right?" Ed asked Laura, his eyes filled with concern.

"Yes, I'm fine," she replied. "Oh, Ed, you shouldn't have come! Didn't you realize they would kill you?"

He summoned a smile. "Well, I knew it was a likely possibility. But, Laura, surely you didn't think I wouldn't come. Don't you realize how much you mean to me?"

Tears burned her eyes. "Yes, I think so. Thanks for coming. I love you, Ed!"

Their exchanged endearments cut deeply into Craig's heart. That they cared about each other was very obvious. He had detected the sincerity in their voices, and had seen the affection in their eyes.

Ed cast Craig a cold perusal. "What's *he* doing here?" he asked Laura.

"The Mitchells kidnapped him, too."

"But not for ransom," Craig quickly clarified, his eyes as cold as Talbert's. "Gus just wants to kill me."

Ed looked away from Craig, content to ignore him. "Laura," he began in a low voice, "Zeb, Jim, and some of my ranch hands are close behind. Gus left his sons to cover any tracks leading to this cabin, but Lobo's on my trail. Zeb is certain the wolf will find me."

"He will," Laura said firmly. "How far behind do you think they are?"

"An hour maybe."

Laura turned to Craig, asking quietly, "Did you hear what Ed said? The others are on their way."

He nodded, but didn't say anything, for he was too preoccupied with the rope binding his hands. He was twisting his wrists back and forth, back and forth.

"What are you doing?" Laura asked.

"I'm trying to loosen this rope." He continued the effort a few minutes longer, then whispered to Laura, "Come here. I think I loosened this rope enough so that I can move my hands more freely. Now I might be able to reach your knife."

With her feet tied, she couldn't ~~walk,~~ so she scooted across the floor. She sat with her boots facing Craig.

Carefully, his fingers slipped down the boot concealing the knife. He touched the handle, grasped it tentatively, and slowly drew it up the high-topped boot and into sight. It fell from his tenuous hold, and dropped to the floor with a clanking sound.

Craig picked it up somewhat awkwardly, and wedged the handle between his palms with the blade pointing forward. He told Laura to hold out her hands, and placing the sharp edge beneath the rope, he sliced easily through the strands.

She rubbed her sore wrists where the rope had cut into her skin, then as she met Craig's eyes, her lips spread into a smile so lovely that it wrenched his heart.

"We're going to get out of this, Craig. All three of us. I just know we will."

He thrust his hands forward. "Cut the rope, then free Talbert. And don't be so damned optimistic, we aren't

391

out of this yet." He didn't mean to sound so curt, but, damn it, that beautiful smile of hers was tearing him to pieces! God, he longed to take her into his arms, hold her close, and never let her go! He wanted to see her lovely smile for the rest of his life, but he had lost her to Ed Talbert! He wished losing her didn't enrage him so, but he couldn't help it.

Laura cut the ropes binding his hands and feet. Her smile had disappeared, and was now replaced with anger. Craig's temperament was exasperating!

She freed her feet, then went to Ed and sliced through his ropes.

Craig's eyes flitted from Laura to Talbert. "Wrap those ropes so it'll look like you're still tied. We'll make our break when Slade and the others get here. To try any sooner would be suicide."

They did as they were told, then moving to lean back against the wall, they sat close together. As Laura nestled her head on Ed's shoulder, he reached down and placed a kiss on her brow.

The gesture intensified the jealous rage burning deeply inside Craig.

Thirty-two

When Ryan and Dave returned, they found their father sitting at the kitchen table ogling the two thousand dollars. Grasping a bottle of whiskey, he waved his sons over and poured them a drink. Gus's spirits were high, and he wanted to celebrate before killing his prisoners and moving on. He had decided that he and his boys would travel to Mexico, and hole up there for a while.

The Mitchells were on their third round of drinks when Zeb and the others arrived. The cabin was located in the midst of trees and shrubbery. The men quickly dismounted, crouched low, and took shelter.

Zeb, standing behind a thick evergreen, looked over at Jim, who was also hiding behind a large tree. "Do you reckon we oughta rush the cabin?"

Slade nodded. "It's risky, but it's still our best choice."

"Our only choice," Zeb mumbled, his expression worried. He knew Laura and Ed could get killed in the cross fire, or that one of the Mitchells might shoot them just for the hell of it.

They checked their guns, then motioned for the wranglers to do likewise. The cowhands Talbert had chosen to ride with Slade and Zeb were straight-shooters, and men who knew how to handle themselves in a dangerous situation. They would do their job well; as they readied their weapons, they did so with quick precision.

Meanwhile, inside the cabin, Dave, needing to relieve himself, stepped to the front door. As he swung it open, the blast from Jim's rifle hit him smack in the chest, knocking him backwards and onto the floor. As blood spewed from his gaping wound, he gasped for a breath that never came. He was dead seconds after he hit the floor.

Gus shoved back his chair and leapt to his feet. An icy snake of fear coiled in his stomach, and blood slid through his veins like cold needles. Momentarily stunned, he watched as Ryan, moving quickly, slammed the door shut.

The cabin had two front windows; Ryan and Joe hurried to take up their positions. They fired randomly into the surrounding thicket, their bullets whizzing through the air. The men, still well concealed, returned rapid gunfire, forcing Ryan and Joe to drop to their knees and duck for cover.

Gus, knowing the woman was their best chance for escape, headed for the storage room. Dave's death didn't prevent his thoughts from spreading a calculated grin across his face. Later he would grieve over his son, now he must save his life and the others. He planned to use the woman as a human shield, then take her with him as a hostage. If the men outside attempted to follow, he'd threaten to kill her.

He opened the door to the storage room, stepped inside, and found only Laura and Talbert! Where the hell was Branston? The question barely had time to cross his mind when, Craig, his body flush against the wall at Gus's back, lunged forward.

He grabbed Gus about the neck tightly, drawing him backwards and off balance. Craig's other hand, holding the knife, moved quickly, and the razor-sharp edge was placed against Gus's throat.

Ed stepped forward and took Mitchell's gun, which was still in its holster.

Craig, keeping the knife at Gus's throat, forced him through the open doorway. "Put down your guns!" he yelled to the brothers. "If you don't, I'll slit your old man from ear to ear!"

Joe was about to lay down his weapon, but noticing that Ryan wasn't cooperating, he decided to hang on to it.

"I don't think you'll kill him in cold blood!" Ryan said to Craig. "You ain't the type!"

Craig pressed the blade into Gus's flesh, drawing a spurt of blood. "You're crazy if you think I won't kill him!"

Ed, standing beside Craig, held Gus's pistol. If Branston cut the man's throat, he planned to shoot Ryan before he could get off a shot.

Craig dug the blade in even deeper, causing more blood to trickle down Mitchell's neck and onto his shirt.

"Goddamn it!" Gus said raspingly, his eyes staring fearfully into Ryan's. "Put your gun down!" He didn't doubt that Branston would kill him.

At that moment, following a thunderous blast, part of the front door was blown off its rusty hinges; what remained crumbled to the floor in a mass of jagged splinters. Zeb, the second barrel of his shotgun still loaded, barged inside. Jim was right behind him.

Ryan and Joe dropped their weapons, and held up their arms in surrender. Craig released Gus and shoved him across the room. Holding his hand to his throat, he took his place beside his sons. Craig hadn't cut him very deeply, and the bleeding was minimal.

The wranglers came inside, and Ed ordered three of them to guard the Mitchells, he then told the others to bury Dave.

Zeb, his arm around Laura, led her from the stuffy cabin and into the fresh air. She breathed in deeply and filled her lungs.

"What's Branston doin' here?" Zeb asked her.

"Craig collected a bounty on Mitchell years ago, and he planned to kill Craig for revenge."

"Bein' held prisoner with Branston must've been mighty hard for you."

"I managed. Besides, it's over now." She sighed wearily. "I just want to go home."

"There's no reason to subject you to travelin' with the Mitchells. I'll see if Jim and the wranglers will take them to Silver Star, then Ed and I can ride home with you. We brought an extra horse."

A look of sadness came to her eyes.

"You're thinkin' 'bout your mare, ain't you?" Zeb guessed.

"I'm going to miss her."

"Miss her? She ain't dead!"

Laura was surprised.

"Ed brought her to the Diamond Cross, and Charlie took out the bullet and patched her up."

"Then she's all right?"

"Well, she ain't goin' to win any races, but you won't have to put her out to pasture."

Laura glanced about. "Where's Lobo?"

"I don't know," Zeb replied, becoming a little concerned. "He brought us here, but then I got to thinkin' about rescuin' you, and I didn't pay him no mind. But he's got to be around here somewhere."

Laura called for Lobo, but he didn't appear.

"Damn!" Zeb cursed, evidently worried.

Laura could see he was upset. "What's wrong?"

"On our way here, we came across a sheep rancher and a few of his hands. The man said a pack of wolves have been attackin' his flock. He and his men were out to kill every wolf they can find. Only us bein' there kept 'em from shootin' Lobo."

"Oh no!" Laura gasped. "If wolves are in this vicinity, then Lobo probably got their scent and left to find them. If that sheep rancher doesn't kill him, those wild wolves will!"

A wrangler stepped outside, holding his rifle. Laura swept it from his hand, and checked to make sure it was loaded. Craig's horse was nearby, she swung up onto its back, slipped the rifle into the scabbard, and said to Zeb, "I'm going to find Lobo!"

Craig came out of the cabin just in time to see Laura leaving. "Where's she going?" he asked Zeb.

"To look for Lobo," he replied curtly. "As soon as I reload my shotgun, I intend to go after her." His countenance was far from friendly.

Craig understood his hostility, but he didn't have time to explain his innocence. The Mitchells' horses—saddled—were tied in a lean-to beside the cabin. He hurried over, mounted Gus's roan gelding, and took out after Laura. He had located his pistol, and it was back in his holster.

* * *

Laura, holding the stallion at a steady gallop, called repeatedly for Lobo. She hoped desperately that he wasn't out of earshot, and would respond to her voice. She was headed toward the mountain; the dense forest that grew there was a natural habitat for wolves.

That she might lose Lobo made her stomach churn with fear. The last few weeks had brought so much tribulation, that she wasn't sure she could take more distress. Craig's betrayal, her ordeal in the desert, then Harry's death—her strength had reached its limit.

The stallion's hooves started up the mountain slope, he was surefooted and scaled the steep incline without a slip. Laura guided the horse onto a narrow path, which was bordered by high bluffs intersected with deep ravines. At the top, evergreens grew abundantly, sheltering small wildlife such as badgers, and skunks. The wooded section, however, also afforded the ideal spot for a mountain lion about to spring an attack.

As Laura rode down the path, on the bluff above, a she-lion, considering Laura a threat to her cubs, crouched low to the ground, peered over the edge, and measured its prey.

The stallion, picking up the lion's scent, whinnied nervously and snorted powerfully through its nostrils. A tremble shook the horse's body, as he suddenly began to prance anxiously. Laura tried to control the animal, but he balked at her commands.

The wild cat leaned back on its strong haunches, let lose with a spine-chilling roar, then sprang its attack.

The stallion reared up on its back legs and threw Laura to the ground, causing the airborne lion to miss hitting its target.

Laura hit the dirt so hard that, for a moment, she

couldn't catch her breath. The stallion, its ears pinned back, made a quick turn and raced back down the path.

The lion had landed a few feet from Laura, it now stood poised to strike. Terror coursed through Laura, and her first instinct was to get up and run. But she knew that was the worst thing she could do. Her only chance to avoid an attack was to remain perfectly still—maybe then the lion would decide to go away. Laura dared to look closer at the cat, she swallowed back a sudden scream, for there was murder in the beast's eyes—it was ready to kill!

The lion's tawny hair bristled, then it roared ferociously, and was about to pounce when, from the cliff above, Lobo made a flying leap. His strong body hit the lion so powerfully that both animals went rolling in the dirt, their deadly jaws snapping at each other viciously.

They broke apart and circled one another, each instinctively waiting for the right moment to launch an attack, and sink its teeth into its adversary's throat.

A pistol shot suddenly rang out, and it sent the lion running for its life. Craig, preferring not to kill the lioness, had shot into the air. He was leading the runaway stallion; it was now calm, and stood by obediently as Craig dismounted his horse and rushed to Laura. She was still on the ground, and he helped her up. "Are you all right?" he asked.

Brushing the dust from her clothes, she replied, "Yes, I think so."

Lobo, remembering Craig, trotted over with his tail wagging vigorously. Branston patted his head, and the wolf's tail moved even faster.

Laura, looking on, sighed with relief. Thank goodness, Lobo hadn't found the wolf pack—or the sheep rancher!

"Well, at least Lobo's happy to see me," Craig said, eyeing Laura carefully.

"That's because he doesn't know you're a weasel!" she muttered, her tone caustic.

Craig, still watching her, folded his arms across his chest. "Laura, I think it's time you stopped behaving so childishly. I realize you think you have cause to despise me, but—"

"Think?" she butted in. Her eyes flashed furiously. "What you did to me in San Francisco was cowardly, rude, and totally inexcusable!"

He quirked an angry brow. "Well, it certainly didn't take you very long to find a replacement for me! What do you do? Fall in love with a snap of your fingers?"

She was seized with fury. How dare he find fault with her! "You despicable son-of-a-she-dog!" she came back, her temper blazing. "I'm warning you, you had better stay away from me!" She tried to shove him out of her way, but he stubbornly held his ground.

"I'm not leaving and neither are you, until you hear what I have to say!"

"You don't have anything to say that I want to hear, you two-timing skunk!"

"Damn it, Laura! Your name-calling is about to try my patience! Now, I want you to control that fiery temper of yours, and listen to me!"

"All right!" she said sharply. "Say your piece and get it over with, so I can leave!"

"It's about what happened in San Francisco," he began, but that was as far as he got, because Zeb and Ed suddenly rode into view. Craig, disappointed, cursed under his breath.

Ed dismounted hastily, went to Laura, and drew her

400

into his arms. "I was worried about you."

She held her brother close. His love was dependable, honest, and unselfish, and, at the moment, she needed the security of his arms. Then, gently, she left his embrace, gazed imploring into his face, and said, "Please take me home!"

He was more than ready to leave, he took her to the horse Craig had ridden, and helped her up. Zeb had remained on horseback, and as Ed was mounting, he looked at Craig and said quietly, "You can ride with Jim and the others."

Craig, his expression inscrutable, watched as they rode away. Lobo trotted beside Laura's horse. Inwardly, Craig was fuming. Twice now, he had been about to tell Laura the truth, and both times he had been interrupted. Well, he'd try again, but the next time there would be no interruptions! He'd make sure of that, one way or another!

He saw no reason to travel with Slade and the others, he'd ride back to town alone. Once there, he'd take a bath, grab a bite to eat, then visit the Diamond Cross. After he told Laura the truth, if she still wanted to marry Talbert, then he'd accept her decision and bow out like a gentleman!

It was a long ride back to Silver Star, and Craig didn't return until late. He paid the desk clerk for another night, then went to his room; his belongings, undisturbed, were still there. He took a quick bath, shaved, put on clean clothes, then went down to the dining room. The kitchen was closed, but the waiter, who hadn't yet gone home, offered to bring Craig coffee and a sandwich.

Branston received quick service, had eaten his sandwich, and was pouring a second cup of coffee, when Jim walked into the room. He had delivered the Mitchells to Sheriff Longley's jail; when the circuit judge came through, they would stand trial. Jim was looking for Branston, and he figured he'd find him at the hotel.

Pulling out a chair, Slade sat down, looked closely at Craig, and asked point-blank, "Why did you marry Deborah?"

"I didn't marry her," he replied.

"What? Then why—?"

"Marsha Donaldson, that's why."

Jim was totally perplexed. "What did Marsha have to do with it?"

Craig told him everything Johnny had learned. Finishing, he said, "For some sick reason, Marsha went to great lengths to hurt Laura."

Jim, amazed, shook his head. "That woman could be as evil as a witch."

Craig agreed. "She not only paid the maid to tell you and the others that Deborah had married me, but paid for my horse's keep, and hired a cabby to deliver her messages."

"I wonder where she got the money?" Jim mused aloud.

"She probably had the funds her husband stole from the bank. I seriously doubt Jerry Donaldson was killed the way Marsha claimed. She most likely shot him herself."

"But if she had the money, where was it? I searched her wagon."

"Did you look for a hidden compartment?"

"No, I didn't," he answered. "Hell, I was so sure she

402

was innocent, that I just halfway searched the wagon."

"After Doyce left you all in the desert, did Marsha keep a bag with her?"

"Yes, she carried her carpetbag. Damn! I bet it was filled with money!"

"What happened to it?"

"It was left beside her grave." A look of wonder fell across his face. "My God, if the money was in there, then it's just lying in the middle of the desert. By now, it's probably covered in sand. Well, I'm not going back to find out. The bank was insured, the citizens in Carson City didn't lose anything. Furthermore, I doubt if I could find where we buried Marsha. I'd probably perish trying to find the spot."

"I don't blame you. This time of year, Death Valley's no place for man or beast."

"Craig, why haven't you told Laura what really happened in San Francisco?"

"I tried to a couple of times, but we were interrupted." He shrugged solemnly. "In the long run, it probably won't matter much one way or another. She seems determined to marry Talbert."

"Ed?" Jim exclaimed.

"She said they're engaged."

Jim laughed, he couldn't help it. "Why, that little minx! She lied to you, Craig. I guess she just wanted to get back at you. She's not planning to marry Ed Talbert. My God, he's her brother!"

"Her brother?" Craig remarked, incredulous.

"After Harry died, Karen told me everything. Years ago, Harry and Laura's mother were in love. Harry was Laura's father, not John Mills. That's why Harry was so concerned about her."

"Well, I'll be damned," Craig replied. "When Laura and Ed were together, I could tell they cared about each other, but it wasn't love! I mean, it wasn't passionate love."

"Laura's still in love with you. She always has been."

Craig bounded to his feet. "Jim, will you do me a favor?"

"Sure, if I can."

"Find the reverend and bring him to the Diamond Cross. There's going to be a wedding."

"This time of night?" Jim exclaimed. "What if the reverend refuses? He's probably in bed."

"Tell him I'll pay him three times what he usually gets. That should get him out of bed!"

Jim got to his feet. "All right, I'll go see him."

"I'm going to head out to the ranch now. That'll give me time to ask Laura to marry me, before you show up with the preacher."

Jim, chuckling, wished him good luck.

Laura was in bed, but she was awake when a persistent pounding sounded at the front door. She got up, slipped into her robe, and left the room.

Charlie Goller had been in the kitchen, enjoying a late night snack. Thus, as Laura stepped into the hall, he was already opening the front door.

Craig was too excited to wonder about the stranger admitting him. "Where's Laura?" he asked.

Craig's voice caused Laura to freeze in her tracks. What was *he* doing here? The nerve of that man!

Branston's noisy arrival had awakened the entire household. The Gollers' bedroom was off the kitchen, and,

Mary Goller, still buttoning her robe, stood poised behind her husband. She was quite taken with the handsome caller, and wondered who he was and why he was calling so late. Karen had also recognized Craig's voice, and as she passed Laura in the hall, she gave her arm an encouraging squeeze. Luckily, Zeb was sleeping in the bunkhouse, otherwise, he would have greeted Branston with a loaded shotgun.

Karen, taking charge, asked Craig, "What do you want?"

"I need to see Laura."

"I don't think that's a good idea."

Laura, listening, suddenly whirled about, stalked into her room, and closed the door. Craig had nothing to say she wanted to hear!

Meanwhile, Craig moved toward Karen and told her, "I'm not married to Deborah. Jim will be here in a few minutes, and he'll explain everything. Which room is Laura's?"

"You and Deborah aren't married?" she asked, surprised.

"Karen," he replied, obviously impatient, "I aim to marry Laura. That is, if I can get a chance to ask her."

Smiling radiantly, Karen said, "Her room is the second one on the left."

He hurried down the hall, found the door unlocked, and barged inside.

Laura, sitting on the edge of the bed, leapt to her feet. "How dare you come in here! If you don't leave, I'll have you thrown out!"

Without a word, Craig went to her, drew her forcefully into his arms, bent his head, and captured her sweet lips in a deep, breathtaking kiss.

Thirty-three

Laura melted in Craig's embrace, as his kiss stole her senses and sent her heart pounding. She recovered quickly, however, pushed out of his arms, and spat harshly, "Have you forgotten you're a married man?" Hands on hips, and eyes flashing furiously, she continued, "The ink on your marriage license isn't even dry yet, and you're already trying to cheat on your wife! Oh, you despicable rake! Get out of my house! Now!"

He smiled, and it reached clear to his heart. "Laura, will you marry me?"

"Marry you?" she exclaimed.

"I love you. You're the only woman I've ever loved."

"Then why did you marry Deborah?"

"I *didn't* marry her."

She was completely taken aback. "What are you saying?"

He reached for her hand, led her to the bed, and sat beside her. She was too numb to object. The room's lone lamp shone dimly, and its soft glow, falling across Laura's long hair, emphasized the golden highlights. Craig gazed deeply into her blue eyes, and their beautiful sapphire depths held him mesmerized.

Laura, gazing back, admired his handsome face. The

beard was gone, but he still sported a well-trimmed moustache. An unruly lock of coal-black hair had fallen across his brow; Laura gently brushed it back into place.

He held her hand firmly, drew a breath, and began to explain. "The morning I left to see Deborah, I was determined to tell her that I was in love with you. Before I could, she told me that she was engaged to a doctor. He had been out of town, but he arrived that very morning. Although I was anxious to tell you the good news, I stayed and had brunch with Deborah and her fiancé. I didn't want to be rude. They decided to get married that afternoon, and leave immediately for Seattle. I wished them luck, and left as quickly as possible—"

"But, Craig—" she interrupted.

"Please! Don't say anything; just let me finish."

She suppressed the questions swirling through her mind.

"On my way back to the Winston, I passed an alleyway. I heard a woman crying. I dismounted and hurried to the alley to see if I could help. She was lying sprawled, her clothes crumpled, and she wasn't moving. As I knelt beside her, two men grabbed me from behind. The woman, of course, wasn't hurt. She took my wallet, then her two friends beat me to a pulp. I was taken in by one of the oldest scams around. One man kicked me in the head, and I was knocked unconscious. Days later, I came to in the hospital. I sent an attendant to the Winston for you, he came back and told me that you and the others had checked out—"

Laura couldn't remain quiet a moment longer. "Oh Craig!" she cried out miserably. "I didn't know!"

He patted her hand soothingly. "I understand, sweetheart. But, back then, I was totally baffled. That you left

San Francisco without me was a terrible blow. I sent for Johnny, hoping he might be able to explain. He didn't know anything, of course. He didn't even know that you and I were in love."

"I never told him," Laura said softly. "I only saw him a couple of times, and his visits were so short, that I didn't have time to talk about us."

"Johnny offered to store my belongings and horse until I got out of the hospital. That was when he learned that Marsha Donaldson had paid a cabbie to deliver a message to the hotel, and also to the livery—"

Again, Laura interjected, "Yes, I heard about those messages! The hotel and the livery were notified to store your belongings for two weeks."

"Apparently, Marsha also paid the maid at the school to tell Zeb and the others that Deborah had married me."

"But *why?*" Laura gasped. "Why did she want to hurt us like that?"

Craig shrugged. "I guess we'll never know for sure. She never liked you, that was obvious. I'm sure she was jealous of you, too."

Marsha's trickery was staggering, and it took a moment for Laura to grasp everything Craig had said.

He continued, "When you came to my hotel room, Gus Mitchell was hiding in the closet. When he was sent to prison, his woman left him, and he blamed me for it. From the things he said, I knew I couldn't let on that I was in love with you. I was afraid he'd kill you out of revenge. That's why I was so cold to you. I was trying to save your life."

"But why haven't you told me all this sooner?"

"I almost told you when we were still prisoners, then I tried to tell you later, after the mountain lion's attack.

408

But we were interrupted by Zeb and Ed." He grinned disarmingly. "Speaking of Ed Talbert, I was so jealous of him that I couldn't see straight."

She spoke haltingly, "Craig . . . about Ed. I lied to you . . ."

"I know," he murmured. "Jim told me everything. I know that Harry Talbert was your father."

Laura, her grief still very real, talked quietly about Harry. She told Craig that she had learned to love him like a father. Later, a tiny smile started at the corners of her mouth before spreading beautifully. "Oh Craig!" she exclaimed, her heart now beating with happiness. "I can hardly believe that I didn't lose you!"

He brought her into his arms, holding her as though he never intended to let her go. "These last few weeks have been hell for us both. But, thank God, it's over! We're together now, and nothing is ever going to separate us again!"

His lips claimed hers in a kiss full of passion and need. Clinging tightly, she responded with all her heart!

He released her somewhat reluctantly, he hated to break their embrace, but he wanted to marry her now without delay. "Laura, put on your prettiest dress."

"Are we going somewhere?"

"Yes, but no farther than your parlor. Jim's bringing the reverend." He arched a brow, smiled wryly, and asked, "You will marry me, won't you?"

"Tonight?" she exclaimed.

"Why should we wait a moment longer?"

"Why indeed!" she remarked, thrilled. She bounded happily from the bed. "If you'll leave, Mr. Branston, I'll dress for our wedding."

"I'll ask Karen to give you a hand." He kissed her again, long and hard, then started out of the room.

"Craig!" Laura called. "I can't get married without Ed and Joshua. Will you ask Zeb to ride to the Circle T?"

He assured her that he would.

An hour later, Laura, poised in front of the mirror, was giving her reflection a final appraisal.

Karen was standing back, watching her. She wondered if Laura realized what a stunning picture she presented. Considering Laura's life-style, her wardrobe consisted mostly of riding attire and everyday dresses. Karen and Laura had been searching through the closet, when Laura suddenly remembered her mother's wedding gown. It had been carefully wrapped and placed in a cedar chest. The ladies removed the elegant dress, and were pleased to find that it was still in perfect condition. It was wrinkled in places, but Karen quickly took care of that with a heated iron.

Now, as Karen perused her friend, she found her a beautiful bride. The white silk gown, edged with rows of applique lace, fit Laura as though it had been made for her. A tulle veil made of whisper-light silk was the final touch.

A knock sounded on the door. It was Zeb, asking permission to come in.

Karen hurried to admit him.

"It's time," he said. His gaze swept lovingly over his niece, she was indeed beautiful.

Karen left and went to the parlor to join the others.

Meanwhile, Zeb, his eyes twinkling, asked Laura, "Are you happy, hon?"

"Yes, I've never been happier! You know how much I love Craig."

"Yep, I sure do. I feel real bad 'bout all those hard feelin's I had toward him. Furthermore, I could kick myself for not investigatin' his alleged marriage. I should've known Craig wouldn't hurt you like that!"

"I'm just as guilty—even more so. I was weak and lost faith in Craig." She lifted her chin resolutely. "That will never happen again!"

Zeb shook his head with wonder. "Jim and Craig told me the whole story, and it's hard to believe that Marsha Donaldson was so devious. Well, she can't ever hurt you again, that's for sure."

"No, she can't," Laura murmured.

This was too happy an occasion to allow Marsha's evilness to put a damper on it, and Zeb changed the subject. "By the way, you'll be pleased to learn that Craig and Ed are now on amiable terms."

"I have a feeling they'll become very good friends."

Zeb went to her side, and offered her an arm. "Are you ready for me to give you away?"

"Oh yes!" she exclaimed. Happiness shone brightly in her eyes.

Dawn was only an hour or so away, and, Craig, sitting on the front porch, knew he should be tired after such a long, anxiety-filled day, but he was too exultant to be fatigued. He was resting on the stoop, and Lobo was at his side. As Craig tried to quell his impatience, he distractedly scratched the wolf behind its ears. Laura was in her room, removing her dress, and slipping into a nightgown. Mary Goller, assisting her, had assured Craig

411

that she'd let him know when he could join his bride.

Craig reflected on their wedding; considering it was arranged so hastily, the affair had turned out extraordinarily well. Following the ceremony, Mary served sandwiches, cake, and coffee. The reception didn't last very long. After all, it was the middle of the night, and everyone was tired. A smile flickered across Craig's lips. Everyone, that is, except for the bride and groom. Following their vows, Laura had discreetly promised Craig a wonderfully passionate wedding night.

Night? Craig suddenly thought impatiently. The night was almost over! Why was Laura taking so long? Didn't she realize whatever she decided to wear to bed would be promptly removed by her eager groom?

The door suddenly opened, sending Craig bounding to his feet.

Grinning cheerfully, Mary told him, "Your bride is waiting for you."

"It's about time," he mumbled, hurrying past the woman and into the house. He made a beeline for Laura's room, went inside, and locked the door.

Laura was in bed; a lamp, burning softly, cast a romantic hue. Craig, despite his eagerness, stood still, watching her. He drank in his wife's beauty, he intended to remember this moment for the rest of his life. The bride, awaiting the groom, was sitting up, a pillow at her back. Laura hadn't bothered to draw up the covers, and Craig's eyes traveled hungrily over her curvaceous form, which her thin nightgown barely concealed.

She held out her arms. "Don't just stand there, darling. Come make love to me."

He moved swiftly, sat on the edge of the bed, and drew her into his arms. "I love you, Mrs. Branston," he uttered thickly, before kissing her with deep longing.

"Get undressed and come to bed," she whispered wantonly in his ear.

He quirked a brow, and a smile filled with anticipation spread across his face. "It seems I married a very passionate young lady."

She remarked saucily, "Yes, you certainly did. But it's all your fault. You shouldn't be such a wonderful lover. If you weren't so desirable, maybe I wouldn't be so wanton."

"I'd have you no other way. Darling, feel free to seduce me anytime you get the notion."

She gave him a very inviting smile. "I have such a notion right now."

"In that case . . ." he said, getting to his feet. He removed his clothes as quickly as possible, letting them drop randomly to the floor.

Her eyes traveled up and down him, admiring his masculine physique. A yearning, fiery in its intensity, sparked her desire into a leaping flame that burned like wildfire.

Craig, his need as powerful as Laura's, took his place beside her and drew her close. He captured her lips in a demanding caress, and, Laura, responding ardently, grasped his broad shoulders, drawing him ever closer.

Anxious to enjoy his wife's naked flesh, Craig deftly removed her gown, and flung it to the floor. It fell feather-soft to rest amidst his own discarded apparel.

Surrendering to their love and urgent passion, they conveyed their need through intimate fondling and questing kisses that fanned the flames of passion.

Their bodies fused into one, and, ecstasy, absolutely fathomless, consumed them. They made love with a fe-

413

verish intensity, each deep thrust carrying them to passion's erotic fulfillment. The lovers reached their peak together, and ultimate rapture embraced them with wondrous sensations.

Craig, his hunger for Laura temporarily appeased, kissed her lips softly, then moved to lie at her side. Content, she snuggled close, and nestled her head on his shoulder.

"Craig?" she murmured.

He kissed her brow. "Yes?"

"We haven't discussed our future."

"We can talk about it now, if you want."

"I know you always planned on building a ranch, but would you consider living at the Diamond Cross?"

"I certainly would. It would be foolish for us to have two ranches."

Laura smiled happily. "I was afraid you might not want to make the Diamond Cross your home."

"This ranch has a lot of potential, and I can hardly wait to start operating it. That is, if you don't mind having me take charge."

"Not in the least," she replied. "You run the ranch, and I'll run our home and take care of our children."

"Sounds good to me."

"However," Laura continued. "I think you should know that the Diamond Cross is heavily in debt. I had to borrow money from Ed to get started again."

"That's no problem. I have money in the bank in Abilene. I'll have it transferred here, and pay Ed back in full."

She wrapped an arm about him, snuggling even closer. "Everything has worked out splendidly, hasn't it?"

"Yes, and I couldn't be happier."

The sun had crested the horizon, and its golden light began to fall across the room.

"It's dawn," Laura murmured. She smiled brightly. "A brand new day, and a brand new life."

Craig agreed. "Our first day as husband and wife."

He took her into his arms and kissed her deeply. They knew that from this moment on, they would spend all their days together. Their love, everlasting, would bind them forever.

PINNACLE BOOKS HAS
SOMETHING FOR EVERYONE—

MAGICIANS, EXPLORERS, WITCHES AND CATS

THE HANDYMAN (377-3, $3.95/$4.95)
He is a magician who likes hands. He likes their comfortable
shape and weight and size. He likes the portability of the hands
once they are severed from the rest of the ponderous body. Detec-
tive Lanark must discover who The Handyman is before more
handless bodies appear.

PASSAGE TO EDEN (538-5, $4.95/$5.95)
Set in a world of prehistoric beauty, here is the epic story of a
courageous seafarer whose wanderings lead him to the ends of
the old world—and to the discovery of a new world in the rugged,
untamed wilderness of northwestern America.

BLACK BODY (505-9, $5.95/$6.95)
An extraordinary chronicle, this is the diary of a witch, a journal
of the secrets of her race kept in return for not being burned for
her "sin." It is the story of Alba, that rarest of creatures, a white
witch: beautiful and able to walk in the human world undetected.

THE WHITE PUMA (532-6, $4.95/NCR)
The white puma has recognized the men who deprived him of his
family. Now, like other predators before him, he has become a
man-hater. This story is a fitting tribute to this magnificent animal that stands for all living creatures that have become, through
man's carelessness, close to disappearing forever from the face of
the earth.